A VOYAGE
TO HYPERBOREA

Novels by John Michael Greer

The Weird of Hali:

I – Innsmouth

II – Kingsport

III – Chorazin

IV – Dreamlands

V – Providence

VI – Red Hook

VII – Arkham

Ariel Moravec Occult Mysteries:

The Witch of Criswell

The Book of Haatan

Others:

The Fires of Shalsha

Star's Reach

Twilight's Last Gleaming

Retrotopia

The Shoggoth Concerto

The Nyogtha Variations

A Voyage to Hyperborea

The Seal of Yueh Lao

Journey Star

A VOYAGE TO HYPERBOREA

A Fantasy with Gill Slits

John Michael Greer

AEON

Published in 2024 by
Aeon Books

British Library Cataloguing in Publication Data

A C.I.P. for this book is available from the British Library

ISBN-13: 978-1-91595-202-8

Cover art by Margaux Carpio
Typeset by Medlar Publishing Solutions Pvt Ltd, India

www.aeonbooks.co.uk

The frozen mountains rise and rise
Above an icebound ocean drear
Where whales evade the swift harpoon
To feed the writhing kraken's beak;
Beneath the stark, storm-tortured skies
Where howl the winds that sailors fear,
Sheet ice the color of the moon
Enshrouds a land gone still and bleak.

It was not thus in bygone days
When Eibon's black enchanted tower
Soared tall above unfrozen seas.
Commoriom! Uzuldaroum!
Thy names still echo with the praise
Once lavished on thy pomp and power,
Thine armies and thine argosies,
Before the dawning of thy doom.

Now ice from far Polarion
Lies heavy on once-verdant plains
And all the fabled pageantry
Of Hyperborea of old.
Of all the glories that are gone,
Scarce whispered rumor now remains;
The kraken writhes beneath the sea,
The ice entombs forgotten gold.

—"Hyperborea" by Justin Geoffrey

CONTENTS

CHAPTER 1

THE COLOR OF THE OCEAN

It was already a bad day, and Toby Gilman knew it was about to get worse. He pasted on a smile anyway and went on into the auditorium.

Outside, a luminous April afternoon spread over Arkham, gilded the brick and concrete of Miskatonic University's cyclopean buildings, glowed on the sagging gambrel roofs of the old New England town and the greenery of the hills around it. Glimpses of that greater reality slipped in through the windows of Morgan Hall, but Toby ignored them, headed for the table between seats and podium where the projector sat. He was in luck this time: the projector actually worked, and a few mouse-clicks on the laptop wired to it brought up his presentation. He went to the podium, found the chair behind it, managed to perch there with an attentive look on his face even though he would rather have hidden beneath any convenient object.

The classroom filled up. Some grad students came in, which was promising, and some undergraduates, which was even more so: both those details spoke of shifts in academic politics that might help him. Most of the people who came through the double doors and settled into seats in the auditorium were professors, though, some from Miskatonic's program in ancient Arctic studies, some from related fields. The three junior professors who made up the search committee, who'd invited him to Arkham and guided him through the less important parts of his campus visit and interview, came up to him and said cheerful things, but he could see past the fixed smiles to the worries beneath. They expected him to fail. He could tell that at a glance.

Half a dozen older professors came in then, and Toby watched them and tried not to blanch. He'd long ago learned how to read the signs that marked the inner circle, the senior professors who made the decisions that mattered, and he also understood the look of implacable hostility they turned toward him. As usual, the task of recruiting a new linguistics professor had been fobbed off on minor players in the program, and they'd invited Toby based on the state of ancient Arctic studies as a whole rather than the internal politics in Miskatonic's program. They were about to get a savage setdown. That Toby's fading chances of an academic career would be crushed in passing, he knew, mattered to only one person in the room.

He kept the smile fixed on his face while the classroom filled up, endured the introduction that followed—one of the members of the search committee, rattling on at more than necessary length about Toby's achievements. All the while Toby braced himself.

How do you tell a group of distinguished scholars that the assumptions on which they built their entire careers turned out to be dead wrong? That was the challenge Toby had grappled with over and over again as he'd prepared his presentation. Ever since Peter Danforth's famous 1939 paper "A Provisional Chronology of Ancient Arctic Inscriptions," most scholars had rejected the traditional claim that Hyperborea had flourished before the ice age and Lomar had its heyday in the last inter-glacial, and tried to squeeze both into the eleven millennia since the ice age ended. It had taken the melting of parts of the Greenland ice sheet, uncovering artifacts that could be carbon-dated, to shatter that conviction and prove that the traditional dates had been right after all. The entire field of ancient Arctic studies was still reeling, and it was Toby's bad luck that he'd helped coauthor two of the crucial papers that had turned his discipline on its head.

The introduction was over and he was about to start talking when one of the doors at the back of the auditorium opened, and another person came in: a spry man in his fifties. He took a seat toward the back of the auditorium. Once that last interruption was over, Toby pressed the button on the remote in his hand; the lights went down, the first slide of his presentation came up on the screen, and he launched into his talk.

He'd sweated blood over the paper and gotten advice from a dozen professors at Case Western, and it showed. He started by talking about other fields of scholarship that had been shaken to their core by new linguistic discoveries—the way the decipherment of Mayan hieroglyphs had turned the entire field of Mesoamerican archeology topsy-turvy, the shockwaves that spread through half a dozen disciplines when the Linear A inscriptions from Crete turned out to be in a language related to the Tamil tongues of southern India, the controversies set off by the Winters-Hall translation of the Eltdown Shards and the recent confirmation of Winters-Hall's work by Whitney and Sloan. From there he surveyed the entire history of ancient Arctic studies, from the first treatises by Johannes Bureus and Arne Saknussemm in the early modern era through the heroic age of nineteenth-century philology, the growth of archeological studies in the twentieth century, and the controversies of the twenty-first.

The radiocarbon evidence came next, and he was careful to present it as a shock to everyone, not (as it had actually been, but you couldn't say this) the vindication of a minority view and a shattering defeat for the established orthodoxy. He was just as careful in the minutes that followed to stress how much could be salvaged from that orthodoxy, how many of the connections drawn by scholars still made sense when, say,

Lomarian turned out to be ancestral to the Hyborian language family and not descended from it. Most of his audience followed along, some of them nodding slowly, some taking notes, but the ones whose opinions counted watched him with cold contemptuous expressions.

He finished with what was supposed to be a rousing call to respect the achievements of existing scholarship in the field, endured the applause that followed, called for questions. As he'd feared, the first response came from one of the people he most needed to convince. He knew that patrician face from a dozen conferences he'd attended: Dr. Hamilton Glynn Broward, one of leading figures in ancient Arctic studies for more than a generation. "What you're telling us," Broward said in an appropriately glacial tone, "is that three quarters of a century of hard work has to be tossed aside because a handful of radiocarbon jockeys think they know what they're talking about."

Toby managed what he hoped was a conciliatory response, but the look on Broward's face showed clearly enough that the old man was having none of it. The next question was less brutal, and then one of the members of the search committee tossed him a lifeline with a question that let him talk about how valuable the work of previous researchers still was. None of it mattered. The scholars who ran the program sat there, radiating silent contempt; Broward made no more comments, and the others who sat near him said nothing at all; grad students and junior professors pelted him with excited questions, and he smiled and responded and tried to tell himself that he still had a chance at the teaching position he needed so badly.

The moment the questions ended, as a second round of applause got under way, Broward stood up and went to the aisle. The others who'd sat close to him did the same. As one, they turned their backs and walked out of the auditorium. The three junior professors from the search committee sent panicked glances after them, and apologetic looks toward Toby.

Once the applause ended, Toby left the podium and went down to the floor in front of the first row of seats, smiled and shook hands, fielded less formal questions from the grad students and the undergraduates. Though his failure twisted in his gut, he made himself go through the charade. It helped that most of the questions he fielded took what he'd said seriously and tried to go further in the same direction. As soon as Broward and his peers died or retired, the ancient Arctic studies program at Miskatonic would join the rest of the discipline and deal with the implications of the radiocarbon evidence: that was clear enough, and Toby tried to convince himself that it mattered more than the end of his hopes.

The questions were winding down when someone else picked his way down from the seats to the floor: the professor who'd arrived at the last minute. Lean and a little stoop-shouldered, his tanned face framed in gray hair worn in a style thirty years out of date, casually dressed in a jacket and slacks, he gave Toby an assessing look through thick wire-framed glasses and then extended his hand. "Phil Dyer," he said. "Department of Geology here at Miskatonic. It's good to hear a solid argument for taking the radiocarbon evidence seriously." With a wry smile: "We've had trouble here getting some people to do that."

Toby didn't have to fake a smile, or the enthusiasm with which he shook the man's hand. "It's great to meet you in person, Dr. Dyer. Your papers on Greenland's preglacial geology have been crucial to my work. I'd have been lost without them."

"Likewise and you're welcome." Dyer considered him. "If you don't mind my asking, do you have a lot of other prospects lined up?"

Everything he'd been told by his professors back at Case Western militated against an honest answer, but he couldn't force himself to keep up the charade any longer. "I wish."

Dyer pulled a business card out of his pocket. "Are you going to be here tomorrow?"

"I'll be staying overnight," Toby admitted.

"If things go the way I think they will, give me a call first thing." He handed Toby the card, and Toby pocketed it. Before he could think of any other response, one of the grad students clustered around him asked him a question, and by the time he'd come up with an answer Dyer was climbing the stairs to the door.

* * *

The rest of the day was as complete a waste of time as Toby had ever experienced. He kept up a genial mask through the rest of the process, asked all the right questions during the hour he spent with the people from the benefits office and the hour he spent with the dean of the College of Arts and Sciences, smiled and fielded questions during a dinner to which all the program faculty were invited but none of the senior professors chose to attend. By the time one of the junior professors drove him back to the off-brand hotel where he was staying, though, he had no doubts about the score. The professor tried to sound cheerful, but when Toby asked him point-blank what his chances were the man looked away and said nothing.

As he rode the elevator up to his hotel room, he had to brace himself to hold panic at bay: old fears jabbed at his awareness of his failure, pushed his nerves to the limit. The silence and privacy of his hotel room helped. He took off his jacket and tie, let himself fall back onto the bed, lay there for some minutes breathing slowly and evenly until the panic passed off and he could get ready for bed.

Despite the state of his nerves, he managed to get to sleep readily enough, and if he had dreams, no scrap of them survived waking. He got up as dawn spread gray across Arkham's roofs, said the old useless prayers he'd learned from his grandmother. Not a week before she died, he promised her that he'd do that every morning, and the mere fact that they hadn't saved her and showed no signs of saving him hadn't convinced him to break the promise.

Other habits offered more comfort. He opened a suitcase and pulled out the squat zippered bag where he kept bathroom gear—his AWOL bag, Aunt Dinah had called it, and he'd kept the phrase. A bottle inside yielded up a salt tablet. He dropped it into a plastic tumbler, added water, set the tumbler on a shelf in the shower stall and then went on to the rest of his morning routine. A shower came last, straight cold. He'd been chaffed by roommates in the SUNY Rochester dorms about that, but it wasn't a religious austerity or a cure for masturbation, as they'd insisted. He stepped into the cold water and let himself enjoy it for a few minutes, before reaching for the soap: a brand he'd chosen after much experimentation, because its scent hid a certain other scent better than anything else he'd tried.

Then it was time for the thing he couldn't reveal to anyone else in the world, the thing that set him apart from the rest of the human race. He twisted the knob on the shower head to get a narrow hard stream, raised his face to it, opened his mouth and squeezed two sets of muscles deep inside his chest. The water streamed in, and three slits on each side of his ribcage—unobtrusive enough under other conditions to pass for scars—gapped open to let it pour out. The gills inside tingled and stung. Fresh water irritated them, especially if it was chlorinated, but they had to be rinsed every day or two to keep the risk of infection down. His family had learned that the hard way after they'd fled to the mountains.

Toby the gill man, he thought, bleakly amused. It was a familiar joke, though he'd never shared it with anyone. His roommates in the SUNY Rochester dorms would have had a good laugh about that, he'd been sure, after they'd finished dousing him in gasoline and setting him on fire, or handing him over to a certain organization not to be named that wouldn't be half so merciful. He'd been raised on too many bitter memories and ugly stories to expect anything else. At least, he told himself, he'd had the webs between his fingers cut away and his feet treated to a knife's rough surgery early in childhood, so he could pass for human otherwise. Though it always hurt a little to walk, he didn't mind the pain; the thought of what would have happened otherwise was considerably worse to contemplate.

Once he'd finished rinsing his gills, he reached for the glass, downed the salt water and pushed it out his gill slits. The stinging stopped promptly. Toby washed his sides again to remove any hint of the salt scent, then shut off the water and got to work with the towel.

Half an hour later he finished convincing his necktie to behave itself, gave his hair an uncharitable look, looked out the window at the gray morning. The business card he'd been given by Professor Dyer sat on the nightstand. Toby had a ticket for a bus that would leave before noon, but that would take him back to Cleveland to wait for a call he knew he wouldn't get. Eleven universities in the United States had programs in ancient Arctic studies and he'd made campus visits to all of them. In a field torn by bitter discords between old certainties and new data, he'd had the bad luck to take up the winning cause too soon.

After a few more minutes staring out the window at the gray hills surrounding Arkham, he found his phone, got the business card, texted Dyer a note saying he was free, and headed downstairs. The university flacks who'd invited him had made cheery noises about restaurants in the student district south of campus, but the thought of wandering through an unfamiliar town in search of breakfast when much could depend on being exactly on time didn't entice him, and he settled for two stale bagels and a cup of unremarkable coffee from the breakfast buffet.

Through the plate glass windows he watched traffic moving up and down Armitage Street, considered the sagging gambrel roofs of the houses on the street's far side and the dim shapes of the old downtown district across the river, rising up a long slope toward distant hills topped with ancient stone circles. Before he'd finished breakfast, his phone buzzed at him, and when he glanced at it he found a text from Dyer waiting: PLS COME BY WILMARTH 226 MAY HAVE SOMETHING TO OFFER YOU. That was enough to convince him to make sure he was still presentable and head out the door into the morning.

The campus was only a few blocks away from the hotel, and he'd already learned enough to find his way there and recognize Wilmarth Hall at a glance: the strangest piece of campus architecture he'd ever seen, a vast rugose shape of gray concrete with walls that bulged and flowed, windows of every shape but the ones he was used to, and a panoply of jagged spires and bulbous cupolas rising toward the sultry sky. The main doorway reminded him a little of a mouth and a little of a less polite orifice, and the mechanical doors in the middle had a sign on them saying OUT OF ORDER; fortunately the doors on either side were unlocked. Once inside, after a few false starts, Toby found a bank of elevators, but before he could push the button to summon one, a silver-haired woman in a black dress and a white sweater came down the corridor and said, "You must be new here. Trust me, you don't want to risk the elevators. The stair's there—" She gestured toward an unobtrusive door. "That's your best bet."

Toby thanked her and went to the door. The stair beyond it wandered up through the heart of the building, spilled him out conveniently onto the second floor. The walls of the corridor outside the stairwell were ridged and rounded in a way that made Toby feel as though he'd somehow strayed into the digestive tract of some vast and somnolent beast, but he found his way without too much trouble to the room numbered 226.

* * *

"Thanks for coming," said Dr. Dyer. "It's really quite a stroke of luck that you decided to visit Miskatonic just now." Toby, watching him, wondered what he meant.

Dyer's office was no less strange than the rest of the building. The window at its far end, which looked out at a parking garage, had five corners whose odd angles didn't quite seem to make sense. The bookshelves seemed to slant, though Toby couldn't tell which way, and the chairs on which he and Dyer sat wobbled slightly on a floor that looked flat but clearly wasn't. Still, standard literature on the ancient Arctic weighed down the shelves. The volumes ranged from Otto Dostmann's 1809 classic *Remnants of Lost Empires*, the first work in any modern language to discuss the Hyperborean and Lomarian civilizations, to Emmeline Grenier's newly published *L'Arctique dans l'Antiquité*, which Toby had in his luggage but hadn't yet read.

"I hope you won't mind my asking," Dyer said then, "whether you can do translations of original texts."

"Of course," said Toby.

Dyer nodded. "That would be an important part of the work you'll be doing if you accept the position I have in mind." He turned, pulled a sheet of paper off his desk, handed it to Toby. "Would you mind a little test?"

Toby considered the paper in his hand and began to smile. On it was a photocopy of half a dozen lines in angular characters that looked like Norse runes but weren't. "Not at all," he said. He pushed the chair over to the edge of the desk, pulled a pen from his jacket pocket, and started writing the translation in between the lines of Hyperborean characters:

Year of the Vermilion Rat, Moon of the Ripening of Tree-fruits, seventeenth day. Ambamethros, great king, king of kings, lord of Uzuldaroum and all Hyperborea, grants to his favored servant—

"You don't need a dictionary," Dyer observed with raised eyebrows.

Toby glanced up at him. "I'll have to use one in a bit. I don't remember what *tuqqoli'qada* means and I need to check the declension of *matam* to make sense of *ammataq*."

"Hard declension," Dyer said. "And *tuqqoli'qada* is 'keepsake, memento'—it's from *tuqqam*, to remember."

Toby nodded, finished the translation:

> —*Ishnuban Dzol, Keeper of the Hawks, this keepsake to recall to him the many years he served the Opal Throne. Let all do him honor and none do him harm, or suffer the king's wrath. The king's scribe Rabannath attests this.*

He handed the paper back to Dyer, who glanced at it and then at him. "It took me half an hour and a good dictionary to translate that."

Toby nodded, and after a moment went on tentatively: "I know this is controversial, but I really don't think you can understand a language unless you know it well enough to read it."

"And speak it?"

"Well, a little." Then: "*Iqqumandoli im'baqqampa oe?*"—Do you speak Hyperborean?

After a moment, slowly, Dyer said, "*Na'djai ish'baqqampa*"— I don't speak it well.

"That puts you way past the people I know at Case Western," said Toby.

"Fair enough," Dyer said after a moment. "I think we can certainly use you." Then, examining a paper on his desk: "Is there any reason you couldn't leave the country?"

Toby kept his surprise off his face. "None in the world. I've already got my passport—I applied to a couple of overseas universities."

"Good. How's your health?"

"Pretty good," Toby said, wondering what on earth Dyer had in mind. "I need some supplements but they're easy to get."

"You'd need enough for a year and a half."

"That's not a problem." Toby gathered up his courage and said, "Dr. Dyer, what exactly are we talking about?"

Unexpectedly, Dyer grinned. "It's simple enough. Miskatonic University's about to send an expedition to Greenland. We've got a research station on the east coast, at a place called Tornarssukalik Inlet. We had to shut things down a few years ago because of budget cuts, but we've secured private funding to reopen it for two summer seasons and the winter between. The location's crucial for archeological research, especially now that so much of the ice is melting—it's in what was the province of Tscho Vulpanomi in Hyperborean times, and only about two hundred miles east of the location of the Lomarian city of Olathoe."

"On the plateau of Sarkia," said Toby.

"That's right, your master's thesis was on the Lomarian fragments of the *Pnakotica*." Dyer considered him. "How's your Lomarian?"

"*Ishkal Lômar-mittu azhrám*," Toby said at once: I speak Lomarian also.

"*Tath âmzad*," he replied slowly: it is well. "Are you interested in the position?"

Toby didn't hesitate. "Of course I am. I need a postdoc, and something like this certainly counts." Then, with a grin: "And the thought of getting my hands on untranslated Hyperborean inscriptions isn't exactly a minus."

"That I can certainly promise you," Dyer said. "We found a couple of steles the last season we were at Tornarssukalik Station, and didn't have time to get more than a few photos." He tilted his head, considering. "Can you stay another day? This evening we're going to have a clambake for the expedition members, and I'd like to introduce you to them before making a final decision. The department can cover your hotel bill if that's an issue."

Of course it was an issue, and Toby had to find a way to accept without sounding too desperate. "I've never been to a New England clambake," he admitted then.

"Well, there's a first time for everything." Dyer considered him and then nodded, as though something had been settled. "I think you'll enjoy it."

* * *

An expedition to Greenland, Toby thought, and shook his head in amazement.

After the conversation with Dyer he perched on a bench in the quad, got his bus ticket changed for one on the next day's run. Once that necessity was taken care of, he plunged into the student ghetto between the Miskatonic University campus and the Miskatonic River, looking for a restaurant that would make up for his dismal breakfast, and found something promptly enough: a hole-in-the-wall Italian place two blocks south of campus, with pinball machines along one wall and plastic plants in baskets hanging at unexpected intervals from the ceiling. The waitress had fake fingernails colored vivid orange—Toby found himself wondering whether someone had cut up a perfectly good traffic cone to make them—but she took his order and brought the food promptly enough.

A decent meatball sandwich and a salad turned the stale bagels into a fading memory, and once the waitress vanished he opened the salt shaker and poured a good shot of the contents into his root beer. It wasn't sea salt but it tasted tolerably good, and once he'd stirred it with his straw, he sipped the root beer and sighed with relief. The need for salt went with the gills, one more legacy of the ancestors who must not be named and the town whose fire-blackened ruins had long since been buried by drifting sand. Table salt would do, but without a good dose of sea salt every few months certain illnesses couldn't be avoided. His family had learned that the hard way, too, and left a few more markers in the family plot before the lesson had been mastered.

He finished lunch and glanced at his cell phone. It was a little past one o'clock, and he had most of five hours to kill until the clambake. A sudden impulse urged him to catch the next bus out of town and hope that one of his other prospects would still come through, but after a few minutes of brooding he decided that an expedition to Greenland was better than nothing, and the latter was what he knew he'd get.

With that in mind, he walked back to the Miskatonic campus. Wilmarth Hall's delirious curves, Morgan Hall's blank brick walls, and the uneven mass of the Armitage Student Union framed the quad. The Gothic arches of Orne Library filled the remaining space, and Toby decided to see what he could find out about the research station that Dyer had mentioned.

He was in luck. The ground floor of Orne Library had shelves displaying new additions to the book collection, and one of the books there was a tall hardback titled *MISKATONIC UNIVERSITY: ONE HUNDRED TWENTY YEARS OF POLAR EXPLORATION*. He picked it up and settled on the nearest chair. The book turned out to be a glossy exercise in self-praise, the sort of thing universities churned out to attract donations from alumni, but it was full of historic photographs. He opened it at random, to a photo from an Antarctic expedition in the late 1920s: bundled figures standing beside a portable wooden derrick while a drill puffed away, extracting core samples from weathered rock. He wondered what they'd found, flipped further back.

That landed him at a black and white image from 1911. Two three-masted ships sat at anchor near a dark inlet reaching back to the ragged face of a glacier, with cliffs rising on one side of the inlet and tundra reaching away to the other. Up on a low hillock well away from the shore, newly erected timber framing half covered with clapboard broke the desolate lines of the tundra. It was Tornarssukalik Station, he guessed, and the caption confirmed it. One of the two ships looked familiar, too; another glance at the caption sent his thoughts chasing down familiar paths, because it identified one of the ships as the barque *Miskatonic*.

The *Miskatonic*—now there was a name to stir childhood dreams. He'd read about her in second grade in a children's magazine that hadn't yet been replaced by the internet, spent rainy afternoons daydreaming about her, wove her history into childhood play: her launching as a mortar ship for the Union navy in 1862, her service in the sieges of Charleston and Mobile, her sale to civilian owners after Appomattox, her career as a whaling vessel, her years as the flagship of Miskatonic University's polar exploration program, and her final home as a tourist attraction in Kingsport, where a foundation begged the money to restore her to her Civil War condition and found eight antique cannon and two mortars to complete the picture. He'd cut out the article, used the information for school assignments more than once—a fourth grade report on voyages of exploration, a seventh grade paper on the rise and fall of the whaling industry—and left it behind only when he'd left his home in the Catskills for good.

It occurred to him then that he was only ten miles away from Kingsport, and might be able to find time to go down and visit the old ship before he left Arkham one way or the other.

He tried to dismiss the thought, paged through the book. It had plenty of other photos from Miskatonic University's Greenland program, chronicling expeditions on the great icebound island, from the early days of tall ships straight through to the current era of glacial melting and rising seas. He tried to imagine himself walking on those sedge-dotted tundras, those gravel slopes, those great sweeping sheets of ice, and ended up feeling dazed.

Greenland, he thought. It really was a green land once—

Iqqumandu. The word surged up in his mind, the name of the land that the legends of a much later age called Hyperborea.

I might be going there, Toby thought, and tried to make himself believe it.

* * *

"Here we go," said the woman in the driver's seat—Louise something, Toby thought he remembered—and pulled the battered compact onto the bare space next to the road. Toby, crammed into the back seat alongside two grad students, braced himself.

As soon as the car lurched to a stop, he opened the door and clambered out. Pines loomed above him, hunched against the salt-scented wind, and above them the vast gray mass of Kingsport Head just across the river rose up stark into a vivid blue sky. Further ahead on the road, a baker's dozen or so of cars sat on the shoulder. Once the car's engine fell silent, a low unsteady rushing sound in the middle distance whispered of the thing Toby dreaded and craved more than anything else.

The others piled out of the car. Toby let himself move with them. He waited beside the trunk, took the case of beer they handed him—at least it was something local, a sturdy brown ale from a microbrewery in Arkham, and not one of the insanely bland national labels. Once the contents of the trunk had been distributed among the car's five occupants, Toby followed the others along the road to a trail that jabbed southward through writhing pines.

The trail veered this way and that around gray boulders half buried in the sandy ground. The wind picked up, carrying a faint murmur of voices, and the salt tang in the air grew stronger. Then the last pines fell behind. The trail wound through low dunes dotted with beach grass that bent in the wind, spilled the five of them out on a long shelving beach that reached out to the surging gray-green waters of the Atlantic.

Toby had wondered for years what he'd do the first time he came within sight and scent of the ocean. The answer, while not exactly a surprise, was reassuringly prosaic. His heart pounded, to be sure, and the thought of dropping the case of beer and sprinting down to the water's edge, shedding every stitch of clothing on the way, occurred to him more than once. Even so, it took him only a modest effort to push the thought aside and keep on walking, following the others down to where half a dozen loose knots of people sat on driftwood logs and beach chairs, and smoke already rose from two robust fires.

He recognized one of the figures a moment before the woman who'd driven addressed him. "Hi, Dr. Dyer." She proffered a tub of clams in water. "Where should these go?"

Dressed in cargo pants, sandals, and an orange and black Miskatonic sweatshirt, Dyer looked in his element. He sent the woman with the clams and the others with their burdens toward a part of the beach not far from the fires, where Toby had already spotted grocery sacks and assorted containers sitting on the sand. When it came Toby's turn, though, Dyer gave him a grin and said, "Thanks for coming." Then, with a glance at the cardboard box he carried: "You have good taste in beer."

"I didn't pick it," Toby admitted.

Dyer's shrug dismissed the matter. "Right over this way." The professor turned and went down toward the water, and Toby followed. A dozen yards of sand brought them to a trench deep enough that sea water welled up into it. Bottles of beer and cans with soft-drink logos on them, scores of each, wallowed in the water.

"That's where the beer goes," said Dyer. "Help yourself." His gesture took in the other hundred or so bottles and cans.

Toby thanked him, plopped down on the sand beside the trench as Dyer walked away, then tore open the box and started loading the beer down into the water to chill. Every time his hands touched salt water a tingling sensation surged through him, but lifelong habit kept his reaction off his face. Once he'd finished emptying the case, he tried to talk himself into taking one of the soft drink cans, failed abjectly, fished out a bottle that looked dark enough and found himself in undisputed possession of an imperial stout from a Rhode Island brewery he'd never heard of. The bottle wasn't screw top and he didn't have anything to open it, but a quick glance toward the box for empties showed a dozen old-fashioned bottle openers stuck in the sand nearby, rising up like so many metal tombstones in a graveyard sized for rats.

Once the bottle was open and a good swallow of the contents had taken the edge off his nerves, he carried the box over to the nearest of the beach fires. In response to the keeper's genial gesture, he tossed it into the flames and stood for a few moments, watching it burn. The salt water sang to him as it rushed up onto the sand and danced playfully back out to sea, urging him to fling himself into the surging glory of the ocean, but the rest of the bottle silenced it. As the box dissolved into twisting black shreds edged in flame, he went back to the trench, discarded the bottle and opened another of the same brand, then walked down to the bare sand just above the highest reach of the waves and stood staring into the great unruly distances of the Atlantic until the bottle in his hand was empty.

A third bottle suggested itself, but he decided against it, walked up toward the fires and the people. Scraps of conversation fluttered past him on the salt breeze as he got close enough. The talk was familiar enough—faculty politics, recent publications in various fields connected wih the ancient Arctic, and the fading prospects for higher education in the face of the economic contraction nobody wanted to acknowledge—but he'd long ago learned to notice when people went out of their way not to talk about something, and this was one of those times. A language of glances and pauses murmured of some issue far more serious than the ordinary details of academic life. What it was he could not tell, but he sensed it in every group he passed.

He'd reached the largest of the knots of people, near where clams and other edibles sat in tubs and boxes and coolers on the sand, when a woman turned toward him, away from the others, and muttered something in an irritable tone. A trick of the unsteady breeze brought the words to him with perfect clarity: *"Sh'pai aqqun ish'tsampa."*

Toby blinked, astonished. His mind, honed by six years' hard work with the languages of the ancient Arctic, identified it at once—Middle Hyperborean, late in the Uzuldaroum period to judge by the contractions—and translated it just as promptly: I waste my time here.

Maybe it was the beers, maybe something else, but before he'd quite finished absorbing the words he said the appropriate response: *"Na'djed mirhastu"*—it is to be regretted.

Her gaze snapped up to his face, and he stared at her, momentarily speechless.

For the rest of Toby's life that moment hovered in his memory, luminous and dazzling as sun on water. She was a little short of thirty, taller than average, with wiry musculature that promised explosive strength and quick decisive movements that doubled down on the promise. She wore blue boat shoes without socks, tan cargo shorts of masculine cut with many pockets, and a blue tee shirt with an illegible logo on it; he could see the lines of her bra beneath the shirt and the curves of her breasts beneath that. White-blonde hair in a practical cut framed a face too lean and angular to be conventionally pretty, and if those lips, eyelids, cheeks had ever been touched with makeup it left no trace behind. Her eyes, though, those were what affected him most. The gray-green color of the deep ocean, they regarded him with a look in which he could find nothing even remotely human. If the ocean itself had suddenly opened eyes and pondered him, he thought later, those eyes might have looked like hers.

An ordinary encounter, or so he tried to convince himself afterwards—but why did her gaze send something through him like electricity? He could not say. He managed with an effort to keep his face from betraying his reaction.

"Iqqumandoli im'baqqampa," she said then: you speak Hyperborean.

"Na'njai ish'baqqampa," he replied: I don't speak it too badly.

She considered that and nodded once. "Your name?"

"Toby Gilman."

She turned back toward the others. "Dr. Dyer!"

Dyers extracted himself from a conversation. "Yes?"

"You didn't tell me that Dr. Tobias Gilman would be here."

Dyer glanced from her to him, and then laughed a short sharp laugh. "Good," he said. "I should have known that you'd find him." He turned to Toby. "Dr. Gilman, this is Wren Kingston-Brown. You might have heard of her."

He hadn't, but made a noncommital nod anyway and said, "Pleased to meet you."

"*Djai iqqol,*" she replied correctly.

"We'll talk tomorrow," said Dyer. He smiled in a way that was probably meant to be reassuring, said something polite, and rejoined the conversation he'd left a few minutes before. Wren Kingston-Brown gave Toby another cool considering glance, nodded once, and headed for a different group of people who were deep in conversation a dozen yards away.

Toby watched her go, wondered why her gaze turned his thoughts to water, and then shook his head, baffled. Nothing about the conversation seemed unusual in any obvious way, but he couldn't shake the feeling that he'd brushed against something very strange.

* * *

The rest of the clambake slipped past in a blur of unfamiliar faces, polite conversations, and foods that he'd never tried before but that sent a jolt of recognition through his deep places, as though he'd hungered for them all his life and never known it. More than once he felt someone's gaze on him; most of those times, a casual glance that way showed Dyer talking with the one who'd turned to look, but three times it was a young woman, short, dark-haired and olive-skinned, who each time gave him what looked like a puzzled glance and then looked away.

Toward evening, when the sun had long since slipped behind the soaring gray mass of Kingsport Head and the last of the iron pots had long since been hauled from under the sand to have its contents shared out among the attendees, he and the young woman happened to be standing together by one of the fires. "I don't think we've met," she said. "I'm Leah Sargent."

"Toby Gilman."

That got him a quick look in which he was sure he caught a flicker of uncertainty. "You're not at Miskatonic, are you?"

"Not yet." He put on a grin the way he'd shrug on a jacket. "Looking for a postdoc."

She nodded, then flicked something invisible off one shoulder with the other hand. "That's not an easy fish to land these days."

"Tell me about it," said Toby. She gave him another quick uncertain look, followed by a silence. "Well, good luck," she said finally, and turned to talk to someone else.

Just then the woman who'd brought him to the clambake came through the crowd. "Oh, there you are, Dr. Gilman. Ready to wind things up?"

"Yes, I think so," he said, and followed her back up the beach to where the other three people she'd brought stood waiting. The woman pulled a flashlight out of her pocket, and by its light the five of them picked their way back up the trail to the road, located the battered compact after a little searching, climbed in.

On the ten-mile drive back to Arkham Toby sat back and said nothing at all while the others chattered enthusiastically about the day. Most of the talk might as well have been empty wind as far as he was concerned, but one exchange made him blink and pay attention. "You know who else was there?" said the grad student sitting next to him, a gangling young man with dull brown hair. "Wren Kingston-Brown."

"Oh, come on," said the young woman sitting next to him, rolling her eyes.

"No, seriously. I recognized her from TV, and I was talking to this guy from the geology department, so I asked him, and he said yeah, she's going with us on the Greenland expedition."

The others laughed and shook their heads and told him he was drunk, and the talk promptly veered off into who'd had how many beers of what kind. They were still on that when the car finished its passage through dark deserted country full of twisted pines and came within sight of the cyclopean buildings of Miskatonic University.

A few minutes later Toby said the usual things and climbed out of the car in front of the hotel, and not long after that, he got off the elevator on the fourth floor and headed down the hallway to his room. He was bone-tired, but made himself stay up long enough to wake his phone and type a name into his favorite search engine: Wren Kingston-Brown. There was an article on her in the big online encyclopedia most people used, but he knew better than to trust a word it said, and scrolled further down. He stopped at an article on a news-and-culture website: Wren Kingston-Brown Opens Up About Her Mental Health Crisis.

A double click brought up the article. It had a picture he recognized instantly—the same lean face, the same unhuman look in the eyes—and a canned biography. Toby read it, rubbed his eyes, and read it again. The daughter of two famous Australian anthropologists, Wren Kingston-Brown had spent much of her childhood with her parents among the Tcho-Tcho people of northern Laos. She was still in middle school when she earned her black belt in tae kwon do, the first of half a dozen in as many martial arts. She'd celebrated her high school graduation with a summer of mountaineering in the Himalayas, during which she'd pioneered a new route up Nanga Parbat and helped rescue a stranded party of climbers on Everest. Then she'd become the first woman to ski across the Antarctic ice cap alone, before spending three years in Japan pursuing her passion for martial arts. When she'd married a Nobel Prize-winning English physicist, a nerdy-looking guy named Harold Phillips, the tabloids insisted it wouldn't last, but as far as he could gather from the article they'd apparently been happy together.

Then, just two years back, a sudden crisis: the article didn't say much, but it sounded to Toby like a full-blown psychotic break. She spent six months in an institution, and when she came out of the mental hospital she left her husband, distanced herself from her friends, and moved to France, where she plunged into the study of obscure corners of folklore and literature. The headline claimed she'd "opened up" about her mental health crisis, but as he read the interview, Toby found himself doubting that. It sounded to him as though she'd assembled a set of clichés about mental illness and deployed them efficiently to stop further questions in their tracks. What she'd done more recently the article didn't say.

Come on, he told himself as he considered the article. You're not fourteen any more. That was true, of course. It was also true, he reminded himself as he walked into the bathroom, that Wren Kingston-Brown was an international celebrity and Toby Gilman was a short, dumpy, unprepossessing linguist who hadn't yet been able to land a postdoc position, much less launch a career worth the name. Shaking his head, he set the phone aside. Only as it shut down did it occur to him that the woman he'd met at the clambake had no trace of an Australian accent.

He was jolted awake the next morning by his phone ringing. After a moment of disorientation, he answered it with a groggy "Hello?"

"Dr. Gilman? Phil Dyer." Toby tried to manage a polite response, but Dyer went on at once. "I've got some good news for you. We've decided that you're the perfect candidate for the position we're trying to fill, and if you're willing to spend sixteen months in Greenland, we'd be delighted to have you."

Despite Dyer's encouraging words earlier, it was quite literally the last thing Toby had anticipated. "Thank you," he said anyway. "Of course I'm willing."

"I'm really glad to hear that," said Dyer. "There's one thing we should settle right away, which is whether you're coming up to Greenland with the advance party three weeks from now or waiting for the main party a month or so later."

Toby processed this. "Is there a difference in when the stipend kicks in?"

"Official university policy," Dyer said, "says that's not something I'm supposed to mention." A little dry laugh followed. "Of course there's a difference. You start getting your stipend when you leave for Greenland, and not a moment earlier. Is that an issue?"

"Kind of," Toby admitted. "I'd be happy to go with the advance party."

"Good," said Dyer, as though he meant it. "You can come over to my office sometime today and we can get the papers signed."

Chapter 2

SAILING TO GREENLAND

The county bus rattled and lurched down the long ragged slope, passing abandoned fields and farmhouses. Toby, craning to see past the passengers ahead of him, caught only broken glimpses of gambrel roofs and gray water off beyond them.

Two weeks had passed since he'd come to Arkham for the campus visit, and he'd spent most of that time scrambling to get ready for the expedition. The bus trip to Cleveland and back again, to gather his meager possessions and clean out the room he'd rented there, at least gave him the chance to read Emmeline Grenier's book on the ancient Arctic. Once he returned to Arkham, he'd spent more hours than he'd thought possible filling out paperwork, ordering the clothing and other gear he needed on Miskatonic's nickel, and dealing with the other details of a journey he'd never imagined making. He had to visit eight drugstores in five nearby towns before he had enough salt pills, and he'd spent the entire process in a cold sweat, trying to convince himself that nobody would connect the dots and realize that he wasn't human.

Then there was the medical exam which every member of the expedition was required to get before embarkation. Toby had been to a doctor precisely once in his life, to fulfill the same requirement before he started classes at SUNY Rochester, and he'd bluffed his way through it, insisting that the his feet had been mangled in a childhood car accident and the odd things the doctor heard through a stethoscope were the result of birth defects he'd long since learned to cope with. He'd prepared himself to do the same thing again, but it turned out to be unnecessary. Dr. Waldron, the elderly physician Dyer recommended, asked a few harmless questions, checked Toby's pulse and blood pressure, declared him perfectly healthy, and filled out the papers that said so. Dizzied with relief, Toby thanked him and left as quickly as courtesy allowed. Only when he'd returned to the hotel room where he was staying did it occur to him to wonder whether Waldron had guessed or known what questions not to ask.

All that was done with, though. His hotel room had a big waterproof duffel sitting in it, stocked with everything he'd need for the voyage out and the first days there. A good deal more, everything he'd need for sixteen months in Greenland, had already been loaded aboard trucks and hauled down to Boston to go aboard the ship. He'd received paperwork back from the Danish consulate, letting him stay on the island longer than the usual six month tourist visa permitted. He'd gotten an advance on his first month's stipend to cover incidental expenses on the voyage out, and he'd met repeatedly with the six other members of the advance party.

It was an odd crew. Phil Dyer was an old Greenland hand, Wren Kingston-Brown had climbed Everest and crossed the Antarctic ice cap, and a postdoc named Bill Allen, a bear of a man with a mostly bald scalp and a booming laugh, had a military background and a more ordinary record as a mountaineer and outdoorsman. Then there were three grad students from Miskatonic, Louise Desrochers, Orrin Bishop, and Susan Eliot, who he'd met en route to the clambake, who were young and healthy, but who had no more experience on arctic expeditions than Toby did. Together they'd sat through briefings, taken copious notes, tried to fit their minds around the adventure ahead.

Finally everything was ready and they had four days to cool their heels before boarding the freighter that would take them to Tornarssukalik Station. Most of the others went off to spend time with their families, but that wasn't an option for Toby. It apparently wasn't an option for Wren either, but he'd learned from Phil Dyer that she'd be spending the interval in New York City doing research in private scholarly libraries there, and it wasn't as though he'd been able to find an excuse to spend time around her. He compromised by looking up the *Miskatonic*, and discovered that it was still in Kingsport, open to the public noon to six daily.

The county bus lurched to a halt, let off two passengers, and moved on. Toby looked up to see eighteenth-century houses on both sides of the street and a scattering of tourists wandering along the sidewalks. The sun had begun to show itself from behind broken clouds, gleaming on small-paned windows and bright maritime-themed banners hanging from the streetlight poles. Up ahead, a forest of masts rose from a marina, and off to the right of that, masts on a different scale—soaring, black, set with yardarms against which square sails once strained—gazed down on the marina like a Great Old One regarding the doings of mere human beings.

Another two blocks and the bus turned onto the street that led past the marina. Toby pulled the bell cord, got off at the next stop, and headed for the *Miskatonic*. The black arc of the hull rose up a good two stories above the sidewalk, pierced with a row of portholes—those had been gun ports originally, Toby knew, before the refitting that prepared her for her voyages to Greenland and Antarctica. A sign said something about hull repairs taking the ship away from Kingsport for a few months that summer, and Toby shook his head and chuckled, imagining what the chamber of commerce would have to say about that. A rickety-looking stair led up to the deck, with a ticket booth at its foot. Toby handed over five dollars to the smiling old woman in the booth, got his ticket and a pamphlet in return, and climbed the stair.

That brought him to the *Miskatonic*'s deck, a single level sweep of wooden planks running more than a hundred feet from stem to stern, broken by three tall masts, a variety of hatches and housings, and an anachronistic line of solar panels—to provide electricity belowdecks, the pamphlet said, though it neglected to mention why. Overhead, spars and rigging loomed cryptic against the broken clouds; to either side, gunwales rose up to waist height, with life rings on ropes in case of emergency. The pamphlet told him that the deck he was on was called the spar deck, that the two shapes like low sheds he saw on deck covered the two mortars that were the heart of the ship's armament, and that the eight short cannon on the foredeck were called carronades officially and "murder guns" by the sailors who'd fired them or had to face them.

It also settled a question he'd wondered about for years, explaining that what made the *Miskatonic* a barque was that the two masts in front, the foremast and mainmast, were square-rigged, while the mizzenmast aft was rigged fore and aft like a schooner. He looked up into the rigging, saw the difference in the way yards and lines were arranged, and wondered about the various ways to rig a tall ship. It wasn't something he'd ever have to know about, he guessed, but the geometries of rope and wood intrigued him.

He wasn't quite alone aboard the ship. A man with broad shoulders, sandy hair, and a neatly trimmed beard paced the deck, escorting a brown-haired girl of five or six who was clearly his daughter. Toby exchanged smiles with the man, then chatted with him briefly as the girl clambered around the stubby iron cannon on the foredeck: ordinary pleasantries, nothing more. When the girl came back over to them, her father turned to her and said, "Fish for dinner tonight?" As he said it, he flicked something invisible off one shoulder with the other hand.

"I hope so," the girl said, beaming. "That's what Mom said." Toby smiled and said nothing; the man glanced at him, nodded, and made some polite comment or other. Not long thereafter, he and his daughter went clattering down the stair. Toby smiled again, watching them, and then his smile faded as he thought about his own family: his mother, dead not long after his birth, and his father, dead half a dozen years later, a dim memory edged with grief.

He shoved the thoughts aside, went below. Placards talking about the *Miskatonic's* many voyages to the cold ends of the planet helped him distract himself. By the time he caught the bus back to Arkham he'd convinced himself that none of it mattered.

* * *

The days before departure crept by. Toby spent most of the time reading everything he could find in the Miskatonic libraries on ancient Arctic studies and working out in the university gym. He tried to tell himself he needed to get ready for the expedition, but he knew perfectly well that he was distracting himself from his worries. That doesn't matter, he told himself. You've got the assistantship. Handle it right, and the next stop's a tenure track position.

Only one thing out of the ordinary happened during those days. He was in Dyer's office, talking about what books were already at Tornarssulalik Station, what books Dyer could order and have shipped there. Just then four raps sounded on the door, and before Dyer could respond the door opened. The young woman Toby had met at the clambake—Leah something, he recalled vaguely—came into the office, her face rigid with some emotion she struggled to keep hidden. "Dr. Dyer," she said, "I need to talk—" She saw Toby, then, and stopped.

"I'm busy right now," said Dyer in a mild tone. "Can it wait until one o'clock?"

Her gaze snapped from Toby to Dyer and back again. "That'll be fine," she said in a wintry voice. "Thank you."

She left the room and closed the door behind her with a click. Toby gave Dyer an uncertain look, but the professor's face was an uncommunicative mask.

Other than that, the time slid past without any sign of trouble. The day before departure, Toby emailed a scholar in Iceland he hoped to meet there on the way out, handed over his luggage, failed to get any sleep that night, and headed for a parking lot by Wilmarth Hall in the small hours of the morning. Stars glittered down cold and hard as he walked east to Garrison Street, turned toward the hills outside of town, and found Phil already in the parking lot. They made a little desultory conversation while the other members of the advance party showed up.

Wren Kingston-Brown appeared out of the fading darkness maybe twenty minutes before the van arrived, noted everyone in the parking lot, and stood by herself a short distance away. Toby tried to think of some excuse to talk to her, failed, and ended up talking to Bill Allen when he showed up a few minutes later. Louise arrived not long after that, went over to where Wren stood, and put on a bright smile. Orrin and Susan showed up moments later, talking enthusiastically, just before the van arrived.

The van was a rental, in mediocre condition. Toby ended up in the back seat, pressed up against the window, irrationally terrified that he hadn't washed well enough and someone would notice the salt scent of his skin. That pointless dread kept him silent and tense as the van drove through the darkness from Arkham to Bolton on the old Aylesbury Pike, found an onramp onto the freeway a little further north, then hurtled through the dim light of an uncertain morning to Boston's harbor district, where cranes rose skeletal against the red-tinted sky and colossal container ships lay silent at their piers.

At first Toby wondered if one of those huge vessels would be their destination, but the van went on into the seedy end of the harbor district, where tramp freighters scrabbled for cargoes the big container ships didn't or wouldn't haul. That was where the MV *Arkham* was tied up: a battered freighter spotted with rust, with cranes along her midline to allow her to offload cargoes where there were no port facilities, and square lines to give her ample room for cargo. The van found a parking place close by the ship, and Toby and the others clambered out into the chill morning air and crossed to the side of the pier. There a ramshackle aluminum stair brought them up to the deck of the *Arkham*, where two officers whose names Toby promptly forgot welcomed them aboard. From there, narrow steel stairs led up to the bridge deck, where they were parceled out among seven bleak little cabins.

Toby's was a cramped space with gray metal walls, lockers underneath the berth, and a single porthole at its far end. He spent fifteen minutes or so getting everything settled for the voyage, then flopped onto the berth and breathed a long sigh of relief. Though he knew he had no idea what waited for him in Greenland, he reminded himself that he'd found the postdoc position he needed, and would have a good many months to prepare articles for publication and try to sort out where his career would go after that. The mere fact that he'd be spending those months in quonset huts in Greenland barely registered just then.

On the drive down Dyer had cautioned them that they might be hours in port before the *Arkham* got under way. To Toby's surprise, though, maybe half an hour after he got his things packed in the lockers, a jolt ran through the deck beneath him, and a low indistinct murmur came rising up after it: the sound of the engines, he realized after a moment. He looked out through the one porthole his cabin had, saw the cranes across the way beginning to slide astern.

He sat up, watched the shapes of the harbor slipping backwards. After a while, longing for fresh air, he left the cabin and walked forward through an equally bleak companionway to the balcony on the bridge deck. Morning light sprawled aimlessly over Boston's skyscrapers and danced over the wind-rumpled surface of Massachusetts Bay. A pair of seagulls flew past, calling to each other in desolate tones. Toby listened until their voices were swallowed by distance and the low murmur of the ship's engines, and then went back to his cabin.

* * *

Most of the others spent the next few days being seasick. Toby was glad to be spared that, judging from what he saw of the faces of the other members of the party. The surging motion of the ship gave him no trouble, and he quickly adapted to the rhythms of life aboard, showing up promptly for meals in the galley three levels down while the other members of the expedition were still hiding from the thought of food. The ship's officers—captain, first mate, and second mate—sat at a little table of their own over to one side and talked in a language Toby quickly identified as Danish. The two dozen crew members, who came from every corner of the planet and talked in an argot that was half English and half anybody's guess, filled three long tables of their own, and that left a fourth table for the expedition.

At each of the first day's meals, Toby sat there in solitary splendor. The second day, Phil Dyer showed up, and though he ate sparingly he seemed to have no trouble keeping his meals down. Wren was the next to appear, and the others trickled in over the next two days. The food was bland but tolerable, and everyone in the expedition seemed to adapt to it readily enough. The one exception was Wren, who ate her share of most meals but wouldn't touch any dish that contained cheese. An allergy? Toby shrugged, filed the detail away among the many other things he didn't know about her.

Between meals, Toby spent much of his time in his cabin, reading books on Greenland's preglacial archeology. Most of the authors thought that Hyperborea had flourished after the ice age, not before it, and Toby kept shaking his head as he turned the pages. Hyperborean texts said that Commoriom and Uzuldaroum, the first two capitals, had been in the center of the great island, where the great river Ambar flowed south toward the port city of Leqquan. Somehow the scholars had managed to cram all three cities into a narrow part of south-eastern Greenland that had been ice-free since the end of the ice age, even though that played merry hob with the distances given in every surviving source. The books really did read, Toby decided, as though their authors knew better, but were deliberately trying to hide something.

When the books got too dull, he composed rude limericks in Hyperborean, and when he finally ran out of indecent words in that language, he went to the little storeroom not far from the galley where, among other odds and ends, the two dozen cheap paperbacks that made up the freighter's library had their home. It was an odd collection, a few mysteries, a few thrill-ers, a few historical novels, a random assortment of nonfiction titles, and a volume titled *The Call of Cthulhu and Other Stories* by H.P. Lovecraft.

Toby knew the name, and remembered a few conversations about the author that he'd overheard in childhood: bitter com-ments about a writer who'd taken the sacred mysteries of the Great Old Ones and turned them into raw material for cheap horror stories. The thought of reading the volume seemed vaguely sacreligious, but none of the other books appealed at all, and he couldn't think of anything in Hyperborean to rhyme with "Lovecraft" and give him raw material for another limerick. After a few moments of indecision, he took the book back to his cabin, perched on the berth, and started reading.

It wasn't cheap horror at all, he decided after finishing the title story. There was nothing especially horrible about it at all, just a good deal of plain common sense about the limits of human knowledge and a set of vivid anecdotes about an attempt to wake Great Cthulhu, the Dreaming Lord who slept in lost R'lyeh; why humans found that frightening was just another of the many riddles he lived with. Toby recalled tales about that attempt, mostly from early in his childhood, though he and his Aunt Dinah had talked about it one bleak spring evening, when she'd tried to cheer him up after a difficult day at high school by reminding him of the far faint hope of their people. He'd recalled dimly that the thing had been tried many years back, before his family had fled to Lefferts Corners, but now he had a date for it, the spring of 1925. There had been more than a thousand of his people then, and if the story was anything to go by, there had been other communities that had joined in the effort. That cheered him, made him wonder if there might just possibly be other survivors scattered across the planet.

He read the other stories one at a time, making himself spend hours between each one studying fine points of Hyperborean grammar and epigraphics, or slogging through chapters on the archeology of Lomarian settlement patterns. Some of the stories reminded him of scraps of lore he'd been told in his childhood, others strayed into realms he'd never encountered before. The last of the stories, "The Shadow out of Time," was one of the latter. It told the story of a scholar who'd apparently suffered a personality change, but had actually exchanged minds with a rugose, cone-shaped creature of the far prehistoric past, a member of a species that called itself the Great Race of Yith. It was a crisp and lively story if you could handle Lovecraft's ornate prose style, and by then Toby was used to the author's vagaries and savored the sense of alienation that ran all through the tale.

He took the volume back to the storeroom with a sense of regret, wishing that more of the man's writing was available. Most of the way there his path crossed Phil Dyer's. The professor glanced at the book in his hand and asked, "Lovecraft? Are you a fan?"

"This is the first thing of his I've read," Toby admitted. "It's pretty good."

Phil nodded. "I wonder. Ever heard of a town called Innsmouth?"

"No," said Toby. "Why?"

The professor gestured dismissively. "Lovecraft wrote about it. No big deal." He went his way, and Toby shrugged and returned the book to its place in the storeroom.

He'd probably have forgotten the incident, except that Phil started engaging him in talk thereafter and asking his help on linguistic questions. The two of them spent hours trying to puzzle out the inscription on a Hyperborean stele from blurry photographs, and even though they didn't get far it was a pleasant interruption to the monotony of the voyage. Toby tried to pretend that the professor's sudden enthusiasm for his company made sense to him.

* * *

One evening well into the voyage, as the sun stood low and red amid clouds, Toby stood near Phil on the bridge deck, looking out over the ocean. They'd started a conversation over dinner and decided to continue it in the open air. Waves rolled dark beneath a steady wind, and high thin clouds made the sky gleam like the inside of an abalone shell. Gulls wheeled around the freighter. Wind whipped spray off the tips of the waves. Off in the distance ahead, a tiny glint showed Iceland's position north-northeast of the *Arkham*. It had come into sight the day before, the first glimpse of land in days.

"It used to be a real problem," said Phil; they had been talking about sea ice. "Back when I first came to the arctic, it was a gamble to get a ship in anywhere on Greenland's east coast even in high summer. The pack ice reached out for miles, and you'd have to wait to find a lead—a gap in the ice—to get to the shore flaw, the open water between the pack and the stranded ice. Nowadays? It's still risky sometimes, but leads are a lot easier to find."

Toby nodded, taking this in. "How long have you been coming to Tornarssukalik Inlet?"

"Thirty-one years." Glancing at Toby: "This end of Greenland was practically my second home before we had to close things down."

"Budget cuts?" Toby thought he remembered.

Phil nodded. "Miskatonic hasn't been able to put much money into the station for years now, and the Université de Vyones is running short of funds too these days—but there's something else. Here's another new term for you: *jokulhlaup.*"

"Okay, I'll bite," said Toby. "What is it?"

"The Icelandic word for a meltwater flood. With all the melting, you get water ponding behind ice dams or under the ice itself, and then sooner or later it breaks through and washes away everything in its path. Greenland's been getting hammered by them for the last few years, and Tornarssukalik Inlet's due for a hell of a big one sometime soon. At the station, we'll keep a helicopter ready twenty-four hours a day, and if something happens we'll have maybe fourteen minutes to get it airborne, with all of us in it, or drown."

Toby gave him a startled look, but the professor didn't seem to notice. He was looking off to windward, his eyes wide and his mouth a narrow line.

"The thing is, the Arctic's like that," Phil said finally. "Let me show you something."

He burrowed inside his coat, brought out a little metal tin that had once held peppermints. "I found this when I was working at a site up on the west coast of Greenland. The archeologist in charge said that it had to be a forgery—I'll explain why in a bit—and told the work crew to throw it away. I managed to pocket it, and I've carried it with me ever since."

He opened the tin, pulled away a layer of cotton wadding. Inside was a piece of ivory not much larger than the last joint of Toby's thumb, carved with exquisite skill in the shape of a face.

It was not a human face, though Toby couldn't quite say what kind of face it was; the eyes were half-hidden beneath heavy lids and the mouth was unhumanly broad, with the tip of the tongue pressing absurdly through it. The expression on the face was the troubling thing, though. There was nothing human about it; it seemed to regard him and the universe with terrible indifference.

Phil glanced at him. "Unnerving, isn't it? It's in the style of the people we call the Dorset culture and the Kalaalit, the native people of Greenland, call the Tuniit—the people who lived in the Arctic before the Kalaalit and the other Inuit peoples got there. A lot of their art is really unsettling, and nobody knows why. Most of them disappeared around 1500 or so. Nobody knows why that happened either."

Wind whistled in the rigging. "That's been happening in this part of the world for a very long time," Phil said. "Ships vanish, people vanish, civilizations vanish. There's a poem from one of the Ice Age civilizations—in English it runs like this." He chanted:

> "Into the west, unknown of man,
> Ships have sailed since the world began.
> Read, if you dare, what Skelos wrote,
> With dead hands fumbling his silken coat,
> And follow the ships through the wind-blown rack,
> Follow the ships that come not back."

"That's spooky," said Toby. "I like it. Who's Skelos?"

"Nobody knows much about him," said Phil. "There's a little about him in the *Nemedian Chronicle* and in recherché Scandinavian writers like Johannes Bureus and Arne Saknussemm. Supposedly he was a loremaster who lived in ancient times."

"Hyperborean times?" Toby asked.

"Long before that. But he wrote a book. It was lost a long time ago, but supposedly part of what's in it is the story of his travels across the Atlantic. The rest—" Phil shrugged.

"Philosophy, sorcery, folklore, the sort of thing you find in the *Necronomicon*, the *Book of Eibon*, and so on. That's what Arne Saknussemm says. He claimed he'd found a few fragments of the book in a wizard's tomb in Sweden."

Toby nodded absently. One of the lines from the poem— "follow the ships that come not back"—circled in his mind, reminding him that the expedition was not without danger, that even in the twenty-first century there were ships that came not back. He tried to push that aside. "So why did the archeologist say the ivory face was a forgery?"

"Because the site where I found it was still inhabited into the 1860s." He looked away, toward the ocean. "Some historians claim that there were a couple of Tuniit villages on islands in Hudson Bay until 1900 or so, when an epidemic killed the last survivors—but you won't see many scholars who accept that these days. They've all been taught that the Dorsets were gone by 1500, and so any evidence that contradicts that—well, it has to be a forgery, right?"

Toby considered the carving again. Tense with unspoken purpose, it seemed to writhe before his eyes. A memory surfaced: a scrap of something he'd read in one of the Lovecraft stories. "You said you found it on the west coast of Greenland," he said. "Way up the coast?"

"On the south end of Melville Bay," said Phil. "That's nearly as far as the coast goes."

"Any chance a professor named William Channing Webb went there in 1860 or so?"

Phil's face lit up. "You've heard of the Webb expedition? I'm impressed."

"Lovecraft mentioned it in 'The Call of Cthulhu.'"

Phil gave him a sudden searching glance, then nodded. "I suppose he did. Yes, as far as we could tell, this was the northernmost village Webb visited—and that's just it. His articles on the Melville Bay people say that they weren't like the Kalaalit, they had different traditions and customs, and some of the details he gives really makes it sound like they were a relict population partly descended from the Late Dorset culture. Smallpox or something killed them off by 1870, but there was a lot that could have been learned from the site if the team had approached it with anything like an open mind." He shook his head.

"They worshipped a *tornasuk*," Toby said then, recallng another detail from Lovecraft.

"*Tornarssuk*," Phil corrected him. "It's a word in all the Inuit languages—'the one who gives power.' That's where the name of the inlet comes from—Tornarssukalik, the place where there's a giver of power."

"I was wondering about that," Toby admitted.

Phil nodded. "To an *angaqoq*, a Kalaalit shaman, the one who gives power is the polar bear, the wolf, the raven, or the walrus—but if Webb was right, the Melville Bay people had a different tradition. Their chief *tornarssuk* was asleep in a great stone house under the sea."

It took an effort for Toby to keep his reaction off his face.

"Their shamans did rituals trying to contact him, to wake him up from his sleep," Phil went on. "This—" He indicated the carving. "—is probably one of the other spirits their shamans invoked. I don't get the sense that it was a particularly easy or safe activity."

He closed the box, put it back inside his coat. "But that's just it. The Arctic is like that. Even nowadays, people die there all the time because they aren't quite careful enough, and do something that wouldn't be any kind of problem back home. In the Arctic, you don't go anywhere alone; you don't take chances; you don't let yourself get out of reach of help—and even then, you can't be entirely sure you'll be going home when the season's over."

* * *

Three more days of steady sailing brought the *Arkham* to port at Reykjavik. All through the last day, the great white mass of the Vatnajokull ice fields hovered above the sea to the north-northeast, a stark soaring presence against blue sky. Toby kept at his work as long as he could stand it, but each morning he lingered on the bridge deck for a quarter hour or so, watching the surging ocean and the mountainous island rising ahead, and three or four times a day he put aside the books and went to stand on deck and taste the wind and the salt spray.

On the last morning before arrival he abandoned all pretense of working, visited the bridge long enough to glance at the chart and figure out where the *Arkham* was, and returned to the deck and stood watching as the Reykjanes peninsula slid past to starboard, a ragged green shape dotted with gray stone. The Garðskagi lighthouse flashed its warning, at first a point of light on the horizon, then a tall shape rising above a distant shoreline. By the time it was off the aft quarter, Reykjavik's brightly painted houses and bland Nordic-modern public buildings could just be made out ahead. Toby stood watching until a tugboat came puffing out from Reykjavik harbor to guide the *Arkham* to its mooring, reminding him that he still had to pack.

He got his cabin cleared, his duffel loaded, and his charged phone in his pocket a few minutes before the lurch that told him the *Arkham* was tied up alongside a pier. Minutes passed. Finally a knock sounded on the cabin door. He answered it with the duffel already slung from his shoulder, and moments later was hurrying along with the others down stair after stair, inside the ship at first and then, after crossing the main deck, down a portable stair to the pier.

Phil led them to the street at the pier's foot and told them to wait. After a few minutes a hotel shuttle came rattling down the access road and the driver got out. He was a big blond-haired man who spoke accented English, grinned at them, got their duffels heaped up in back and drove them to a nondescript hotel on the edge of Reykjavik's downtown district. There they checked into their rooms and then assembled again, all but Wren, in the stark glass and aluminum wilderness of the hotel lobby.

The next few hours went into tourist things—"Might as well get it out of our systems," Phil said, and Toby couldn't disagree. The six of them walked down to Lækjartorg, Reykjavik's central square, past rows of brightly colored houses roofed in corrugated iron. From there they strolled around, took in a couple of museums and a few of the town's other sites, and wound up in a little restaurant close to the harbor where seafood dishes outnumbered everything else on the menu and no two beers on tap were from the same continent. "If we had a little more time," Bill said, "we could go out Laugavegur to the weirdest museum in town, the Hið Íslenzka Reðasafn."

"Okay, I'll bite," said Orrin. "What's weird about it?"

"It's a museum of the phallus." Louise choked on her beer. Bill grinned and went on. "Seriously. They've got like three hundred penises in jars of formaldehyde. Whale penises, walrus penises, human penises, you name it."

Susan turned to Louise and said, "I'm waiting for the first person to make a joke about logical phallusies." Louise choked on her beer again.

"Logical," said Bill, "is the last word I'd use for that particular organ."

"Compared with a uterus," Susan told him, "it's a marvel of rationality. Ask any woman when she's having menstrual cramps." Orrin turned bright red, and Bill and Phil laughed. Toby, for whom the female body was still purely theoretical territory, kept his expression bland and added a mental note to his limited knowledge on the subject.

A leisurely walk brought them back to the hotel, and they were most of the way to the elevators when one of them opened and Wren came out of it. "What's up?" Phil asked her.

She paused, for all the world as though she didn't know the idiom and had to parse it. "I'm driving up to the University," she told him.

All at once, the excuse Toby had longed for opened up in front of him. "Reykjavik University?" he asked, and when she nodded: "Do you mind giving me a ride? I was hoping to talk to Dr. Ragnhild Ormsdóttir."

The sea-colored eyes turned toward him. "Does she know you're coming?"

"I emailed her before we left," said Toby.

That was apparently enough. She motioned with her head: follow me. Toby stifled a grin, nodded to the others, and followed her back out the doors to the street, and then three blocks down to a car rental office. While Wren filled out paperwork and handed over her credit card, he sent a text to Dr. Ormsdóttir, letting her know that he'd arrived and would like to come by. He was startled to get an immediate reply welcoming him to Iceland and inviting him to stop in at her office as soon as he could find the time.

By the time he'd responded to that, Wren had rented a car, a little yellow Fiat with two doors, two seats, and barely enough room to take a deep breath. As he settled into the passenger seat and Wren steered the car onto the street outside with precise motions, Toby tried to figure out something to say to her and failed completely. The thought of trying to make casual chat with her embarrassed him, the thought of spreading his feelings out before her horrified him, and if there was a third alternative he couldn't think of it. With those thoughts circling in his head, Toby kept his silence until Wren found a parking space within a block of Reykjavik University.

Once the car stopped, she turned toward him. "Thank you."

Toby gave her a baffled look. "For what?"

"You don't chatter. I appreciate that."

He took that in. "You're welcome."

She nodded and opened the door. Toby did the same, and tried not to blush too hard as he clambered out of the Fiat.

* * *

Dr. Ragnhild Ormsdóttir was tall and statuesque, with blonde hair gone mostly silver and clothing a good deal more formal than Toby's: skirt and jacket in brown tweed wool and a silk blouse with ruffles in front. She greeted him with a broad smile and the Hyperborean words "*Oqqol ish'matampa oe?*"—in what way may I be of service? Toby, unsurprised, grinned and responded appropriately: "*Djai im'ayampa*"—you are kind. The formalities out of the way, and greetings from Toby's teachers at Case Western passed on, she waved him to a seat, settled in her own chair, and said in crisp Oxford-accented English, "But tell me about this expedition of yours. Where in Greenland will you be going, again? And how long will you stay?"

Over the next quarter hour or so he passed on most of what he knew about the voyage to Tornarssukalik Station and the sixteen months he'd be spending there, and she beamed and nodded. "A fine plan," she said when he was finished. "I visited the station half a dozen times back when it was occupied regularly. My last summer there they found one of the inscriptions the Webb expedition went looking for, and I got into the most frightful quarrel with Hamilton Broward over a subjunctive absolute." She shook her head, laughing.

It took Toby a moment to remember where he'd heard of the Webb expedition. "What was the inscription?"

"A *tuqqoli niunda*," she said, and his eyes went wide. "Yes, that was the summer that turned up." She got to her feet, went to a cabinet, pulled out a folded sheet of thin paper and unfolded it to its full size, maybe three feet by eighteen inches. Handing it to Toby: "You've only had transcriptions to work with, correct? Here's the rubbing I made. A little more interesting, wouldn't you say?"

Toby managed to fumble his way through a response. Rubbings were old technology but still useful even in an age of computer scanning, and Toby had taken paper and wax crayons to a cemetery or two as part of his university classwork to get some basic skill in the technique. It was one thing to copy the inscription on a nineteenth-century headstone, though; it was quite another to handle a rubbing made of a *tuqqoli niunda*, a stone of remembrance from ancient Hyperborea, and know that the weathered and pitted inscription on the stone had been carved three quarters of a million years ago by hands that had not quite finished becoming human. He could make out a few entries in the long list of place-names and distances, somber testimony to the grief of a vanished people for the homeland they had lost.

The two of them discussed the text and its source, and went from there to a free mix of ancient Arctic linguistics and gossip about other scholars in the field. After more than an hour of conversation, recalling an approaching appointment, Dr. Ormsdóttir took Toby to the university library and arranged for him to have access to the Hyperborean and Lomarian collections while the *Arkham* remained in port, a stroke of luck he hadn't expected. When she went back to her office, he checked the time, found that he still had most of an hour before he'd agreed to meet Wren, headed for the collection of early texts on Hyperborea, and found Wren there ahead of him, sitting at a wooden table, and turning the pages of a big Latin folio as though she was skimming casually through a magazine.

She glanced up at him, nodded a silent greeting. Toby nodded in response, went into the stacks and found an unexpected treasure, a copy of the rare first edition of Friedrich von Junzt's *Unaussprechlichen Kulten*, with its lengthy narrative history of the preglacial past. He carried his prize to the table and paged through the book until the headings in jagged *fraktur* script read 𝕰𝖗𝖟ä𝖍𝖑𝖚𝖓𝖌 𝖉𝖊𝖗 ä𝖑𝖙𝖊𝖗𝖊𝖓 𝖂𝖊𝖑𝖙, "Narrative of the Elder World." A little further searching found him the description of Hyperborea's rise and fall, and his mastery of German was more than sufficient to allow him to follow von Junzt's tale: the settlement of the great northern island by a legendary species of primitive hominids called voormis, the arrival of the first protohumans millions of years later, the diffusion of civilization and literacy from long-vanished Nemedis, the three great Hyperborean dynasties. Then, in the traditional account, came the Ice Age, the long hopeless struggle against the spreading glaciers, and the flight of the last refugees to new homes on the island of Atlantis in its earliest days, the days of the Witch-Kings, before golden cities rose out of green jungle and the empire of Atlantis spread over four continents.

He'd read the same section before more than once in English translation, but von Junzt's ornate nineteenth-century German made the story a little more real for him, and reminded him of another place that had risen and fallen far more recently. There were no stones of remembrance for the little town on the New Jersey coast that had once been called Pine Harbor. You couldn't even find the name on maps made after 1955 or so, the town's erasure had been that complete. Nor had the handful who'd made it to Lefferts Corners found a destiny there anything as bright as the one that waited for the Hyperboreans in Atlantis, where families of Hyperborean descent played important roles straight through Atlantean history.

Instead, the folk of Pine Harbor dwindled and died, leaving only one descendant. The descendant in question tried to drag his thoughts back to Hyperborea, with little success.

* * *

"I've got some good news," Phil said first thing the next morning. "We have reservations at the Blue Lagoon at eleven. I figure we should enjoy ourselves while we can. We'll be under way as soon as the ship's loaded, and in Greenland a couple of days after that."

"What's the Blue Lagoon?' Toby asked. He was feeling unusually cheerful just then. His conversation with Dr. Ormsdóttir the day before had encouraged his academic hopes, and Wren had responded to his carefully maintained silence in the library and on the ride back to the hotel with what looked remarkably like relief. Some people just don't like chatter, he reminded himself. *If she's like that, I can deal.*

"Hot springs," Bill told him, grinning. "It's famous, the kind of place celebrities go. You don't want to miss it."

Toby, appalled, managed somehow to keep his reaction off his face. "I'll pass. I'm going to be going up to the university again this morning."

Phil shot a quizzical look his way. "You're sure? Bill's right, it's worth doing."

Toby forced a grin. "I'm sure. You've got tenure, you can afford to relax."

"Gotcha," Susan said to Phil, and the professor nodded ruefully, acknowledging.

"You," Bill said, turning to Toby, "are seriously going to regret this. When it's February and we're all taking cold showers to save fuel, you're going to *dream* of hot springs."

Toby kept his grin fixed in place and said something inoffensive to turn the conversation toward something less risky. As he took the elevator down to the lobby at eight-thirty, though, Bill's words still stung. It would be so easy if he could just explain to them why the thought of cold showers didn't bother him at all and why climbing into a seething hot spring was his idea of Hell, but the secret had to be kept.

By the time the elevator got to the lobby, though, he'd changed his plans for the morning and took it right back up to his room. He'd readied an excuse in case he ran into someone from the expedition, but his luck held. It took him only a moment to put on swim trunks under his jeans and stuff a spare set of underwear and a hotel towel into an innocuous bag, and then he headed back down and went straight to the same car rental place Wren had used. Half an hour later he was perched in the driver's seat of a little Renault, weaving through sparse traffic on his way to one of the beaches he'd read about in the tourist book in his hotel room.

The morning had turned gray and cold. The GPS unit atop the dashboard guided him in its mindless way to an empty parking lot just above a beach of black sand in a cove bounded by stark headlands. He stripped down to the swim trunks in the car, then got out, found the trail through the low dunes, and walked down to the wet sand just above the surf.

Aunt Dinah had warned him over and over again about going into the sea, but she'd meant the coast of New Jersey and New York, he was sure of it. The Deep Ones off the shores of Iceland, if any of them happened to be there, wouldn't be waiting for a chance to avenge whatever the people of Pine Harbor had done to earn their silent wrath: he was sure of that, too. It still took an effort to go rest of the way, to wade out into the surging green water and then, when he'd gotten chest deep, to plunge forward into the water, open his mouth and his gills, and let his body do what it was born to do.

He wasn't prepared for the electric rush that went through him as his gills swept up oxygen from the churning waters, the sense that he'd never before been able to take a really deep breath, the surge of strength that shot through his muscles as the frigid water stripped away years of weary heat. Those startled him so much that he rose to the surface again and trod water for a few moments while he blinked and gasped and tried to clear his thoughts. Then, bracing himself, he plunged again, swam deeper. His eyes adjusted effortlessly to the dim light and the water. He could see the sand on the bottom of the cove with perfect clarity, watched fish darting out of his way. He let himself enjoy the cold oxygenated water, and then rose to the surface again.

He heard the voice while he was still blinking water from his eyes. What it said was a mystery to him—something in Icelandic, he guessed—but the voice was a man's, and obviously concerned. "I'm fine," Toby shouted back, hoping the words would communicate, and swam shorewards, allowing himself one more blissful rush of salt water across his gills. Once he was close enough to shore he forced the water out of his gills, clamped the muscles shut, hauled himself to his feet and filled his lungs again.

He blinked and blinked again, and finally saw something more than a blur on the beach in front of him. Stark naked, barrel-chested, and furry as a bear, a big blond Icelander stood knee deep in the surf, facing him with a radiant grin. Toby walked toward him, and the man called out in English, "Damn! You're American, aren't you? I never met an American who had the balls to go swimming in the ocean here."

"You've met one now," Toby said.

The Icelander laughed, as though Toby had cracked a joke. "Damn!" he said again. "You tell everyone else in America they ought to try it. It's good for you." Still grinning, he waded out to sea as Toby climbed up on the beach. Toby turned and watched him as he plunged into the water with a tremendous splash, surfaced, and headed further out with a powerful breast stroke, for all the world as though he meant to swim straight to Newfoundland that day.

An east wind blew pleasantly chill as Toby headed back to his rented car. The Icelander's car, a four-wheeler well caked with mud, was parked two spaces from Toby's. The cars screened Toby as he shed the swim trunks, toweled off, and dressed. A glance back to the beach showed the Icelander still swimming—he'd apparently decided that Newfoundland was dull that time of year, and was heading back toward the beach. Laughing, Toby climbed behind the wheel of the Renault, got the engine started, and headed back toward Reykjavik.

He spent the rest of the morning and all the afternoon at the library again—alone, this time, for Wren had found somewhere else to go. When he took the car back to the rental office, though, he asked the clerk about used bookstores. He returned to the hotel an hour or so later with two battered paperback collections of stories by H.P. Lovecraft.

CHAPTER 3

TORNARSSUKALIK STATION

I t took five days for the *Arkham* to take on the rest of the supplies for the expedition and for its captain to gather reports about the ice near the Greenland shore, long enough for Toby to take copious notes from obscure books in the university library, and learn a little more about the place where he'd be spending most of a year and a half. "A little more" was the relevant phrase, for there wasn't much to find. Miskatonic University had put its research station in one of the most isolated parts of the great icebound island, a desolate coastal region where not even the native Greenlanders went if they could help it. Shards of pottery and a single bronze arrowhead from late in the Uzuldaroum period hinted at Hyperborean settlements, in the days when that stretch of coast was part of the province of Tscho Vulpanomi; shards of another style of pottery told of a Lomarian presence during the last interglacial; rings of stones south of Tornarssukalik Station marked a campsite of the Dorset people perhaps a thousand years back, and after that, nothing until the first two ships from Miskatonic, the *Manuxet* and the *Sarah Orne*, struggled their way in through the pack ice to drop anchor in Tornarssukalik Inlet.

The day of departure finally arrived. The morning turned out gray and chill, with a harsh wind flicking spray from the tips of waves in the harbor. The hotel van took the seven of

49

them back to the ship. Twenty minutes or so after Toby got settled in his cabin, he felt the jolt and murmur that told of the ship's engines getting under way. A glance out the porthole showed the roofs of Reykjavik beginning to slide away.

Before long fog flowed in, blotting out sky and horizon alike, and the *Arkham* rounded the long peninsula of Snaefellsnes without anyone aboard catching a glimpse of the great white cone of Snaefellsjokul at its end. When the last shelter of the land fell away and the *Arkham* set out across Denmark Strait, Toby could feel the great rolling swells of the deep ocean rising up under the surface waves. Bundled up in wet-weather gear, he headed for the bridge deck and stood at the rail for a long while, drinking in the salt air and wondering what lay ahead.

He'd been there half an hour or so when a sudden gurgling rush sounded off to left—port, he reminded himself, on a ship it's called port. Maybe a quarter mile from the *Arkham*, maybe less, a whale had risen to the surface, black and glistening, its breath rising in a great plume of vapor from its blowhole. It stayed long enough to fill its lungs and then plunged back into the deeps, showing the broad flukes of its tail before it vanished. He watched the water churn where it had been, let out a breath he hadn't been conscious of holding. His grandmother had said once that the Deep Ones knew the languages of the different nations of whales, and he wondered what whales talked about and what they and the Deep Ones said to one another.

That brought back colder memories. When the people at Pine Harbor realized that an armed mob was heading their way, he'd been told many times in childhood, they'd sent an urgent message into the sea—a call for help to the Deep Ones—and waited for the waters to roil and the green-skinned folk of the depths to arrive in force, armed with weapons more deadly than human rifles and torches. It wasn't the first time they'd had to send such a message, but this time they waited in vain. No help came, the unequal fight ended the only way it could, and flames rose over Pine Harbor's houses as the mob threw corpses into the marshes behind the town, where no one would look for them. Fourteen survivors had reached deep water in time, and for years thereafter they'd wondered, silently or aloud, what Pine Harbor had done to make the Deep Ones turn their backs on their relatives ashore.

What had been said, or left unsaid, to make that happen? Toby kept that with all the other unanswered questions about his past. It circled through his mind as he watched the sea for a while longer, then turned and went inside.

None of the members of the advance party said much at lunch or dinner, as the *Arkham* drove northwest through gray troubled seas. Toward late afternoon a huge white iceberg loomed up in the middle distance, and Toby joined the others on the bridge deck and watched it slip past: a stark shape bordered with soaring cliffs on every side he could see. It looked alien, a shard fallen into the ocean from some otherworldly kingdom. Seagulls wheeled around it crying in plaintive voices, and here and there skeins of blue water plunged from it into the sea.

Toby watched it in silence. He recalled enough maritime history to know that if it so much as brushed against the *Arkham* in passing, they'd have to run for the life rafts and hope for rescue in some of the worst seas on the planet. The crew of the *Arkham* knew their business, though. They gave it a wide berth, and did the same to the two other bergs that moved past later.

The sun never set that night. Toby got what sleep he could, but every time he woke he saw light coming in through the porthole, and when he finally gave up and went on the bridge deck for a little while, a piece of the northern horizon was the livid mottled color of an old bruise and a glow stretched out to either side. Ahead of the *Arkham*, a different light hovered low and ghostly above the horizon; it took Toby some minutes to remember something he'd read about Arctic voyages, and recognize it as the ice blink, reflected light from the ice pack around Greenland. He stood staring at it for a long while, finally made himself go back to his cabin.

After a while, he slept, and somewhere in the deep places of the night he dreamed.

He was in a lightless place, where cold air sighed against cold stone. Though he could see nothing, the air echoed in a way that suggested caverns and underground vaults. He was lying on his back, hard stone beneath him. As he lay there, footsteps whispered in the unquiet air, and a pale light began to spread through the space, as though some unexpectedly small and distant moon rose in the sky. The light revealed a dark shape looming over him, and Toby froze in dread until the light became strong enough for him to see what the shape was.

A man bent over him, staring at his face, as though seeking something in it. The man was clothed in bulky garments of sealskin and fur that looked a little like Inuit clothing, but only a little, and his face was hidden behind a circular shape daubed with bright colors—a wooden mask, Toby realized after a moment of baffled dread. It had one eye contracted to a narrow crescent and the other round as the full moon, and the mouth was another round hole; the other features were reduced to abstractions; downy tufts of white feather surrounded the outer edge, interspersed with little glinting bits of native copper. Toby stared up at the masked figure for what seemed like a long time, until the dream went spinning away into darkness again.

* * *

Toby was up early and joined the others for breakfast. "We're about three hours out," Phil told them all, grinning. "Ready for our adventure?" The other members of the advance party nodded with varying degrees of enthusiasm. Toby tried to show an eagerness he didn't feel. The fact that he was about to spend sixteen months in a collection of quonset huts in the high arctic was beginning to weigh on him.

Once breakfast was over he went to his cabin, filled his duffel and hauled his gear down to add to the heap on deck.

The weather was bright and cold with a crisp wind out of the west. Dolphins darted and veered through the water ahead of the *Arkham*. Sea birds Toby didn't recognize circled the big steel cranes amidships. The wind danced and the cold air burned in his nostrils, but something else caught his attention. Ahead, the gray churning sea had given way to something new and unsettling: a line of white, not quite even, that spread across the horizon from starboard to port as far as sight could reach. Beyond it a faint darkness seemed to hover close to the horizon. Greenland, Toby thought, and then: Hyperborea.

He wasn't the only one who stared. The three grad students, Louise, Susan, and Orrin, gathered on the main deck not far away from him and watched in awed silence as the shore drew nearer. A little further away, Bill stood with his arms crossed, facing the shore as though he expected it to fling down a challenge at his feet. Further still, Phil Dyer stood with his chin up, grinning, for all the world like a traveler returning home.

Soft footfalls on the stairs announced Wren. She glanced at the approaching ice pack as she came on deck, then added her duffel to the others and sat down on a deck fitting, looking at nothing in particular, wrapped in thoughts Toby didn't even try to guess.

The three hours passed. The *Arkham* veered to starboard to avoid the thickest of the ice ahead, pushed through scattered floes, and finally broke through into the shore lead. Ahead, Greenland rose stark against the morning. Though he'd read plenty about climate change, Toby half expected to see images like the ones in old photos, mountains wrapped in ice and glaciers plowing their way down to the sea. Instead, the mountains ahead rose bare and brown. Rounded valleys gaped between them where glaciers once flowed. White patches still crouched on north-facing slopes, but that was all the ice Toby saw on land, and the sea ice was a fraction of what old photos showed. He stared, tried to process the immensity of the change.

At the feet of the mountains, a dim shoreline spread out, mottled in a dozen subtle shades of green and gray and spotted here and there with snow that hadn't melted yet. Ahead, an inlet stretched off toward the mountains. Cliffs rose sheer from the water's edge to the north, and a broad stretch of tundra dotted with low hills spread to the south. As the ship drew closer still, little black dots moved over the tundra, and eventually the dots became musk oxen grazing on grasses and sedges. Toby recognized the landscape at once, knew where to look to spot the gray quonset huts of Tornarssukalik Station, the big fuel tank rising behind them, the antennas on another hill further off, alien shapes against the contours of the land.

Another quarter hour brought the *Arkham* close to shore just south of the inlet. The anchor chain rattled and the anchor splashed. "Okay," said Phil. "Now we've got work to do."

The four hours or so after the *Arkham* dropped anchor went past in a blur. A first helping of supplies and gear had to be loaded onto the *Arkham*'s two motor launches, taken ashore, and then hauled to the quonset huts atop the hillock. That was easier than it could have been, as Phil hurried up to the Station while the others were unloading the first launch, and came back driving a battered pickup with no doors and a flat bed someone had pretty clearly built by hand. The wind rushed past, keening to itself. Voices, the pickup's engine, crunch of wheels and boots on gravel blended with the wind's song, but Toby had no attention to spare for the landscape around him. His world consisted of an endless sequence of cardboard boxes and five-gallon buckets of white plastic that had to be hauled off the launches, stacked on the beach, loaded onto the pickup, and piled temporarily just inside the doors of the station.

By the time Phil called a halt, Toby's muscles were aching with exhaustion. It took nearly all the strength he had left to climb into the launch that took them back to the *Arkham* and haul himself up the stairs to the messroom for one more shipboard meal. A full belly and an hour off his feet made more of a difference than he'd expected, though, and he had no trouble heading back down again to the launch and bracing himself for another round of work as the launch pulled away from the *Arkham*'s side and crossed to the shore.

Then it was four more hours of offloading as the sun circled behind the mountains to the west. "Good," Dyer said finally, as Bill drove the pickup to the station with its last load. "Let's get things set for tonight and then turn in. We've got a lot more to do tomorrow."

They walked up the gravel-covered trail to the station in a loose file. No one spoke. To the north, across the inlet, the gray cliffs rose up stark and sheer a good two thousand feet. To the south, tundra still half covered with snow reached away into the middle distance, stopped at the foot of steep ragged hills. Ahead, to the west, the hills closed in, and Tornarssukalik Inlet went through a gap and bent southward out of sight. Behind, to eastward, icebergs punctuated the horizon, luminous white against the subtler colors of sea and sky. The wind whistled past, and a bird Toby didn't recognize—a golden plover, he learned later—came fluttering out from the grass to one side of the path, then stopped to watch the newcomers pass by.

The main doors of the station slid open when Dyer pulled on them. Inside, dim light from yellowed fiberglass skylights filtered down into the central corridor. More work had to be done, and Toby ended up helping Bill Allen roll a barrel of diesel oil to the generator shed behind the station, and handed over tools while Bill took on an assortment of intricate tasks about which Toby knew precisely nothing. In due time the generator growled awake, lights sprang on, appliances whirred and hummed, and Toby helped haul boxes into the kitchen until enough food had been put away for the next few days and a meal of canned beef stew and pilot bread was ready. By then the others had finished whatever tasks they'd been assigned. Once the meal was over, Dyer assigned the next day's chores and told everyone to get some sleep.

Toby was more than ready to do just that. His room was a cramped but comfortable little space just off the central corridor, with a narrow bed in a metal bedstead that reminded him of college dorms, and a few other pieces of furniture—desk, dresser, bookshelf, chair—that echoed the cheap furnished apartments he'd rented in his graduate years. His pillow, sheets and blankets had been tossed onto the mattress by whoever had unpacked them. He used the last of his energy to get the bed made and himself into tee shirt and boxers, tossed his clothing all anyhow onto the desk, got settled under the covers and fell asleep within moments.

* * *

The next three days were variations on the same theme, except that Toby and the others didn't return to the *Arkham* and the station began to feel more like home with each meal cooked and eaten there, each hour of welcome sleep. Sixteen months of supplies all had to be offloaded from the *Arkham's* launches, hauled up to the station one pickup load at a time, and then stored in some kind of order in their proper places. Toby quickly settled into a role unloading the launches, which sometimes involved getting splashed with sea water he knew humans would consider cold. Some of the others asked him whether he was okay, and Toby grinned and said something about his family's metabolism. They nodded and seemed to accept it. Wren, for her part, gave him a measuring look he couldn't interpret, said nothing, did her own share of the unloading with tireless patience and precision.

Late the fourth morning, one of the launches brought a few stray buckets and a big box of waterproof flares to finish the offloading, and that was that. Phil Dyer went aboard to confer with the captain, came back half an hour later, and not long after that the *Arkham* hauled up its anchors and began to back out of the inlet. Most of the advance party stood out in front of the main door of the station to watch it leave. When the freighter had vanished from sight beyond an iceberg, they trickled in one by one. Toby lingered outside longer than most, feeling the immense solitude and silence of Greenland. The briefings they'd all received before leaving Arkham had mentioned the nearest settlement, a little Kalaalit village called Tulugaqtak more than a hundred miles further south, but the only route there involved a boat and a long, risky trip along the shore flaw—inland the mountains were too rugged for anyone but an expert mountaineer to traverse, and there was only one of those in the expedition.

At lunch Bill announced that he'd made radio contact with Arkham and the rest of the expedition would be on its way soon. Afterward, they settled the chore rotation that would last until the main party arrived, and got to work on the preparations and minor repairs the station needed. That was less strenuous than the offloading but just as busy. The station had come through the three years since the last expedition in fairly good shape, but there were leaks to be patched, pipes and tanks to be tested, two more diesel generators in the shed that had to be checked carefully, refueled, and then fired up, and the helicopter and the four snowmobiles in the hangar next to the station had to go through the same process.

Toby learned more about the helicopter than he'd expected. It was a big two-rotor Bell, military surplus from the mid-twentieth century, and it had been in the hangar except for short flights since before most of the advance party's members were born. In an emergency, Phil Dyer said, it could lift twenty-four people and get them to high ground, and that was its job. "The ice dam's about twelve miles inland," Phil told them; they'd all heard it before, but the reminder didn't seem out of place. "Once the sensors tell us it's started to crack and the alarms go off, we've got just a few minutes to get up in the air before the *jokulhlaup* hits and this station and everything in it goes out to sea. That's why all of you are going to learn how to start the engine and get the copter into the air."

In the days that followed, between long stints at other chores, Toby got used to sitting in the pilot's seat, reaching for the necessary buttons and switches, and then pulling back on the controls as though taking off. Outside the blurred windows in front, he could see the clutter of spare parts and tools. To one side of those were the big electric motors that made the hangar roof slide open in a hurry; to the other were two old refrigerators holding extra food, some big cardboard boxes of freeze-dried meals for trips inland, and a rack loaded with big orange duffels full of emergency supplies, one marked with the name of each member of the expedition, to be scooped up and taken aboard the helicopter if the big siren atop the hangar sounded. The snowmobiles were by the roll-up door; on the other end of the hangar, a rack of electronics and big backup batteries monitored the sensors in the ice dam. More than once, after his turn at the copter's controls, he went to look at the screens, saw straight green lines traced across black, reassuring him. If those lines suddenly jumped, he knew, the siren overhead would sound.

The one interruption to the routine came two days after the freighter left, when another ship nosed its way into Tornarssukalik Inlet. "Oil tanker," Phil said as he headed for the doors. "It's here to fill up the main tank." That involved watching big burly men stretch what amounted to a big hose from the ship to the tank back behind the quonset huts— underground pipes weren't an option, Toby gathered, not with the slowly melting permafrost—and go about complicated tasks for most of a day, after which they waved goodbye to Phil and returned to the tanker. Half an hour later the tanker had vanished beyond the pack ice, leaving the station and the advance party to the silence of the tundra.

Thereafter the days settled into a rhythm that soon became familiar. Toby got used to taking turns at the cookstove, the dishwashing sink, the big industrial washer and dryer where everyone's laundry went in together. He and the others had enough to do that no one went outside for long or walked far. During those first days, going to and from the helicopter hangar or hauling spare parts and fuel out to the generator shed gave Toby what contact he had with the wild stark land around the station.

Those brief glimpses showed him more than he expected. Now and again he spotted musk oxen in the distance, moving slowly as though drifting with the wind. Birds soared and darted all through the long days, and once the massive white shape of a polar bear came pacing along Tornarssukalik Inlet, sniffing the air as it went. It plunged into the water not far from where they'd unloaded the supplies from the launches, and went swimming out toward the pack ice. "You see?" Phil said over dinner that evening. "They're around, and as far as they're concerned, you're just another piece of meat. That's why you don't ever go anywhere in Greenland alone, or without a rifle."

"They're also meat," Wren said.

Everyone turned to look at her. "Sure," said Bill. "But you'd better have a rifle or the bear's going to be the one enjoying the meal."

She considered that, nodded, took another bite of her chicken curry. After a few moments, the conversation picked up again, but everyone but Wren looked slightly unnerved.

* * *

Over the days that followed, Bill kept them posted on the movements of the rest of the expedition. A commercial flight got the whole team to Gander in Newfoundland, the nearest big airport to the west; three flights on smaller planes, one of them delayed by atrocious weather over Davis Strait, got them to Nuuk, the capital of Greenland: but then a storm off Baffin Bay had Nuuk socked in for three days. Finally, late one morning, Bill came out of the radio room grinning. "The first copter's up," he said. "Guests in about eight hours."

That meant another round of chores: getting rooms ready for the newcomers, mostly, and beginning to get ready for the work the expedition would be doing once everyone had arrived. Just after six that evening, as Toby helped roll another barrel of lubricating oil to the hangar for the snowmobiles and the sun gleamed red over the mountains to the west, a low faint murmur that didn't sound like the wind spread through the air. Once he and Orrin got the barrel where it belonged, they stopped outside to listen. The murmur became a rhythm, and after a little while Orrin pointed at a tiny dot up above the mountain crests. "Here we go," he said, grinning.

By the time the copter settled down on the flat space behind the quonset huts, the whole advance party was outside to welcome them. The big doors on the side of the copter slid open. Four people clambered down, crouching against the downdraft from the rotors, clutching duffels and rucksacks. One of them slid the door shut, and they hurried over to the waiting party as the helicopter pilot waved and the copter rose up again and headed back west.

Three of the newcomers shook Phil's hand and then headed into the station. The fourth, a stocky woman with gray hair in a short practical cut, went at once to Wren and talked with her in a low voice, then went to Phil and threw her arms around him and said something else inaudible, then followed Phil over to where Toby was standing. "Toby," Phil said, "this is Emmeline Grenier. Emmeline, Toby Gilman."

Toby didn't have to fake a grin. "Dr. Grenier," he said. "It's an honor to meet you."

"*Docteur* Grenier?" she said, with a strong French accent. "Bah! You will call me Emmeline, of course. We are, how you say it, in the fields." She considered him with her head at an angle. "So you are the Toby Gilman who has so very many linguists running this and that way like the chickens without heads. Sometime soon we will talk, eh?"

He said something agreeable. She nodded once as though the matter had been settled, and headed for the quonset huts with Phil, talking rapidly in French the whole time. Toby turned to go, realized suddenly that he and Wren were the only two people still standing on the landing area, and she was regarding him with a look he couldn't read at all.

"I would speak," she said then in flawless Middle Hyperborean.

"*Djai iqqol,*" he responded politely, covering his surprise and uncertainty.

"It is well." A quick glance made sure no one else was in earshot. "I will need your help in the days ahead."

"*Qed gadi ish'qadaun,*" he said at once: if it can be done I will do it.

"*Ish'silampa,*" she replied: I know. While he was still processing that, she went on in English: "Is Emmeline correct about names?"

It took him a moment to process the question. "I don't know," he admitted. "I haven't been on an expedition before."

She nodded, more or less: a stiff deliberate movement, the head dipping and then rising after an instant. "Thank you, Toby," she said, and set out at once for the quonset huts. Toby stared at her for a moment, and then hurried after her.

All that evening, as the newly arrived members of the expedition settled in and the advance party helped them, Toby wondered about what she'd said, about the dazed warm feelings she waked in him, and most of all about Wren herself. The strange way she'd nodded left him baffled: it was as though she'd learned to make the motion out of a book. Maybe it had something to do with her nervous breakdown, he told himself.

He had little spare time for wondering over the next few days. The copter returned with four more members of the expedition early the following evening; it was back with four more the next day, and brought the last four the day after that. Chores and duties had to be reassigned, more supplies broken out of storage, and the library made ready—the last team at Tornarssukalik Station had put every book into a plastic envelope and then covered the shelving with tarps to keep leaks in the roof from spoiling the collection, and that meant nearly a thousand books had to be freed of their wrappings and then put back onto the shelves in some semblance of order.

He and Susan were in the middle of that when voices shouting in the hallway outside told him that the helicopter had come. It was traditional for everyone to go meet the new arrivals, so he set down the book he was unwrapping and followed the others out to the landing area. The copter came down as before, the new arrivals hefted their luggage and hurried out from under the downwash, and the pilot waved and took off: it was no different from the last two times, except that one of the newcomers—a short, olive-skinned woman he almost remembered—glanced at him, gave him an icy glare, turned sharply and went toward the quonset huts. Bill Allen, who was standing next to Toby, gave him an amused look and said, "So what's that about?"

"No clue," Toby said. A moment later the face found a memory: the woman who'd spoken to him at the clambake and then come barging into Phil Dyer's office. It was most of a day later that he found time to leaf through paperwork, remind himself of her name—Leah Sargent—and find out that she had a Ph.D. in archeology from Miskatonic and was there on a postdoc fellowship, the same way he was. He shrugged, went back to the books.

* * *

Well before the last helicopter arrived, the station was more or less ready for sixteen months of occupancy, and some of the more experienced hands got busy in the dining hall as soon as lunch was over, doing something Toby couldn't figure out at first. As the afternoon lengthened, he made an excuse to go past Phil's office and ask him what was up.

"A party," the professor told him. "There's always one as soon as the last people arrive, and another the night before the first group leaves. It's one of those things." He considered Toby for a moment, and then said, "I know you haven't been in the field before, and I don't know if you have any sense of what it's like. You know the saying about Las Vegas? It's true here—what happens in Greenland stays in Greenland. Your job, everyone's job, is to do your work and your share of the chores and do your best to get along with the rest of the team, and other than that—" His shrug sent uncertainties spilling into the air. "What happens, happens."

Toby thanked him, made sure nothing else needed to be done, and retreated to the library, where sunlight filtered in through the fiberglass skylights and the swinging double door shut out the central corridor and the dining hall across it. He found an unexpected treasure, a reprint of Arne Saknussemm's 1559 classic *De Mirabilia Septentrionalibus*, and flopped on the battered library sofa to read it. Turning the pages past accounts of Saknussemm's journeys across Iceland and Greenland and his adventures in caverns far below Snaefellsjokul, he found a lengthy passage on an indecipherable "Norse runestone" from southeast Greenland—a Hyperborean stele, though Saknussemm had had no way of knowing that. A copperplate engraving gave the inscription clearly enough that Toby could read it at a glance: an edict of the Emperor Vardanax proclaiming a new governor for the province of Leqquan.

Interesting though that was to any student of ancient Arctic studies, he had trouble keeping his mind on it. It began to sink in that he was going to be spending sixteen months at Tornarssukalik Station with twenty-two people he didn't know at all, and whatever scholarly work he managed to get done would be only a small part of what would happen to him there. He squelched a sudden surge of panic before it could get a foothold in him, took the book back to its place, headed for the doors, and nearly ran into Leah Sargent as she walked through them.

A moment of mutual shock, a sudden cold glare on her side and a mumbled apology on his, and he stepped around her and pushed through the swinging doors into the station's central corridor. A glance back through the gap in the still-moving doors showed her heading for one of the shelves, her shoulders drawn up hard. Toby shook his head, considered going to Phil's office to see if he knew what the issue was, but discarded the notion.

He ended up spending the next hour helping Bill Allen with a recalcitrant water heater. His assistance consisted mostly of handing over tools and turning valves on and off on request, but it distracted him more effectively than Saknussemm's book had. It was far from the first time he'd helped Bill, either, and when Bill finally closed things up and wiped sweat off his forehead, he glanced at Toby and said, "Thanks. I ought to show you how to do some of this stuff."

"That'd be great," Toby told him. "I don't know how much translation I'm going to get to do, so I might as well learn something else useful."

"True enough," said Bill. Tightening a final screw: "Okay, that does it. Care for a beer?"

Toby had already learned that there were spare refrigerators in a couple of quiet corners of the station, antique oil-burning models with labels on the back in an assortment of minor European languages, and it didn't surprise him at all that Bill went straight to one or that it turned out to contain an unexpected cargo of cheap beer. They took a can each, sat on rickety chairs, listened to dim voices and footfalls in the middle distance.

"You just up and signed onto this thing at the last minute," Bill said.

"I had to get an assistantship," said Toby. He took a sip of the beer. "This is what turned up." He considered the can, took a more substantial swallow. "I'm not complaining."

"I bet." Bill copied the motion, emptying his can, and then crushed it in his hand with a sudden movement. He glanced at Toby, grinned, tossed the crumpled can into a recycle bin next to the refrigerator, and said, "Ever heard of a place in Massachusetts called Innsmouth?"

The question took Toby by surprise. "No. Why?"

"I knew a guy from there who looked a little like you."

"Well, I'm from the Catskills," said Toby, and downed another good-sized swallow. "As far as I know nobody in my family's from Massachusetts at all. When I went to Miskatonic for the campus visit this spring, that was the first time I'd ever been in the state."

Bill nodded as though it didn't matter at all, but behind the easy smile something shifted. Toby wasn't sure if his answer had passed a test or failed one, but it mattered, he knew that for certain. He finished his beer, tried to copy the sudden movement that had flattened Bill's can; the attempt didn't accomplish much. Bill grinned, said nothing.

* * *

Dinner was far more lavish than Toby expected. He'd gotten used to the plain bland industrial food that the kitchen seemed set up to turn out: stew or chili or ravioli from hefty #10 cans, biscuits or corn bread or rice pilaf from boxes, next to nothing that might not have been there for three years already and couldn't just as well be left for three more. When he passed the dining hall an hour before the meal, though, the scents that came out through the swinging doors couldn't have come from cans. Someone had been roasting meat, he could tell that at a sniff, and the rich warm yeasty smell of freshly baked bread followed it.

Well before six o'clock people began to gather outside the dining hall doors, talking in quick lively tones. Toby glanced at them on the way past, went somewhere else. He was back right at six, filed in with the others, lined up along one wall, picked up a plastic tray, napkins, cheap metal tableware: the usual routine, familiar enough from university dormitories. When he got to the serving line, though, what waited for him was baked cod, roast pork, a thick peppery soup full of vegetables, croissants that looked homemade, and much more. He loaded up, found a place at a table with Orrin and Susan.

"If this is the kind of food we get," said Orrin, "I want to come back next year."

Susan made a skeptical noise in her throat. "I bet this is our last good meal." They smiled at each other, and Toby, watching, guessed that if they weren't an item yet it was at most a matter of days. He tried not to think of Wren, and when that didn't work, mocked himself mercilessly in the silence inside his head.

When the meal was maybe half over, Phil Dyer stood in the middle of the dining hall and said, "You won't hear me say this very often until we're ready to head for home, but there's plenty for seconds. And for those of you who haven't been here before—don't go anywhere when dinner's over. We've got some bottles to empty, and once the tables aren't needed, some space to dance and some music."

"Performed by Emmeline Grenier on the bagpipe," said Mike Brezinsky, one of the archeologists, getting a general laugh.

"*Chut, bête!*" Emmeline retorted. "Or *la cabrette* maybe will sing outside your room at four in the morning."

"She's got you, Mike," Bill Allen said, getting another laugh. Toby, feeling even more on the outside of things than usual, pasted on a smile.

Once the meal was over, he joined some of the others pushing the tables over to the sides of the dining hall to clear room for dancing. The chairs followed, forming a rough circuit around the hall, and the promised bottles made an appearance on the counter by the serving line. The cleaning crew hurried through their chores, and all at once four of them, old timers at the station, started singing in deep voices, off key:

> "You scrub sixteen pots, what do you get?
> A face full of bubbles and an apron that's wet.
> Phil Dyer don't you call me 'cause I can't go,
> I washed my soul down the drain overflow."

That got another round of laughter. By then the bottles had a crowd around them, and Bill Allen extracted himself from it, crossed the hall, and handed Toby a glass with a cup or so of bourbon in it. That was more than Toby usually drank in an entire evening, but he raised the glass anyway and thanked him. Lacking anything else to do, he followed Bill over to the nearest part of the ring of chairs, sat down.

He sipped at the bourbon, let it take the edges off his nerves. "What's the business about Emmeline and a bagpipe?"

"She plays one." Bill raised his glass, downed a shot. "Not the Scottish kind—they play different kinds in some parts of France, and where she's from they've got one that sounds like a nanny goat in heat." Toby choked, and Bill grinned and went on. "She always brings hers, and practices it out in the helicopter hangar because nobody else can stand the thing."

Toby was spared the need to respond by the sound of a cheap CD player belting out the opening bars of a strident rock tune he didn't recognize—something about a land of ice and snow, midnight sun, and hot springs. Bill grinned again. "They always start with that," he said. "When I was in my teens my friends and I would borrow my older brother's Led Zep CDs and play them and get really ripped. Fun times."

"I bet," said Toby, faking a response he didn't feel. Memories from his own teen years replayed themselves. He'd always been the odd one out, partly because of the secrets he'd had to hide but also because he'd never learned how to be anything else, and it didn't help that most of the other families in Lefferts Corners had been there since the Dutch settlement and his hadn't. Sitting around with friends listening to music and smoking pot hadn't been an option, or maybe it had been but he'd missed it somehow. He'd put countless solitary afternoons and evenings into his schoolbooks instead, and when he'd won a four-year scholarship to SUNY Rochester he'd told himself that it had all been worth it—but had it?

A swallow of the bourbon took the edge off the memories, so he followed it with another. The song about ice and snow gave way to something else he didn't recognize. A few people were already dancing, Phil and Emmeline among them.

"Another?" Bill asked him. Toby glanced up at him, blinking, and then noticed that his glass was empty. Bad idea, he told himself, but said "Thanks" anyway and handed the glass over. Bill wove past the dancing couples to the forest of bottles. Laughter sounded just then on the other side of the dining hall, followed by a burst of voices and a sudden decisive motion: Leah Sargent hurrying to the door and out it. It occurred to Toby that he could do the same thing, go somewhere that wouldn't make him feel quite so out of place. Later, he told himself.

"Here you go," said Bill, returning with two full glasses. More couples started dancing, Orrin and Susan among them. Watching the two of them, Toby felt sure they'd be sharing a bed within a few hours. The idea clawed at him, reminded him of his own loneliness.

As though he'd heard the thought, Bill leaned toward him. "You ought to ask Kingston-Brown to dance."

"Yeah, right," Toby said dismissively, and downed more of the bourbon.

"No, I mean it." Bill gestured across the hall. Wren sat there by herself, watching the proceedings with her usual cool reserve, for all the world as though she was observing the mating rituals of arctic birds from miles away. "She's just sitting there. Go ask her."

The image of the two of them dancing like Orrin and Susan surged up, dizzying, and then collapsed. Was it his own insecurities that shredded it, or was there something deeper and colder? He could not tell. He turned away, said, "Not a chance."

"Then I will," said Bill, and lurched to his feet.

For Toby, that was the last straw. He waited only long enough for Bill to turn his back, then set down the half-empty glass, got up, and left the dining hall.

* * *

The music faded behind him as the door swung shut. Between the bourbon and his own tangled thoughts, he scarcely noticed where he was or where he was going until he stumbled into the swinging doors of the library and went right through them. The midnight sun spilled a dim glow through the skylights. It took Toby a moment to notice Leah Sargent sitting on the sofa, and another to process the fact, redden, and say, "Sorry."

She glanced up at him. "It's okay," she said, her voice faintly slurred. Then, before he could back out of the library: "Drunk?"

"Yeah."

"Me too. Over there—" A gesture indicated the door behind Toby and the mess hall beyond it. "—last place on earth you want to be, right?"

"Yeah," Toby admitted with a little bleak laugh.

"Me too." She waved vaguely at the other end of the sofa. When he didn't cross the room at once: "I know. You're thinking I've been a complete bitch to you, and you're right. Ever do something stupid you know is stupid but you do it anyway?"

"Yeah," Toby said. "Way too often." Lacking anything better to do, he went to the sofa, sat facing her. Maybe it was the bourbon, maybe the way he'd watched Orrin and Susan, but all at once he was aware of the curves of her body, the full breasts under the tee shirt, the angle between her thighs drawing his gaze. He tried to come up with something to say, but all he could think of was, "Why?"

She gave him a blank look, then: "You took Ham's place." Seeing his baffled expression: "Ham. Dr. Hamilton Glynn Broward. You know. He was supposed to come here with us. He was the chair of my dissertation committee. Phil Dyer hired you instead."

Toby winced. Even through the bourbon-induced haze, he could see the tangle of faculty politics he'd stumbled into. "I didn't know," he said, knowing how little that mattered. "Dyer didn't tell me any of that."

"I bet," said Leah. "That's Phil all over."

"And—and you, and Broward—" There were words he could use to ask what he wanted to know about their professional relationship, but none of them came to mind.

The lack didn't seem to confuse her. "Yeah. Not that it matters, 'cause Ham's as gay as a tree full of parrots. Wasting my time. I do that a lot."

Her face was close to his. Had he moved, or had she? Toby couldn't tell, but he could smell the faint sweet scent of her breath. She was looking at him with an expression that seemed to be blended half of puzzlement and half of a kind of reluctant affection.

"Feeling stupid?" she asked then.

"Yeah," he said, and let his lips meet hers.

That kept them busy for a few minutes. When he drew back to catch his breath, she blinked and said, "Let's do that again."

This time her lips opened beneath his. By the time they both drew back, panting for air, Toby's mind was reeling. He could think of nothing but Leah's body and the sheer pointlessness of the layers of clothing that separated it from his.

"Come on," she said, and got unsteadily to her feet. Her hand grasped his, helped him stand. "Your room's just around the corner, right?"

"Yeah," he managed to say, and followed her lead.

Voices and music still sounded from inside the dining hall when they stumbled out of the library, but it all seemed a million miles away. The dim glow from the skylights above guided them to the turn, around it. Toby had just enough clarity left to make sure the right number was on the door, and to feel a vague momentary panic at the thought that she might turn the light on, though he couldn't remember why that mattered. The light stayed off; the dim glow from around the door and the hint of midnight sun through the curtains guided him to the bed, and she got there first, started shedding her clothes. He managed to struggle out of his, joined her on the bed, reached for her as she reached for him.

Afterwards he remembered only splintered fragments: the taste of her crotch, the way one of her nipples popped between his lips, the moment when he slid into her and she cried out and wrapped arms and legs around him. At the time, though, the whiskey turned those things and more into a seamless shape of vague motion and confused delight. There was plenty of fumbling on both sides, but they both laughed more than once at that—or was it something else? He couldn't remember. Finally he flopped onto his back and she nestled up against him, both of them groggy and spent, and he tried to think of a reason why her body seemed so comfortable but drifted off to sleep before the thought could finish taking shape.

CHAPTER 4

THE PLACES OF THE DEAD

He was alone when murky dreams finally released him. He blinked, wondered vaguely why his head hurt so much, sat up, and barely had time to lurch sideways and get his face above the plastic wastepaper basket beside the bed before a good share of what he'd eaten the night before came up in a rush. He crouched there on the bed, gasping, as the spasms shook him.

Memories of the night before tumbled past him in fragments: images of the party as clear and sharp-edged as ice, dim warm recollections of Leah's face and body as he'd felt and tasted them in the near-darkness. He wondered for a moment whether he might have dreamed the latter, but the smell of her musk on his body and the bed was strong enough that he could smell it even through the stink of his vomit, and when he shifted to sit on the side of the bed—slowly, hoping not to set off his stomach again—he spotted something white on the floor that proved to be her panties. That made him laugh, and the laugh undid all the good his careful movements had done and left him bending over the wastepaper basket again.

His clothes were scattered on the floor where they'd fallen. He pulled on pants and a tee shirt as another biological need made itself felt, grabbed his AWOL bag, stumbled out of the room and made it to the bathroom at the end of the main corridor before the rest of what he'd eaten the night before came surging up. That ended in a series of dry heaves that left him wrung out and miserable. Once those were over and he'd used the toilet for its more accustomed purpose, he went to one of the shower cubicles, skinned out of his clothes, turned the cold water tap all the way on and stepped into the stream.

The frigid water shocked his mind back to clarity. After a while he stepped out of the shower, got a salt pill dissolving in his plastic tumbler, fetched his soap, and plunged back into the water. The raw cold impact of it helped again, and by the time he toweled off and skinned back into his clothes the wretchedness had become a background murmur, no more intrusive than the low hum of machinery in the station.

He stumbled back to his room, told himself he was going to lay down just for a minute or two to gather his strength, woke up again an hour or so later. The vomit in the wastepaper basket stank abominably, and the bedding under him was less unpleasant but no less pungent. He got up carefully, rubbed his eyes. Hell of a way to lose my virginity, he thought. I bet she doesn't want anything to do with me once she's sober.

Lacking anything else to do, he dressed in clean clothes, gathered up the dirty clothes and Leah's panties, and dumped them into the laundry bag. A moment's reflection, and he added the bedsheets to the bag; they reeked of sex and also of salt, and a moment of panic shot through him, wondering if Leah had noticed the latter. That brought on another burst of nausea but it faded without bringing anything else up. Once his stomach settled, he repeated the old useless prayers he'd learned from his grandmother, then picked up the wastebasket and the laundry bag and headed back out into the corridor.

Except for the sounds of machinery, the station was as quiet as a tomb. Gray light filtered in through the skylights; it was early yet, and Toby guessed most of the others had been up much later than he had. He tossed the laundry bag into the bin for dirty laundry, then took the wastepaper basket into the bathroom and rinsed the vomit out of it. Back in his room again, he paused, then headed for the dining hall. Food was the last thing on his mind just then, but the thought of sipping some hot tea made him feel as though he might get better someday.

The dining hall was not quite as empty as the rest of the station. Phil Dyer was sitting at one of the tables, hands circling a cup of coffee, looking only slightly the worse for wear. He glanced up as Toby came in and said, "Hung over?"

"Yeah. I don't usually drink like that."

Phil nodded. "Get some crackers from the basket. No, seriously—just a nibble at a time, and some fluids. It'll make your stomach behave."

Toby decided to give it a try. A cup of weak tea and a packet of saltines found their way onto a tray, and he sat across from Phil.

"As I said," the professor told him then, "what happens in Greenland stays in Greenland. Unless you want to take it somewhere else, of course."

Was he talking about Leah? Toby knew better than to guess, but he thought he knew a way around to the answer. "Like you and Emmeline."

He glanced up at Toby with a wry smile. "Pretty much. She's got a husband, but he doesn't object to her affairs and she doesn't object to his mistresses. Me, I got married once, and came back from my second long stay in the Arctic to find divorce papers waiting for me. She'd already sold the house and spent the proceeds. I didn't make that mistake again." He shrugged. "So when Emmeline and I are both in the field, which happens fairly often, yeah, we're an item. It's some consolation for the risks we run."

Toby nodded slowly. One of the lines from the poem Phil recited aboard the *Arkham*—"follow the ships that come not back"—circled in his mind. It reminded him of the ivory face the professor had shown him, and he glanced at Phil. "Could I ask a favor?"

"Sure."

"Do you still have that ivory amulet with you? I'd like another look at it."

Phil gave him a long unreadable look. "Do you want it?"

Toby, taken aback, tried to find something to say.

"Seriously," said Phil then. "If you want it, it's yours. I've known all along that it's not for me." With a shrug that looked casual. "You may think that's crazy, but there it is."

"No, it isn't crazy," said Toby. He opened his mouth to say something else, some polite evasion or other, and found to his astonishment that only one set of words would let themselves be said: "Please—I'd like to have it."

"Done," said Phil. He pulled the peppermint tin out from inside his coat and handed it over. Toby wondered at the flicker of fear and relief that showed for just an instant in his eyes.

* * *

A silence passed. Toby pocketed the tin and sipped tea. When Phil spoke again, it was to ask about *uqqayab*, an obscure Hyperborean noun that seemed to refer to some kind of animal. That pleasantly neutral subject kept them talking through two respective refills of coffee and tea, and once the first blinking and unshaven member of that day's kitchen crew showed up, a lunch of chicken noodle soup and dry toast.

Others trickled in, a few at a time, most of them bleary and red-eyed. Emmeline was an exception; she showed up an hour after Toby did, looking cheerful and well-rested, with a contraption of leather and wooden pipes tucked under one arm. She came over to the table, gave Phil a kiss, greeted Toby, set down the contraption, went to the kitchen, and returned with a plate full of leftovers and a steaming mug of coffee. In the meantime Toby had the chance to examine what he guessed was the bagpipe Bill had mentioned: two long pipes of black wood with silver fittings, a loose bag of black leather, and what looked like a little leather-sided bellows hooked up to the bag.

"Ah, so you have met *la cabrette noire*," Emmeline said to Toby when she returned to the table. "The part of France I am from, the old province of Averoigne, this is the bagpipe they play there. I should play it for you—a *bourée*, that is a dance tune, or a *regret*, that is, how do you say it, a lament. Maybe you will like it."

"If you play that in here," Phil said calmly, "you'll start a riot."

Emmeline gave him an unsanitary look, then softened it with a laugh. "You are probably right," she said. "In a little while I will go to the hangar as usual."

"Sometime when you're going to play, let me know," said Toby. "I'll come listen."

That got him a broad smile. "But not today, eh? No matter. Of course I will tell you. It does not surprise me even a little that you have so many people in linguistics clucking like the hens." She applied herself to her breakfast. Toby glanced at Phil, caught his amused look.

All the while, Toby kept watch on the door, though he did his best not to be caught at it. Wren would come through it sooner or later and so would Leah, and though he dreaded both those moments he couldn't make himself evade either one. As it was, Wren's appearance was total anticlimax; she came through the door as though it was any other morning, looking well-rested and freshly showered, and got soup, toast, and a glass of water from the serving line. She came to the table and sat next to Emmeline, who smiled and said nothing.

Toby did the same, and was rewarded by a nod and a glance from those gray-green eyes. He wanted to ask her whether she'd danced with Bill Allen, but embarrassment kept him silent; he didn't even want to think about whether she'd done anything else with him—it was obvious enough to Toby from the way people trickled in by twos that he and Leah had been far from the only people there to end up unexpectedly in bed together, but the thought of Wren having sex at all, with anyone, seemed wrong in some sense he couldn't define. Don't be stupid, he told himself. She's got a husband, doesn't she? Sound as it was, the logic did nothing to shake the irrational conviction that sexuality was wholly alien to her.

Leah came in a half hour later, when Toby was about to give up and head for some welcome silence and solitude. She looked as hung over as Toby felt, and when she caught sight of him she turned as red as her complexion allowed and was careful not to look his way thereafter. The reaction didn't bother him. He'd been afraid, if anything, that she would pretend that nothing had happened between them. Once she'd found a place at another table, he decided to reduce her embarrassment and got up. Careful not to make eye contact with her, he took his tray and dishes to the dishwashers' station, started for the door.

Phil waved him over before he got there. "Got anything planned this afternoon?"

"Nothing at all. Why?"

"I might just be able to show you an *uqqayab*."

Toby gave him an uncertain look, but agreed on a time two hours later, and left the dining hall. A glance at the library brought back too many memories of the night before, and he headed for his room instead, telling himself he could read something by Lovecraft.

Before he got one of the paperbacks from Reykjavik from its place atop the dresser, though, he pulled the little tin from his pocket, opened it and pulled aside the cotton wadding. The not-human face stared up at him, its expression suggesting that it felt a faint amusement at his troubles if it felt anything at all. It seemed to be saying to him: this is the way the universe would think about you, if it ever bothered.

"Yeah," he said to it. "I know."

* * *

Two hours later Toby slung a rifle over his shoulder and followed Phil out the door into the clear light of a Greenland afternoon. Unfamiliar birds moved through the bright air. So, closer to the ground, did mosquitoes and biting flies, which buzzed around Phil and the other two who came with them— Orrin Bishop and Susan Eliot—but ignored Toby completely. He wondered about that, but didn't dare bring it up.

All around them fireweed and cotton grass bent before the steady wind, and lichen of a dozen colors clung to masses of broken gray rock. High clouds had blown in to veil the sun, turning the sky the shimmering hue of mother-of-pearl. By that directionless light Toby and the others followed Phil up the trail. They passed the station's radio antenna, rising up from its hillock with heavy cables guying it against the wind, and the satellite antenna close by. Further on, the trail passed between thickets of low sprawling willows, wound down into another shallow swale full of sedges, and then began to climb toward a low cliff topped with willows a quarter mile away. A glance back showed the station on its hillock, bright in the veiled sunlight.

What struck him most, as the four of them picked their way south across the tundra from there, was the immense silence of the land. Above, birds soared and swooped; muskoxen, black dots in the distance, moved at a leisurely pace, cropping the greenery; wind tasting of distant ice came rushing past, bending the sedges like the sea under a light breeze. None of that touched the deeper stillness that surrounded Toby as he kept pace with the others and tried not to twist an ankle on the uneven ground. It felt as though the glaciers of the ice age had scoured away every human measure of time, leaving behind only the slow pulse of geological epochs.

This used to be Tscho Vulpanomi, Toby told himself, and called to mind the scraps of lore he knew about that Hyperborean province. The Gulf Stream flowed north along its shores, or so paleoclimatologists theorized, turned from its later course by the great island of Atlantis; semitropical forests burgeoned there; smoke rose from time to time from the white conical peak of Mount Achoravomas. Farmers tilled the rich volcanic soils, foresters cut scented *apha*-wood for coffins and saved the sawdust for incense, archers bent longbows tipped with horn or marched north to serve in the armies of Hyperborean kings and emperors. Toby tried to imagine those scenes around him, but the wind picked them up and sent them tumbling away toward the ocean, leaving only the clear light and the sweep of the tundra behind.

A few more minutes brought the four of them to the foot of the cliff, where a ramshackle shelter made of lumber and heavy plastic tarps stood out from the face, visibly battered by three years of neglect and occasional falls of clay lumps from the cliff face. Above, maybe ten feet past the shelter's roof, willows hunched and twisted, sending stray roots over the bank into empty air. Phil and Orrin pulled the tarp aside. Under it, a portion of the cliff face had been cleared of rubble, and pale shapes showed faintly against brown clay.

Orrin and Susan made the kind of noises Toby associated with cute kitten pictures. Phil breathed a sigh of relief and turned to Toby. "Okay," he said. "You've been reading Lovecraft. Here are some primal horrors he didn't know about."

Toby considered the pale marks, and realized they were bones. After a moment he could trace the line of a leg, the curve of a long tail, the delicate structure of a skull and a toothy jaw. "That looks kind of like a small dinosaur," he ventured.

That got him sudden grins from the other three. "Let's hear it for science education," Phil said. "That's exactly what it is—a fierce little coelurosaur about four feet tall. Half a dozen of them, probably a family group like a wolf pack, got caught by a mudslide here a long time ago. What you don't know, and we didn't know until we got a lab to run the dating and half a dozen more to confirm it, is that the mudslide only happened about eight million years ago."

Toby gave him a startled look. "That sounds pretty recent for dinosaurs."

"Two for two," said Phil. "Exactly. We found two closely related species of dinosaurs that survived the end of the Mesozoic era, and kept going most of the way through the Tertiary, until the ice slid over the last of their refuges here in Greenland." He shrugged. "We shipped a bunch of bones from this site three years ago, but I came out here to do some clearing and found this skeleton two days ago. It's better preserved—it's a good type specimen, good enough that we can put some species names into circulation. I plan on calling this one *Omegasaurus groenlandicus*. The other species I'm modestly naming *Omegasaurus dyeri*."

"Omegasaurus," Toby said, tasting the name. "The last dinosaur."

"Bingo. I'm guessing—though it's only a guess—that that's what the Hyperboreans meant when they talked about *uqqayab*."

Toby considered the skeleton in the clay, trying to imagine what it looked like back when it ran through the undergrowth of a Hyperborean forest. "What else lived here back then?"

Phil glanced at Susan, who beamed and said, "Mostly your usual Miocene and Pliocene North American fauna: bears, mastodons, ground sloths, sabertooth cats, an interesting early elk, and one real oddity, a bird so primitive it had claws on its wings and teeth in its beak."

Phil gave Toby an unreadable look. "Emmeline named it *Raphtontis hyperborica*, after something in the *Book of Eibon*."

It took Toby a moment to place that. "Oh, of course," he said. "The legend of Ralibar Vooz and Ezdagor."

Orrin looked up from the clay. "You've read the *Book of Eibon*?"

"It's one of the main sources for Hyperborean mythology," said Toby, "and the names in it are most of what we've got from the Mhu Thulani dialect, so I've read it a couple of times."

Orrin nodded as if that was the most ordinary thing in the world, but Toby caught the quick glance that passed between Susan and Phil, and sensed that he'd brushed against the edges of something stranger than dinosaurs.

* * *

There were other times during those first few weeks at the station that Toby sensed something else of the same kind. Another happened a week after the party, when the pickup came lumbering back from an archeological site a few miles upstream. Toby went out to help haul whatever they'd found back to one of the laboratories, heard high shrill sounds from the helicopter hangar, recognized their source after a moment as Emmeline's bagpipe. He'd spent an hour listening to it a few days previously, and decided it sounded like a dental drill had decided to take up a second career in music—though he hadn't mentioned that to Emmeline.

"Just the guy I want to see," Louise said to Toby as she got out of the cab. "We found a stone with an inscription."

Toby grinned. "Music to my ears." She glanced at the hangar, started laughing.

Half a dozen sturdy plastic bins full of carefully packed artifacts had to be hauled into one of the labs. "Here we go," said Mike Brezinsky once all the bins were against one wall and the bagpipe music was inaudible at last. He and Louise pulled a stone slab a few feet long out from its wrappings and set it on a table, the dim marks of an inscription facing up. "I don't know whether there's enough left to read."

Toby, in his element for once, found rubbing paper and one of the glorified wax crayons the station stocked for such purposes, spread the paper over the inscription, and rubbed the blue wax over the top just hard enough to bring out every subtle marking on the stone. The angular Hyperborean script sprang to life, spelling out a woman's name and below it a familiar sentence with an unusual ending. "It's a funerary inscription," he said. "There was a grave close by."

Leah, who was busy with pottery fragments on the other side of the room, glanced briefly his way and then looked away again. Toby caught both motions but said nothing. He was sure by then that most of the others had guessed what had happened between them the night of the party. It had occurred to him more than once that he'd like it to happen again, but he was far from sure Leah shared that opinion and he had no idea how to talk to her about it—and there was the way he felt whenever Wren looked at him, which he still couldn't process.

"Got it in one," said Louise, breaking into his thoughts. "Adult female, almost certainly, from the grave goods."

"Her name was Ellara," Toby said. "No clan name, so she didn't belong to the nobility. Her husband was really torn up by her death, too."

Orrin came over from the work table where he and Susan had been laying out omegasaur bones for close-up photography. "Okay, I'll bite," he said. "How do you know?"

"The word for love down here." He tapped the paper, touching the sentence under the name. Glancing up: "How much do you want to hear? I can get really boring really fast."

"Go ahead," said Louise. "This is interesting."

"Okay." Toby turned to face her. "The Hyperboreans thought there were three kinds of love, one for each part of the self. They thought each of us has a body, *usul*, solid like the earth. Each of us has vital fluids, *sirau*, liquid like the ocean, and each of us has a soul or spirit, *paha*, which is also breath, like the air. So there's a love that belongs to the body, called *aqqat*."

"So, sex," Orrin said.

Toby shook his head. "No, to the Hyperboreans what the body wants is a home, a family, a place in the *iqqibal shalsholi*, the cord that ties the generations together. It's the vital fluids that want sex. That kind of love is *nen*, which means wetness." Susan choked, and Leah turned red and looked away again. "Then there's *ilul*, the love that belongs to the *paha*, the soul or spirit. That's love at first sight, infatuation, Romeo and Juliet, or Vardaban and Dathli if you want to put it in Hyperborean terms. Most of the time when you get a funerary inscription like this it says *a'qada niunoli ish'adaq sh'aqqambe*, this thing of stone I made on account of my *aqqat*, my marital love. This one says *a'qada niunoli ish'adaq sh'ilumbe*, this thing of stone I made on account of my *ilul*, my—" He paused, searching for words. "My adoration, my being crazy in love. Something like that."

"Okay," said Susan. "But how do you say 'I love you' in Hyperborean?" Orrin gave her a glance and a smile that confirmed all Toby's guesses.

"Depends on what kind of love you mean," said Toby. "*M'aqqat ish'djampa* means I want to marry you. *M'nen ish'djampa* means—"

"I want to jump your body," Mike said when Toby paused. "Got it."

"Basically, yeah. And *m'ilul ish'djampa* isn't something you'd say; it would be 'I want you to adore me.' You'd say *m'ayad sh'ilumpa*, I adore you, I adore the quality of who you are, or *m'ayad da'e sh'ilumpa*, I adore every single one of the qualities of your being."

"Now that's romantic," said Susan. "*Really* romantic."

"Dathli said that to Vardaban in the thirty-fourth canto of the *Song of Iqqua* when they rode to Mount Voormithadreth, so yeah."

All at once the room got very quiet, and then everyone started talking at once. Toby wondered whether he'd said something inappropriate, but the conversation veered elsewhere and it was only much later that he finally understood what no one had wanted to mention.

* * *

Other than necessary chores and those brief encounters with the unspoken, Toby had very little to occupy his time during those first few weeks at Tornarssukalik Station. A few more inscribed gravestones turned up, but none of them offered any particular difficulties in translation; an altar dedicated to the elk-goddess Yhoundeh had two sentences, equally easy to decipher. Lacking anything else to do, he read the stories in the Lovecraft paperbacks he'd brought with him, and alternated those with long hours in the library reading the obscure books that made up so much of the collection.

Those two sources of reading material turned out to cover more of the same ground than he'd had any reason to expect. Time and again, he'd turn a page in some photocopied volume in the library and find something that he'd already encountered in Lovecraft's stories. An old legend that Arne Saknussemm mentioned in *De Mirabilia Septentrionalis*, about shapeless creatures in the deep places of the earth and the alien beings who had made them and then been destroyed by them, sent him back to Lovecraft's story "At the Mountains of Madness," which told the same story. Another passage in Saknussemm sent him to von Junzt—the library had a photocopy of the first edition of *Unaussprechlichen Kulten*—and then back to "The Shadow out of Time." It was unnerving, he thought, to realize that Lovecraft hadn't invented the Great Race of Yith or their habit of possessing the bodies of beings in future ages, and even more so to see just how much evidence von Junzt had gathered, during a trip to the Australian desert, that seemed to show the legend was founded on a basis of hard fact.

Even so, he was more than ready for a better alternative to boredom when one finally showed up. "We've got a real puzzle," Louise told him over lunch. "A bunch of pieces of a broken stele. It looks like someone went after it with a hammer. It had text all over it, but trying to figure out what it said—" Her shrug finished the sentence.

"You ought to be able to sort out at least a little of it on linguistic grounds," said Toby.

That fielded him a grin. "Why do you think I'm telling the expedition linguist?"

After lunch, accordingly, he went with her to one of the labs and looked over the shattered remains of the stele. At first glance it was a hopeless mess, but books from the library yielded the texts of other steles and they were formulaic enough that he knew there was a chance he'd be able to make some sense of it. The rest of the day went into making careful rubbings of each of the pieces. On one of those he hit pay dirt: the Hyperborean letters YRENE followed by AQQ, the first letters of the Hyperborean words for "emperor" or "empress."

"I think it could be one of the Empress Amphyrene's edicts," he explained to a circle of listeners at dinner. "This was during the Uzuldaroum period, when Hyperborea was an empire instead of a kingdom. The histories say that when Amphyrene died and Charnamethros took the imperial throne he ordered all her edicts revoked and all the inscriptions destroyed. This might be archeological evidence of that." That earned him an appreciative whistle from Mike Brezinsky, excited questions from two others, and a promise from all the archeologists that they'd look for more pieces of the stele in that part of the dig the next day.

The next morning he was back at work, busy trying to reconstruct a bit of text, when he heard hurrying feet in the corridor outside and looked up. It was too early for anyone to be back from the dig, and the emergency siren didn't go off, so he shrugged, turned back to the text, and all at once saw how two words might fit together to make a bit of formal prose.

At lunch, though, Phil tapped on one of the tables with the handle of a knife and said, "If I can have your attention for a moment." Conversations hushed, and he went on. "I'd like to introduce you to Anna Slange from the University of Oslo." Toby craned his neck and caught a glimpse of white-blonde hair. "It turns out we weren't the only people planning on using the station this summer. Professor Slange's here to study the local botany, so she'll be joining us on and off for the next few months. I hope you'll make her welcome."

Various approving noises provided what answer there was, and the dining hall filled with the usual buzz of conversation thereafter. Toby got a glimpse at the newcomer once he finished his lunch and hauled his tray and dishes to the kitchen: a woman in her twenties, with big blue eyes, blonde hair in a braid down her back, and the kind of face and body for which the word "gorgeous" was invented. She was taking part in a conversation with Phil and Emmeline, and it took Toby no more than a glance to see how every straight man and lesbian in earshot was sizing her up and every gay man and straight woman in the same range was bristling with jealousy. Then there was Wren, who watched the newcomer with cool detachment. Was it his imagination, Toby wondered, or was there a hint of wariness in Wren's calm regard?

He shrugged, put the matter aside. With all the other things on his mind, he told himself, rivalries over an attractive newcomer weren't something he had to worry about.

Nonetheless he could hardly ignore what happened over the weeks that followed, as Anna Slange cut a swath through the expedition. She'd bedded Phil the day of her arrival, Toby guessed from their body language, and if she spent a night alone thereafter he saw no sign of it. One morning, Orrin and Susan were sitting at different tables for the first time since they boarded the MV *Arkham*, Orrin embarrassed and ashamed, Susan tearful and angry, though they apparently patched things up that night and were sitting together the next morning. A few mornings later Bill was grinning from ear to ear and wouldn't tell anybody why, and the morning after that Louise, who Toby had thought was as straight as a geometrical line, got flustered and red-faced whenever Professor Slange came into view. Toby watched from the sidelines with amusement not unmixed with envy, and noticed Wren watching as well.

* * *

Meanwhile he labored over the text from the shattered stele. Three times over the week or so that followed, the truck came back from the dig with new fragments of the same rock, some of them with letters or words on them. Those that didn't surrender their message to rubbings yielded it up to a complicated device in another lab, something involving lasers and computers, which Toby left in Mike Brezinsky's capable hands. Phrase by phrase, the text came together—nothing out of the ordinary, just a typical edict proclaiming a forgotten noble as provincial governor in Tscho Vulpanomi, but it was an edict of the empress Amphyrene with what looked very much like damage from hammers, and thus a scrap of evidence for the accuracy of the surviving sources on Hyperborean history.

The work fascinated him enough that he had to make an effort not to grudge the time that had to go into station chores or questions tossed his way by some of the others. Anna Slange was responsible for several of those. Her English was flawless but she didn't know Latin, and she needed help several times with passages from old Latin botanical texts. The first time he wondered if she was going to proposition him—partly wishful thinking, he decided later, partly the clothing she had on, a skintight tee shirt and jeans that left very little to the imagination—and was at once disappointed and relieved when she was friendly but wholly professional.

As soon as he had a preliminary reconstruction of the text on the stele, Toby drafted a letter announcing the find and discussed his options with Phil in private. "*The Bulletin of Ancient Arctic Antiquities*," Phil said at once. "I hope I don't have to tell you not to bother with the linguistic journals. If you don't mind having a coauthor or two—"

"Of course not," Toby said at once. "Interested?"

"Nah, it's too far out of my field—though you can quote me if you need to cite something about the geology." He paused. "The logical person would be Leah Sargent. I know you two are on opposite sides of the date business, but if you like, I can sound her out."

Toby agreed to that, and later the same day Phil and Leah came to the lab to talk it over. Leah looked as uneasy as Toby felt, but Phil set a smooth professional tone and both of them followed suit. After a little careful negotiation Phil left, Leah pulled a chair over, Toby slid the laptop her way, and she put three precise paragraphs into the letter and corrected a few details. Since the edict was dated in the Hyperborean calendar—*Year of the Amber Toad, Moon of the Salmon Returning, eleventh day*—they could tacitly ignore the entire question of whether that year had been before or after the ice age, and focus on the details that mattered.

"You're good with it?" Toby said finally.

She nodded. "I think it's pretty solid." He thanked her, and she gave him a glance he couldn't read and said, "Would it be okay if I asked a personal question?"

Toby, who'd spent the previous quarter hour fighting an urge to slip an arm around her, draw her close, and kiss her, tried to keep his reaction off his face. "Sure."

"Did you ever hear of a Massachusetts town called Innsmouth?"

"No." The question startled him. An instant later he remembered that Bill Allen and Phil Dyer had asked him the same thing. "Why?"

Leah shrugged. "You look a little like some people I know who were from there."

"My family's from the Catskills," he said. "A little place called Lefferts Corners."

"Oh. I just wondered." She got up from the chair. They said the usual things, and she hurried out of the lab while he busied himself with the laptop and got the letter on its way over the station's balky satellite link to the journal.

Hours later he was still brooding over the text as a way to try to keep from brooding over Leah. *Okay, we had sex,* he told himself irritably while closing things down before dinner. *But that was just once, and she still acts like she doesn't want me here.* The remonstrance didn't do any good he noticed, and he ate dinner in a wretched mood.

Afterwards, desperate for distraction, he went back to the lab and busied himself getting images of all the fragments of the stele numbered, indexed, and copied into a zip file to be forwarded to three scholars back home. He was most of the way through that process, and the station had taken on its late-night hush, when the door of the lab opened behind him. He glanced back and found Anna Slange looking in.

"I was hoping I would find you here," she said. "Yes, it's more Latin."

"Sure thing." He motioned at the chair where Leah had sat as she came to the desk, but she stood next to him and set the book down on the desk. One of her breasts nearly brushed his face. She was wearing another tight tee shirt, and the bra under it didn't conceal much.

The paragraph of Latin she needed put into English made a temporary distraction. He jotted down a quick translation. "Thank you," she said. "I hope you aren't planning on spending all night here in the lab."

"No." He forced a shrug. "Just finishing something up."

"Good." One of her hands settled on his shoulder, slid to turn his face toward hers. He stiffened, and she laughed a soft breathy laugh. "You're shy," she said. "I like that."

His gaze met hers. For an instant he sensed something behind the big blue eyes, something cold and intent, but then his thoughts scattered like clouds.

Anna smiled. "Your room's close by, isn't it?"

"Yeah." He tried to say something else, could not.

"Come on." She drew him to his feet and the two of them left the lab. Blood drummed in Toby's ears and his thoughts spun; he could do nothing but follow her through the silent station. Once in the dimness of his room, she pulled off her clothes with sinuous grace as he struggled out of his, and then she pushed him backwards onto the bed and followed him there.

It was nothing like his lovemaking with Leah: no laughter, no fumbling. Her hands and tongue and womanhood set him writhing and groaning, not once but many times, and now and then when he struggled to a moment's clarity he caught the same sense of focused purpose, and something more: something urgent, almost desperate.

How the night ended he could never remember afterwards. All he knew was that he blinked awake late the next morning, alone in his bed. She'd pulled the covers over him and left a pleasant little note on the nightstand. He went to the showers, tried to make sense of it all, and gave up after a little while. He'd missed breakfast but the kitchen crew found him some cold cereal and reconstituted milk. In the lab, his laptop was still on, and someone had gone through the scrap paper where he'd jotted down scraps of translation of the fragmentary edict.

* * *

As the arctic summer deepened and the clouds of insects over the soggy tundra made going outside miserable for everyone but Toby, the sense of something moving below the surface became even harder to miss. A guarded quality showed in low earnest conversations, most of them between Phil and Wren, or between one of them and Emmeline; a certain tension moved through the station when some of the archeologists went out. It took Toby many days to be sure that whatever it was centered on a particular dig in the hills south of the station, where the diggers had uncovered the ruins of a settlement from very late in Hyperborea's history.

Pottery shards brought back from the dig, Leah announced, could be dated to the late Cerngoth period, no more than a century before the last Hyperborean cities were abandoned, and maybe less than that. A few days later, a stone stele with a half-legible inscription came back to the station. Among the words that came clear when Toby made careful rubbings was the name *Haalor* followed by the first words of the usual royal titulary, and that had everyone in the station talking. The name of Haalor was known from the king-lists, right at the end of the dynasty of Cerngoth. If an early Atlantean chronicle was to be believed, his granddaughter Amalea had sailed with the last ships from Iqquan at the very end of Hyperborean history.

That was exciting enough, and Mike Brezinsky used his laser gear to bring out nearly all the text, which was more exciting still. "The village was named Ulut," Toby said to the others at dinner that evening. "In the Year of the White Serpent the village elders sent a ship all the way around the southern end of Hyperborea and then north again to the royal court at Cerngoth, to find out if there was still anyone there. King Haalor sent back a letter telling them to choose one of their elders as provincial governor for all of Tscho Vulpanomi that wasn't under ice, and they set up the stone to commemorate that. I'm sure they knew it didn't mean much, but it made them feel like they were still part of the kingdom."

"All of it that wasn't under ice," Phil said, suddenly intent. "Did it say that?"

"Yeah. The text was—" Toby paused, recalling the passage. "*Sha mirhanda abbanoli iqqumololi tsed'ulumbe ni am'matastu,* 'he is to serve as governor of that part of the province not laid waste on account of ice.'"

That end of the dining hall went utterly still. "None of the glaciers here advanced much after the glacial maximum," Phil said then. "So you're saying that you've got contemporary written evidence that Hyperborea rose and fell before the ice age."

Toby stared at him for a moment, then managed a nod. "I hadn't thought of that," he said, "but yeah, that is what I'm saying, isn't it?"

Phil turned to look at Leah, who swallowed visibly. "There's something else," she said after a moment. "The whole site is buried under glacial till. We only found it because a gully turned up some potsherds. We can send samples of organic material for carbon dating to confirm that, but—" She gestured, admitting defeat. "It looks like you were right."

"This needs to be published right away," Phil said.

Toby turned to face him. "I'd be happy to be a coauthor but it needs someone with more of a reputation as the lead author—and the geology of the site's your field."

"Fair enough," said Phil. With a sudden grin: "Ham Broward hates my guts anyway, so I'm not going to lose anything. How soon can you get the inscription written up and translated?"

"A day or two." He turned back toward Leah, but the effort was wasted. Her place at the table was empty, and the door of the mess hall swung shut a moment after.

Later, once the meal was over, Toby went to the lab again and looked at the stele from Ulut for a long while. He was nearly alone in the lab. Wren sat over near the omegasaur bones in the pool of light from a lamp. She was assembling a device of metal and glass he didn't recognize, but he recognized the look of perfect concentration on her face and left her alone.

The inscription, blurred by the changes of three quarters of a million years, caught the light sidelong. Toby pondered it and thought about the villagers of Ulut who'd sent a dozen young men to the court at Cerngoth. Stories of Pine Harbor whispered themselves in his mind, but what pressed forward was a memory of his own, the day he'd sold the family farm in Lefferts Corners. He'd wanted to go back to the farm between Aunt Dinah's funeral and the closing, and couldn't make himself do it. Instead, he'd signed the final papers in the realtor's office, shaken hands, headed straight to the bus station four blocks away and sat there, seeing nothing, until the bus came rolling up to take him back to Cleveland.

He forced his mind clear and turned away from the stone. Wren had finished putting together the thing of glass and metal, slipped it into a pocket of her cargo pants, and pushed the chair back. Toby, suddenly desperate for a scrap of human contact, came over. The omegasaur bones had been set out neatly, forming what looked like a complete skeleton. For want of anything else, Toby said, "They've done a great job on the *uqqayab*."

She glanced at him. "It's not an *uqqayab*. Those were larger."

Toby nodded, then caught himself, turned to look at her. "How do you know that? How—" He stopped, and then all at once it sank in that he knew of every university program in the world that taught the Hyperborean language and she'd attended none of them "Wren, where did you learn Hyperborean?"

"I think you know the answer," she said.

He stared at her. An answer occurred to him, one that explained all the strangenesses that surrounded her—the apparent nervous breakdown, the movements that seemed rehearsed, the lack of the accent she'd been raised with, all the way to her perfect mastery of a language that had gone extinct before humanity had finished evolving—but his mind drew back from it.

"That's correct," Wren said.

A moment passed before he could respond at all. "Can you hear my thoughts?"

"No, but I can anticipate them." She leaned forward a little: another rehearsed movement, he guessed. "You said earlier that you would help me. We're close to the time when I'll need that, and you're one of the only people here I know I can trust."

He stared at her again, trying to find a meaning for her words other than the obvious one. In the faintest of whispers: "Do you know what I am?"

"No. But I don't think you're entirely human."

It took an immense effort to answer. "No. No, I'm not." Then: "And you're—Yithian."

"Yes." Her voice went low. "Listen carefully. Not everyone here is what they appear to be. My name—one of my names— is Vrispaa. Repeat it." He did so. "Good. I may ask you to say it later, to prove that you are who you seem to be. I may say it to you, to prove that I am myself. Do you understand?" He nodded, and she got up from her chair. "Not a word to anyone else. The survival of this world depends on it."

He stared after her as she went to the door and left the room.

* * *

Shaken by the encounter, he still had work to do, and he flung himself into it to keep his thoughts at bay. He had the transcription, translation, and commentary of the edict from Ulut done the next evening, and two days later a preliminary paper and photos were on their way over the balky internet connection to the editors of *Arctic Prehistory*, one of the top journals in the field. "Next time a copter comes by I'm going to get the stone on its way out of here," Phil said. "That and the omegasaur fossil. The sooner they get proper curation, the better." Then, with a wry look: "Université de Vyones, not Miskatonic. That edict is going to be a bombshell, and I want it someplace where everyone already accepts the preglacial dating."

The stele was still in the lab when the pickup came rumbling back from the southern site with another inscribed stone wrapped in burlap and plastic. "Toby," Mike Brezinsky said on finding him in the library. "Got something for you." With a grin: "*Tuqqoli niunda.* No, I'm not kidding. It was just west of Ulut and it's in pretty good condition."

Maybe ten minutes later, Toby watched as Mike and Phil and Emmeline unwrapped the stone in one of the labs. He could tell at a glance that Mike hadn't been mistaken. The three stones of remembrance that had been found by earlier expeditions had been slabs of sturdy fine-grained gray stone four or five feet tall, a foot and a half wide, and a few inches thick, covered with closely written text on one side. This was another, and the briefest glance over the writing showed place names and distances, the remembered geography of a vanished land.

He spent the next half hour making rubbings, getting as much of the text as he could. Some it leapt out at him even before he completed the rubbings: *Uzuldaroum, greatest of cities, seat of emperors. Distance, of* shol, *one hundred ninety-one.* It took him a moment to convert Hyperborean measures into those he was more familiar with, and place the city some four hundred miles away. The text didn't mention which direction it was; the Hyperborean language had only two words for directions—*iisil* which meant "inland" or "toward the shore" or "uphill," and *chosil* which meant "toward the ocean" or "out to sea" or "downhill"—but the library had texts from the other stones of remembrance, and that raised the possibility of triangulation. The thought of being able to pin down the location of Hyperborean sites that might soon be free of ice set his mind racing.

It didn't take long for him to discover that Phil had similar ideas. "How long do you think it'll take you to get that into English?" the professor said. They were sitting in Phil's office, a cramped little space lined with bookshelves and filing cabinets.

"I've already made a rough transcription of what I can read," Toby said. "Once Mike gets me his scans, I can to work out the rest of it, and get going on the translation. Then I'm going to sit down with the translation and the other remembrance texts, and figure out how to use the mapping program. Do you realize we could get the location of Commoriom?"

"I'll walk you through the program," Phil promised. "Any other major landmarks?"

Toby nodded. "Most of the major cities of central Hyperborea are listed, and so are a couple of mountains—Mount Achoravomas is one of them."

"Mount Voormithadreth?"

"I think so. I'll have to wait for the scans to be sure, though."

The scans took another day. In the meantime, Toby buried himself in the library, made a list of all the Hyperborean place-names he could find. When that was done, a stray thought sent him looking for Warren Rice's classic work *The Myth-Cycle of Commoriom*, and he turned to the chapter on Mount Voormithadreth. That had been the tallest mountain in Hyperborea, a mighty volcano astride the central spine of the Eiglophian Mountains. One of its four black peaks had issued smoke occasionally in predynastic times, but it was otherwise extinct. The prehuman voormis lived in caves high up on the mountain, and gave it its name. Legends spoke of tunnels within it reaching deep into the earth, and strange things and beings that had once been found there. Toby shook his head slowly, thinking: and sometime soon I might know where it is.

Mike handed over the scans just after breakfast the next day, and Toby arranged to spend nearly all that day in the lab with the scans, his rubbings, and a few reference works. The stone of remembrance itself sat on its table close by, in case he needed to try to puzzle out an obscure character on it. All day, other members of the expedition came in to look at it, and though they didn't interrupt Toby at his work, most of them came over to the desk where he was busy and looked over his shoulder as he transcribed the text.

Just before dinner, Toby briefed Phil and Emmeline in Phil's office before the three of them trooped into the dining hall. "About eighty per cent of it is readable, and I'm working on the translation now. There's nothing west of the Eiglophians or north of Mount Voormithadreth, but it's got the cities of Leqquan, Commoriom, and Uzuldaroum, and just about every other place I've heard of from Tscho Vulpanomi to the Ambar valley."

"And Mount Voormithadreth, what of that?" Emmeline asked.

Toby nodded. "That part of the stone was pretty badly worn but Mike's photos did a really good job on it. I just have to get that far."

The two of them nodded as though it was the most ordinary thing in the world, but Toby sensed something tense and waiting behind the apparent calm, and Phil's next words confirmed it. "Have you mentioned that to anybody else?"

"No," Toby said. Then: "Shouldn't I?"

"There were treasures buried in the mountain," said Phil. "The last thing we need is looters messing up the archeological sites there before we can get to them."

That seemed reasonable enough, Toby reflected later, but why had they shown no concern about any of the other sites that might attract looters?

CHAPTER 5

A TIME OF BLOOD

Until then the only trips he'd made away from the station were the hike to the dinosaur bones and a day trip out to an archeological dig in the hills to the west, to see what sense he could make of words carved on a stone too massive to move. Nearly everyone else in the expedition did more traveling than that, sometimes on missions that concerned them and sometimes not. Phil insisted that nobody leave the station by themselves; when Anna Slange decided to set out on a long research trip to catalog plants south and west of the station, he tried to talk her into taking someone with her, and only let her go because she wasn't part of the expedition. For those who'd come from Miskatonic, there was no such flexibility, and if that meant a marine biologist who had nothing to do for a few days got to hike inland to help one of the archeologists look for potsherds, that was what it meant.

Toby had wondered more than once when his turn would come, and so he wasn't unduly surprised when Emmeline waved him over one day as he came into the dining hall for lunch. "You are between the projects?" she asked. "A journey inland, it will not be a problem?"

He assured her it wouldn't, got his lunch, sat at the table next to her and asked for the details. "It is maybe, how you say it, chasing the wild duck, but the fortress of Dal Uqqul—you remember, from the *Song of Iqqua*? *Bon*. I am thinking that it may be not so far from here. A few days looking for traces is perhaps a waste of time but perhaps not."

That was more than enough to catch Toby's interest. After they settled the details, he took a few hours that evening off more useful work to go back to Rice's *The Myth-Cycle of Commoriom*. In it, toward the back, was the *Song of Iqqua*, and he paged through it, found the passage in the sixteenth canto where Aleema Ral passed the fortress of Dal Uqqul on her way into Tscho Vulpanomi. The poem spoke of forests full of brightly colored birds, of hills rounded like breasts, of the stark walls and soaring towers of the fortress. Gone, he thought, another place of the dead—but was it? The thought that he and Emmeline might spot some fragment of stone from the fortress dazzled him.

The next morning, to his surprise, a helicopter came over the mountains to the west and landed at the station. "*Trés bon!*" said Emmeline, coming to find him in an otherwise empty lab. "Can you pack soon? The copter is taking the stele and the fossils to Nuuk, and the pilot says he will take us to the place I want to camp."

"Sure," Toby said. "Anything I should bring besides the usual?"

That got him a sudden assessing look he couldn't read at all. "The translation," she said. "The stone, with *Mont Voormithadreth*." In response to his baffled look: "The helicopter will be back in a few days. Wren wants to see if she can find the mountain. She will go from there, and it will be less trouble if you have the thing with you."

There was more to it than that, Toby was sure of it, but he was just as sure that Emmeline wouldn't tell him more than she had to, and he had to pack. He got the text he'd copied from the *tuqqoli niunda*, his tentative translation, and a good Hyperborean dictionary, and stuffed those in a rucksack along with clothes and outdoor gear. After a moment's hesitation, he got out the little peppermint tin with the ivory figurine and tucked it into an inside pocket of his coat. By the time he'd finished, the helicopter was ready to leave, and he grabbed the rucksack, slung it over one shoulder, hurried outside to board the copter.

To his surprise, Phil was coming with them, though he didn't bring a rucksack and said he'd be going on to Nuuk. He climbed in and sat in the cabin alongside Toby, right in front of the masses of bubble wrap that protected the fossils and the stele from Ulut, while Emmeline went to sit beside the pilot in front.

"Flown before?" Phil asked, and when Toby shook his head, he grinned. "You're in for some spectacular sights. Hang on."

The engine roared, and the copter lurched and began to rise. Toby leaned over to look out the window, saw the station falling away. Up ahead, as the copter cleared the hills, the inlet reached back toward a steep-sided valley the Tornarssukalik glacier had once filled. In the glacier's place, a river wound among rocks. Blue pools of meltwater dotted the landscape, and a ragged green carpet of plants veiled the harsh edges of the land. In the distance, Toby spotted the source of the river, a jumbled mass of dirty white ice nestled in a gap between mountains.

The copter rose further and flew straight toward the glacier. Toby craned, expecting to see a modest lake beyond it, but on the far side of the glacier, open water reached out as far as he could see. For a moment he wondered whether it was an arm of the ocean.

"I told you about the *jokulhlaup*," Phil said then, pitching his voice to be heard over the roar of the engine. He gestured out the window at the water. "That's all meltwater, and the ice there is what's left of the Tornarssukalik Glacier. Once the ice dam breaks, more than two thousand cubic miles of water go down the inlet in a few days."

Toby gave him a worried look. "What's that going to do to sea level?"

"An inch or so worldwide," Phil said with a shrug. "The oceans are pretty big. Of course that's on top of all the rest—but it's what it'll do on the way out that matters."

The copter passed the ice and soared out over the water, then veered, flew north along a ragged coastline dotted with masses of beached ice. To the left, the meltwater lake stretched away to the edge of sight, where a hint of white suggested distant glaciers. To the right, rugged mountains gouged and battered by millennia of ice age conditions hid the ocean further east.

Half an hour passed, maybe more, and then the copter turned, dropped down to within a hundred feet of the water and headed back the way they had come. Toby sent a wary glance Phil's way; Phil put on a bland uncommunicative look and turned to consider the view. More time passed, and finally the helicopter slowed and descended to a flat stretch of tundra close to the shore of the meltwater lake.

The engines slowed but didn't stop. "Here you go," Phil said. "You've got a hike ahead of you, and I'm sorry to say it's all uphill."

Toby gave him another wary look, didn't bother to answer. A moment was enough to scoop up his rucksack, and by then Emmeline had come aft from her seat beside the pilot, shouldered a hunting rifle, and motioned at the pile of gear in nylon sacks further back in the cabin. Phil slid the door open; Toby climbed out onto bare gravel dotted with little huddled plants, took the gear as Phil and Emmeline handed it out to him, turned his back briefly as the two of them embraced, and then gave Emmeline a hand she didn't need but took anyway. They gathered up the gear as best they could and hurried away from the copter as the engine roared again. Downdraft from the rotors set dust billowing; the copter rose, turned, and headed due west, toward Nuuk and the inhabited parts of Greenland.

* * *

"Now to the camp," said Emmeline then. "You can fasten these to your rucksack, eh? *Bon*. I will take these others, and the rifle. We can stop to rest as often as we like." The whole time she watched Toby with a faint smile. She was waiting for his reaction, he knew.

He got the nylon bags strapped to his rucksack first. "We can't be more than ten miles from the station," he said. "Why did the helicopter take us the long way around?"

The smile did not change at all. "Wren gave you her name," she said. "A thing she gives to very few. I give it to you now also, so you know I can be trusted: Vrispaa."

Toby nodded. "Okay." Then: "You're not going to tell me what the reason is."

"That is correct." With a little shrug: "I know it is a difficult thing. If it helps, you know more about this business than most."

He opened his mouth to say something irritable, and stopped, remembering the things Wren had told him. "Okay," he said again. "I'll trust you. Are we actually near Dal Uqqul?"

To his surprise, that earned him a sudden broad smile. "*Oui*. Maybe we will even find the traces." She motioned toward the long barren slope that rose up into the mountains beyond, indicating the trail, and Toby nodded and shouldered his rucksack.

Phil hadn't been entirely correct when he said the hike was all uphill, but he was close. There was no trail, just a series of slopes angling up toward a gash between two mountain peaks, dotted here and there with dwarf willows that rose only a few inches above the hard brown soil. A few birds soared high overhead, and once something Toby guessed was a lemming darted out of their way and vanished down a burrow, but other than those he saw no signs of animal life. Now and again he glanced back the way they had come, saw the vast meltwater lake stretching out into distance, white icebergs glowing in the sun at intervals.

They stopped to catch their breath halfway up to the gap between peaks, and then again when they reached the gap.

Off to the east, he could see rugged country, slopes rising up toward the cliffs that overlooked Tornarssukalik Inlet, the great headland north of the inlet's mouth.

"Another two miles," Emmeline said then, "there is level ground north of the hills. If I am right Dal Uqqul is there, or close. We will camp near there, in a place not easy to find." Toby nodded, wondered if he'd ever learn the reason for the secrecy.

They reached the level ground, turned toward the hills and reached the campsite, a place on one side of a valley where a vanished glacier had left four big ragged boulders close together, forming a rough stockade with four narrow entrances. Nearby, a stream splashed and pooled; when they followed the stream uphill to its source, they found a big mass of ice not yet finished melting, and beyond that the edge of the cliffs overlooking the inlet, with a fine view of Tornarssukalik Station in the middle distance. "Très bon," said Emmeline. "Maybe it is pointless, but—" She shrugged. Toby didn't expect an explanation and didn't get one.

They picked their way back down the place among the boulders, and made camp there. Once the tent was set up, she unpacked something else that looked like a tent, made of fabric the same dull gray-brown color as the landscape around them. It was only as she unfolded it and started assembling the long poles that Toby realized it was camouflage netting, meant to make their camp invisible from the air.

They finished setting up camp, made lunch over a little hissing camp stove, spent the rest of the day doing a rough search of the area where the fortress of Dal Uqqul might once have stood. That was tiring work, for the ground was flat only in the sense that it didn't slope one way or the other; mounds and hummocks showed by their shape where something had resisted the slow grinding movement of the ice. The cyclopean stones of a Hyperborean fortress? They talked about that over dinner, reached no conclusions.

Later still, before crawling into his sleeping bag, Toby went to empty his bladder. The sun was hidden beyond hills to the northwest but broken clouds caught a little of its glow. He had the rifle with him in case of polar bears, but the landscape stretched out silent and empty around him. It was only when he finished and turned to go back into the camp that he caught a hint of movement; he froze, realized a moment later that the movement was up in the air.

Something moved up beyond the clouds. Toby caught a brief glimpse and then another, not enough to make sense of it, and then all at once it crossed a gap in the clouds and he saw it clearly. Humanlike in shape but titanic in size, gaunt, naked, with white hair and a white beard all aswirl about the huge haggard head, and eyes that glowed like coals: that was the figure he saw striding across the empty wind.

Lessons he'd learned at his grandmother's knee screamed at him to hide himself, warned of what could happen if that shape reached for him out of the sky. He stood staring anyway. Though he'd grown up with tales of the Great Old Ones and murmured his prayers to them every morning since childhood, they had always been abstract to him. It shook him to his core to see one of them, Ithaqua the Wind-Walker, stalking through the sky in the unhuman flesh.

The figure passed out of sight behind the hills to the north. Toby stood there for a while, gazing at the place where it had been, and then finally shook his head and went back to the tent.

That night, for the first time in weeks, he dreamed again of the man in sealskin garments and the strange mask. It was the same dream, or nearly: the place underground, the cold air sighing on cold stone, the pale sourceless light, the figure bending over him, the dark eyes visible through the mask, searching, intent.

* * *

He wondered later if the Great Old One's presence and the dream had been omens, for the next morning brought an abrupt answer to some of his questions.

He woke early, went to the stream to wash, and had gotten dressed again and started back to camp when he heard the distant drumbeat of a helicopter in flight. He grinned, remembering what Emmeline had said about Wren flying out to meet them, and hurried back through one of the gaps between the boulders. "Emmeline?" he called out. "There's a copter coming."

That got a sleepy "Hmm?" in response, so he repeated the words, and heard her sit up inside the tent. "You are sure? It is too soon."

The rhythm had become loud enough to hear faintly even inside the circle of boulders. "Yeah," said Toby. "Can you hear—"

Sudden and unmistakable, the rolling boom of a distant explosion set the air trembling.

"*Saint Crapaud*." Emmeline's voice was ashen.

She came out of the tent a moment later, still fastening her clothes. Toby scarcely noticed. He was facing south, toward the inlet and the station, listening to the distant sounds. It wasn't just a single helicopter, he was sure of that. How many? He could not tell, but there seemed to be more of them with each moment that passed.

"This is bad," said Emmeline. "This is very bad."

He turned to face her. "What's happening?"

"I cannot be sure."

"We can go look," said Toby, and turned toward the nearest gap between boulders.

"*Non!*" She caught him by the arm. "If they see you they will shoot you dead."

He turned toward her, staring. In the distance, the mutter of helicopter rotors changed in a way he recognized after a moment: one of the copters had landed.

"Once they are all down," Emmeline said then, "we can see." She turned, went back into the tent, emerged a moment later with a pair of binoculars.

Minutes passed. The sound of the helicopters faded out as it had begun. Before the last one fell silent, Emmeline motioned toward the gap between the boulders and led the way. The two of them scrambled up along the stream to the mass of melting ice, where Emmeline gestured again: down. On their hands and knees, they crept up to the cliff's edge.

Looking south, Toby could see the station on its hill and the fuel tank nearby. Ten black dots he guessed were the helicopters formed a ragged ring well out from the station. It took him a moment to realize that something else had changed: the station's antenna was a crumpled mass sprawled over the tundra. Blackening near its base placed the blast he'd heard.

"*Non, non, non,*" Emmeline murmured next to him, her voice low and desperate. "It should not have been this soon."

Toby turned also. "Can I—" She shoved the binoculars into his hands. Tears streaked her face, though she made no sound.

He raised the binoculars, spotted one of the helicopters: a black military-style machine. A little more searching caught the tiny figures of men in camouflage fatigues. Tiny flashes caught his gaze. A moment passed before he heard a faint dim sound in the still air and realized that he was seeing gunfire. What they were shooting at he could not see, and did not want to see.

"Come," Emmeline said then.

He looked back at her, his mind blank with shock.

"Come," she repeated. "We can do nothing here." When he did not move at once, she took hold of his arm and pulled. Numb, he followed, crept down to the far side of the ice, rose unsteadily to his feet.

"If they catch us, everything is lost," she said then. "I brought you here once the thing, *la traduction*, was done, in case, but we did not think—" Her voice broke. Once she'd mastered herself: "There is a place we can go, if we are lucky, if we move fast."

He nodded after a moment, followed her down the slope.

* * *

They broke camp as quickly as they could manage, hurried across the place where Dal Uqqul might have been, followed the little stream north though its narrow valley until they got out of the hills. From there the ground swept away north into the distance and east to the sea, a bare brown landscape dotted with patches of cinquefoil and moss campion, slashed here and there by creeks edged with the brilliant green of sedges and grass. Numb and silent, Toby let himself be led, paid only as much attention to the path as would keep him from stumbling. Mosquitoes and flies gathered above the creeks but shunned the windswept open ground, so it was only now and then that they had to squint and hurry through the swirling cloud and scramble up into clear air. Every such passage left Emmeline with more bites, to be checked quickly with a probing finger and a low French curse. Toby glanced at his unbroken skin and hurried on.

Now and then the numb feeling gave way. When it did, what came through was dread. The land offered no shelter from watching eyes, and the sky soared clear and blue to the edge of space. If one of the black helicopters happened to rise above the cliffs behind them, he knew, their chances of escaping being spotted and shot from the air were too slight to worry about. A dozen times, more, his imagination turned some trick of the keening wind into the distant beat of rotor blades, set his pulse pounding and sweat breaking from his forehead, and he could think only of the gunfire he'd seen. Each time, though, the imagined noise faded, leaving only the whispering sounds of the tundra in their place.

Hours passed. Once they were well north of the cliffs, the crannied bare uplands gave way to a broad stretch of lower, greener ground tenanted by a dozen musk oxen. The great hairy beasts left off their grazing to watch Toby and Emmeline hurry past a quarter mile off, and the wind brought Toby their rank sweetish scent. Further north an arctic fox spotted them and matched their pace at a safe distance for some time, until it decided they weren't likely to leave carrion behind for its benefit and veered off. Jaegers circled overhead, patient.

The sun had circled around well to the west, and long shadows reached across the landscape from the mountains of Tscho Vulpanomi, when Emmeline tapped Toby's sleeve, demanding his attention. She brought a finger to her mouth, urging silence, then motioned for him to follow her seaward, into a gully that veered northeast. They moved along it as quietly as they could, while the ground rose up to northward into a hill spotted with dwarf willow and cotton grass and the sea came closer. Finally she gestured for him to wait, and moved noiselessly up the slope and over it, out of sight.

In the moments that followed, a stillness that was more than the tundra's ordinary silence closed around Toby, vast enough that the whispering wind, the distant rhythmic rush of waves on the shore, and the buzzing of unsatisfied flies and mosquitoes couldn't break it. He thought of the people he'd left behind at Tornarssukalik Station—Wren, first and foremost, but not Wren alone. Face after face rose and faded in his mind's eye, and last of all Leah Sargent's, not the look of rigid hostility she'd turned on him at first or the wary respect with which she'd regarded him later, but the look he'd gotten from her just before their half-drunken tryst, half puzzlement and half reluctant affection.

They were all dead. He had no doubt of that, not after seeing the men spreading out around the station, the flashes of their assault rifles. Just like Pine Harbor: the thought rose suddenly in his mind. The folk there had been caught the same way, taken by surprise with no time for more than a few to escape. This time, though, there'd been no water to hide the survivors and no Lefferts Corners waiting to give them a temporary home. And the survivors—

So many of the people he'd known in childhood were dead that he'd thought about his own death many times, but always in the abstract, as something hovering in the distance. Now it stood in front of him, maybe imminent, maybe delayed by a few days or weeks, and he wondered if it mattered. The thought of giving up, letting himself sink into the despair that pressed up hard against him, whispered with the wind's voice, seductive. Had the ones who'd died at Pine Harbor felt the same thing as the gunmen closed in on them? Had it made the end easier?

Motion seen out of the corner of his eye caught his attention, and he glanced that way. A little brown shape scurried among the sedges: a collared lemming, he realized after an instant. The turning of his head startled it, and it rose up suddenly on its hindquarters, regarding him with eyes like little polished stones, its gaze unwavering.

Toby considered the little creature for a long moment, and it considered him. Things he'd read about lemmings rose from memory. Jaws of fox or weasel, beak of jaeger or snowy owl— the little life in front of him would end between those, but there it sat, wary and unyielding, facing a being more than a thousand times its own size with no sign of fear.

Toby drew in a ragged breath, another. Damn it, he thought. Damn it. If a lemming can face the world with that kind of courage, then so can I.

"Toby!" Emmeline's voice came down from above. Toby stood and turned, spotted her on the hillside, and sensed rather than saw the lemming take advantage of his distracted attention and dart to safety in a clump of sedges. Emmeline motioned for him to come up, and he scrambled up out of the gully, climbed the barren slope to her.

"We are, how you say it, in the good luck," she said. "The place, North Station, it is unharmed, there is food inside, and I did not even have to kill anyone. Come."

He gave her a startled look at the last phrase but one, but she had already turned to lead the way over the crest of the hill. Holding tight to his newfound resolve, he followed.

* * *

North Station was a single quonset hut maybe twenty feet long, streaked with rust but still intact, huddled against the lee of the hill. Off past it, beyond a steep slope and a gravel beach, the sea spread out into distance, stirred by low rolling waves and dotted with floating cakes of ice. They hurried down to the hut, ducked in through the narrow door on the seaward side. "You see?" Emmeline said, gesturing at the bare little space inside with evident pleasure. "It will serve *parfaitement*. No fuel for the stove, but we could not risk that anyway, no, not if the others might have infrared gear, and they might. But we will hide here, use our camp stove to cook, be safe from *bêtes* human and otherwise, and I can try to call for help."

"There's a radio?" Toby asked—puzzled, for he'd seen no antenna. "Is that safe?"

"A radio? Oh, *non, non*. They would be on us *à l'instant*." She turned to face him. "Toby, there are things I cannot tell you— someday, maybe, but now, no. I must ask you to let that happen. I know it is not easy."

"I said I'd trust you," Toby reminded her.

She beamed. "*Bon*. Let us see what else is in this place, and then, food."

Inside was a big rectangular space with a kitchen and a little walled-off bathroom at the far end. Four iron bedsteads with cheap foam mattresses stood more or less in a row against one wall; a big stove made of two 55 gallon drums and various ironwork and stovepipes stood well away from the other wall; a table and four chairs stood close to the kitchen; random crates and boxes stood in the corners and edges of the space. A trickle of light came in through brown fiberglass skylights in the ceiling and small barred windows in the walls at each of the hut's ends. By that dim glow, Toby shed his backpack and his coat, then helped Emmeline search the crates, the boxes, and the kitchen cupboards.

The food consisted of foil packets of freeze-dried meals, decades old from the look of the labels; there were close to a dozen of them in one of the kitchen cupboards. The boxes and crates contained the most random assortment of gear Toby had ever seen in one place, everything from snowshoes and a signal mirror through spare blankets and canvas buckets to an old pair of binoculars and a hefty volume with the cryptic words *Proc. Misk. Gree. Conf.* on the spine. The canvas buckets were helpful, at least, and Toby shouldered the rifle in case of polar bears, went outside, and started bringing back buckets of water from a stream a dozen yards away, two at a time, to fill the big steel reservoir that provided for the toilet and the sink.

By the time he'd finished that task, Emmeline had boiled water and used it to reconstitute two packets of freeze-dried tuna noodle casserole. The resulting meal tasted like warm cardboard and the texture wasn't even that appetizing, but it filled his stomach. Cups of hot boiled water had to make do in place of coffee or tea. Neither of them spoke much; Toby guessed from the fixed expression on Emmeline's face that she was thinking, as he was, about the people at Tornarssukalik Station.

"So," she said after they'd finished washing up the dishes. "It should be time. I will go outside, and you will please stay inside. I will return in, hmm, let us say twenty minutes." Toby nodded and held out the rifle. She gave him a sly smile and said, "*Trés bon.* If *M'sieur le* Polar Bear comes to pay a visit, why, we will eat better tomorrow than today." She shrugged on her coat, took the rifle, and went outside.

Lacking anything else to do, Toby got up and fetched the book he'd found in one of the crates. The arcane words on the spine turned out to be abbreviations for *Proceedings of the Miskatonic Greenland Conference*, with a date in the middle of the last century. He turned to the table of contents, slid a finger along it. Most of the papers were of little interest to him—*Stratigraphic Analysis of Subglacial Soils at Nanuqtak, A Tentative Periodization of Uzuldaroum IIa-IVc Ceramics*—or covered material he already knew inside and out—*Newly Discovered Inscriptions from*

Inukiviq III, Hieratic Naacal Loanwords in Old Lomarian—but one caught his eye: *Hyperborean Artifacts in Norse Greenland?*

He paged through it, then went back and read it more carefully. Apparently the seventeenth-century Swedish scholar Johannes Bureus quoted lost twelfth- and thirteenth-century records that seemed to refer to Hyperborean weapons, metalwork, and jewelry in the hands of the Norse settlers in Greenland. Blurry images from Bureus' book seemed to show two-handed scimitars, axes with strange sawtoothed blades, broad flat bowls carved with the faces of many-eyed gods, hexagonal coins with exotic markings on them: none of them at all like the plain sturdy Norse gear Toby remembered from the museums in Reykjavik. He read on, nodded slowly at the author's speculation that some rich Hyperborean grave or buried treasury must have been found by a Norse settler and plundered a little at a time.

A map reminded him that the Norse settlements in Greenland had been on the southwest shores of the great island, where the verdant provinces of Leqquan and Aquil once stretched out toward a blue sea unburdened by ice: more than a thousand miles from Tscho Vulpanomi, Toby reminded himself, and from him. He sat back, found himself thinking of the Norse colonists, who'd dwelt there for five centuries, before—what? Nobody knew. In the fifteenth century, the colonists had vanished or died, leaving behind ruined houses and stone churches, their lives erased as completely as the glaciers had erased the cities of Hyperborea. Absurd as the thought was, Toby found himself wondering if they'd been killed by the same secret organization that had gunned down the people of Pine Harbor. Had that same organization sent the helicopters to Tornarssukalik Station?

"The Radiance." He made himself whisper the name aloud.

A moment later the door rattled and swung open. Toby sat bolt upright, but it proved to be Emmeline, coming back in with a relieved look on her broad plain face. "It is done," she said. "The message is sent. It will be days, but help is coming."

"From Nuuk?" Toby asked, naming Greenland's capital.

"Oh, *non, non.*" She shook her head, dismissing the thought. "There is still much to happen." An upraised hand forestalled his questions. "You will see."

* * *

They spent three days in all at North Station: waiting was one way to think of it, hiding was another, but either way it would have been unbearable if Toby had had any other choice. He ended up reading the whole volume of *Proceedings of the Miskatonic Greenland Conference* twice through just to keep his mind off the images that circled through his thoughts and dreams, the grief and the helpless rage. Going outside for more than a few minutes at a time wasn't an option; twice they'd heard the distant beat of a helicopter off to the south, and though each time it stayed too far off to endanger them, they both knew the risk was real.

Late the third day Emmeline slipped out again, cautioning him to stay inside, and was gone for ten minutes or so. When she came back in she was all smiles. "Tonight," she said. "Just after midnight, the fog will come, and something else with it. We must be ready to go."

He took that in and nodded after a moment, weighing the possibility that she had cracked under the strain and would start raving shortly. Instead, she packed her rucksack, and so did Toby. They fixed one more meal of freeze-dried food, a packet that claimed to be turkey tetrazzini and would probably have tasted less chemical if the label had read turkey tetrachloride. As the skylights darkened and the light through the dim little windows took on the blue tinge of an arctic summer night, Emmeline sat down to wait, and after a while Toby did the same thing.

Then the fog came. Toby scarcely noticed the fading light at first, but the room around him darkened until he could see almost nothing. He shouldered his rucksack, got to his feet and went to the nearest of the little windows. He could see precisely nothing outside.

"It is time," Emmeline said then. In the hush, Toby could hear her get to her feet, but the darkness was so thick that he could see nothing at all. A moment passed, another, and the door opened, letting in a faint pallid light. He could see Emmeline silhouetted against it, motioning to him, and he hefted his rucksack and went after her, pulling the door shut behind him.

Gravel crunched beneath their boots as they picked their way to the shore. Low hissing sounds spoke of waves flowing onto the beach and slipping back again. Nothing else moved. They stopped a few paces back from the waves. He gave Emmeline a puzzled look; she stood looking out to sea as though she could glimpse something through the pallid wall of the fog.

Then, as though from a great distance, a faint repeated noise sounded across the water: a rhythm slower and harsher than the waves. Toby gave Emmeline another look, startled, but he could not see her expression. The sound grew louder, took on definition, and finally Toby recognized it: the rhythmic splash of oars breaking the water's surface.

Light flared suddenly: a flashlight in Emmeline's hand, on and then just as quickly off. She waited a few moments, then repeated the signal twice; another pause of a few moments, then three times. Off in the distance, as though in response, came the low dim sound of a human voice, saying something Toby couldn't make out.

The sound of the oars drew closer. A low dark shape emerged from the fog a little at a time: a longboat, Toby saw, rowed by three pairs of oarsmen with a seventh man sitting aft at the stern. One more pull at the long wooden oars sent the boat skimming toward the beach, and the man at the stern growled, "Oars up!" Up they went, and the longboat beached its prow neatly in the gravel only a few yards from where Toby and Emmeline stood.

"Mistress Grenier?" the man by the stern called out.

"Yes, that is me," Emmeline said. "And this one, he is Dr. Gilman."

"Aye, then, come aboard, both of ye, and make it lively." The man's voice had an accent Toby couldn't place, not quite English, not quite New England. "We've a deal o' rowing yet ahead of us."

Emmeline clambered aboard, and Toby followed her. They picked their way past the oarsmen, who glanced up as they passed. Toby considered them and wondered if he was the one who had cracked under the strain. Tough and heavily muscled, they wore clothing centuries out of date: knee breeches, bloused shirts, leather waistcoats, stout belts or bright sashes bristling with long knives and pistols of a style Toby thought had gone out of fashion by the War of 1812. Some wore tricorn hats, others had brightly colored kerchiefs tied about their heads. All in all, he thought, they looked like extras in an unusually authentic pirate movie.

Emmeline sat on one of the thwarts just aft of the oarsmen, motioned to Toby to sit next to her. He complied, took off his rucksack as she did and set it with hers, in front of their feet and close to the keel. "Push off!" the man behind them growled, and the two oarsmen amidships turned their oars end for end and used the butts to push the longboat free of the beach. More quick movements and two more orders, and the longboat pulled away from the beach, turned neatly, and slid across the dark water into the silent fog.

Toby sat on the thwart, watched the oarsmen pull at the oars with practiced ease, and wondered if he was hallucinating, or maybe dead and on his way to an afterlife more colorful than he'd had any reason to expect. Next to him, Emmeline beamed, as though skimming into the unknown on a longboat crewed by pirates who couldn't exist was a frequent pleasure of hers. Floating cakes of ice drifted past, ghostly in the dim light. Once a seal put its head up out of the water and watched them, and Toby wondered if it was as baffled by the view as he was.

Time passed, marked by the steady metronome of the oars-men's rhythm. The fog began to thin. Then, impossibly, the masts and rigging of a tall ship loomed up ahead, black against the dim gray fog. Toby stared at it and muttered a profanity under his breath.

"You see?" Emmeline said to him. "It is not over yet, not by the long shot. The other side, they have done their worst, *non*? Now it is our turn."

He gave her an incredulous glance, stared at the ship again. The hull loomed up out of the fog ahead, long and black from the jutting bowsprit to the rounded stern, and Toby wondered why it somehow seemed familiar to him. He spotted shapes on the forecastle, thrusting over the gunwales, that could only be old-fashioned muzzle-loading cannon. The longboat sped closer and closer still, until another growled order brought it alongside the tall black side of the hull. The pirates backed water, stopping the boat alongside a ladder of cleats that rose up, flanked by ropes in stanchions, to the deck a good two storeys above.

The man at the stern motioned for them to go up. Toby got his rucksack back on his shoulders, took hold of the ropes, and scrambled up the ladder. There was, he thought, some-thing unnervingly familiar about the black wall of the ship's side he climbed, the line of portholes that pierced it in place of gun ports, the gangway at the ladder's top that let him onto the great sweep of the spar deck. Only when he glanced for-ward and spotted two low shedlike structures along the deck's midline, one forward of the foremast and the other between foremast and mainmast, did he realize why he recognized everything around him.

He turned to Emmeline as she hauled herself up through the gangway. "My God," he said. "This is the *Miskatonic*."

"*Mas oui*," said Emmeline, beaming. "I said it, *non*? Now it is our turn."

* * *

More pirates hurried past them, got to work hauling the long-boat aboard, as the longboat's crew scrambled up the ladder to the spar deck. Toby watched them, tried to make sense of what he was seeing, and failed utterly.

"The ship, it is owned by a foundation in Kingsport," said Emmeline then. "The people in charge are on our side of all this. The *Miskatonic* needs to have work done on the hull, so it must go to a drydock in Maine—that is what they said. So away it sailed, but not to a drydock."

Toby was still staring at her. "But—but why this ship?"

"A ship of steel can be seen with the radar. Wood and canvas, not so. Clever, no?" Then, gesturing: "The captain, he will want to see you. Come this way."

Just forward of the mizzenmast, the ship's wheel rose up, dark and spectral. The compass in its binnacle nearby had a hooded oil lamp to light it, and by that diffuse golden glow he saw the captain of the *Miskatonic*. Resplendent in a cocked hat, a gray greatcoat with gold buttons, brown knee breeches, stockings, and shoes with buckles, he looked ready to command a crew even more piratical than the one that swarmed over the ship. His face, framed with a short white beard, was tanned and wrinkled as old leather and looked far more ancient than any human face should be. The thing that caught Toby's attention first, though, were his eyes. The yellow of polished gold, they gleamed in a way that the dim light from the lamp didn't quite explain.

"Captain Coldcroft," Emmeline said. "One more time I am in your debt. This is the young person I spoke of, Doctor Toby Gilman."

"Pleased to meet you," Toby said, then remembered to say, "sir."

The yellow eyes turned toward him, and the captain nodded, acknowledging. He turned to Emmeline, said in a voice rich with the old New England accent: "I sent men ashore south o' the inlet. Ye weren't wrong."

Emmeline stared at him for a moment, then clenched her eyes shut and muttered what sounded like a malediction under her breath.

"Save the curse," Coldcroft told her. "Ye'll have use of it soon enough." She gave him a bleak look and walked a short distance away, and the captain turned abruptly to Toby. "Ye have the words from the remembrancin' stone."

Toby blinked in surprise, but said, "Yes. Yes, I do."

"And ye know how to read 'em?" When Toby nodded: "D'ye know what hangs 'pon it?"

"Not really," Toby admitted. "I know that it's important."

"Ye might call it that." He turned, called out to the pirates: "Jack, take the wheel. The rest of ye, set the tops'ls and spanker and break her out."

The pirates had apparently been waiting for that command, and moments later some swarmed up the ratlines to loose the sails while others took hold of lines from the deck. The topsails, Toby was startled to find, weren't actually the top sails but the middle set; they flapped and wavered as the crew hauled the great yards up and then moved them to two different angles. The spanker, though the name was no less confusing to him, was simply the lowest of the sails rigged fore and aft on the mizzenmast. Once set, the sails aft filled gently with wind, while the one forward billowed back against the mast. Somewhere forward, rough voices rose in a song:

> "Where is the trader o' London town?
> His gold's on the capstan, his blood's on his gown
> And it's up and away to Saint Mary's Bay
> Where the liquor is good and the lasses are gay!"

Toby felt the lurch of the deck as the anchor came up, felt another shift as the ship began to move. Only then did he realize why the sails had been set the way they were: the sail in front caught the wind one way, pivoting the bow away from land, while the others caught it a different way and got the ship in motion.

Waves slapped the sides of the hull and the rigging creaked as the *Miskatonic* swung toward the open ocean, but the thing that struck Toby most about those first few minutes under way was the lack of engine noise. Each of the few other times he'd been out on the water, there had been either an outboard motor roaring at the stern or an engine below setting the decks thrumming. It seemed uncanny to him to be picking up speed steadily with no sounds but those of wind and wave.

Once the bow was pointed toward the sea, the crew got the forward topsail braced at the same angle as the one behind it, and then set the rest of the sails. One after another, white shapes filled with wind, and the *Miskatonic* picked up speed. A glance back showed Toby the pack ice and the dim shore of Greenland already some distance away, across an ocean the color of night.

"Where are we going?" Toby asked the captain then.

Yellow eyes glinted as the man turned to face him. "For the nonce, the open sea. Once we're well clear o' Greenland, that'll be time to choose a new course."

Toby bowed his head, guessing that the course would lead away from Greenland and any hope of doing something about Wren and the others. The captain made a harsh amused noise in his throat, though, and said, "Think ye so? By the Black Goat and all Her Young!" Toby stared, astonished as much by the oath as by the way the captain seemed to hear his thoughts, but the old man went on before he could speak. "I didn't sail here with men such as these only to turn around and sail home. We'll speak o' that in a matter o' days." He turned. "Peters!" One of the pirates, a lean man with a pale pockmarked face and red hair, crossed the deck to him. "Give these gentlefolk their cabins and see to it they have all they need."

"Aye, sir," said Peters, and turned to Toby. "If ye'll come with me, I'll show ye below." He turned to Emmeline: "Ma'am—"

"I am coming," Emmeline said, turning back toward Toby.

The way down was a hatch between mainmast and mizzenmast, forward of the wheel, with a wooden ladder slanting down into darkness. Peters led the way, gathered up a lantern from a hook beside the ladder. They went to the deck immediately below, then headed aft a short distance to where doors opened off to either side of the companionway. "Ellis and me, we're to starboard," Peters said, "and the two of ye can take yer pick o' the cabins to port."

Emmeline gave Toby a questioning look. He shrugged, motioned to her, and she went through the forward door. Toby got a brief look at a little cabin inside, and then Emmeline nodded to him, to Peters, and closed the door. Toby said something vaguely suitable to Peters and went into the cabin further aft. It had a pleasant little berth up against the forward wall, with latched drawers below for clothing and the like; on the other side, fastened to the wall, were a chair and a washstand with a metal mirror. Between the bed and the other furnishings there was just barely enough room to turn around.

He closed the door, stowed his gear, considered his options, then stripped down to boxers and tee shirt and got into bed. Tired though he was, he didn't expect to get to sleep easily, but he managed it after a while. Pale meaningless dreams wandered past him for a time before he found himself in the empty space where cold air conversed mindlessly with cold stone. The dim shape that loomed over him was almost familiar by then, the bleak eyes staring out through the holes in the round mask. What it saw as it looked at him Toby could not tell, but after a moment it nodded slowly, as though some guess had turned out correct.

CHAPTER 6

THE SHADOW OF THE ROPE

Toby woke suddenly out of a nightmare of gunfire and flames. It took him a moment to realize the images were dreams, and a longer one to remember why the bed was rolling slowly beneath him. He sat up slowly, tried to make himself think of anything but Tornarssukalik Station and the people he'd left there. The porthole on the wall past his head let in a dim gray light. Through it he could see little but featureless cloud.

After a while he sat up, pulled on his clothing and left the cabin. Glass prisms set into the ceiling at intervals let in a glimmer of daylight from the deck above, and a stronger light came down the hatch. Nobody seemed to be moving belowdecks, and he went to the ladder and hauled himself up into the open air.

On deck a cold wind sent salt spray whipping past, with thick clouds above and surging green water stretching out unbroken to every side. The *Miskatonic*, her sails bellying before the wind, was making headway toward some unknown destination, setting the water foaming along her flanks. A red-faced man in knee breeches and a ragged waistcoat, with a yellow sash around his waist, a red kerchief on his head, and a patch over one eye, stood by the ship's wheel and held it steady. Others who looked just as piratical lounged about the deck or stood in platforms high up on the two forward masts, evidently keeping watch, and a crew hauled on lines, doing something to the mainsail. Toby could hear a man's voice rising in a rough song over the keening of the wind: "Of a pirate bold I'll sing to ye,"

Other voices joined in: "Hey, ho, the winds do blow!"

The first voice repeated: "Of a pirate bold I'll sing to ye,"

The others answered in chorus: "Yo ho ho and a rumbelow!"

The first went on:

"Of a pirate bold I'll sing to ye
Who ventured out on the rollin' sea,
But never came back to Saint Maree,"

A chorus rang out again: "Yo ho ho and a rumbelow!"

As they were starting a second verse, a bearded black man in a greatcoat and tricorn hat came aft. "Dr. Gilman? I'm Ellis. The Old Man told Peters and me to make sure you're well."

Toby shook his hand. "Is it Mr. Ellis?"

"On board, it's Mate Ellis. I'm first mate and Peters is second, and that means any hour of day or night you'll find one of us on deck."

"That's good to know," said Toby. "What time is it?"

"Just past five bells," said Ellis. Seeing Toby's puzzlement, he grinned. "Meaning a bit after six-thirty in the morning, landlubbers' time. Breakfast's at seven bells, seven-thirty, but you can get something hot to drink in the galley before then if you fancy that. It's down on the orlop deck—listen for the clanging pots and you won't miss it."

"Thanks," said Toby, and then asked the other obvious question. Ellis laughed and said, "Of course. Back down to the main deck—that's the one your cabin's on—and then for'ard as far as you can go. There's one on either side."

Following the directions, Toby went back down the ladder to the main deck, made his way from there by the pale light that came through the prisms. Forward of the hatch, the mainmast plunged through the space, and forward of that stood two massive structures of timber, arranged fore and aft, that he guessed had to do with the mortars. Alongside these, swinging as the ship rolled, hammocks hung from the beams overhead, and every other hammock had a figure asleep in it. Toby picked his way past these to the forward hatch, where he heard the clattering of pots from the galley below, and then past the foremast. Beyond that, on either side of the great slanting timber of the bowsprit, were the doors Ellis had mentioned.

It was a little unnerving, Toby decided, to be sitting with nothing between the cold surging sea and certain tender portions of his anatomy but a few yards of spray-filled air. A placard on the inside of the door, no doubt put there for the benefit of tourists back in the day, answered a question that had puzzled him for years:

> IF YOU'RE WONDERING WHY THE HEADS
> AND THE GALLEY ARE AT THE SHIP'S
> BOW, ASK YOURSELF THIS: WHEN A
> SAILING VESSEL IS UNDER WAY,
> WHICH WAY IS THE WIND BLOWING?

He laughed at that, but it made sense, and when he'd finished he went to the forward hatch and climbed down to the orlop deck and the galley, a cramped space outfitted with modern kitchen gear and lit by a pair of electric lights. A big round-bellied man with white hair and a wooden leg labored there, sleeves rolled up. His shirt and the kerchief on his head were damp with sweat as he boiled up something in a big copper kettle, but when he spotted Toby he nodded a greeting, filled a mug with coffee from a pot on the back of the stove and handed it to him. Toby thanked him, and the cook responded with an amiable grunt and turned back to his kettle.

Toby considered climbing the ladder again, but the cup was full enough that he decided against it, and headed aft along the orlop deck. The same massive timber structures he'd seen on the deck above filled much of the space between the foremast and mainmast on the lower deck as well, and there were more metal eyebolts to hang hammocks on the timbers overhead, back to the aft hatch and beyond it. The coffee, he decided, was far and away the worst he'd ever tasted, but it took the chill off him, and by the time he'd reached the aft hatch he'd downed enough that he was able to haul himself and the coffee up the ladder without spilling a drop.

He was back in his cabin by the time the bell rang six times, and guessed after a moment's calculation that this meant it was seven o'clock. The thought of lying back down on the bed occurred to him, but there was no sleep left in him. Once he'd finished the dreadful coffee, and spent some time staring out the porthole, lacking anything better to do, he headed back up on deck. There the same pirates labored at the same tasks as before, the sails strained before a brisk wind, and the *Miskatonic*'s black hull sliced through gray turbulent waters.

He'd hoped to find Captain Coldcroft on deck, so he could ask about where they were going and what they would do when they got there, but he was nowhere to be seen, and Emmeline remained out of sight as well. Instead, Ellis nodded a greeting. Once one of the sailors rang the ship's bell seven times, the ship's mate motioned to the hatch and said, "Breakfast's in the messroom aft—unless you're feeling seasick."

"No," said Toby. "So far, so good."

Ellis laughed and went to the hatch ahead of him. Just then a flurry of cold raindrops spattered on the deck.

* * *

Over the next two days, as the *Miskatonic* surged ahead with blustery winds in her sails, Toby found his sea legs again. He got used to thinking of the side of the ship toward the wind as windward and the other as leeward; he watched the pirates labor at the ship's eight black iron cannon, cleaning them for use, and blinked as they slid open the two low shedlike structures between the foremast and mainmast to reveal the mortars, short massive guns that could send explosive shells soaring high in the air, to drop from above onto targets on shore. The thought of trying to use weapons so archaic against helicopters and assault rifles seemed absurd to Toby, but the pirates seemed in earnest, and watching them gave him something to do besides stare at the walls of his cabin and try not to think of the people he'd left at Tornarssukalik Station.

He tried to get used to the abominable coffee without much success, but it helped him deal with the aftermath of broken sleep and hideous dreams. The rest of the shipboard fare was less of a challenge: a molasses-laced porridge for breakfast that the pirates called burgoo, and for the other two meals of the day, a variety of stews, salmagundis, and slumgullions mostly spiced to the point of incandescence, with hard crisp rounds of crackerlike bread called ship's biscuit to fill in the corners. Most of what he had to learn, though, was how to stand on deck with only the sea for company when the weather was fair, and when it rained or sleeted or snowed, which was often, how to sit in his cabin with nothing to do but stare out the porthole and try to silence his mind.

The pirates didn't seem to care about the weather at all. Rain or shine, one of the two mates stood on deck and the crew scrambled into the rigging, trimming the sails to the unsteady winds and keeping the *Miskatonic* under way. Toby heard their footsteps on the deck above his cabin and shook his head. Those footfalls and the mournful cries of sea birds were sometimes the only sounds of life he heard between one meal and the next. The meals were not much improvement, for Ellis and Peters were friendly enough but said little, and Emmeline was nowhere to be seen. Where she'd gone and what she was doing he had no idea.

Toward the end of the second day he went up on deck, he stood watching the gray waves as they slid past, and seriously thought about finding a knife somewhere and cutting his own throat. The lemming he'd seen was far astern, and his memory of its fierce uncompromising gaze offered little protection against the other memories that tumbled around him in the cold wind, the bitter grief and the pointless but inescapable sense of guilt that he was alive and all the others were dead. He was standing in the same place half an hour later, still watching the water rush by and still unable to get past a decision he couldn't make and couldn't avoid, when he heard footfalls on the ladder and turned.

It was Emmeline. "Ah, there you are!" she said. "You are busy? No? *Bon*. The captain, he wants to talk to you."

He didn't have to force a smile. "Sure thing." Answering her gesture, he followed her belowdecks, then aft past cabins and the messroom to the captain's cabin at the after end of the main deck. Her fist tapped briskly on the door, and she followed it with words: "Captain Coldcroft? He is here." Whatever answer she got missed Toby's ears completely, but she opened the door a moment later and motioned him in.

The cabin beyond reached from side to side of the ship and had a row of windows stretching across the stern, looking out on the *Miskatonic*'s wake and the gray turbulent sweep of the Atlantic beyond. A bed to port, a table and chairs to starboard, two chests bound with iron: that was the extent of the furnishings. Coldcroft stood by the windows, looking out over the ocean, but turned as Toby came in. His first words, though, were directed past Toby to Emmeline: "Ye've told him?"

"*Non*," she said. "You said only to bring him."

"Aye, that I did." He motioned for her to speak, turned away again.

"Toby," Emmeline said. Toby turned toward her, uncertain. "Maybe you wondered what we were doing all this time, eh? We wasted none of it. We have been in contact with others, to find out what happened at Tornarssukalik Station, to send for help. All this is *trés importante*, more than a university expedition, more than you were maybe told."

Toby took that in, thought of Wren's words and his promise, and abruptly decided to speak. "I know."

Coldcroft turned, regarded him with golden eyes. Emmeline considered him, too, with a look of utmost gravity. "How do you know?"

"Wren told me." He drew in a breath. "She—she said the survival of the world depended on something she was here to do."

"And you believed her."

"Yes," he said, knowing how absurd it sounded. "Yes, I did."

"*Bon*," said Emmeline. "It is true, all of it. Did she tell you more?"

"No—but I know what she was."

That earned him another silence. Coldcroft broke it with a harsh laugh. "'Tis well. I guessed ye knew more than ye let on. What would ye say if I told ye she's still drawin' breath?"

Toby turned to stare at him. He opened his mouth, closed it, tried again. "I'd want to know how you knew that."

"You know she puts on the bodies as we put on the clothes," said Emmeline. "There is another body waiting for her. It is still waiting. So the body of Wren, it still lives. The people who came, they could not permit that, and they do not know about the other body, so—" She made an expressive shrug. "I do not know how, but she is alive."

Toby, his mind reeling, tried to process that. "So," said Coldcroft then, "we have two deals o' work afore us. The first one's to find her, and any other such as got clear o' the station. The second's to keep sartain others from what they have in mind to do. The first might need the sheddin' of blood, the second surely will. If that's not somethin' ye can face, I can have ye put ashore in a safe place wi' friends of our cause until all's done with."

"No," said Toby. "Thank you, but no. I want to do something to help. If Wren's alive I want to help find her, and if the people who killed the others were from the Radiance—" He stopped abruptly, realizing a moment too late what he'd said.

A third silence, longer, filled the cabin. "So you know about them," said Emmeline.

"Just a little," Toby admitted.

"'Tis well." Coldcroft nodded once, as though satisfied. "Aye, they were. And if I tell ye, Dr. Gilman, I mean to serve 'em as they served those ye knew?"

"Then I'll do whatever you want me to do." Toby's voice went ragged. "But you're seriously going to take on helicopters and assault rifles with—" His gesture jabbed out to indicate the ship around them and its pirate crew.

In answer, Coldcroft smiled. The bared teeth reminded Toby suddenly of a shark's mouth. "Aye," said the captain. "Ye haven't yet taken the measure o' this ship or the manner o' men that crew it. We'll see which is the better once it comes to a fight."

"Then I want to be there," Toby said. "I want to help." It stung to admit a weakness, but he made himself go on: "And if there's anything I can do before that happens, please tell me. It's been kind of hard sitting around doing nothing."

Coldcroft glanced at Emmeline, read something in her face Toby couldn't see. "Aye, there's work to be done. We're short-handed for a ship this size, if ye can haul on a line."

The thought of helping to sail a tall ship hadn't occurred to Toby since his childhood, but he didn't hesitate. "Please. I don't know a thing about sailing but I can learn."

Without another word Coldcroft stepped past him, went to the door, and called out, "Mate Ellis!" A moment passed, another, and then Ellis came down the companionway to the door. "You know Gilman? 'Tis well. He's asked to serve along-side the crew. See to it."

Ellis took that in and said, "Aye, sir." Then, to Toby. "Come on. It's near time for the watch to change."

* * *

Up on deck the wind was sharp, flinging spray from the tops of gray rolling waves. Ellis gave Toby a hard look. "You might want to think twice about this."

"I've already thought about it." That wasn't strictly true, but having something to occupy his hours felt very nearly like salvation to him.

"You won't sleep more than four hours at a stretch."

Toby gave him a bleak look. "I'd settle for four hours."

Ellis considered that, led him amidships, and shouted forward, "Long Tom! Get your pox-ridden bones aft."

One of the pirates ambled aft from the fo'c'sle, a long lean gangling man with a short rough beard and unruly brown hair. "Aye?"

"Gilman here wants to stand watch with the rest of us. Show him the ropes, will you?"

Long Tom grinned. "Aye, that I can do. Come for'ard, then."

Toby followed him. "Glad to have ye," said Tom. "Ye'll be in the larboard watch with me, and that means first and third watch tonight, second on the morrow. T'other half o' the crew's the starboard watch, and ye needn't consarn yerself with 'em. When our watch is on, look lively and do what needs doin'; when we're off, sleep while ye can—ah, here's the bell."

The ship's bell rang eight times, and half a dozen pirates who'd been on the fo'c'sle headed below. The rest, joined by others from belowdecks, came amidships.

"Jack, take the wheel," said Mate Ellis. "Geoff, Spanish Joe, up to the tops with you, and keep a smart eye out. The rest of you, get the mainsail and fore mainsail in and reef the topgallants. I don't like the taste of this wind."

Within moments Toby was hauling on a rope alongside Long Tom and two other pirates, helping to pull the mainsail up against the yard from which it hung. Tom started singing as soon as he got his hands on the rope: "There once was a ship called *Miskatonic* ..."

The other pirates joined the shanty: "Father Dagon and Mother Hydra!" It had been years since Toby had heard the names of the Adam and Eve of the Deep Ones spoken aloud, and he could not keep a grin off his face.

"Poor lot o' bastards sailed upon it," Tom sang.

"Down to the heart o' the cold, cold sea," came the refrain.

"East out o' Greenland they was sailin' ..."

Toby joined in the chorus: "Father Dagon and Mother Hydra!"

"Any sane man would've jumped the railin' ..."

"Down to the heart o' the cold, cold sea."

Toby thought then of how close he'd come to cutting his throat and heading down to the sea's cold heart, and threw himself into the work. He sang and hauled along with the pirates, and caught more than one of them glance at him and nod approvingly.

Once the line was made fast, the two other pirates leapt for the ratlines and began to climb. "Up wi' the both of us now," said Long Tom. "But ye'll want to leave the shoon. Bare feet are better to hold to spar and rope."

Toby kicked off his shoes, pulled off his socks, gathered up his courage, climbed onto the ratlines and hauled himself step by step up to the lowest yard, where the bunted mainsail still billowed in the wind.

The others had already worked their way out along the yard to starboard, their feet braced on a stout rope that hung from supports a few feet below the yard. Long Tom clambered along the yard to port, motioned with his head for Toby to follow. "Feet on the footline," he shouted over the wind, "back to the backrope, belly to the yard. Watch what I do, and do the like."

Toby made himself clamber out along the yard and slip under the backrope—a length of rope strung just behind the yard, which he guessed was there to keep him from being blown back into empty air if the wind changed suddenly. That offered a little security, so did the footline, and so did the strong wooden mass of the yard itself beneath his middle, but he was exquisitely aware of the long drop that separated him from the deck. Still, he leaned over the yard and helped haul the sail up and roll it in a bundle atop the yard, where one set of short ropes whose name he didn't know fastened it between two other equally unknown ropes that ran along the top of the yard, one a short distance behind the other. (The first set, he learned later, were gaskets, and the second were jackstays.) He fumbled and strained, but finally got a portion of the sail rolled and gasketed and settled in place, then moved outward to the next.

By the time he was finished with his share, the rest of the sail was bundled. Long Tom glanced over his work, nodded, and then jerked his head upwards, toward the topgallant mainsail high above. The others were already climbing toward it. Toby swallowed, his throat suddenly dry, but climbed unsteadily after them.

That was the way his first watch went: up into the rigging to do tasks he didn't pretend to understand, then back down on deck for a while until the wind changed or Mate Ellis decided a little more or less canvas would speed them better on their way. When the watch was over, Toby stumbled into his cabin in a state of utter exhaustion, got himself partly undressed, and fell into bed. He didn't wake at all until Mate Ellis' fist pounded on his door, rousing him for the third watch of the night. Minutes later he clambered groggily up on deck, to find every sail the *Miskatonic*'s masts could carry bellying out above him in the cold moonlight. The wind had slackened and veered to the west, and the ship surged on steadily through choppy seas.

Toby had no time to admire the view, though. The yards had to be braced to angle the sails to the wind's new direction, which involved hauling in a set of ropes on one side of the ship while paying out an identical set on the other, and then the wind picked up again and up he went into the rigging, to help reef the mainsail and then the foresail, shortening each sail by a third or so to keep from dipping the lee rail or driving the bow too deep.

After that was done, Mate Ellis put him at the ship's wheel for an hour. That took effort of a different kind: standing to windward of the wheel, holding it steady, and all the while watching the compass in its binnacle to be sure the *Miskatonic* stayed on course. For moments here and there, with the deck slanting beneath him, the sails straining overhead, and the wheel's well-worn handles in his grip, he could feel the entire ship from keel to mainmast-top and bowsprit to rudder, all its intricacies bent to the single purpose of harnessing winds to cross the ocean. It was exhilarating but exhausting, and he was glad when another pirate took the wheel and Ellis sent him forward to help Jack and Long Tom with a recalcitrant spritsail.

He was happier still when it was time to go below. Breakfast was waiting in the galley; he got a bowl of burgoo and a cup of atrocious coffee, then nearly dozed off at the table with food and drink sitting in front of him. It took an effort to hold off sleep long enough to eat, but the hot food and drink helped take the chill off him. Once he was finished, he went to his cabin, got himself undressed, crawled into bed, and fell asleep within moments.

Somewhere in the few hours that followed, as the ship rolled and the starboard watch labored above, he slipped back into the dream he'd had before. Once again he found himself in a vast lightless place where cold air whistled and sighed against cold stone; once again the sourceless glow like moonlight flowed around him, and the man in bulky sealskin garments with the mask on his face seemed to bend over him, silent and intent. Then a noise like roaring waves burst over them, and the man in the mask looked to one side, as though he'd heard. The dream broke apart, and Toby woke to hear Mate Ellis pounding on the door to rouse him.

"Dinner," the mate said once Toby opened the door, "then both watches are topside—the Old Man wants the gun crews drilling, so the rest of you get to keep her on her heading."

"Fair enough," said Toby. "Let me know what to do and I'll do it."

"Still up to standing watch?"

"It beats the hell out of staring at the wall."

Ellis nodded, and then headed aft to the messroom.

* * *

When he started standing watch, Toby wondered if he'd be as much a burden to the rest of the crew as a help, but somehow that didn't happen. Part of it, he guessed, was that sailing ships in their heyday took on landlubbers often enough, and every sailor got used to teaching a new man how to make himself useful aboard. Another part was simply that keeping his mind on the work to be done kept it away from questions he didn't want to ask and answers he didn't want to think about. The work itself was no harder than he'd done growing up on a farm, and hands that had been used to rakes and pitchforks turned out well suited to ropes and spars. He soon took to wearing clothing out of the common store that Cooper the ship's cook kept belowdecks—bloused shirt, woolen waistcoat, trousers that went only a little below the knee, a cloth tied around his head to keep sweat out of his eyes—and going barefoot in all weathers as the crew did. The clothes were more practical than the gear he'd brought onto the ship, and the cold didn't trouble him.

Within a few days, he'd gotten used to going aloft to set or shorten sail, hauling on lines, taking watches at the wheel, and lending a hand to the hundred other tasks of sailors aboard a tall ship: not well, compared to the deft muscular men alongside him, but well enough to help the ship and the crew along. There was plenty he knew he didn't know and might never learn, but there was never a shortage of things to do that demanded nothing more of him than taut muscles and a willingness to follow instructions. Despite the constant labor and the stark memories of Tornarssukalik Station, he was happier than he had been in years. It mattered, too, that for the first time since childhood he was among people who swore oaths by the Great Old Ones and knew something about the hidden lore Toby had grown up with. How much they knew, he had no idea and wasn't sure it was wise to ask, but that hardly mattered to him, it was so cheering to be able to growl "Father Dagon!" aloud when a rope he was trying to belay fought back, and have the men around him treat it as an ordinary profanity.

Other changes waited for him, unexpected. The first day, right after the noonday dinner, Coldcroft called him forward with a motion of his head. "Time to see what manner of man ye are, Gilman." That sounded unsettling, but Toby followed him to the windward side of the mortars, where most of the pirates lounged at their ease. They straightened up when Coldcroft came into sight, and Toby noticed that most of them were carrying cutlasses, and the rest had wooden sticks with handguards of stout basketwork around them.

"Show him what to do, lads," the captain said, and stepped back without another word. Toby glanced at him and then turned to face the pirates.

"Gilman," said one of them, a short wiry man with dark hair and a scar from sword or knife disfiguring the left side of his face, "ye ever fought?"

"No, but I can learn," Toby said.

The pirate's wry look showed what he thought of that. "Here," he said, handing Toby one of the cutlasses. "Do as we do."

What they did turned out to be a sword drill: step forward, step back, cut this way, parry, cut the other way, parry, and on and on for something like ten minutes, until Toby's right arm ached with the unfamiliar exertion. They repeated it twice more, and all the while Coldcroft stood beside the foremast and watched the proceedings with narrowed eyes. "Enough," he said then. "Gilman, practice that as often as ye may. If it comes to boarding, it might just get ye through with a whole skin. Peters, put the gun crews through their paces."

Each day thereafter they drilled again, and once Toby knew the sword drill well enough to get by, he was handed one of the wooden sticks with the handguards and set to spar with one or more of the pirates. That meant painful bruises, but after a few of those he started to learn how to get his weapon in the way first, and how to follow up fast so that now and again he got a stick past the other man's guard. He would never be as good at cutlass-play as they were, he knew, but there were other reasons for the practice. "When a man can take a blow without flinching," Ellis said one cold afternoon when the wind gusted down out of the north, "there's plenty else he can do the same way—stay at his post no matter what, for one." He considered Toby for a moment, and nodded. "I think you'll do."

Meanwhile the *Miskatonic* drove east and then south under sullen gray skies, now catching light breezes with every yard of canvas she had, now riding before gales under two topsails and the spanker alone. Sometimes rain fell hard, and Toby finished his watch soaked to the skin, feeling like the bedraggled sea birds that hunched on the topgallant yards. In better weather, porpoises danced ahead of the bow wave and sea birds wheeled. Now and then the great curve of a whale's back surfaced within a mile or so, and a white plume of breath shot up with a great gurgling rush before the whale plunged into deep waters again. He saw Emmeline only now and again, for she was rarely on deck. What she did the rest of the time he had no idea.

Coldcroft was waiting for something. Ellis mentioned that, one night when the skies were clear and cold. "I've got no notion what he waits on," he said, as the two of them sat in the messroom over the remains of supper; Peters had already left to take charge of the watch and Emmeline, silent and indrawn, had gone back to her cabin. "But I know the Old Man's ways. Your other captains, they'd sail right ahead and take their chances, but not him. He'll get everything in place and then strike. It's no accident folk used to call him the Terrible Old Man."

The phrase rang a dim bell somewhere in Toby's memory, but he couldn't trace it. "You've sailed with him for a long time," he ventured.

"I suppose so," said Ellis. "It doesn't do to think on such things." He rose to his feet, raised his tankard, wished Toby's health, drained the last of his beer and left the messroom. Toby gathered up the dishes and tankards—one of the tasks he'd taken on as part of his anomalous status aboard, half sailor, half passenger, not at all an officer though he slept in an officer's cabin—and hauled them back down to the galley.

* * *

That night was clear and pleasant, with a light breeze blowing out of the northeast and stars splashed across the blackness so thick that Toby couldn't make out the constellations he knew. When the bell sounded for his watch, he went amidships as usual, but the half dozen or so men who kept the ship scudding along under full sail stayed at their posts and the larboard watch didn't appear. After a few moments he went forward, past the mainmast and the wooden covers that hid the mortars, and past Peters, who was standing watch just then and acknowledged him with a nod. Further forward, half a dozen pirates lounged about the foremast in the light of a lantern. Long Tom was one of them, and he spotted Toby and beckoned to him. "Why, we was just talkin' of ye, and here ye be. Come cant down a caulker or two!"

"Two," said another of the pirates, the man with an eyepatch Toby had seen at the wheel his first morning aboard. "Just one, why, that would be a crime for so fine an evenin,' seein' as we're celebratin' Joe's skill wi' the dice cup." He nudged the man next to him with his elbow.

"Aye, dice are my friends," laughed the one he'd elbowed, a thin-faced man with black hair and a strong Spanish accent. "I smile at them, they smile at me."

That got a general laugh. "Damme if I'll argue," Tom said. Then, grinning at Toby: "We diced wi' the starboard watch, and by the Goat, Joe won every toss. So long as the weather holds fair, the ship's theirs to sail 'til the sun comes up, and yon bottles, they're ours to drink 'til we're drunk as Davy's sow. Ours and yours, I should say, if ye'll share a drink wi' the lot of us."

"Sure thing," said Toby, and sat on the deck with them. "Is the captain okay with that?"

One of the others, a black man with the rich accent of Jamaica in his voice, laughed. "Oh, if the wind comes up it's damn sure he'll have us up in the rigging, rum or no. But maybe Mother Hydra will be kind to us tonight."

"Here's to that!" said the one with the eyepatch. Tom pressed a glass into Toby's hand, and he raised it and drank. The rum burnt its way down his throat, but he managed not to choke.

"Now, then," said Tom. "Me ye know, and ye'll have met Jack O'Driscoll." He nodded at the man with the eyepatch, then the thin-faced man: "This is Spanish Joe—"

"José Medina y Gomes, *servidor de usted*," said Spanish Joe, half-bowing where he sat.

Tom went on. "That one's Geoff Walker—" He motioned toward the Jamaican. "—and next to him's Scar-Face." The pirate gave Toby a grin that twisted his namesake scar.

"Just Scar-Face?" Toby asked.

The grin turned unpleasant. "I drowned me other name in a bottle o' London gin long since. Didn't have a use for it, and Scar-Face suits me well enough."

Toby raised his glass, acknowledging the words, and Scar-Face laughed, drained his, and refilled it. "Feelin' brave?" he asked. "Ye're among cutthroats, I'll have ye know."

"You're pirates, aren't you?" Toby asked.

"Aye," said Tom, "and mutineers, too, some of us."

"Don't give yerself airs," said Scar-face, and tried to cuff him.

Tom brushed aside the blow, drank, went on. "Me, I got pressed aboard one o' King George's ships, and the captain was a right bastard—a rogue as we was used to say, the kind o' man who'd as soon flog ye as look at ye. One moonless night when we was off the Windwards, a good lot of us had more'n enough, and so we got the guffies drunk, pinched cutlasses and boarding pikes from the stands belowdecks, and a quarter hour on the ship was ours and what was left o' the captain went over the rail for the fish to nibble at." He emptied his glass, refilled it. "We scuttled the ship in deep water and made for land in the longboats, and I asked the first folk I met ashore to point me somewhere I could find a captain plyin' the sweet trade. Me, I reckoned I'd be hanged one way or t'other, and might as well earn it."

"And there he came," said Geoff, "straight down the beach where Red Barnaby had the *Sea Falcon* careened and we were scraping barnacles off her belly. He walks up to the captain and says, 'Ye look like proper pirates. I'd be glad to sail wi' ye if ye'll have me.' The captain says, 'What have ye done that we should want ye?' and Tom says, 'I cut the throat of a man-o-war's captain not three days past.' Barnaby, he laughed and said, 'S'blood, that'll do.'"

The pirates laughed too, and Tom said, "And that's how I met Barnaby Dwale, and Geoff here, and Stephen Magbane, and many another man—and how I ended up after a good few voyages in the Kingsport jail in the year 1731 with not a thing to look forward to but a rope 'round my neck, 'til the Old Man came to speak to me, and away I went with him."

Rum splashed into glasses, and one of the other pirates started telling his own story. As the night deepened, Toby listened, and sipped rum at a pace he hoped wouldn't leave him flat on his back. Every story was different and every story was the same: hard choices in a hard time, with the shadow of the rope looming up close until the Terrible Old Man offered a way out. Toby listened, and tried to shake the feeling that he was listening to ghosts.

"On a night like this I could almost bless the old bastard," said Geoff. "And damn, but it beats dancing a jig at the rope's end." The others laughed. Glasses rose and rum splashed, and suddenly every pirate fell silent. Their heads rose, for all the world like hunting dogs catching a scent. Toby blinked, and then realized that the wind had shifted, blowing suddenly from a different quarter. For a few minutes it whispered past, and then veered back and settled down to a light breeze again. "Just a passin' trick o' the weather," said Jack, and Geoff: "Maybe."

High above, thin clouds blurred the stars. Spanish Joe started talking then, about a voyage he'd made under Henry Every around the Cape of Good Hope to raid the fleets of the Great Mogul. That got others reminiscing about times they'd sailed with Thomas Tew and Calico Jack Rackham, the terrible Edward Teach whom every soul afloat called Blackbeard, Barnaby Dwale and a dozen other captains who'd followed the sweet trade, as they called piracy: treasures won and lost, fights they'd been in, storms they'd weathered, long hours they'd spent crossing the ocean no faster than the wind would carry them, and other hours, sweeter and not long enough, when rum flowed freely and women pressed close.

Another puff of cold wind blew by, and Tom sighed, shook his head, and filled the glasses. "Drink up," he said, "we'll be up in the top hamper afore the night's much older."

They raised the glasses, drank, and laughed at him. They were still laughing when the wind wheeled around and blew hard, flinging drops of rain in their faces.

The pirates were on their feet at once, and Jack scooped up bottles and glasses and went down the forward hatch with them. By the time he scrambled back on deck, Peters had finished shouting something to the men on watch and came forward. "Up wi' ye," he said. "Tom, Scar-Face, help the rest of 'em get the main topgallant in and the topsail reefed. The rest of ye, do the like wi' the fore topgallant and fore topsail."

Toby was on his feet long before Peters finished talking, and knew enough to go at once to the foremast pinrail, where the lines from the upper sails came down and wrapped around belaying pins. Geoff got there before him and loosed the lines, and moments later Long Tom's voice rose over the wind as they hauled: "What d'ye do with a drunken Deep One?"

Toby managed not to choke, but it took an effort. The other pirates joined in:

> "What d'ye do with a drunken Deep One?
> What d'ye do with a drunken Deep One?
> Early in the mornin'."

They pronounced "early" as though it was spelled "earl-eye," the way Toby had heard it years ago on a recording of one of the last of the old shanty singers. The rope was coarse in his hands; he leaned his back into the work, joined in the chorus:

> "Way, hey, and up she rises,
> Way, hey, and up she rises,
> Way, hey, and up she rises,
> Early in the mornin'."

Tom launched into the next verse at once: "Put 'im on a plate with a slice o' lemon!" The others joined in, and Toby, grinning, joined in with them:

> "Put 'im on a plate with a slice o' lemon!
> Put 'im on a plate with a slice o' lemon!
> Early in the mornin'."

They got through three more verses, each specifying some colorful indignity or other, before the sail was close up against the yard. Then it was up the foremast ratlines all the way to the topgallant head and out along the yard, the footrope beneath him and the backrope behind him frail protections against the harsh wind. The rum made Toby clumsy but he still managed to cling to the yard, haul up the canvas, and get the sail bundled and tied between the jackstays. Then it was down to the foresail yard to reef in the sail, another struggle with flapping canvas and keening wind, before they could clamber down to the deck and help with the jibs.

They had only an hour left of their watch by then, but by the time the bell finally rang eight times and Toby stumbled down the ladder he felt as though he'd been on deck all night. "Come on, Toby," said Jack, who was in front of him. "Ye ought to have somewhat to warm ye after that, and by the Black Goat, so will I."

He let himself be led down to the galley, where Cooper was ladling out mugs of a hot brown concoction that smelled of spices and lemon. "What is it?" Toby asked.

"Yard o' Flannel," said Cooper. "Best thing ye can drink on a raw night."

Toby took a mug, sipped at it, then drank a good swallow. It had rum in it, no question of that, not to mention sugar, lemon juice, and a good half dozen spices as well, and it sent something warm and soft surging out to the tips of his fingers and toes. As soon as they'd downed their mugs the pirates headed to their hammocks and Toby went to his cabin. Tom slapped him on the shoulder as they parted. He said nothing, nor did he need to.

* * *

A week passed, maybe, while Coldcroft waited, cold and patient as a heron watching a fish. Toby stood watch with the pirates, clung to ropes and spars for dear life when a storm came sweeping down on the *Miskatonic*, rejoiced with the rest of the crew when the weather turned clear and the wind blew less fiercely, tried not to think too often of Tornarssukalik Station and by and large succeeded. He and Ellis talked now and again, especially when it was Peters' turn to haul himself out of his chair after a meal and head up onto the deck to take charge of the watch. That helped, not least because the first mate knew tall ships inside and out and had a knack for explaining them so they made sense to a landlubber like Toby.

Finally, one cold gray morning when the wind blew in gusts, Toby ventured a question about the pirates' stories about the captain. Ellis sat back in his chair and nodded. "You've heard of that? Oh, it's true enough: the Old Man bought us from the hangman, one and all."

"Were you a pirate?" Toby asked.

"Me? No, a mutineer. I was born in Boston, ran off to sea when I was ten—that was in 1822—worked my way up from cabin boy to able seaman, and ended up as second mate when yellow fever got aboard and took half the crew. We got becalmed on the way home, and after two weeks in the doldrums the captain lost his wits and tried to set the ship on fire. The cook, the purser, the first mate, and me kept him tied up in his cabin until we got to port, and then the bastard turned around and had us arrested for mutiny." With a bleak smile: "I'll let you guess which three white men were found innocent, and which black man got sentenced to hang."

Toby tried without much luck to think of something to say in response. Ellis sipped at his tea and went on. "But that was how I met the Old Man. You heard stories about him in every seaport in New England back then, so I wasn't too surprised when he came to my cell the night before I was supposed to hang. He told me he needed a first mate and we made our bargain. And since then, why, when he sails I sail with him."

"And when he doesn't sail?"

"Why, that's something else again," said Ellis. He finished his tea, got up, and said, "A good morning to you." A moment later he was gone, leaving Toby to stare after him.

All that day the wind stayed gusty, filling the sails and then veering around or falling off suddenly: hard going for the crew, who had to haul yards this way and that, scramble up the ratlines again and again, change the set of jibs and then change them back again. Toward late afternoon, when every man of the larboard watch was weary and grumbling, the wind veered again, fell off, and suddenly blew hard from another quarter. Toby, who'd just gotten a line fast, heard a cry, a splash, and then the shout that sailors dread, "Man overboard!"

He turned toward the splash, saw the water falling back and a flailing figure in it. Instinct took over. He pulled off shirt and waistcoat together, flung them aside, and took a running leap as the deck dipped toward that side. A minute of rushing air, and then he plunged into salt water. Mouth and gills opened by reflex, flooding his muscles with oxygen; he could see the figure in the middle distance, still flailing, and felt him as well—some other sense his family had never mentioned to him? He had no idea, nor time to think. He went deep and came up from below, gripping the man's flailing feet and shoving upwards. He could feel the pirate break the surface and catch a breath. A moment later something else hit the water nearby—a life ring on a rope, he saw—and Toby shoved again, sending the man toward the ring. Water splashed and churned, but he'd gauged the distance well enough; the man flailed and then clung to the ring, the rope tautened, and ring and pirate went together toward the ship.

Toby surfaced, saw that the men aboard had backed the sails to bring the *Miskatonic* to a halt, and swam for the ladder. Once he got to the ship, he had to wait until the waves rolled the ladder within reach, but by then he'd seen the pirate he'd rescued being hauled onto a hastily launched longboat, and realized that it was Long Tom. He grinned, and scrambled up the ladder.

He got to the top to find Mate Ellis next to the gunwale and most of the larboard watch close by. Ellis turned toward him with a grim expression. "By the Goat, Gilman—" and stopped, staring at Toby's bare torso. After an instant Toby realized why: his gills were open and dripping water. A hot sick surge of fear went through him.

"Gilman," Ellis said again, and started laughing. The pirates gave him startled looks, glanced at Toby, and started to laugh as well.

"Toby me lad," said Jack, grinning from ear to ear. "Damn ye, why didn't ye tell us ye had kinfolk on both sides o' the shore?" He slapped Toby on the shoulder, then turned and helped the others lift Tom over the gunwale.

"You're okay with that?" Toby asked Ellis. "Me being part Deep One, I mean."

The mate gave him a startled look and said, "If you think you're the first sailor who's had Deep Ones in the family, think again. Back in my day there were plenty of 'em. And here I thought you'd come near to throwing your life away. Gilman." He laughed again and shook his head, savoring the joke. Then, to Tom, who was sitting on the deck catching his breath: "It's belowdecks for you, and don't let me catch your scurvy bones on deck until Cooper says you're well." To Toby: "The same for you. Gills or no, that water's damned cold."

Toby, half dazed, didn't argue. He went for his shirt and waistcoat, followed Tom.

* * *

A few minutes later, fully dressed again, he sat near the galley next to Tom and sipped at a cup of Cooper's abhorrent coffee. Tom was bundled up in a spare blanket, looking shaken; in the galley, Cooper labored over a big cauldron of salmagundi. After a while, Tom let out a long ragged breath and said, "Well, Toby me lad, I'm not sure whether to thank ye or to curse ye for bein' six kinds o' fool."

"I don't have to worry about drowning, you know," Toby said.

"Aye, I saw. But it was still a chancy deed."

"Well, I wasn't about to just stand there when I could save your life."

That got him a long silent look that lasted until Toby had begun to wonder if he'd somehow said the wrong thing. "That's just what ye can't ever do," said Tom then. "Ye truly don't know what manner o' captain ye serve or what manner o' men we are?"

Toby, uncertain, shook his head.

"We're dead men all." Tom stared past him, at nothing Toby could see. "The Old Man bought no living hands for his crew. He keeps bottles o' glass, with a piece o' lead hangin' from a string and more lead to seal 'em. If I'd drowned this day, he'd just say his words over one o' the bottles, and there I'd be again, with no least scrap o' remembrance o' what I'd done since the day we made our bargain. There my soul's held, and there it'll stay until Great Cthulhu rises out o' the sea and he sets us free as livin' men again—that's the bargain we made with 'im."

Toby took that in. After a minute or two: "You really don't remember anything that's happened since you made the bargain?"

"Oh, I dream of it betimes." Then, putting on a grin: "Me old granny told me more'n once that I'd end up face down on a griddle in Hell. Next to that, why, this is right pleasant." He started talking about something else, and Toby took the hint and let the matter drop.

That night, when the larboard watch was belowdecks, he thought about it again, for all the members of the watch gathered in a circle on the orlop deck by the light of a single lantern and had him sit with them. Ghosts, Toby thought, for that was what they looked like: shadows of a vanished age sitting in judgment over Toby's own time. Judgment was indeed what they had in mind, and Toby wasn't wholly surprised to find himself the subject.

Jack spoke first once the others had assembled. "A good many of ye saw what Toby Gilman here did this day just past, and the rest of ye'd have to be stone deaf not to have heard it by now. The Goat knows it's been a good long while, but there was a day when such as did the like would ha' been greeted by all as a proper brother o' the coast. Some of us got to talkin' about whether the same thing's worth doin' even now."

That earned a murmur of agreement, but Scar-Face said, "I grant ye the thing was well done, but 'tis no hard thing to jump in the sea when ye know ye can't drown. I'd want to see him stay at his post in a couple of sea fights afore I'd grant him that."

"And ye, Gilman?" said Jack, turning to Toby. "What say ye?"

By that point Toby had enough experience with the rough democracy of the pirates that this didn't take him by surprise, and he also knew his shipmates well enough to know what the answer had to be. "I think Scar-Face is right. I'm glad I could help Tom, but for someone like me, jumping into the water's not that big of a deal. If we get into a sea fight, then we'll see."

"If?" Geoff said, and shook his head. "When, rather."

"Aye," said Jack. "D'ye recall how Red Barnaby was used to wait off the Windwards for days, weeks, even a month or more, knowin' that soon or late the king o' Spain's viceroy would send ships his way? The Old Man's doin' the same, though it's no ship he waits for."

"And when the time comes?" Scar-Face asked Toby.

"Then we'll see," Toby repeated. Then, meeting his gaze: "You've hit me often enough with that stick of yours when we practiced. Did you see me flinch?"

Scar-Face regarded him, and after a moment said, "No, I didn't. But sticks are one thing, gunshot's quite another."

"I know." Memories tumbled through Toby's mind: the men he'd seen spreading out from the helicopters, the muzzle flashes of their guns. "You—all of you—know what happened at the station." Nods answered him. "The people there were friends of mine. Two of them were—were more than friends. Most of them are dead now. And the ones who did it—"

He'd felt the helpless rage at the fate of his friends gnawing at him ever since he and Emmeline had hurried down the slope from the cliffs over Tornarssukalik Inlet, but all at once the rage wasn't helpless any more. Sitting there on the orlop deck of a ship of war, surrounded by men who'd killed for a living and held their own lives cheap, he felt cold fury build in him and knew the one thing that would satisfy it. "I want them dead." His voice sounded ragged. "All of them. I don't know a lot about fighting—less than I know about sailing, and all of you know how much more I have to learn about that—but if there's something I can do to see that those goddamn bastards get treated the way they treated my friends, I'll do it, whatever it is." Then: "And if I'm dead when it's done with, you know, I honestly don't think I care."

The men around him grinned, and Jack said, "Good on ye, Toby me lad." The response that mattered most, though was Scar-Face's. He took in Toby's words, and nodded once. Something stirred in his eyes, and Toby found himself wondering whether some similar turn of events had driven Scar-Face to the sweet trade and the gallows.

The inevitable bottle of rum made its appearance, and Toby gulped some down with the rest of them. He went to his cabin not long thereafter and the pirates headed for their hammocks, for the next watch wasn't far off. He was up for four hours in the dim sepulchral light of the waning midnight sun, then back to his berth for the third watch of the night.

He woke in the gray dawn to the sound of Ellis' crisp rap on his cabin door, and felt something cold and wet on his cheek and something hard against one shoulder. Blinking, he reached for the cold wet thing, and discovered that one of his crewmates had come into his cabin while he'd slept, slipped a plate under his pillow, and put a slice of lemon on his cheek. A moment of sheer incomprehension passed before he remembered the shanty about the drunken Deep One, and started laughing. He was still laughing about that, and so was the rest of the larboard watch, as they finished a breakfast of burgoo and detestable coffee and climbed the ladder onto the deck.

Ellis was waiting for them amidships. "Jack, take the wheel," he said. "Geoff, it's the foremast top for you." He handed the Jamaican a spyglass. "The rest of you, make ready to bring her about. The Old Man says take her in to shore, and be ready for a fight."

CHAPTER 7

THE VOICES OF FLAME

All that day the *Miskatonic* sailed west through gray choppy seas. Toby worked with the others, helped haul cannonballs to the main deck during the dog watches, went topside with the rest of the larboard watch as the bell sounded eight times. Ellis sent him to the foremast top, where Matt, one of the pirates from the starboard watch, stood scanning the horizon with a spyglass. Icebergs drifted by, silent and menacing.

"Anything?" Toby asked.

"Plenty o' sea and a berg or two," said the pirate. "Not a thing else."

Toby nodded, took the spyglass from him, and began searching the horizon. Meanwhile Matt climbed down to the deck and headed below with the rest of his watch.

He was aloft for two hours, and then Spanish Joe came up to take his place. When he got back down to the deck, Ellis came over to him. "Anything in sight, Gilman?"

"Bergs and a lot of ocean."

The mate nodded, went aft to talk to the Old Man. Toby went to join three of the pirates hauling on a line—the wind had strengthened, and Ellis wanted the fore topgallant furled. Long Tom was hauling on the same line, and so of course there was a shanty.

"Red Barnaby and all his crew sailed off to Nicarag-you-ay,"
Tom belted out.

"Way, haul away, way, haul away, Joe," was the chorus, and
Toby knew it well enough by then to join in from the beginning.

"Lookin' for a temple what was sacred to Tsathogg-you-ay,"

"Way, haul away, way, haul away, Joe!"

Then, all together:

"Way, haul away, 'til Great Cthulhu rises up,

"Way, haul away, way, haul away, Joe."

Ellis and the captain came forward as Tom began a second
verse:

"A statue of a toad o' gold excited their cupid-eye-tee,"

The chorus rang out: "Way, haul away, way, haul away, Joe."

"But all what laid a hand on it, they died o' their
stupid-eye-tee—"

"Captain, sir!" Spanish Joe's voice, from above. "Ship
port abeam."

The shanty stopped, and they finished hauling on the line
in silence. Coldcroft turned, pulled out his spyglass. As Tom
got the line tied, Toby looked past him at the ice-strewn sea.
Off in the distance, between two bergs, a dark dot had come
into sight.

"Diesel freighter," said Coldcroft after a moment of staring
through the spyglass. "Armed, I'll warrant." He leaned back.
"Watch every quarter," he shouted up to Spanish Joe. "There
might be more than just the one."

"Aye, sir," came the response.

By then Toby was on his way up the ratlines to gasket up
the fore topgallant. From the insecure vantage of the topgallant
spar, he could see the dot more clearly: a ship with two streams
of smoke rising from it. He got his share of the work done and
came back down to the spar deck, to find the starboard watch
boiling out of the hatches and Peters on the foredeck barking
orders to knots of men Toby realized, after a moment, were
gun crews.

Mate Ellis came forward a moment later, having been giving orders further aft. "Gilman, take the wheel," he said. "Scar-Face, Long Tom, take charge of the swivel guns. The rest of you, lend a hand and make ready."

Toby hurried aft and took the wheel from Geoff, who grinned and went forward. Men scrambled aloft to furl the mainsail and foresail, clambered up again with long shapes of wood and steel that looked as though a rifle and a small cannon had run off together and had a litter of offspring. "Steady as she goes, Gilman," said Coldcroft, standing close by, and Toby braced the wheel, watched the ship draw closer. His heart pounded, and he could feel sweat beading on his brow. Steady as she goes, he repeated silently, aiming the words at himself.

Ellis came aft again moments later. "Captain," he said, "all's ready."

"Hold fire 'til they're close at hand," said Coldcroft.

"Aye, sir." The mate went forward, and Toby could hear him barking orders to the crew.

Minutes passed. After a few of them Toby could see the freighter more clearly, smoke belching from its stacks, little dark shapes of men on the foredeck with what had to be guns in their hands. Fear spiked hard in him, but there was nowhere he could run. He knew that, knew also that holding the helm steady meant that every other man on board could be spared for the cannons, the swivel guns, and whatever else Coldcroft and the pirates might be able to do.

The low grumbling of the freighter's engines rose above the wind. A glance to port showed Toby that it headed straight toward the *Miskatonic*, closing the distance fast. Coldcroft raised his spyglass, looked through it, lowered it. The men on the diesel freighter aimed their guns, and one of them raised what looked like a bullhorn. Toby made himself check the binnacle to be sure of the course, then braced himself and looked to port again.

At that instant, the four carronades on the Miskatonic's port foredeck roared and vomited flame. The deck lurched hard.

Vast clouds of stinging smoke swept past. When he could see again, Toby looked to port and gasped aloud. The freighter's superstructure looked as though it had been punched by a giant's fist, and the foredeck was clear of men. Murder guns, the sailors of old called carronades; Toby remembered that and understood why.

Pirates hauled the carronades back, swarmed over them, rolled them back out, and a second volley thundered out, shaking the Miskatonic's deck. When the smoke cleared, the superstructure had been hit again, but so had the hull: a hole gaped in the bow, and the freighter had begun to settle awkwardly in the water.

"One more," Coldcroft shouted forward. "Send 'em to the bottom."

Another few minutes to reload, and the guns roared flame again. This time, when the smoke cleared, the broadside proved to have punched through the bow and port forequarters just above the waterline. The freighter settled at a steeper angle and with ghastly slowness began to sink, the stern rising as the bow went down. Toby could see men struggling in the water, knew that the terrible cold wouldn't leave them to struggle for long.

"Cack-handed lubbers," the Terrible Old Man said appreciatively, watching them drown. The freighter's stern rose higher and higher. He turned to Toby. "I recall ye wondered whether I'd take this ship and crew against such as they. Ye see the answer." The smile that reminded Toby of a shark's teeth creased his face. "It's fools alone who think that a thing can't be both old and deadly. The sea's older than us all, and it's not slow to kill even yet."

* * *

Belowdecks, rum and a bowl of salmagundi helped Toby keep from brooding about what he'd seen. It helped, too, that Scar-Face gave him a long assessing look and nodded slowly, as though approving. When the larboard watch came on deck for the first watch that night, clouds veiled the sky but a colorless light shone through them, so that masts and rigging stood out black against the livid sky and the sails seemed like billowing ghosts. In that spectral setting Toby helped trim the sails, then took an hour at the wheel while black water foamed and bits of broken ice slid past. A pale glow hovered above the horizon. Toby recognized the ice blink and knew that Greenland was close. Greenland, and what else? He knew better than to try to guess.

By the end of the night watches the wind slackened and the air off the sea turned cold. Past the off-white wedges of the spritsails, the gray churning sea had given way to a line of white, not quite even, that spread across the horizon from starboard to port as far as sight could reach. At first it seemed unbroken and impenetrable, but that was an illusion of distance. A quarter hour later, as the *Miskatonic* drew near the ice, gaps became visible, where some trick of wind and current had driven floes apart to reveal black water between them. Guided by watchful eyes at the foremast top, the *Miskatonic* slid into the largest of the leads, while Toby helped get every scrap of canvas out to catch the light fitful breezes off the ice.

By afternoon they were in sight of land. "Point to port," Coldcroft said. Toby turned the wheel. The wind off the pack ice was barely enough to keep the ship moving, but it clawed at Toby's hands and face, brought cracking and groaning sounds from the floes. The water to either side looked black as ink against the gray-white of the pack. Seals hauled out on the ice watched them, or slid off into the water. Mist rose from the sea in little plumes like smoke.

"One more." The ship turned again, following the course of the lead. The ice to starboard fell away to a skin on the surface of the sea. Then the pack ice was behind them, the mist over the water cleared, and the mountains of Greenland loomed up against a cold blue sky.

"Hard to starboard," said the captain, and the *Miskatonic* ghosted into the shore flaw.

Where they were in relation to Tornarssukalik Station Toby had no idea, and the landscape didn't look familiar in the least. Past the shore flaw and a little inshore ice, a wall of sheer gray mountains rose straight up out of the ocean, pierced here and there by steep-walled valleys carved out by vanished glaciers. Sea birds wheeled and cried along the rocky shore, but he could see nothing that grew or moved on land.

Time passed: more than two hours, by the ship's bell, and Toby and the larboard watch were off duty by the time it was done, though Toby stayed on deck and watched the rugged coast of Greenland slip by. Ahead, the mountains slumped and tumbled down to a ragged peninsula that jutted out into the shore lead. Beyond it, dim in the distance, rose a crag Toby recognized after most of an hour: the headland just north of Tornarssukalik Inlet. The sight chilled him.

Orders rang out aft, and the starboard watch scrambled to haul on lines. As yards swung and sails billowed back into the masts, the *Miskatonic* slowed to a halt. A splash off the bows told of the anchor plunging down from the cathead. Toby watched, uncertain. The bare gray slopes of the land to port were less rugged than they'd been further south but no more inviting. Why Coldcroft had ordered the ship to drop anchor he had no idea.

"Gilman!" Peters called out, coming forward. "The Old Man wants ye aft."

Toby got to his feet, said something suitable, and went to the quarterdeck. Coldcroft and Emmeline stood there, looking at the shore. The captain glanced over one shoulder as Toby approached. "Gilman," he said, "can ye go ashore?"

"Of course, sir," Toby said, startled.

"'Tis well. If the folk we're seekin' are hereabouts, they'll know ye by sight, ye and Doctor Grenier. I'll have some o' the crew with ye in case there's trouble."

Shoes felt unfamiliar and clumsy as he got them on his feet, but a few minutes later he and Emmeline were climbing down the ladder on the *Miskatonic*'s port side to board a longboat. Scar-Face sat aft, in command as usual, and half a dozen pirates of the larboard watch held oars upright, waiting. Once the two passengers were settled on a thwart, Scar-Face barked an order and the longboat's crew pushed off and began to row. Cold fitful breezes caught drops of spray and flung them into Toby's face. The pirates leaned into the work, pulling long and steady on the oars. The longboat sped across the dark unquiet waters, weaving past floating masses of ice, toward the ragged line of the shore more than a mile away.

In due time two curt orders from Scar-Face brought the boat up onto a little scallop of sand flanked by ragged gray rock and a scattering of bleached driftwood. Toby clambered over the bows with the other pirates, offered Emmeline a hand onto the shore, then helped drag the boat up onto the sand for safety. "Geoff, Spanish Joe, stay here and guard the boat," Scar-Face said. "The rest o' ye, follow me, keep quiet, and stay close to hand. There's no small danger."

He led the way up the ragged slope behind the beach. Wind hissed against the bare rock, and a few ragged clouds sped by overhead, as they clambered up to a low barren crest. On the far side the slope descended just as unsteadily, in a wreckage of boulders and steep gullies, toward a stretch of tundra where signs of digging interrupted the sweep of gravel and scattered wildflowers. Beyond that, hills rose crest upon crest into evening dimness, ended at the jagged line of mountains against crimson sky.

Scar-Face gestured: spread out, move silently. Toby complied. He ended up at one end of a ragged line. It occurred to him that all the pirates were armed with pistols and long knives but he had no weapons at all. When I get back to the ship, he told himself, I'm going to talk to Ellis and see if there's at least a knife I can use.

The slope stretched on. Toby passed a boulder the size of a car, left there casually by some vanished glacier, and looked this way, that.

Then an arm tightened around his neck and pulled him back hard. A hand clamped over his mouth, stifling a cry. An instant later he was flat on his back behind the boulder, the point of a knife pressed against his throat. In the dim light he could see little of his assailant, just a lean shape crouched over him. Then a voice hissed, "Say the word!"—and the voice was Wren's.

* * *

He sagged in relief and delight, said, "Vrispaa." Then: "You're okay?"

"Yes." The knife left his throat. "Who are the men?"

"Sailors. Enoch Coldcroft's crew. Dr. Grenier's with us."

Abruptly she stood and called out: "Emmeline!"

The pirates turned fast, drawing pistols, but Emmeline turned also and let out a delighted shout. "*Par Saint Crapaud!* Wren, it is you?"

Toby picked himself up, called out, "It's her." Then, to Wren: "Did anyone else—"

"Yes." She glanced at him. In a low voice: "I'm glad you're well. I hoped for that."

If she had leaned over and kissed him Toby would not have been more surprised. He gaped and tried to think of something to say, but she turned at once and strode out of the shelter of the boulder. He squeezed his eyes shut, opened them again, got a neutral expression on his face by sheer effort, and followed her.

"You are alone?" Emmeline asked. "Or any of the others, did they escape with you?"

Instead of answering, Wren faced the pirates. "You belong to Enoch Coldcroft?"

A moment of silence passed, punctuated by the hissing wind. Then Scar-Face allowed a harsh laugh. "Aye, that we do."

"He's here?"

"Back aboard the ship."

"Good." She turned to Emmeline. "I knew of eight who escaped. If you and Toby were alone, ten. Three others are here. Phil's one of them."

Emmeline stared at her, then: "And the three, where are they?"

Wren turned to face across the slope, raised both hands to her mouth, and made a flawless imitation of a jaeger's shrill cry: once, twice, a long pause, and then a third time. Something stirred on the rim of one of the gullies nearby; and then a lean figure hauled itself out of the gully, got to its feet. Another followed, smaller, and a third, massive. It took Toby a long moment to recognize the first and third—Phil Dyer and Bill Allen—and another, longer still, to be sure that the one between them was Leah Sargent.

"If that's the lot of ye," said Scar-Face, "the Old Man said to take ye back to the ship right quick. Have ye gear to bring? Fetch it."

Emmeline paid no attention. The moment she saw Phil, she hurried across the slope to him. "There's gear," Wren said to Scar-Face. "We can leave it if necessary." The pirate gave her a quizzical look, nodded.

Meanwhile Toby crossed the slope to the other two others, said, "I'm glad you're okay." Off beyond them, he could see camouflage netting in the gully, knew where they'd hidden.

"Likewise," said Bill. He looked haggard, but managed a grin. Leah said something inaudible. Bill glanced past Toby at the pirates and said, "You'll have to tell me how you found those guys. The one with the scar said get our gear, right? I'll grab it." To Leah, who turned to help: "Don't worry about it. I can get it."

Leah glanced up at Toby, looked away. Toby tried to figure out something to say. Fortunately Phil and Emmeline let go of each other just then and saved him the trouble. "Toby!" Phil said, coming over to him and taking his hands. "You're okay? Good. I thought you and Emmeline would be able to get away."

"Here we go," said Bill then, clambering back up out of the gully with four rucksacks draped all anyhow about his shoulders. "Let's get out of this godforsaken place."

Not much more than a minute later they were hurrying back up the slope, Scar-Face and Wren in the lead, the survivors of the expedition in the middle, pirates with drawn pistols bringing up the rear. Otherwise, nothing moved in sight except the wind, but Toby could see all too clearly beyond the hills to northward the headland that marked the entrance to Tornarssukalik Inlet. If the Radiance force was still at the station—

They crested the hill, hurried down the other side. The *Miskatonic* stood at anchor, and Toby could see tiny figures in the mainmast top keeping watch. Below, the longboat waited.

They reached the little crescent beach without incident. "The boat won't hold all of ye," Scar-Face said then, glancing over them. "It'll be two goes for sartain."

"I can wait," Toby said.

Leah glanced at him, turned to Scar-Face. "So can I."

Scar-Face nodded curtly, turned to Phil and Bill. "I'd wager the two of ye might be fit to haul on an oar," he said.

"I can do that also," said Wren. Scar-Face gave her a scornful look, turned and said, "Geoff, Spanish Joe, ye'll wait for the nonce. We'll be back soon enough."

The other pirates hauled the longboat down to the water. Before Bill could go after them, Wren stepped neatly into his path and then climbed into the boat, picked up an oar, and headed for the foremost thwart. The pirates turned to look at Scar-Face, waiting for orders, and that gave Phil the chance to clamber on board after her and sit beside her, taking another oar.

Scar-Face let out a snort of derision and waved the pirates aboard. Bill shrugged and followed Emmeline into the boat, sitting aft of the rowers with her. A shove from the pirates' oars, a clatter as Scar-Face sprang aboard and took his place, and the longboat slid out into the sea. Oars dipped and caught the water, Wren's moving with the precision of a well-tuned machine. Moments later the boat was tracing a line straight for the *Miskatonic*.

* * *

Leah went over to a nearby driftwood log and sat on it, letting out a long uneven breath, as though the last of her strength had given out. Toby considered the options, sat next to her. The pirates stood some distance away, keeping watch. After a moment, he said, "Is it okay if I ask how you and the others got away?"

That got him an uncertain look, and then a nod. "Phil took a bunch of us to the Ulut dig—that's what you saw, down below the place we were hiding. The day after you left, Louise got a bad tooth infection—she had to go to Nuuk to see a dentist. Phil sent three others with her to pick up some extra supplies and ship some artifacts to Miskatonic University, and then took us to Ulut the day after that. I think he knew something was going to happen and wanted to get people to safety. He tried to talk Mike and Susan and Orrin into staying at the dig, but they wanted to haul some things back to the station." Her eyes clenched shut. "They left in the pickup about three hours before the copters came."

Toby flinched. "I'm sorry."

"I don't know if you saw what happened."

"Emmeline and I were on the cliffs north of the inlet," said Toby, "and we had binoculars. I thought everybody was dead."

She glanced at him again, managed a fragile smile. "Not quite." Then: "Dr. Grenier must have taken you someplace safe."

"North Station," said Toby. "She got in touch with Captain Coldcroft from there, I don't know how, and we got picked up by a longboat three days later." She nodded as though that was the most obvious thing in the world, and he gave her a puzzled look and went on: "Did you know that the *Miskatonic* was up here?"

She opened her mouth, then closed it again, and he realized what that had to mean. "Don't worry about it," he said. "I know there's a lot going on I can't be told about."

That earned him a long assessing look. "Yes," she said then. "I didn't know the *Miskatonic* was in these waters, but I knew there would be help. You're right, there's a lot going on. I wish I could tell you more."

"Thank you," he said, and she smiled at him again and then suddenly reddened and looked away. He scarcely noticed, for all at once he had to cope with a sudden longing to put an arm around her, draw her close, comfort her and take what comfort he could from her presence. Their one drunken tryst and the wary regard they'd worked out thereafter didn't justify that, and he knew it, but the desire remained. He wondered for a wild moment if she wanted the same thing he did—or had she blushed for some other reason?

The returning boat made a convenient distraction. He got to his feet, held out a hand; she took it, smiled, held it a moment longer than necessary. They went down to the shore, waited with Geoff and Spanish Joe as the boat drove its prow up onto the sand, climbed aboard. Only four oarsmen had come back with them, so the two pirates took oars and helped drive the boat back off the beach and across the water, leaving Toby and Leah sitting side by side on one of the aft thwarts. She was almost close enough for her arm to touch his, but not quite. Unnervingly, he could feel the warmth of her body across the fraction of an inch separating them. He tried to think of something other than her, and failed.

They reached the side of the *Miskatonic* without incident, and she scrambled up the ladder ahead of him. On the spar deck, as a dozen pirates of the starboard watch ran lines through the davits to haul the longboat up, Ellis came over and said to Leah, "Welcome aboard, miss." To Toby's surprise, she responded with a smile and a neatly done curtsey.

"Gilman," Ellis said then, "we're one cabin short. Can you handle sleeping in a hammock so the lady can take your place?"

"Sure thing," Toby said. "Let me get my gear." Then, turning to Leah: "Come on. I'll show you where it is." Leah thanked him and Ellis both, and followed him to the aft hatch.

"Here you go," Toby said, opening the door into the cramped little cabin a few moments later. "Let me clear my stuff out and it's all yours."

"Thank you," Leah said, following him into the dimly lit space. "Are you sure?"

"I've been standing watches with the crew." In response to her startled look: "I had to do something to keep from thinking."

In answer she started to cry. He reached for her out of raw instinct, drew her close, and she clung to him and buried her face in his shoulder and wept. Every inch of her body that pressed against his set his blood pounding. Wait, he told himself. Wait—and then, when she'd cried herself out, she raised her face toward his with wet eyes and a luminous smile, and he could not keep himself from bringing his lips down to meet hers. Both their mouths opened; their tongues twined around each other.

He drew back when he was nearly out of breath. "Leah."

"Please," she said, and he knew exactly what she meant by it, knew also that he could do nothing else. Which of them closed the cabin door, and how exactly they struggled out of their clothes and got onto the berth, he was never afterwards sure; all he could recall was how she'd felt and tasted, how she'd cried out and clutched him, how the two of them lay close afterwards, her pulse quick and strong enough that he could see it fluttering in the hollow of her neck.

She laughed a little shaken laugh after a while. "We've got to stop doing this."

"Yeah." He kissed the nearest portion of her, which happened to be one of her breasts, and she reached for him and clung to him for a long moment.

"I know you have to go," she said then, and he mumbled something, untangled himself from her, extracted his clothing from the heap on the floor. Naked except for a pair of socks, she watched him as he dressed and put what little gear he had into the battered rucksack, then got herself under the covers before they fumbled through a few more words and he left the cabin.

* * *

The pirates didn't need to be told where he'd been or what he'd been doing there, and he endured a certain amount of rough teasing over the watch that followed. Still, when he slung himself into the hammock Long Tom found for him, he fell asleep readily enough, and he turned out with the others when it was time for the larboard watch to go abovedecks. There was little for him to do; the *Miskatonic* rode at anchor, waiting for word from Coldcroft, and other than an hour keeping watch from the mainmast top, he spent the four hours listening to the dim rhythms of the sea, and thinking about Wren and Leah.

The English language seemed a miserably blunt instrument as he brooded over the two of them. How did it help to say that he loved them both, when the feelings he had for them were so different? The thought of making love with Wren would have shocked him if it hadn't been so absurd: whatever the habits of the body she wore temporarily, her people had no sense of touch and reproduced by spores, and the responses she summoned from him didn't seem to have anything sexual in them at all. Leah was another matter. He could guess easily enough that if the two of them survived, they'd end up in bed again promptly and in some kind of relationship thereafter. That had perils of its own, for he had no way of guessing what she'd do when she found out he wasn't human and had gills; only the dim light that sheltered him both the times they'd made love had kept that from happening already.

Ilul, he thought, turning to the Hyperborean word, the love that's of the spirit, and *nen*, the love that's of the vital fluids. And *aqqat*, the love that's of the body, the love that turns toward home and family? He choked back a bitter laugh. That's not an option for me, he reminded himself, and tried to divert his thoughts to some less difficult theme.

A sudden low murmur nearby caught his attention, and he glanced that way. Jack was saying something to Long Tom, pointing up into the starry sky. Toby knew what he would see there before he followed the gesture: a gaunt shape striding across the sky as though walking on the wind. It was heading east—no, northeast, he realized, and wondered what that meant.

After it had vanished from sight beyond distant crags, he went to the two pirates and said, "That was the Wind-Walker."

They looked at him. "Aye," said Jack. "And not the first time one o' the crew's spotted him on this voyage. Not a thing I like to see."

"The cold lands are his," said Long Tom. "Might be no more than that."

"Aye, might be," said Jack, but his expression showed how little he believed that.

The sun circled around from north to east. The bell rang eight times, and after breakfast and a few hours of sleep, eight times again. Ellis set the larboard watch drilling with cutlasses and then fencing with sticks, as much to keep them busy as for any other reason. Partway through the drill Wren came on deck, perched on one of the mortar housings, and watched the proceedings with every sign of interest. Toby tried not to notice her, concentrated on Jack, who was trying his level best just then to get past his guard and deal him another bruise. The bruise got dealt in due time anyway, but Toby managed to land a solid blow of his own on Jack's sword arm, getting a good-natured curse and a grin.

Later on, Bill came on deck, spotted Toby, came over to him, and in a low voice said, "Do you have any idea what's going on? I can't get anyone to give me a straight answer."

"They probably don't know any more than I do," Toby admitted. "You probably have to ask the captain, and I doubt he'll tell you."

That got an uncharacteristic shudder from Bill. "No, thank you. That guy gives me a serious case of the creeps."

They talked a little more, and then Ellis came on deck and called Toby and a few of his shipmates to go aloft and tighten the foremast stays, ending the conversation.

The day was mostly over and Toby was off duty, standing alone near the bowsprit and wondering when the *Miskatonic* would sail and where it would go, when Emmeline came forward and said, "Toby? Ah, here you are. You will come with me, please. The captain, he wants to speak with you, and you should bring the papers about the *pierre de souvenir*."

A few minutes later, following Emmeline, he brought the notebook with his translation of the text from the stone of remembrance into Captain Coldcroft's cabin at the aft end of the main deck. Coldcroft was waiting there, looking out the windows at the sea. Phil and Wren stood by the table, breaking off a conversation in low tones to look at him. Tension filled the cabin.

"Toby," Phil said, waving him to a chair. "Wren tells me you can be trusted, and so we've decided it's time to tell you a little more about this business—not least because you've got the key of it with you right now." A quick motion of his head indicated the notebook. "You've got the whole text from the *tuqqoli niunda* translated, right?" When Toby nodded, uncertain: "Do you recall what it says about Mount Voormithadreth?"

"Not offhand," Toby replied. "I can find it."

"Please," said Phil. "Read it aloud."

Toby paged through the notebook and found the passage. "'Mount Voormithadreth, highest of flame-crowned peaks,'" he quoted. "'On its heights, beside the fourth peak, the Uppermost Gate; it is of bronze. In its deeps, barring the way to those secrets which may not be named or approached, the Lowermost Gate; it too is of bronze. Distance, of *shol*, two hundred twenty-one.'" He looked up. "So?"

"The Lowermost Gate," said Emmeline. "That is the thing those *cochons de merde* hope to find, and if they pass through it and reach what is beyond, it is all up with everyone."

Toby gave her a baffled look. "Why?"

It was Wren who answered. "You know the story of Ralibar Vooz and Ezdagor." When he nodded, uncertain: "In that story, what's in the lowest depths of Mount Voormithadreth?"

"Abhoth," said Toby after a moment. "Abhoth, the source of all generation."

"And what is Abhoth?"

Toby took another moment to recall what he knew of Hyperborean mythology. "It's the last remaining part of Ubbo-Sathla, the first of all living things." He glanced up at her. "But that's just an old legend, isn't it?"

"I wish," said Phil.

"And what is it that Ubbo-Sathla guarded?" Wren went on.

"Stone tablets," said Toby. He was staring at her, feeling as though he had suddenly been caught up in a nightmare. "Tablets of star-quarried stone, bearing the secret magic of a race of gods who died before the Earth was born. That's what the *Book of Eibon* says. But—"

"It's true," Phil said. "All of it. That's the ghastly danger we're facing. The Radiance—you know about them, right? They're trying to get a force down through Mount Voormithadreth to the Deep of Abhoth. If they manage it, there's a real chance that they can take the tablets, bring them back to one of their bases, decipher them."

The blood drained from Toby's face. "They'd be unstoppable then."

A sudden harsh laugh broke through the cold horror that filled him. "Unstoppable?" Enoch Coldcroft said, turning away from the windows, still laughing. "Aye, could they master those powers. Let 'em try to turn aside a hurricane wi' the wind off a butterfly's wings afore that. No. Should they get the tablets, they'll speak such words as will loose powers they can't hope to command. They'll perish one and all, but that won't spare the rest of us."

"Toby," said Wren. He turned to face her. "You know that my people visit the future. The future always changes, and that is one of the sources of our power, for we visit every future and learn what it has discovered. But that stopped not long after I was spawned. My people found that there was no more future—that all that will be left of Earth sixty-three days from now is a cloud of dust circling the Sun. I'm here to stop that. I was trained from the creche for that."

Toby's mouth felt dry. With an effort, he forced out words: "What do I need to do?"

"You've already done the thing that matters most," said Phil. "Two hundred twenty-one *shol* is a little over four hundred ninety-one miles. We know where the village of Ulut was, we know which landscape features on today's maps were the Eiglophian Mountains back in Hyperborean times, and that means we know exactly where Mount Voormithadreth is— where they're headed, and where they can be stopped."

"If we are very lucky," said Emmeline, "the Radiance has not figured that out yet. If we are not so lucky, we know where they have gone."

"But—" Toby tried to pull together the chaos of his thoughts. "The—the Great Old Ones. Can't they do something?"

Coldcroft fixed his unnerving golden gaze on Toby. "Ye know the other side has sartain powers," he said, "sartain bindings they put on the Great Old Ones when the seven temples fell all that time ago. They don't use those lightly, for there's only so many times ye can wield such things afore they lose their strength—but they've called on all of it now. Nor for here alone."

"Right now," said Phil, "they've got a force of something like five thousand armed men, with more than a hundred of their initiates, heading from northern Laos up onto the plateau of Leng. They must have spent millions to bribe Laotian officials and the opium gangs in that region. You've probably heard of a monastery on that plateau. They're trying to get to it."

Toby stared at him, aghast. "They've got to be crazy."

Phil shrugged. "Another force of theirs, nearly as large, has gone to Lake Mlolo in Uganda to search the megalithic ruins there. That's even crazier—if they find what they're looking for, that'll be the end of them—but there they are. They've got another force, even bigger, deployed to Antarctica. There are people on our side of things trying to stop them in each of those places, but we're stretched very thin right now."

"Not so thin as all that," said Coldcroft. Something in his voice made Toby look up at him suddenly, startled. A slight smile creased the leathery face, but there was no humor in it at all. In that moment Toby understood exactly why the sailors called him the Terrible Old Man.

"Not so thin as all that," the captain repeated. "This is a stout ship o' war, well armed, and I've a crew to match. This very night we sail against the station, and we'll see what stuff yon whoresons are made of."

Toby made himself speak: "I'm good with that." Then: "And afterwards?"

"If they've gone to the mountain," said Wren, "I'll go after them. If not, I'll go anyway, to be sure they've failed. We can worry about that later."

"Okay," Toby said, trying not to let his dread show in his voice.

"Toby," said Phil then. "I know this is tough to deal with, but we don't have much choice. I'm going to ask you to do two things. The first is to leave the translation with me." Toby considered that, handed over the notebook, and Phil nodded. "The second," the professor said, "is not to mention any of this to anybody who isn't in this room, no matter what. Okay?"

"Okay," Toby said. "Do Bill and Leah know what's going on?"

"No, and they're not to hear about it from you. Will you promise me that?"

"Of course."

"Will ye bind yerself by oath?" Coldcroft asked then.

"Yes, I will," Toby said, nettled. Facing the captain, he recalled an ancient oath he'd heard a few times in childhood and read a few times in strange old books. "I swear myself to silence about this by the bones of the King in Yellow."

That got a moment of utter silence, and then Coldcroft nodded. "Well enough. Ye asked o' the Great Old Ones earlier, and I'll tell ye this much: sartain o' Them are about, and They'll do their part if we but do ours. There's more movin' here than ye know."

That offered some reassurance, but not enough to stem the tide of Toby's fears. It didn't help that when he and Emmeline left the cabin a little later, she turned to him and said, "A word with you, *s'il vous plait*." When he turned to her: "Wren says we are to trust you, and she knows more than any of us. But the Radiance, those *sous-merdes*, heard about the stone and its message much sooner than they should have. We would have had everyone safe in time, but—" A harsh and expressive shrug punctuated the sentence. "If Wren is wrong and it was you who told them, then you will die in very great pain if I can make that happen. I want you to know that." She turned sharply and went into her cabin, leaving Toby to stare after her.

* * *

Mate Ellis' voice sounded low and urgent. "All hands. We sail at once."

Toby blinked awake, scrambled out of his hammock. Around him the rest of the larboard watch did the same. A few minutes sufficed to pull on clothes and rub sleep from his eyes, and then he was heading with the others toward the hatch. As he neared the ladder Scar-Face stopped him and pushed something at him. A moment's struggle to focus in the dim light from above, and he recognized it: a cutlass in its sheath on a stout leather belt. He put it on, hurried up the ladder.

On deck the starboard watch was already at the capstan, making the anchor chain taut. A drowned uncertain light spilled over the rocky headland to the north, showing the hour: two in the morning, Toby guessed. A light breeze came hissing off the mountains to the west, rippling the water's surface; a few stray clouds hurried by overhead, and mist rose like smoke from the ice-dotted surface of the sea.

Within moments he was hauling on a line, following Mate Ellis' terse orders. Others scrambled aloft, loosing the top-sails and the spanker. The anchor came up, and the *Miskatonic* turned neatly eastward and got under way. By then Toby was helping to haul the covers off the two great mortars while gun crews readied the cannons on the foredeck and the swivel guns went up onto the fighting tops.

Coldcroft came on deck then. "Peters, ye've seen to the guns? 'Tis well. Have the murder guns loaded wi' grapeshot; we'll need 'em afore all this is over. Ellis, take charge o' the sailin'. When our guests come topside, put 'em to work as ye will." He turned. "Gilman, take the wheel."

"Aye, sir," Toby said, and went aft. Matt from the starboard watch stood there, but handed it over to Toby and went forward to join one of the gun crews. Toby took the wheel, standing to windward, feeling himself part of the living thing that was a ship of war under sail. Ahead, the crew moved with brisk effi-ciency to tasks Toby didn't pretend to understand, though he guessed the point of it all readily enough. How the *Miskatonic*'s archaic weaponry would fare against the modern gear of the Radiance wasn't a question he wanted to think about just then.

The *Miskatonic* cleared the headland after a few minutes. Coldcroft pulled a chart from one of the pockets of his great-coat, glanced at it and said, "Hard to port." Toby turned the wheel and felt the ship respond, while the pirates hauled on lines to angle the yards and sails. As the headland slipped past, Toby glanced to port toward the great sweep of tundra north of it, but saw only white fog, blotting out everything between the shore and the distant mountains. The mist rising from the water flowed inland, joining the bank of fog. A moment passed before Toby realized that it was moving against the wind.

As the survivors of the station came on deck one at a time, Ellis sent them to this duty or that, mostly belowdecks. Meanwhile the fog thickened. Ahead, the great crag that marked the entrance to Tornarssukalik Inlet rose up dark against the midnight sun. Coldcroft stopped his pacing briefly, and said, "Gilman, in a little while, like as not all hell'll come loose in a hurry. See to it that ye hold her steady."

"Aye, sir," Toby said.

The great crag ahead drew closer with agonizing slowness. Toby checked the ship's heading, glanced forward. The pirate crew stood at their stations, and the harsh scent of burning slow matches came drifting aft when the wind paused.

Then, all at once, something that didn't look like wind rippled through the fog inland, dispersing it. Toby caught sight of a half-familiar hill in the distance and a tiny cluster of shapes atop it. His breath caught, recognizing the station. At first the scene seemed unchanged, but then he noticed the signs of the enemy's presence. A short way up the inlet, a diesel freighter like the one the Miskatonic had sent to the bottom earlier sat at anchor, a few lights glinting on its superstructure. Toby glanced toward the station again, and spotted something off beyond it: four black helicopters, crouching like predatory insects.

Coldcroft raised his hand and brought it down, giving the signal. "For'ard mortar," Peters barked. "Three ... two ... one ... fire."

An instant later, it felt as though some vast hand slapped the *Miskatonic* down into the water. The forward mortar roared and belched flame, and something half-seen soared high up into the dimly lit sky, then plunged. A sudden flash burst off past the helicopters, and after a moment a great rolling boom reached the *Miskatonic*, swept past it, came echoing back from the cliffs to the north.

While the echoes resounded, Toby saw Peters conferring with the gun crews. "Aft mortar," Peters called out. "Three ... two ... one ... fire."

Again the sudden shock drove the *Miskatonic* down as the mortar roared. Again the half-seen shape rose and plunged, and the explosion was closer to the copters. By the time the boom came echoing back, Toby could see tiny shapes of men sprinting from the quonset huts, and not long after that the rotor blades of the copters began to turn.

"For'ard mortar," called Peters. "Three ... two ... one ... fire."

Another shot jolted the *Miskatonic* down to her keel, another mortar shell soared and plunged, and this one blew up between the copters and the quonset huts, leaving men sprawled and motionless in its wake. Smoke began to rise from one of the copters. More men came out of the quonset huts, heading down toward the shore, but two of the copters had their rotors going fast enough to dissolve into blurs, and would be airborne in moments.

Peters barked, "Aft mortar, three ... two ... one ... fire."

The shell soared and plunged like the others, but chance or skillful aim brought it down on the main fuel tank. The flash of the shell's explosion was followed an instant later by a massive fireball that engulfed the whole area where the copters sat. The sound came a moment later, a tremendous roar that landed like a physical blow.

* * *

The pirates yelled in triumph. Through the billowing smoke from the mortars and the thickening mist, they looked to Toby like phantoms of a vanished age. "By Dagon, that'll do," said Coldcroft, watching through his spyglass. To Toby: "Point to port."

The great wheel turned, and the ship responded.

By then smoke was rising from the freighter's stacks, and the men running toward the shore were most of the way to the water. Toby tried to gauge the distance, hoped the *Miska-tonic* was still out of their range, held the wheel steady. The forward mortar roared again, jolting the barque down to its keel; the shell soared and plunged, and a great spout of water rose from the inlet fifty yards or so from the freighter.

All at once something stung one of Toby's arms. An instant later the crack of gunfire shook the air. Another instant, and he saw the torn cloth and blood welling up, and realized that a bullet had nicked the arm on its way past. Panic surged, but he fought it back, stayed at the wheel though he knew the next bullet might well kill him.

Half-muffled, assault rifles chattered, and wood splintered further forward. Toby braced himself. "Steady as she goes," Coldcroft said, and Toby forced his attention back to the wheel.

An instant later the four port carronades roared, spitting flame toward the shore. The sound of the assault rifles stopped as though someone had thrown a switch. Once the smoke cleared, Toby looked to port and wished he hadn't. Dark shapes that had been men lay contorted on the tundra. Those who had survived were backing away, rifles flashing ineffectually.

The aft mortar spoke then, jolting the *Miskatonic* and sending a shell on a steep trajectory up and down. This time the aim was better, and the shell came down amidships on the freighter. The superstructure dissolved in a flash and a rolling boom. As the smoke cleared, Toby could see men leaping off the freighter's deck, flinging themselves into the water. A moment later the forward mortar added its voice, and the shell traced a perfect arc up and then down into the gap blown open by the previous shell. Another flash and boom was followed by a deeper rumble and a great rolling cloud of smoke and flame. The freighter's fuel tank? Toby guessed so.

The pirates yelled again and Peters barked orders. "Hard to port," Coldcroft ordered, and then turned to shout orders forward. The *Miskatonic* turned into the wind. As it slowed to a halt, the anchor chain rattled, and men scrambled aloft to furl the sails. Coldcroft watched them, nodded once, and then strode forward to the bow, picking up a brass shape that looked like a megaphone—an old-fashioned speaking trumpet, Toby realized after a moment.

"Ye o' the Radiance," he shouted. Toby looked that way, astonished; Coldcroft's voice was louder than any human voice should have been. "Surrender or die like dogs."

A silence gathered, and then the men still standing raised their hands high above their heads. A few others came out from inside the station and joined them.

"Ye o' the Radiance," Coldcroft called out again. "Come down to the water's edge with hands high. My men have more grapeshot loaded, so don't be fools."

They obeyed as though dazed. Coldcroft barked orders, and the longboat swung over the side on davits, settled on the water, took on a crew of pirates, and sped to the shore, then returned for a second load. The pirates knew their trade; moments after they'd landed, most of them were patting down their prisoners for concealed weapons and trussing them up with ropes. Weapons went into the longboat and returned to the ship as a heavily armed party went up the gravel road to the clustered quonset huts.

Whisper of shoes on wood announced Leah, who climbed up through the aft hatch with the stench of gunpowder around her. She came up to Toby, gave the scene ashore a long astonished look, started at the sight of his wounded arm, and then asked in a low voice, "Any word yet about the others?"

"I don't know," Toby replied. "I think they're checking."

Leah nodded, said nothing more.

CHAPTER 8

MOUNT VOORMITHADRETH

A little later Coldcroft stopped his pacing, turned toward the shore. Toby craned to look, saw a pair of pirates marching a man in gray and white fatigues down to the longboat. A few minutes later the same man hauled himself through the gangway just ahead of the pirates. He saw Enoch Coldcroft in his greatcoat and cocked hat, and blanched.

"Aye, ye may well stare," Coldcroft said. "Some o' those ye thought to kill are yet livin', and the ship ye sent after us went down with all hands." He fixed the officer with a hard look. "There were some deal o' folk here when ye came. I'll know what befell 'em."

The man glared at him through narrowed eyes and remained silent.

"I'll have tidings soon enough," said Coldcroft. "Baulk me and it'll go hard for ye."

Wind in the rigging and waves against the hull gave the only answer. Coldcroft's leathery face did not waver at all.

After a time, up on the hill, someone stepped out the main door of Tornarssukalik Station: one of the pirates, Toby guessed, from the bits of bright color he could make out even at that distance. Something flashed, once, twice, again, to the right of the figure. A moment passed before Toby realized that the pirate had swung a cutlass three times to his own left side.

Seeing the same sign, Coldcroft said, "Enough o' this. Ye killed the lot of 'em, did ye? By the Goat and all Her Young, I'll know why."

The yellow eyes narrowed. The Radiant officer tried to clench his own eyes shut, but Toby watched, fascinated, as some unseen influence forced the man to look at Coldcroft.

"Who are ye?" the Terrible Old Man demanded.

"Curtis Rathkeller," the Radiant officer said, as though the words had been dragged out from between his teeth.

"The rank ye hold in the Radiance?"

Just as unwillingly: "Level three negation team coordinator."

"Where be the others—no, ye shan't baulk me that way." A sudden motion of the man's mouth and jaw, just as suddenly arrested, told Toby that he'd tried to bite through his tongue. "Answer me. Where be the others that came wi' ye?"

He struggled hard and turned half away, but finally burst out, "Inland. Voormithadreth."

"Aye, I thought as much. And the ones ye found here—who gave the word to kill 'em?"

With an effort that made the veins in his temples stand out, the man kept his mouth shut, made himself turn half away. Coldcroft allowed a thin smile and said, "Ye did it, then. Why?"

All at once the man rounded on Coldcroft, eyes blazing. "Why? Because we knew your side was behind this entire expedition. We know what they found and what it means. Do you think we weren't watching when your side's lackeys started digging in the hills south of here? Do you think we didn't know what they'd find? Everyone at the station was either a member of one of your foul cults or a puppet of the ones who were. They deserved to die. We had our orders and we carried them out."

"Enough," Coldcroft said in a tone of cold disgust.

"You can't stop us!" the man shouted at him, his voice rising unsteadily. "No matter what you do, no matter what vile powers you summon, you can't take this world back from us. We are light and reason and you are darkness and ancient foulness—"

Coldcroft brought his hand suddenly across the man's face, and the Radiant officer's voice went suddenly still. Looking on, Toby wondered what was wrong with his face, and realized an instant later, staring, that the man no longer had a mouth.

"Ye spoke of orders," said Coldcroft, in the same icy tone. "By the King's cold bones, I can give the like." He turned his back on the man. "Mate Ellis."

"Aye, sir."

"It's the yardarm for this one. Call up the crew and have a rope reeved."

"Aye, sir."

Toby stared blankly at captain and first mate for a moment, then realized what the words meant and blanched. Ellis called to six of the pirates, and in moments a rope was run through the yardarm block and tossed back down to the railing, where Spanish Joe knotted it neatly into the traditional noose. By then, despite his struggles, the Radiant officer had his hands bound behind his back and a lump of iron ballast tied to his feet, and his guards hauled him to the rail.

Only the keening wind and the splash of waves broke the silence. Off in the middle distance, past the quonset huts, flames and smoke still rose from what was left of the fuel tank and the helicopters. Beyond them, mountains climbed toward ragged ice-capped summits stained red with the sunlight, and thin streamers of cloud blew by above them.

"Ready?" Ellis asked, and got a nod from the pirates who held the rope; the noose was already in place. "Heave away." A sudden sharp movement, and a shape in gray and white camouflage lurched up from the deck, swung out over the open water, writhed for a time, and then was still. Ellis said something Toby couldn't make out; a knife glinted, and the silent shape beneath the yardarm fell free into the still waters of the inlet.

Toby turned away then, and found himself looking at Bill Allen, who'd come up the aft hatch from below. His face was bloodless, but he was nodding slowly, as though he'd seen something he'd long expected.

* * *

Once the ship was at rest Ellis came aft and sent Toby below to get his arm bound up, a process that involved an evil-smelling salve and a scrap of rag that didn't look especially clean, though Cooper swore he'd boiled it. The wound stung but the muscle hadn't been harmed.

"What d'ye say now?" Jack asked Scar-Face, seemingly apropos of nothing. The two of them had both taken minor wounds, one grazed by a bullet as Toby had been, the other cut by flying splinters when another bullet pierced a gunwale. No one aboard had been killed or seriously hurt, though there had been close calls.

Scar-Face glanced at Toby and said simply, "He'll do."

Jack turned. "Cooper! Two tots o' rum, by Mother Hydra." The cook grunted something in response, brought out two glasses with a shot of rum in each. Jack took one, then suddenly dumped it over Toby's head. "There," he said as Toby blinked and spluttered. "Now drink this down." He put the other glass in Toby's hand, and Toby gamely downed it. "And that makes ye a true brother o' the coast. Damme if ye'll ever find a ship plyin' the sweet trade in these times, but ye earned the thing."

"Thank you," Toby said, meaning it. "Jack, Scar-Face—thank you."

A cup of Cooper's execrable coffee helped keep the rum from making him tipsy, and he had just enough time to drink it before Phil came down the ladder. "Toby? The captain says we can go ashore and salvage what we can. Are you up for that?"

"Sure thing," said Toby, who'd caught the professor's level glance and knew there was more going on than the words suggested.

"Keep the cutlass," Phil said, confirming it. "And you'll want shoes."

For good measure, Toby changed into clothes better suited to the twenty-first century and put on his coat, and a few minutes later they were clambering down the side to a waiting longboat. Wren, Bill, and Leah were already waiting on the beach. The surviving negation team members were sitting on the ground a few yards from the sea, arms tied behind their backs, guarded by a dozen grim-looking pirates. More of Coldcroft's crew waited to haul the salvage of the expedition aboard the *Miskatonic*.

The walk from the landing up the gravel road to the station brought back memories turned bitter with grief. It didn't help that when they got inside the station, bullet holes pocked the internal walls and most of the doors looked as though they had been kicked in. Toby found it painfully easy to imagine the last moments of the people he'd known, the blazing assault rifles, the impacts and the screams.

"Okay, get your personal gear and put it by the main doors," said Phil once they'd looked around. "Once that's done, let's see what else we can save. Leah, you're our remaining archeologist— sort out what's valuable and get it packed as quickly as you can."

Toby went to his room, gathered a first helping of his belongings, got them stowed in a duffel and hauled it back to the main doors. He got there just as Leah did, and she gave him a shaken smile and then hurried off to the archeology lab. Before Toby could go back for more of his possessions, Emmeline came and dropped two heavy duffels and her bagpipe case by the doors. "*Bon*," she said. "Toby, perhaps you will help me? There are books in the library that should not be left."

"Sure," Toby said. Just then Wren and Phil returned with their gear, added it to the pile. Phil called to the pirates, got them hauling the luggage toward the shore. Emmeline went toward the library with Toby at her heels, and Wren followed them to the swinging doors. Just before they went in, she said, "Where's Bill?"

Emmeline gave her a startled look. Toby looked at them both, and realized that Bill was the only one who hadn't brought his gear to the main doors. "His room—" Emmeline began.

"Toby," Wren said, "please go to the helicopter hangar. I think he'll be there."

Toby, puzzled, nodded anyway and went to the far doors. Outside smoke drifted past from the wreckage of the helicopters. Flames still rose from them, and from what was left of the fuel tank. He crossed the gap between the station and the hangar, trying not to notice the sprawled scorched shapes that had been men, the sickly-sweet smell of burnt flesh. The small door in the hangar's side was open, and he slipped through into dim light and low noises.

The helicopter and the snowmobiles still sat in their places, and unfamiliar crates with cryptic markings on their sides showed where the Radiance force had stockpiled some of their own stores. Toby looked past the crates, saw nothing out of the ordinary, then suddenly saw a hint of movement low down. He waited, saw it again, moved closer.

Off past the helicopter, against the electronic gear on the far wall, someone crouched in shadows. It took Toby a moment to realize that the screens with their steady green lines had gone black, and another to see the cables that had been pulled from their sockets, the circuit boards scattered across the floor, the sudden motion as another circuit board joined them.

Then he came close enough to recognize the figure bent over the devices.

"Bill," he said aloud.

Bill Allen turned suddenly, startled. A quick glance moved from Toby to the door, assessing, and then a familiar smile creased the man's face. "Toby," he said. "Good. You'd probably better go tell the others that the Radiance disabled these. I figured I'd check."

"You're lying," Toby said.

"Toby," Bill said again, still smiling, and sprang at him.

If Toby hadn't been expecting something of the sort he would have been knocked down in an instant. Instead, he lunged to one side, dodging Bill's rush, and drew the cutlass from its sheath. Hours of practice on shipboard brought it up suddenly, guarding.

"Put that toy down," Bill said then. "It's not going to help you."

He sprang again, and Toby slashed. Bill was quick enough to jump out of the way of the blade, but the tip traced a sudden red line across one of his arms. He let out a hiss of pain.

"It was you," Toby said then, his voice ragged. "You're the one who let the Radiance know what we found. You filthy lying son of a bitch—"

All at once Bill lunged for one of the workbenches. Toby went after him, but Bill got there first, caught up a big pipe wrench and sprang at Toby, swinging the wrench like a mace. Toby managed to jump back out of the way. Bill swung again, fast and hard, and again Toby dodged, but it was a narrower thing.

Then a flash of light, blinding, filled the hangar. Bill cried out in sudden agony and dropped the wrench. It thudded to the concrete floor, dull red and smoking.

"Think again, apeling," Wren's voice said.

Another flash followed. This time Toby could trace it: blue-white and jagged as a lightning bolt. It caught Bill at knee level and knocked his feet out from under him. He landed hard. Toby risked a quick glance the way the shots had come, and saw Wren standing in the doorway, a strange shape of metal and glass in one hand. He recognized it after a moment as the thing he'd seen her assembling in the lab, the night she'd revealed her secret to him.

"He must not survive," she said.

Toby nodded, understanding. Before second thoughts could stop him, he stepped forward and raised the cutlass. His fingers knotted in Bill's hair, yanking the head up, exposing the man's neck. Half-glazed eyes stared up at him, still conscious. "This is for the people who thought you were their friend," Toby said, and brought the cutlass down with all his strength.

* * *

"We must go at once," Wren said then. Her voice seemed unnaturally loud in the sudden silence of the hangar. "There's little time—and he may not be the only spy."

Toby looked at her blankly, then suddenly realized what he still had in his left hand. He dropped Bill's head, fought back an urge to vomit, and only then processed the words. "Go?"

"To Mount Voormithadreth. Will you come with me? It's too risky to go alone."

"Of—of course." He blinked, tried to clear his mind. "We'll need—"

"Get our survival packs, two others, and extra food," Wren said, gesturing toward the refrigerators and the boxes near them. He nodded, then looked at the bloody cutlass in his hand, wiped the blade on Bill's clothing, and sheathed it. That done, he went to the shelves where the packs waited. Meanwhile she went back to the door, locked it, and then went to the switch that opened the roof. By the time he'd hauled the heavy survival packs one at a time to the copter, gotten the cabin door open, loaded the packs onboard, and made two trips for food, light spilled down from above.

Moments later, as he was stowing the food in the survival bags, Wren climbed in, slid the cabin door shut, and sat in the pilot's chair, leaning forward to adjust the controls as though she'd been flying antique helicopters her entire life. Scattered flakes of snow drifted down from above as the roof finished opening, and a deep vibration shook the copter as the engine started. Wren leaned forward again, adjusted a dial, then took hold of the controls and gunned the throttle. The rumble of the engine turned into a roar. The copter lurched and rose into the air.

Toby braced himself, looked out the windows as the hangar fell away beneath them. Tornarssukalik Station spread out below, the patched and battered quonset huts against brown tundra, the blackened wreckage of the Radiance helicopters further off and further still, past them, the crater where the fuel tank had been. Behind, the *Miskatonic* rode at anchor; craning his neck, he could see pirates ashore, and wondered what they would think as they saw the copter rise; wondered, too, what Leah and Phil would think of the same sight. He turned his gaze forward. The mountains of Tscho Vulpanomi rose ahead, harsh and snow-edged, jabbing up toward the heavy gray clouds that hung over all. The mass of ice that was all that remained of Tornarssukalik Glacier slid past as the copter soared upwards, and the great freshwater sea beyond the mountains glinted in the distance.

Only then did he let himself think about what had happened and what had almost happened, another death narrowly averted, another mystery unraveled. It occurred to him then that Wren must have sent him to the hangar knowing or guessing why Bill was there, and followed at a moment she'd timed precisely. He drew in an unsteady breath, another. He was still alive, so was she, and the spy who'd betrayed the expedition and doomed so many of Toby's friends was dead: all those counted for something.

The mountains slid past beneath them and the inland sea stretched out for miles before them, unnervingly blue, rippling with waves. He looked ahead, then at Wren, and a question occurred to him. "What did you call him? 'Apeling'?"

"I apologize," she said, not looking at him. "I should not have used that word."

Toby pondered that. "That's what we are to you, isn't it?"

"I still should not have used it. Your species can't be blamed for its ancestry." He managed a shaken laugh, and she gave him a puzzled look. "That's amusing to you?"

"Kind of. I know vertebrates are at the bottom of the list when it comes to intelligence."

"You learned that from Lovecraft," she said, and when he nodded: "He misunderstood. Some vertebrates have high intelligence."

"But not us."

That earned him another glance, assessing. "No. Hominids, shoggoths, and two species of the far future—their ancestors are freshwater clams now—they're lowest on the scale of sentient beings." Then: "I hope that doesn't distress you."

"Thank you," he said. "No. It's something to know that we're not alone at the bottom."

The helicopter flew on, its shadow a flitting presence on the water north of them. "Can I ask another question?" Toby asked, and when she nodded: "What did you shoot him with?"

"A lightning gun." Her glance took in his puzzled look, then the flicker of recognition as he recalled a bit from von Junzt. "Some of my people came to America years ago to make the components and hide them where I could get them." After a moment: "At full strength it would have reduced him to ash, but that would have wasted too much power. Your cutlass was a better option." He thought about that, said nothing more.

A quarter hour later, maybe, she glanced at him and said, "A minor vanity, maybe, but now that we're away from the others I'd appreciate it if you could call me by my own name."

"Vrispaa," he said, and when she made her semblance of a nod: "Thank you."

That got him a look he couldn't read. "Why?"

"Among humans that's a sign of trust."

She made her awkward almost-nod again. "I'll keep that in mind."

The water stretched on and on. After half an hour or so, when the shores of the meltwater lake were hidden in haze in every direction, Vrispaa pulled back gently on the controls and the helicopter began gaining height. After another five minutes of flying time a stark white line marked the horizon ahead, just visible in the front windows. The line deepened and broadened into sheer blue-white cliffs stained here and there with dirt and shattered stone. Vrispaa pulled back further on the controls. The copter fought for height and won, and then the huge lake was falling behind and the landscape below and to either side became a vast and ragged sheet of glacial ice, a memento of the Greenland that had been and would soon be no more.

Time stretched into meaninglessness. Rivers of meltwater, gray as iron beneath the bleak sky, surged across the disintegrating ice sheet, writhing in temporary beds and plunging into unexpected chasms. Each of them resembled the others closely enough that Toby soon lost count. Nothing moved on the white surface but the surging water, and now and then a mass of ice undercut by the water toppled into a stream or plunged down into the darkness of a seemingly bottomless crevasse. If their goal was drawing near, he had no way of knowing.

Then something black and massive rose up in the middle distance: the crest of a mountain, Toby guessed after a moment. The helicopter turned. On its new heading, the front window showed the top of a great uneven peak bursting out of the ice, soaring in stark majesty maybe a thousand feet above the glacial surface.

Mount Voormithadreth, Toby thought. It's got to be.

The helicopter flew straight toward it. The great mass had been battered and sculpted by the long millennia of ice, but Toby could still make out the rough outlines of the four volcanic cones atop it that had long ago sent flame and ash billowing into Hyperborean skies. It drew closer and closer still, and the copter climbed over the first outflung shoulders of stone.

Vrispaa pointed suddenly to one side. Toby craned his neck to see, and spotted the black helicopters, crouched on the ice like so many wasps. There were six of the smaller ones that had landed at Tornarssukalik Station and two others, big twin-rotor transports. He gave Vrispaa a worried look, thinking of how many armed men those could hold, but she had turned her attention back to their route.

Their copter cleared one more outflung mass of rock, slowed, and settled gently down onto an ice field close to bare stone. Toby's blood was pounding in his ears, drowning out even the roar of the engines, as the helicopter settled down onto the ice upon Mount Voormithadreth.

* * *

Toby went back into the cabin, flung open the cabin door, hauled the emergency packs two at a time to the door and threw them out, then scrambled out after them. The down-wash of air from the slowing rotors rushed past him. A moment later Vrispaa clambered out, shouldered two of the bags, and motioned toward the black slope nearby. He hefted the other two, got them more or less settled on his shoulders, and fol-lowed her lead.

The two of them picked their way across the ice and then up the slope toward the lowest of the four cones. Fragments of shattered rock shifted and slid under their boots. Above, a bitter wind hissed in the crags. Not far below, the ice sheet stretched away to the edge of sight and beyond, marked at intervals with pools and writhing streams of meltwater, and a line of low black crags just barely clearing the surface of the ice marked what remained of the crest of the Eiglophian Mountains, the rocky backbone of ancient Hyperborea.

"We're close to the Uppermost Gate," Vrispaa said. She pointed off around the curve of the cone. "A mile, maybe."

"You've been up here before," Toby said.

"A very long time ago," she told him. Toby gave her an uncertain look, but gestured for her to lead the way.

There was no trail, just an uneven slope of black basalt, crumbling in places, stark and smooth in others. Nothing grew on it yet, and Toby guessed that it hadn't been free of ice for long. He picked his way in Vrispaa's wake, trying to ignore the weight of the emergency packs, keeping a careful eye on his footing, sparing only the very occasional glance at the glacial sheet stretching out to eastward or the ragged crown of the volcano above. That kept him from noticing the corpses until he was nearly beside them.

There were maybe twenty of them, three huge sprawled shapes covered with white fur, surrounded by human figures in military gear. The furred shapes looked a little like bears grown monstrous. It took Toby a moment to notice that each of them had six legs, but that was because he was staring at their faces: like caricatures of humanity, with staring eyes and fanged mouths bent in what looked like crazed smiles. Few of the human figures were intact, and the stink of blood filled the air. Toby stopped, then hurried after Vrispaa, whose pace hadn't slowed.

"Gnophkehs," Vrispaa said. "Ithaqua's servitors. He must be nearby."

"I saw him twice," Toby said, catching up to her. "Once before the Radiance came, and then again last night."

"They'll face other dangers underground," said Vrispaa. "They bound the Great Old Ones, but their servitors remain free—and so do we."

They hurried on. After another half mile or so, the slope gave way to a flat space that looked as though it had been fashioned by human or unhuman hands, and there Vrispaa stopped. Toby turned, and drew in a sudden sharp breath.

There before him stood the Uppermost Gate: a massive archway hewn from the mountainside, some sixty feet from side to side and easily a hundred feet in height, cracked and riven and partly blocked with rubble. Back maybe twenty feet from the face of the sheltering arch rose a flat wall of stone, pierced at its lower end by three squared openings maybe ten feet high, and the whole soaring wall between the top of the openings and the crest of the arch was worked in bas-reliefs as mighty as those of the temples of Karnak or the gates of Babylon.

On the right side the carvings showed a monarch in ornate tasseled robes and a conical crown, one hand raised in a stylized gesture of greeting. On the left stood a being not quite human, shorter than the king and half bent over, with great eyes, a protruding muzzle, and a furred body partly covered by a loincloth and a sleeveless tunic; it also raised one hand. Between them was an altar heaped with offerings, and back beyond it, facing outward as though looking on, rose a vaster and stranger shape: rather like a toad, something like a bat, a little like a sloth, gazing down at the king and the other being through half-lidded eyes. It was Tsathoggua, Toby knew, the toad god, eldest of the Great Old Ones on Earth, but something about it reminded him of a memory that would not quite surface.

Here and there vertical columns of angular characters spilled down the stone face, blurred by the millennia but still legible. "I wish I had a camera," Toby said, as they started toward the gate. "Those texts are pretty substantial."

"A treaty," said Vrispaa. "The human figure is Saphirion, second emperor of the dynasty of Uzuldaroum. The others are a voormi and a god." She glanced at him. "I was at the signing." Toby gave her a startled look, but she turned back toward the gate, and he followed.

The rubble had been cleared from one side of the arch—recently, too, or so Toby guessed from the signs. He gave Vrispaa an uncertain look, but followed her past what remained of the rubble to the midmost of the three openings. Within, a stone chamber—no natural cave, but a room with smooth floor and walls and a low ceiling supported by heavy pillars spaced well apart—gave onto a corridor that led straight away into darkness. Water pooled here and there on the floor close to the doors, a last trace of the vanished ice, but further in all was dry.

"Before we go further," said Vrispaa, "these packs can be lightened." She motioned with her head to an alcove over to one side. Toby, who'd been trying not to notice how heavy the duffels were, followed her and let go a ragged sigh as the two packs slid to the ground.

It didn't take long to unpack. Each duffel contained the same items—sleeping bag and ground pad, tarp for shelter, cooking pot and camp stove, bottles of fuel, bottles of water, packets of food he recognized as military surplus MREs, and a few other odds and ends—along with two changes of clothing and a pair of spare boots. Then there was the food Toby had stuffed into the packs: packets of beef jerky, foil packs of freeze-dried camper's meals, a box of energy bars, a bag of apples, and twelve plastic-wrapped bricks of bright orange American cheese.

Vrispaa considered those bleakly when she opened her second bag, where half of them had ended up. "I have no idea why humans think of this as food," she said.

"Are you allergic to cheese?" Toby asked.

She gave him a blank look. "No. I find it distasteful."

"Okay, but it's still food."

"True—and it might keep us from starving." She didn't look pleased at the prospect.

Discarding two sets of spare clothing and boots, two extra sleeping bags, three camp stoves and pots, and all the tarps decreased the load to the point that it could be put in two duffels rather than four. A little creative work with the straps of the extra duffels rigged the ones they would be taking so they could be worn like backpacks, which also helped. They stuffed the things they weren't taking in the spare bags, and left those over by one wall; once everything was repacked, they shouldered their lightened burdens and went on.

Further in, dust formed a thin layer on the floor. Masses of fallen stone from the cracked and riven ceiling above marred the dust, and so did the prints of military boots, many of them, going deeper into the mountain.

"The Radiance came this way," Toby said then in a low voice.

"Yes. They got here three days ago. I watched their helicopters leave the station."

"What are we going to do if we catch them?"

"Leave that to me," said Vrispaa.

The light faded as they went further back into the corridor. As the last of it guttered out, Vrispaa pulled out a small flashlight from her parka pocket and handed it to Toby, then brought out another for herself. "For the time being," she said, "these are safe. Use the lowest setting."

Toby's eyes had already adapted to the dark, and so the lowest setting was more than enough for him. By that pallid glow, they followed the corridor to its end, where a stair zigzagged down into darkness. At the top of the stair sprawled two human corpses and three not quite human, with jutting muzzles and umber fur. The overfamiliar stink of blood tainted the air.

"Voormis," Vrispaa said. "I was told that they would try to get here in time."

"I didn't know they still existed," Toby said.

"There are seven intelligent species on Earth now," Vrispaa told him. "They're one. Humans are one. You may see a third. The fourth, fifth, and sixth—" A shrug left the matter undecided. Then, in a low troubled tone Toby had never heard her use before: "And may the Makers of Destinies grant that we don't encounter the last." She motioned toward the stair, and they stepped around the corpses and began the descent.

* * *

The stair went down, down, and further down, zigzagging into the heart of Mount Voormithadreth. Neither of them spoke, and the rustle of their footfalls on the stone stairs was the only sound. Here and there the walls to either side had cracked and crumbled, and debris lay across the steps, but the way remained open. A steady cold current of air swept down the stairs. What dust still managed to cling to the steps showed bootprints here and there.

Hours later, or so Toby guessed, the stair finally ended at one side of a pillared hall that reached away into utter darkness. Vrispaa motioned for him to follow and led the way straight out across the hall, following the bootprints. On the far side an archway loomed up, leading into a broad corridor with bas-reliefs on both walls. Stiff and half-abstract, they were in a style utterly unlike the carvings on the Uppermost Gate; they showed curious figures, half bent over, with wide bulging eyes and protruding muzzles, engaged in some unknown activity that might have been dance or formal combat.

"Voormis?" Toby asked.

"Yes. After your people drove them underground and they learned from the serpent folk how to smelt metals, they lived here until the ice drove them away. It's a sacred place to them."

Toby considered that. "Are they going to be okay about us being here?"

"They've been told," said Vrispaa. She motioned, and they went on.

The corridor ended in another pillared hall reaching into distance, maybe a hundred feet long and half that in width, with doors around it leading into shadow. Between the doors, more bas-reliefs showed the doings of voormis: hunting parties, mostly, with packs of spear-armed voormis chasing down sabertooth cats, small oddly shaped elephants he guessed were probably some kind of mastodon, and fleet little long-necked dinosaurs that pretty much had to be Phil Dyer's omegasaurs. The carvings cheered him, reminded him of the world of sunlight and wind he'd left far above.

Beyond the hall was a short corridor and then another stair zigzagging into blackness. "Before we go on," Vrispaa said, "food and rest. We have a very long journey ahead."

Toby sat down on the stone floor not far from the stair. "Works for me," he said. "All the way to the Lowermost Gate?"

"Yes, and then back up again."

One MRE packet each and a pair of apples made their first meal inside the mountain. They ate and drank in silence. Around them, air whispered, but nothing else stirred. Once they'd finished the meal, they started down the stair. Hours passed. So little seemed to change that Toby had to fight the feeling that he and Vrispaa were descending the same hundred steps over and over again. Now and then doorways opened into blackness off a landing, but the bootprints kept going down the stair and so did they.

Finally the stair ended in another set of halls and rooms with bas-reliefs on the walls. "We should find a safe place and sleep," Vrispaa said.

"Thank you," said Toby.

A little searching found a small room well away from the stair with only a little dust on the floor. The room lacked bas-reliefs, but two letters had been carved roughly on the far wall:

$$\uparrow \; \mathsf{h}$$

"Do you recognize those?" Vrispaa asked. "I don't."

Toby examined them. "They're Norse runes," he said, recalling a detail from one of his undergraduate classes. "The equivalent of A and S."

She pondered that for a moment and then said, "Arne Saknussemm."

Toby gave her a startled look. "How could he have gotten here? This whole region was deep under the glaciers until a few decades ago."

"I don't know," she admitted. "Do you have another hypothesis?" He didn't, and went to work on a meal instead.

One of the foil packets of freeze-dried food, reconstituted with boiling water, turned into something that was supposed to be chicken a la king. Bland and pasty, it made Toby long for one of Cooper's salmagundis, but he wolfed it down anyway, followed it up with an apple.

"Do you think we need to keep watch?" he asked her then.

A shake of her head, just as deliberate as her nod, denied it. "I can do certain things to keep us from being found."

With that reassurance he shed his boots and coat, unrolled his sleeping bag and ground pad, and settled down for the night. It took a while for sleep to find him, but some time thereafter he strayed out of vague unremembered wanderings into the same dream he'd had so many times before, where he'd been lying in a vast lightless place where cold air whistled and sighed against cold stone. Slowly, just as in those previous dreams, the dim colorless light came trickling in, as though the rays of a rising moon had found their way in through a distant window.

Then, as in those other dreams, the man in the sealskin clothing bent over him, and the dark desperate eyes considered him through the holes in the strange mask. Toby stared up at the man as he pulled off one of his gloves and reached out a brown muscular hand, palm up, as if pleading for something.

Then Toby understood. He pulled off one glove, fumbled with his garments, pulled out the little metal tin that held the ivory amulet. His fingers felt leaden and clumsy as he opened the thing and extracted the little pale object, but he managed to slip his hand outside the sleeping bag, and placed the amulet in the palm that waited for it.

A sudden broad smile creased the face behind the mask. The man seemed to say something, then, though Toby couldn't hear any sounds at all. He gestured downwards emphatically several times. Lips just visible through the mouth-hole of the mask moved again, as though he was explaining what he meant. Finally he smiled again, folded the ivory amulet in his hand, curled his other gloved hand around it, and vanished.

Toby woke from the dream in utter darkness, lay there for a long moment before he remembered where he was and how he'd gotten there. He could hear the soft sounds of Vrispaa's breath close by, gathered that she was still asleep. After a while he pulled himself out of the sleeping bag, found his flashlight and clicked it on, shielding it so that the light wouldn't fall anywhere near Vrispaa's face.

As he moved, something shifted inside his clothing. He remembered the dream, reached through the half-unfastened front of his shirt, and found the little tin, still in the inside pocket where he'd placed it before boarding the helicopter with Emmeline.

He pulled it out and opened it. The ivory amulet was gone. He could see the cotton wadding clearly by the faint glow from the flashlight. He stared at the wadding for a time, and then shook his head slowly and closed the box.

* * *

That day they followed the tracks of booted feet down what seemed like an endless series of stairs and echoing stone halls, stopping only at long intervals. Once, in a hall where they rested briefly, they saw the same two runes as before—Arne Saknussemm's? Toby wondered about that, and guessed he might never know. Twice they caught the stench of gunpowder and blood, and in due time came to a place where sprawled corpses, some human, some voormi, lay contorted on the flagstoned floor. Once something fouler tainted the air—a smell of blood, gasoline, burned flesh, and something acrid Toby didn't recognize at all—and when they reached its source they found carnage: more than twenty negation team members with heads ripped off and bodies smeared with a black stinking goo, two shapeless charred masses that Toby guessed had once been shoggoths, and oily smoke hanging in the air. "Flamethrowers," Vrispaa said. "Phil and Emmeline warned me they would likely bring those."

Not long after that Vrispaa gestured away from the trail they were following. "The Radiance has some knowledge of the tunnels down here—old records, maybe—but there are routes its people clearly don't know about. We can use one to catch up with them."

"How come you know so much about what's down here?" Toby asked.

"We exchanged minds with voormis," said Vrispaa. "This way."

She led him across another pillared hall, down a long corridor and two short flights of steps, and then through a narrow passage that veered off from the geometry of the rooms and passages through which he'd been traveling. That passage angled downward for what seemed like several hours of walking, and finally let onto an open space unlike anything Toby had yet seen under Mount Voormithadreth: a hall made for giants, easily a quarter mile in width, with a groined and vaulted ceiling half hidden in the shadows far above, and a floor of great octagonal flagstones. The crumbling stone walls looked even older than the ones he'd seen further up; they were carved with curvilinear mathematical designs that meant nothing to Toby, and long rows of hieroglyphs of a style he was sure he'd never seen before.

"Good," said Vrispaa, in a very low voice. "We're only a few levels above the Lowermost Gate. Do you recognize the architecture?"

Toby gazed up into the vast dim space, and memory stirred. "Your people made this."

"Yes. There was a city of ours here two hundred twenty million years ago. They experimented with geothermal power."

"Because of Mount Voormithadreth?" Toby asked.

She shook her head, the motion awkward as ever. "Mount Voormithadreth exists because they got careless." Then, in a still lower voice: "Either we're perfectly safe here or we're in more danger than you can imagine. We'll find out which one in the next hour." She motioned, and they started walking down the length of the immense hall.

Time passed and their footfalls whispered in the stillness. The hall came to an end after what must have been more than a mile; they passed through arched doorways made for beings many times their size, and down smooth ramps that seemed to replace stairs. Here and there the flashlights' glow showed corridors half choked with what looked like long-cooled lava, and great chasms running through the walls where some vast convulsion of the earth had torn the stonework apart. More than once they had to clamber over a mass of broken stone that had fallen from above, and glimpsed the ruins of other halls and rooms through gaps in the vaulted ceiling.

It was as they crossed the last heap of rubble that Toby spotted the trapdoor. It was in the middle of a vast and otherwise empty circular space walled with square-cut black stonework of an unfamiliar style. From the top of the fallen mass of stone he could see only a square of absolute darkness cut into the paving stones of the floor, surrounded by faint dim shapes he couldn't identify at first. Vrispaa's sudden halt told him that she'd seen it as well.

She started down the slope of rubble after a moment, though, and he followed. As they came closer he was able to see the trapdoor more clearly. It was maybe twenty feet across, opening onto a shaft that plunged straight down into the unknown. Once, to judge from the corroded remnants of metal bands and fastenings, it had been sealed shut, but now it stood open, and a steady cold wind flowed out from it.

Vrispaa's urgent gesture called for perfect silence. Toby nodded, and the two of them finished picking their way down the heap of rubble. He followed her to the outer edge of the huge circular chamber, as far from the trapdoor as possible. Quick and silent, they slipped around the chamber and reached its far end, where the square-cut black stonework ended abruptly and another great vaulted hallway with curvilinear designs and strange hieroglyphs on the walls reached away out of sight.

At the end of that hall a ramp led off to one side, and Vrispaa led the way down it and stopped at the bottom, where another vaulted hall of slightly smaller scale reached out into the darkness ahead. "We should rest and eat," she said. "Another two levels down and we'll be within reach of the Lowermost Gate."

"What if the Radiance gets through the gate first?" Toby asked.

"They won't." She set her bag on the floor, got out a stove and a pan. Toby let his own bag slide from his shoulder and went to help her.

"The trap door," he said, as they ate beef stew that smelled and tasted remarkably like vinyl. Scraps of lore he recalled dimly from von Junzt and a Lovecraft story circled through his mind. "That's the seventh species—the flying polyps."

She glanced up at him. In a low voice: "I don't know if they're still present here or not. They were there once, and we know they still exist in a few parts of the world." She ate more of the beef stew, went on. "They're the only intelligent species on Earth whose minds we've never been able to borrow, and you know what kind of history we've had with them."

Toby nodded and finished his meal without saying anything else. The spare account in von Junzt gave few details of the terrible wars between the Yithians and the flying polyps, just hints of whole regions laid waste and cities wiped out in an instant, but the ruins of the Yithian city around him made those hints unpleasantly vivid. He thought of the other Paleozoic races still on Earth, the shoggoths and the serpent folk, and wondered what parts of their long histories they kept in memory, what horrors from their past made them speak in low tones. The whispering darkness, around the little pool of light their flashlights cast, offered no answers.

He reached for his pack again, got out some of the cleaning wipes the emergency packs had for dishwashing. "Time to go, I guess," he said to Vrispaa.

"No," said a half-familiar voice out of the darkness. "You've gone rather too far already. If you try to draw a weapon I'll shoot you dead."

"Too late," Vrispaa said. A shape of glass and metal glinted in her hand.

"The fact remains," said the voice, "that I have a clear shot at your head." Then: "Dr. Gilman, stay right where you are. If you try to get between us or approach me, I'll shoot her dead and then empty the rest of the magazine into you." That was when Toby recognized the voice as Anna Slange's.

CHAPTER 9

THE GATE OF THE WATERS

A frozen moment followed. "So you're with the Radiance too," Toby said bitterly.

"The Radiance? No." A hint of amusement tinged Slange's voice. "But thank you for that piece of information. I suspected they were the third player in this little game. I gather that you're after the same thing they are."

"And you?" Vrispaa asked.

"Of course."

The lightning gun in Vrispaa's hand did not waver. "Then we're at an impasse. My mission is to keep anyone from reaching it."

"I find that hard to believe," said Slange. "Humans rarely have that much sense."

"Thank you," said Vrispaa. "You've just told me what species you belong to."

Toby blinked, tried to process that. A tense moment passed. "You intrigue me," Slange said then. "How?"

"You appear fully human. That means serpent folk or Yithian, and you're not Yithian."

"You seem very certain of that."

"For good reason. I know the current identities of the other Yithians in this time."

That got a much longer silence. "Then you're correct," Slange said. "We're at an impasse. If you're Yithian, your claim that you simply want to keep others from reaching our common target makes no sense, and my intention remains unchanged."

A longer silence passed. Toby looked from one of them to the other, uncertain. He tried to fit their words together and kept on stumbling over a gap between meanings. "You know," he said finally, "I don't think you're both talking about the same thing."

Slange allowed a little laugh; it sounded just a little like a hiss. "How like a human."

"Nonetheless," Vrispaa said, "he may be right. What are you here for?"

A moment of silence, then: "The *Book of Skelos*, of course."

"I thought that was lost forever," said Toby.

"Very nearly," said Slange. "One copy hasn't been accounted for. It may be here. Do you pretend that that's not of interest to you?"

"There's no reason it should be," Vrispaa said. "In my time there were copies of fourteen editions in the archives at Pnakotus, including one of the Hyperborean redaction. The oldest was made from Skelos' own manuscript before he left Yanyoga."

A longer silence slipped past. "Tell me this," said Slange. "If you aren't here after the *Book of Skelos*, what do you claim you're after?"

"The Radiance force," said Vrispaa, "is trying to reach the Deep of Abhoth and steal the tablets that Abhoth guards."

Slange's eyes narrowed. "Not even humans could be that foolish."

"Thanks," Toby said sourly.

"Your people must know about the Radiance and its ways," Vrispaa went on. "In what way is blind hubris out of character?"

"I read your companion's mind some weeks ago, and he knew nothing of this."

"Of course not," said Vrispaa. "He wasn't instructed in advance of this mission."

"Hold it," Toby said. "If you can read my mind, why can't you look into it now to see that we're telling you the truth?"

"My dear human," said Slange, "if I wanted to read your mind now I would have to place myself in much the same position as I did then, and you must admit it's both undignified and rather vulnerable."

Toby turned bright red as the implication sank in.

"You didn't realize that was what I did?" Slange went on. "So you were quite serious just now in offering to let me read your mind." After a brief silence, she said to Vrispaa: "I'm prepared to shift the muzzle of my weapon one degree of arc downward and to the left, and to repeat the motion if you copy it."

"That's acceptable," said Vrispaa. Fractional movements on both sides turned into a slow fluid arc, until both weapons pointed at the floor between the two of them.

"Are you willing to put your weapon away if I do the same?" Vrispaa asked.

"Of course." Equally careful movements brought the pistol and the lightning gun to their respective pockets, and left them there.

"You're serious about the Deep of Abhoth," Slange said.

"Yes. I was sent to this time to stop them."

"You and one human? There must be fifty to sixty of them."

"I know. I've made arrangements." Then: "Your help would be welcome, if you're willing to give it, and I can offer you something in return. The book you're looking for was buried in the tomb of King Viramethros, wasn't it? It's not there any more."

"I'm curious how you know that."

"Because my people have been borrowing minds in these tunnels since they were first built, of course. I know where the treasures of the royal tombs of the Commoriom necropolis were taken, and that's where the *Book of Skelos* will be. If you help us, I'll lead you there once we've finished with this business. It won't be long."

"Very well," Slange said. "I'll need to know more about your plans, though."

"I mean to follow them to the Lowermost Gate. They won't get further."

Another silence passed, even more edged than before. "I know what lies behind that gate," Slange said, "and if you intend to open it, nothing you can offer is enough to convince me to be there with you."

"That won't be necessary," said Vrispaa. "I want you to guard the stair up to the levels above the Gate, with that pistol of yours ready. We may be pursued when we come that way. All I ask is that you shoot the pursuers."

"That's acceptable," Slange said.

"In that case," said Vrispaa, "we should go. It isn't far."

* * *

For the next quarter hour or so they hurried down stairs. Toby kept a wary eye on Anna Slange the whole way, and especially on the pistol in her coat pocket. Though he had no weapon other than his cutlass, he surreptitiously made sure it was loose in its scabbard, resolved to draw it and try to cut Slange down if she reached for her gun. An amused glance she sent his way early on made him suspect that she was fully aware of this.

When exactly he first noticed the light and the sounds, he could not afterwards have said for sure. All he knew was that some point during their descent, the blackness below took on a slight tinge of red, and at another point—before, after, he could not recall—the whisper of cold air on cold stone began to blend with fainter, harsher sounds. As they went further, though, the tinge of red turned into a faint glow and the sounds became separate from the background noise of the depths of Mount Voormithadreth. Once another few minutes had passed, the reddish glow became clear enough to outline the portal at the foot of the stair, and the sounds opened up into voices interspersed with the sounds of machinery.

Vrispaa gestured for silence, turned her flashlight off. Toby did the same. Anna Slange didn't carry one—could she see in the dark? And was she really one of the serpent folk of old Valusia, as Vrispaa had hinted? He shoved the questions aside, waited.

"This is where I wish you to wait," Vrispaa whispered to Slange. "If we could leave our packs here with you?" Slange nodded, and motioned toward a shadowed alcove with a view of the stair heading down. Vrispaa and Toby dropped their duffels there, and Slange nodded and gestured at the stair: after you. Vrispaa made her equivalent of a nod, then motioned for Toby to follow her. The two of them started down the last stair.

She stopped partway down, motioned him to lean close, and said in less than a whisper: "This stair ends just behind a balcony. Another stair goes further. Stay on the balcony. Watch if you wish but make no sound, and—" Her voice went lower still. "You must trust me. No matter what you hear, you must trust me."

"Okay," he whispered back.

She made her awkward nod, motioned for them to continue.

The stair ended in a hall with pillars, carved to represent trees, rising from floor to ceiling. The far wall, though, was absent; a cracked and battered stone railing took its place and red light poured out of a vaster space beyond that. Vrispaa gestured, indicating a nearby stair that slanted back into darkness, and then motioned for Toby to stay low and out of sight. He nodded, and she hurried to the stair and vanished from sight.

He waited for a while, in case she needed help and came back up to get it, but nothing happened. Finally he dropped to hands and knees and crept across the pavement toward the balcony, staying in the shadows the whole way. As he got nearer he could hear the noises from the space beyond more clearly: someone giving orders he couldn't quite make out, shrill sound of a motor being pushed past its limits, a shout, and then a grinding sound as machinery failed.

He reached the balcony, found a convenient gap angled so no light streamed through it, flattened himself on the floor, and raised his head slowly until he could just glimpse what was in the huge and echoing space beyond.

* * *

The red light showed a vast open chamber. Below a vaulted ceiling high in the dimness above, it gaped perhaps half a mile across; the stone-railed balcony went around three sides of the chamber, and stairs descended from the balcony, ending at a broad stone floor fifty feet down, scattered with huge masses of fallen masonry that had apparently dropped from the vault above. Flares burnt crimson here and there on the floor, casting an unearthly glow over everything; figures in camouflage uniform stood in clusters, busy with tasks he could not identify. At first Toby barely noticed them, for he had seen the gate.

It pierced the one wall the balcony did not cross, off to Toby's right, a double portal soaring high into the shadows above. Light from the flares gleamed and flickered off the intricate arabesques on its surface, glinted off the machines at its base—the Radiance team had brought those, Toby guessed, to try to open the way. The soaring gate was of bronze, he knew, and not just because the stone of remembrance had said so. Fragments of Hyperborean myth and legend came together around it, helped him make sense of what he was seeing.

The Lowermost Gate, he thought. The way to Abhoth and the stone tablets.

He was still staring at the gate when he heard a shout from below: a male voice, raised in sudden alarm. "Freeze."

"Of course," said Vrispaa's voice. Toby could not see her, and guessed she was beneath the balcony, directly under him or close to it

A dozen uniformed men had turned, leveling assault rifles. Voices stopped elsewhere. From a group close to the gate, another figure crossed the stone floor to approach her. A new voice, female, cold and precise, spoke: "You're Wren Kingston-Brown."

"This is her body, certainly," said Vrispaa.

The uniformed woman gestured to one of the others, who came over, did something with a device Toby couldn't see clearly, spoke in a low voice and backed away. "You're Yithian," the woman said then.

"Good," said Vrispaa. "Your species' technology is improving nicely, I see."

"Why are you here?" the woman demanded. Then, before Vrispaa could answer: "If you plan on trying to stop us you're wasting your time."

"If I wished to stop you," Vrispaa said then, "I wouldn't bother showing myself. We have military technologies you don't, and the bindings you put on the Great Old Ones don't affect us. No, I'm here to assist you."

Listening, Toby froze, unbelieving.

"Why?"

"There are real dangers involved in approaching Abhoth," Vrispaa said then. "Serious enough that my people have no interest in running them. If you do the work for us and succeed in taking the tablets back to one of your bases, we can easily exchange minds with someone who has access to them, and get the information we want that way. If your General Directorate is willing to negotiate with our representatives, for that matter, we can offer certain technological insights in exchange for unrestricted access."

A silence passed. "I can't speak for the General Directorate," said the woman.

"We can work that out later," Vrispaa said. "The relevant point now is getting you through the Lowermost Gate. I imagine you've tried all the simpler options."

"We're prepared to use explosive charges."

"Which would bring down the vault on top of you, plus three to five thousand tons of stonework from further up. I don't recommend that approach. On the other hand, the spell that opens the Lowermost Gate was recorded in the archives of Pnakotus a very long time ago. I'm prepared to give it to you."

In the dead silence that followed, Toby crouched behind the balcony railing, feeling once again as though he was caught up in a nightmare. The only thing he had to cling to was Vrispaa's words earlier: "You must trust me." I'm going to trust her, he told himself. I'm going to trust her. And if that means that the Earth turns into a dust cloud ...

"That's acceptable," said the woman.

"Do I have permission to approach you?" Vrispaa asked.

One of the men turned toward the woman. "Coordinator—"

She made a sharp dismissive gesture. "I'll take responsibility. If anything happens to me, Logan's in charge and the Yithian's to be negated at once."

The man turned back toward Vrispaa without another word, leveled his assault rifle. "You can approach me," said the coordinator.

Vrispaa came forward to stand in front of her. "I'll use sorcery to place three words in your mind. You'll know how to speak them and they'll do you no harm. Go to the Gate, place one hand against each side, and speak the words. That's the spell. The Gate will open when you do that. Understood?"

"Understood," the coordinator said after a moment.

Vrispaa did nothing Toby could see, but the woman lurched as though a weight had struck her. Her hands jerked up to clutch her head, drew back slowly.

"You have them?" Vrispaa asked.

"Yes."

Vrispaa indicated the gate with a gesture, then turned and started walking away. "Not a chance," said one of the men. "Stay where we can see you."

"As you wish," said Vrispaa. She stopped near one of the masses of fallen masonry.

"Alton, Gurevich, cover me," said the coordinator. "The rest of you, get ready to move." She turned, and crossed the pavement toward the gate.

Moments stretched out into vastness. The coordinator reached the gate, raised her hands, placed one palm on each side of the join between the gate's two halves, and spoke three short sibilant words. For a moment thereafter, the Lowermost Gate gazed down on her in silence.

Then an immense shapeless darkness flung the gate open and crashed down upon the pavement with a tremendous roar.

* * *

The Radiance coordinator vanished instantly beneath it. Some of the other negation team members were overwhelmed just as quickly. The ones who stood near Vrispaa froze in horror for an instant, and that was all the time she needed; she flung herself behind the mass of fallen stone as the shapeless darkness shot waist-high out to the edges of the pavement, sheltered behind it as guns flashed. More of the darkness came rushing in through the open gate with a sound like thunder, and the rest of the negation team turned and ran or were swallowed. It was only when Toby noticed streaks of foam on the flanks of the descending mass, and saw the flares still struggling to burn on the submerged pavement, that he realized that what was pouring through the gate was a vast torrent of water.

He sprang to his feet as Vrispaa reappeared, surging up out of the chaos of water at the foot of a stairway. She set off up it at a run, but then a great tumbling wave swept up from behind her and pulled her back in.

Instinct took over then, just as it had aboard the *Miskatonic* when Long Tom had gone overboard. Toby flung off his sword belt and cutlass, shed coat and shirt and shoes in a fraction of a minute, scrambled to the top of the balcony railing, and dove.

Water rushed through his gills as he plunged into it, but this time it stung and burnt: fresh water, he guessed. He scarcely noticed. The torrent that roared through the Lowermost Gate turned the rising water into a vast confusion of tumbling movements, in which human forms were caught here and there. The waterproof flares flickered in the depths, casting a fitful lurid glow over everything. That and the senses he'd inherited along with his gills helped him spot one slim shape struggling up toward air with powerful strokes.

In the turbulence, it took Toby longer to reach her than he wanted, but he still got there soon enough. She wasn't flailing, though, and so he couldn't simply push up on her feet. Instead, he swam up where she could see him, saw the sudden look of recognition on her face, then took hold of her waist with his hands and added his own kicking to hers. That got her up above the water's surface long enough to draw in a deep breath. Another wave crashed over them, but Toby pointed toward the calmer water he could sense, and they swam hard, reached it, surfaced again. The roar of the inflow was too loud to allow speech; Toby glanced around, sensed a route that could get them to a stair, showed it with a gesture. Vrispaa made her awkward nod, and they plunged one more time into the turbulence.

Moments later they scrambled up onto a stairway. "Thank you," Vrispaa gasped.

"Any time," said Toby. "Which way?"

Vrispaa motioned: straight up, and fast. They ran, and the water rose behind them.

The dim drowned light from below faded as the water deepened and the flares went out. Vrispaa pulled a flashlight from her sodden pocket, shook it, got it to turn on. By its flickering yellow light they reached the top of the stair a few yards above the water, sprinted down the corridor beyond it, reached the stair they'd crept down a quarter hour before.

By the time they reached the top of that stair both of them were winded and gasping, but they'd outdistanced the water for the moment. Vrispaa gestured, indicating that they could stop. "Five minutes," Vrispaa said once she'd begun to catch her breath. "We have—that long. There are—enough rooms—below here—for the water to fill first." Then, after drawing in a deep breath: "I hope we can find Anna Slange again."

"That won't be a problem," Slange said, emerging out of shadows that Toby was sure had been empty a moment before. She had both their emergency bags in her hands. "That," she said to Vrispaa, "was remarkably elegant. I have underestimated your species."

"If you don't mind putting it in words humans can understand," Toby said then, "what the hell just happened? Why was there water behind the Lowermost Gate?"

Vrispaa turned toward him. "There was no Lowermost Gate until my people built one, and it never led down to the Deep of Abhoth. It simply opens onto a deep valley under the ice full of ten or eleven cubic miles of meltwater."

"But the inscription—" Toby started to say, and then stopped, beginning to understand.

"Exactly. My people put that there too. All the references to the Lowermost Gate in Hyperborean texts and legends were our doing. It was easy for us to possess the right people at the right time, all through the last few centuries of Hyperborean history, to make sure the Radiance thought that they could only get to Abhoth through a bronze gate. My job was to make sure that they opened the gate, and to report back on what happened to them." Then, intent: "You must not say too much about these lower levels to any human. There really is a way down to the Deep of Abhoth, and I don't want divers to try to find it."

Toby nodded slowly. "I won't say anything." Then: "I hope nobody from the negation team got away."

"If they did they won't get far," said Slange. "I had some visitors while I was waiting for you: voormis and shoggoths.

Fortunately I can speak both their languages and took on my more usual form so they could be sure they could trust me. The voormis are spreading through all the passages and halls above water level, and the shoggoths have gone into the water—they breathe it as well as you do. When the shoggoths are underwater the Radiance flamethrowers can't hurt them, and a foot of standing water is more than enough for a shoggoth to spread out thin, slide along, and drag someone down to tear their head off."

Toby nodded again, trying not to think about the final image. His emergency pack made a useful distraction, and he pulled socks, boots, t-shirt, and shirt from it, got a little more of him covered. His gills still stung from the fresh water; he found the spare bottle of salt tablets he'd stashed in the emergency bag, gulped down two for good measure.

* * *

By then the sounds of the rising water could be heard again. "We should go," Slange said. "We don't have long before this level floods."

Toby nodded wordlessly, got his pack slung from his shoulders, picked up Vrispaa's. "I can take that," Vrispaa said, and he handed it over. Slange glanced at Vrispaa, who gestured toward one of the nearby corridors.

They hurried along it as the sound of the waters grew closer. By the time the corridor ended at another of the great stone stairways, water was spreading in a thin dark sheet across the floor behind them. A few quick glances and a gesture, and up they went. No one spoke, or needed to. The pools of light from their flashlights, the vast darkness pressing down on them, and the rush and splash of the rising waters made up as much of the world as they needed to think about, and the mathematics that mattered—how fast the water was flowing in, how much space there was for it to fill, and how high it would rise—were wholly outside Toby's reckoning. He hurried, and the stair rose up into blackness above him.

Time passed and the sound of the waters faded. "We can stop for a little while, I think," Vrispaa said after something like an hour, when they reached one of the landings. Slange nodded, and Toby simply let himself slump down onto the stone. They shared out water and food: energy bars from the emergency packs, and strips of dried pale meat from Slange's rucksack—"Dried cave lizard meat," she said, handing them out. "Most humans like it." Toby bit off one corner experimentally, chewed it. Inevitably, it tasted like chicken.

A few minutes, and they were on their feet again. The water sounds were a little louder than when they'd stopped, but not as much as Toby had feared. He slung the pack from his shoulders again and started up the stair with the others.

Another hour or so and they reached the top of the stair, stopped for another brief rest, and then made their way through echoing halls to a crumbling stone ramp built in a style Toby recognized at once. "Good," Vrispaa said. Her voice sounded dull, almost slurred. "Four more levels and we'll be above the meltwater."

Slange took that in, nodded, and motioned for her to lead the way. Vrispaa headed up the ramp, which opened onto another of the vast Yithian halls with mathematical diagrams on the walls and groined and vaulted ceilings half lost in the darkness above. Lava had forced its way into one end of the hall but no further, and the three of them were able to weave their way around tumbled masses of fallen stone and great cracks in the floor to another ramp.

By the time they reached the top of that and entered another Yithian hall, Vrispaa wasn't quite steady on her feet. "Are you okay?" Toby asked her.

"I'll be fine," she said, but her voice was not much more than a mumble.

He took a long look at her, and all at once thought of the icy water they'd plunged through and knew what the problem had to be. "You've got hypothermia."

"Can't stop," she managed to say. "Above the water."

"Yeah." He took her emergency pack from her. "Come on."

Two more ramps, two more halls, and finally she said, "S'okay."

"We're above water level?" Slange asked, and got a mumbled "yes" in response.

Back in Arkham, during the weeks before the expedition, Toby had been drilled over and over in what to do about hypothermia. As soon as they found a place that looked safe to camp, he pulled out his sleeping bag and unrolled it, got Vrispaa to strip down to her underwear and climb into the bag, spread her clothing on a fallen block of stone to dry a little, and then did the same thing himself, pressing himself close up against her back and putting his arms around her. Her body felt cold to the touch. "I'll get something hot made," Slange said, and busied herself with the camp stove.

Minutes passed. The stove hissed and splashed pallid blue light across the octagonal flagstones. Vrispaa's body warmed slowly. "Here," Slange said. She had a saucepan of instant soup, and filled a cup with it. Toby woke Vrispaa, got her into a half-sitting position, held her up, and coaxed her to drink. Once the soup was down her, Slange handed him another cup and said, "For you. I know you don't have to worry about hypothermia but it's been a hard day for all of us." He took it and said something polite, and she poured a third cup for herself.

By the time he'd finished his share of the soup he was blinking and trying to clear his mind, without much success. Exhaustion from long days of journeying made every muscle in his body feel like lead—or was it something else? He could not tell. He set the empty cup aside, tried to remember why he needed to stay awake, and then nestled down with Vrispaa close against him and went to sleep.

* * *

He woke slowly in total darkness. Vrispaa was still pressed against him, but her skin was warm and her breath came steadily. After a little while it occurred to him that he'd just spent some unknown number of hours lying next to her in a state two thin layers of cloth removed from nudity. Before his body could react to that, he slipped out of the sleeping bag, zipped it back up, felt around in the darkness for his clothing and by sheer luck found a flashlight. He clicked it on, glanced around and realized that Anna Slange was nowhere in sight.

As he pulled spare clothes from his emergency pack and put them on, he thought about her, wondered if she'd decided to find her own way back to the surface and forego whatever help finding the *Book of Skelos* Vrispaa might be able to give her. He'd almost decided that something of the sort must have happened when a point of light appeared in the middle distance and the faint sound of footfalls whispered through the air.

"Good morning," Slange said as she came back to their temporary camp. "I've just checked the last ramp we came up. She was right—the level below us is half flooded, but the water doesn't seem to be rising any more."

"That's good to hear," said Toby. Glancing at Vrispaa: "I hope she's going to be okay."

"She'll be fine. The drug I put in the soup was dosed to make both of you sleep until you'd recovered." Toby gave her a startled look and she shrugged. "It seemed like a good idea. Your work is done but mine isn't, and the stronger you both are, the sooner we'll be able to finish this business, find the *Book of Skelos*, and get out of here." She squatted down, busied herself getting things out of her rucksack. "First things first, though. If you're less hungry than I am I'll be very surprised."

They fixed a meal together, pooling what they had. The dried cave-lizard meat worked surprisingly well with freeze-dried chili, though Toby doubted he'd appreciate the combination in a different setting, and something better than energy bars and lukewarm water to accompany it would have been welcome. Still, once they'd dished out two thirds and wrapped the pot in one of Anna Slange's spare sweaters to keep the rest warm for Vrispaa, he tucked into the meal and felt noticeably better once it was in him.

Vrispaa showed no signs of waking. They sat in silence for a while, and Toby finally said, "Do you mind if I ask a couple of questions?"

"Go ahead." With a little smile: "You've earned a few honest answers, which is more than most of your species ever manage."

"You're really one of the serpent folk von Junzt wrote about?"

"Of course. Shall I introduce myself formally? I am Ss'hss'thhi ss'tss Ss'mei'shh. You may call me Ss'mei if you like."

"Thank you. And you can take any form you want to."

"I can make you see any form I want to," she said. "See, feel—it affects all the senses. Human senses, at least. You're more easily misled than most species."

He gulped as an insecurity forced its way into his thoughs. He tried to find a graceful way to ask what he wanted to know, and finally blurted out, "Um, are you actually female?"

That got a laugh from her. "You humans," she said. "Yes. Does that surprise you? We're like most reptiles—the females of my species are larger and stronger than the males—and so once we've finished our egg-laying years, we tend to take on the more challenging tasks."

"Okay," Toby said, embarrassed. Another question came to mind. "How did you know we were at Tornarssukalik Inlet?"

"You told me yourself," she said. He gave her a baffled look, and she smiled. An instant later Ragnhild Ormsdóttir, the professor he'd met in Reykjavik, sat across from him. "You didn't guess?" she said in the professor's voice. "Yes, this is my usual appearance and identity just now. In a few decades she'll be lost at sea in a tragic accident, no body will ever be found, and I'll take on a new identity and find some other way to do my job."

"Okay." He considered that for a long moment. "If you don't mind my asking, what do you actually look like?"

"Actually," Anna Slange said, sitting across from him. "I wonder if you have any idea how many complexities are in that little word. Still, if I were dead or my powers were taken from me, this is what you would see."

Another instant, and the creature that sat by the stove was a biped a little shorter than Toby but not even remotely human. Leathery reptilian skin, a protuberant forehead between small horns, flame-colored eyes with vertical pupils, fanged jaws like a small alligator's—that was what met Toby's appalled and fascinated gaze. The creature wore ornate robes of yellow cloth ornamented with plaques of gold, and footgear that covered clawed three-toed feet.

"Okay," Toby said after a moment. "I'm surprised."

The flame-colored eyes regarded him. "Not what you were expecting?"

"No," Toby admitted. "I don't think that's what von Junzt described."

"That's true." Before him sat a muscular figure that loomed over him; he guessed the creature would have stood eight feet tall on its hind legs. Light from the little flashlight shone on glittering scales, the gleaming arc of a tail, a head like a viper's, twin curved fangs jutting down like sabers from the upper jaw. "More like this."

"Yeah," said Toby.

"That was long ago," Ss'mei said, reverting to the yellow-clad form. "Those who went into what you'd call hibernation when old Valusia fell, they still look that way, and so do their descendants, but those whose ancestors went to live underground—" The creature shrugged. "Two hundred twenty-five million years is ample time for genetic drift. You may find it amusing that my people consider me quite attractive."

"Not really," said Toby. "I bet we look pretty horrible to you."

"No, just ungainly." She took on Anna Slange's appearance again, smiled. "And absurd. Those tiny little teeth."

Toby laughed aloud, and Vrispaa blinked awake and said groggily, "What is it?"

"Tiny little teeth," Toby said, still laughing. She gave him a bleary look, closed her eyes, and went back to sleep.

* * *

Vrispaa finally woke maybe two hours later, sat up slowly and rubbed her eyes. They said the usual things, and then she looked around at the vast shadows of the hall and said, "I have no memory at all of coming here."

"You were pretty far into hypothermia from the water," Toby said. "You got here on your own feet but not by much."

"You warmed this body, didn't you?" she asked him. Toby nodded, his face reddening, but she simply said, "Thank you."

"There's food," Ss'mei said then. "It should still be warm." Vrispaa thanked her, too, then ate her share of the odd breakfast and dressed while the others cleared the makeshift camp and made ready to leave.

"Now where?" Toby asked.

"I'll have to remember." Vrispaa raised her chin and closed her eyes for a time. Opening them: "We need to go much further west. The Valley of the Silent Ones, the old necropolis of Commoriom, was many miles east of here, but the shoggoths took everything they gathered to tunnels closer to the Norse settlements. It made trade easier."

"Sensible of them," said Ss'mei. "And it will save me a great deal of searching." She gestured, inviting Vrispaa to lead the way.

Their route took them out of the ruins of the Yithian city, up six levels via one of the great stairways, and then along straight tunnels that ran for miles without any fallen stones on the floor. "Shoggoths," Vrispaa said when Toby asked about that. "They're surprisingly fussy about their surroundings, and good at building repair." Her flashlight beam turned upwards and slid along the ceiling of the tunnel, stopped at a place where fallen pieces of stone had clearly been fitted back into place and patched with some unknown mortar.

The three of them stopped, ate and drank, went further. The tunnels stretched on. After another hour or two Vrispaa's flashlight beam darted to the wall on one side. In place of the smooth surfaces they'd passed for hours, someone or something had carved a band of bas-relief with its bottom edge a few inches above the floor and its top edge maybe three feet higher. Bold spirals and geometrical shapes, wholly abstract, filled the band. Toby walked over to it and turned his own light on it, and found the carvings rounded and smoothed as though countless hands had brushed over them. "Shoggoths?" he asked.

"They carve these wherever they have a permanent home," said Ss'mei. "One of their art forms, if I understand correctly." The thought of shoggoths as makers and connoisseurs of art hadn't occurred to Toby, but he shrugged and kept going.

The carved band continued on the one side of the tunnel, started on the other. Openings began to appear now and again in the walls, not the squared and linteled doorways of voormi architecture Toby had gotten used to, but half-circles that rose only waist high from the floor. A faint acrid scent tinged the air like a memory. The tunnel ran another mile or so, and then ended in an echoing cavern, natural from the look of it, with stalactites hanging from the ceiling and stalagmites jutting up from the floor. By the entrance, on a flat stone wall, were carved the two familiar runes A S.

Vrispaa stopped briefly, considered the runes, then turned. "This way. It hasn't changed much." She led the way through a gap between two masses of stalagmites, down a slope that looked as though it had been shaped by flowing water, and then to a flat area where the cavern ended and a narrow passage led off into the unknown. Close to the passage, their flashlight beams brushed a dark shape, caught on things that gleamed and sparkled. A moment of surprise passed before Toby realized that he was looking at a mound of treasure.

The heap was maybe twenty feet across and six feet high in the middle, all of gold and silver and precious things. As Toby came closer, he saw crowns and bracelets and rings, ornate plaques set with gems, swords with golden hilts and bronze blades, shapes of gold and silver and jade he couldn't identify, all piled together at random. He stopped, stared at the heap. Ss'mei stepped past him, began examining the heap of treasures carefully.

"They brought it all here," Vrispaa said then. "A long time ago, the shoggoths chose this place to put the treasures from the royal tombs, and they let the humans come here and pick what they wanted when they bartered, one thing for one thing. A wheel of cheese, a barrel of salt fish, a cask of honey, for a crown or a necklace or a golden cup worth a thousand times as much." She turned to face Toby. "The shoggoths were happy. They had no use for the gold, they liked the food they got in exchange, and they didn't know that the trinkets they handed out wrote the death warrant for the entire Norse settlement."

Toby turned. "Why?"

"Because the Radiance found out about it," said Vrispaa. "So I suspect."

"That's quite correct." Ss'mei glanced back at them from the heap.

"I'm curious how you know that," said Vrispaa.

"Because I was there at the time," she said, and kept searching the treasure.

Vrispaa watched her for a moment, and then went around the pile. "Over here," she said to Toby. "You should see this."

Toby headed that way, rounded the glittering heap and stopped. There, a little past her, a circle of pale crumpled shapes sprawled across the bare stone of the floor. It took a moment before Toby realized they were skeletons, surrounding a little heap of ash and charcoal that had once been a fire.

"Look!" said Vrispaa, and pointed her flashlight at the wall not far away. A long string of angular letters had been carved into the rock there. "That isn't Hyperborean."

Toby nodded after a moment. "No, it's more Norse runes," he said. "The text is in Latin." He read it aloud: *"Maere audas viator gentis ultimis groenlandici superstetibus kibus hic cum sociis skraelingis iaceant. A. S."* He turned to face her. "Saknussemm's Latin wasn't that good but the meaning's clear enough. 'Mourn, bold traveler, for the last survivors of the people of Greenland who lie here with their native allies.'"

He turned, stared down for a moment at the ashes of the long-extinct fire. Scraps of clothing remained on the bones, leather and wool on some, sealskin and caribou hide on others. One of the latter had something flat lying under the skull, where its face had been, and after a moment of incomprehension Toby realized that the shape was the crumbling remnant of a mask he had seen over and over again in his dreams. Not far away, clutched in the bones of one hand, was a little shape of carved ivory Toby recognized instantly.

Just then, as he stood there staring, a low complex whistling tone sounded in the darkness nearby. "Turn around slowly," Ss'mei said, "and don't raise your hands or reach for a weapon. We have company."

* * *

Toby turned, his pulse racing. At first all he could see was blackness, but as his eyes adjusted he saw pale luminous dots low down, and glimpsed an iridescent mass in which the dots appeared and disappeared. A black blobby shape maybe four feet high and twice that in width and length, it slid out of the darkness. Further back, hints of movement further away suggested another. The acrid smell he'd noted in the tunnels came with them, stronger and sharper.

He had almost processed that when something else moved in the darkness, smaller and less uncanny. For a moment he thought that a human was with the shoggoths—for shoggoths they were, that he knew at a glance—but the being that came past them stirred a different memory. Shorter than Toby, it stood half bent over and so looked shorter still; it had short sturdy legs and long heavily muscled arms that ended in hooked yellow claws; yellow umber fur covered its body, though it wore a loincloth as well; the glow of the flashlights gleamed in its huge pale eyes and glinted off the hooked knife it held in one hand. Toby had seen carved images in the tunnels higher up and corpses sprawled where the negation team had fought skirmishes on the way down, but it still startled him to see a voormi in the flesh—and it startled him even more as other voormis came out of the darkness to join the shoggoths.

Ss'mei made an odd, crouching bow, and the voormis did the same. One of the voormis spoke in a language that sounded like the yapping and baying of hounds, and she responded in kind, then whistled a melody covering two octaves. Toby glanced at Vrispaa, noted the look of calm regard in her eyes, tried to tell himself that they were in less danger than it seemed.

The conversation went on for a while, and then Ss'mei turned toward Toby and Vrispaa. "Thank you," she said, "for following my advice. They wanted to be sure we weren't negation team members who'd escaped drowning, and since the negation team had flamethrowers and grenades, the shoggoths were quite ready to kill us and then figure out who we were." Then: "But we've settled that."

Toby took that in. "Do they know if anybody else got away?"

Ss'mei turned back to the shoggoths and voormis, spoke to them in their languages, listened to the replies. "Not as far as they know," she told him, "but the searchers haven't all reported back yet." She motioned to the two of them. "Go ahead and sit down if you like. I'm going to have to bargain for the *Book of Skelos*, and it may be a while."

Toby glanced at Vrispaa, then sat down on the bare stone floor a yard or so away from the circle of the dead. Vrispaa sat as well. Ss'mei perched on a heap of treasure and all at once took on her yellow-clad reptilian form, gesturing with three-clawed hands as she spoke and the voormis gathered around to listen.

Minutes passed. The nearer of the shoggoths slid around the heap of treasure and approached Toby in what looked like a hesitant manner. He considered it, decided that it wasn't as unnerving up close as he'd expected. It looked, he decided, like a cluster of black soap bubbles covered with a half-transparent layer of gelatin; the pale green eyes rose from amid the bubbles to regard him, slid back into the depths after a few moments. The acrid smell had vanished, and the creature emitted an odor that reminded him a little of Brie.

"Hi," he said.

It opened an orifice and made a complex whistling sound.

"I wish I knew your language," Toby replied. "Or you knew mine."

It whistled at him again, then slid away to join the voormis and whistle to one of them. The voormi responded in kind, and then said something in its own language to Ss'mei, who turned to Toby. "The shoggoth," she said, "would like me to ask you a question. It smells cheese with you, and it would like to know if you're willing to trade."

Toby blinked, astonished, and turned to Vrispaa. "Please," she said, before he could ask her anything. "I'd rather go hungry."

"We've got twelve blocks of cheese," Toby said to Ss'mei. "Sure, we'll trade it to them." Then, curiosity getting the better of him: "How do shoggoths know about cheese?"

A conversation in musical notes followed. "These shoggoths came from Newfoundland," said Ss'mei then, "and they trade with humans there who worship the Great Old Ones. They bring the humans things from underground the humans want, and the humans give them food. They apparently like cheese a great deal." The reptilian head canted to one side, regarded Toby. "Lay out the cheese in a row, with some space between each block. You don't need to remove the wrappings; I've told them to expect an outer layer of plastic."

Remembering the warning not to move fast, Toby opened his emergency bag and got out blocks of cheese, then got the rest from Vrispaa's bag. The shoggoth slid closer, extended what looked like a snout from its iridescent flesh, sniffed appreciatively. He gave the creature an uncertain glance, and then laid out the blocks of cheese in a rough line on the floor.

More shoggoth-whistling followed, and Ss'mei said, "Now choose one smallish thing from the heap of treasure for each block of cheese. That's how they trade."

Toby blinked in astonishment, but got to his feet and offered Vrispaa a hand; she let him help her up. "Six each?" she said, and when he nodded, she went at once to the heap as though she knew what she wanted to find. Toby watched her go, then turned to the heap himself, trying to figure out what he should take. He'd just begun to gauge the difficulties involved in bringing archeological treasures home with him when he noticed a narrow cylinder of pale brown metal sticking out from under a gilt bronze shield, and every other thought went away in a hurry.

He had to scramble over priceless gems and the crowns of forgotten kings to get to the cylinder, but those scarcely registered. He lifted the shield out of the way, picked the cylinder up, opened the cap on the end, and drew in a sudden sharp breath as he realized his guess had been right. In the tube were two rods of metal with a scroll of bluish-white membrane wrapped around one and anchored to the other. The scroll-case and the rods were a bronze made with *lagh*-metal, he knew that at a glance, and the membrane was *pthagon* parchment, prepared from the skin of the long-extinct *yikilth*-lizard in a way that made it endure for ages. He slid the scroll just far enough out of the tube to see Hyperborean letters inside.

There was another scroll-case beneath it. He took those as well, then looked for others. A few minutes of searching turned up three more, and then just as he turned to go he spotted a sixth. A glance inside each showed more *pthagon* parchment, and when he pulled another out slightly, more Hyperborean writing met his gaze. Beaming, he closed it again and carried his finds back to where the shoggoth waited.

CHAPTER 10

A PRAYER TO THE TOAD GOD

By then Vrispaa had already set things down beside half the blocks of cheese. Toby didn't manage to deflect enough of his attention to notice what they were. His thoughts circled frantically around the scrolls: original Hyperborean writings, without the errors inescapable in a text copied and recopied over hundreds of millennia. If they were known writings, that was exciting enough, but the two he'd glanced at didn't seem to be parts of any surviving texts he knew. He managed to put the six scroll cases alongside blocks of cheese, but his heart was pounding and his hands shook at the thought of what he might have found.

The shoggoth seemed just as delighted by the blocks of cheese. Once treasures and cheese had been set down together, it gathered up the cheese with a deft pseudopod and slid over to the other to share them out, to the accompaniment of sounds like an orchestra's woodwind section warming up. Ss'mei kept talking with the voormis in their language. Toby glanced at her, at the scrolls, and then at Vrispaa, who had knelt down and was gathering up whatever she'd taken and putting it into her bag. He did the same thing, wrapping the scroll cases carefully in his sleeping bag for the time being.

The shoggoths finished their conversation about the cheese, if that was what it had been, and both of them slid back over to the

221

voormis and Ss'mei. A few flurries of whistled notes, and the colloquy finished. Ss'mei got up and, accompanied by a shoggoth and two voormis, went to the far end of the heap of treasure. When she returned alone, she had a book in her hands, bound with straps of iron that showed no sign of rust despite the book's age. Behind her, the voormis made off, and the shoggoths waited.

"We should leave at once," Ss'mei said. "The voormis said that the tunnel there's blocked." She motioned toward the narrow passage leading further. "A pity—we could get to within a few days' hike of Nuuk if it were open. So it's back the way we came and then up."

"I'm not looking forward to that," Toby admitted. Ss'mei gave him an amused look, and motioned toward the slope they'd come down. They started that way, and the shoggoths watched from beside the heap of treasure.

"Did they have people try to steal from them often?" Toby asked.

"Never more than once," said Ss'mei.

The long straight tunnels stretched out into distance before them. They walked for hours, stopped to eat and rest, walked further. When they reached the ancient halls and stairs of the voormis again, they found a safe place to camp. "The next few days won't be easy," said Vrispaa. "Sleep and a meal will help."

"So you got the Book of Skelos," Toby said to Ss'mei a little later as the camp stove hissed and Vrispaa dozed, sitting back against a fallen block of stone with her eyes shut.

"Yes. As far as anyone knows, the last copy anywhere on Earth. It has lore of ours we lost when Yanyoga fell, and so finding it has been a goal of ours for a very long time." With a half-smile: "The two of you made it easier than it might have been. The shoggoths were pleased that you were willing to share your food with them."

"We certainly got our money's worth," said Toby.

Ss'mei shrugged. "They don't care much for objects. Why should they, when they can make their bodies take any form they want? Food, though, that's another matter. I'm not sure why. I think it has something to do with their notions of hospitality."

"It makes sense to me." Remembering something that Vrispaa had said: "Aren't shoggoths about as intelligent as humans?"

"Yes." She considered him. "I'm surprised your two species don't associate more than you do. You ought to get along well together."

The pan of water on the stove boiled, and they got busy making a meal and then sharing it out: freeze-dried beef stroganoff, a gelid brown mass that Toby supposed counted as food by some definitions, with energy bars and more lukewarm water as accompaniments. Vrispaa blinked awake long enough to eat her share, then curled up in her sleeping bag and went to sleep at once. As soon as they'd gotten the cleanup done, Toby sat for a while looking at her, glanced up to see Ss'mei's cool assessing gaze considering him. He smiled and shrugged, then unfolded his sleeping bag from around the six precious scroll cases and got ready for bed.

He fell asleep promptly, and after unmeasured time slipped into a familiar dream. Once again he was in the same dark place where cold air sighed against cold stone, though a new sound, the distant splashing and gurgling of water, joined the voice of the wind. Once again the pale sourceless light came trickling in, and once again the figure in the sealskin clothing and the strange mask bent over him, the dark eyes intent. The desperation had vanished from those eyes, though, and through the mask's round mouth-hole Toby could see a broad smile.

The man held out his hand, showing the ivory carving Toby knew so well, and gestured at it. Toby tried to find words to ask him about the carving, where it had come from, what it had meant, but the man simply nodded and motioned upward, his lips shaping words that Toby could not hear. Then he was gone, and Toby's dreams wandered off into dim journeys where the sound of flowing water was never far away.

Hours later he blinked awake to find Ss'mei and Vrispaa already up, and the stove hissing to itself, boiling water. Toby pulled himself out of his sleeping bag and sat up. The image of the little ivory carving with its look of terrible indifference hovered before his mind's eye. He sat there for a long moment, wondering what strange tale of sorcery he'd become part of when Phil Dyer had given the little image to him.

That was when he realized where else he'd seen the same image. Though the artistic styles were three quarters of a million years apart, the one formal and abstract, the other lifelike and shot through with harsh emotions, the figure in the Tuniit carving was the same as the figure in the great Hyperborean bas-reliefs above the Uppermost Gate: Tsathoggua the toad god, the lord of sorcery, the first of the Great Old Ones to descend from the stars to Earth.

The prayers he'd learned from his grandmother all those years ago included a prayer to Tsathoggua in the Aklo language. He thought about saying it then, but the faintly amused look he recalled on the toad god's face made the effort seem even more pointless than usual. He compromised by silently repeating the old prayers before getting out of the sleeping bag and getting ready for a challenging day.

* * *

"It's an ugly story," said Ss'mei.

Freeze-dried tuna noodle casserole gave off steam into the cold still air. It was even less appetizing than the beef stroganoff, and another round of lukewarm water made Toby long for anything else, even Cooper's cacodemoniacal coffee. He made himself eat and drink anyway, and listened. They had a long day of climbing stairs ahead of them, but Ss'mei had agreed to start by telling what she knew about the fate of the Norse settlements.

"I first visited the Eastern Settlement in 1264," she went on. "I was young then, and had colorful notions about finding some way into Mount Voormithadreth and recovering the lost *Book of Skelos*. Of course I got nowhere. The settlers hadn't started trading with the Tuniit, and it took the Tuniit and the shoggoths a while to figure out that they could both get anything they wanted from the Norse in exchange for gold. As far as I can tell, it wasn't much before 1400 that the first Hyperborean gold got to the Greenland settlements, and at first the Norse did the sensible thing, melted it down, and told the traders from Europe that they'd gotten it the hard way, panning gold dust out of glacial streams."

"But someone finally got greedy in 1451, and sold the traders a cache of gold items that hadn't been melted down. The Radiance had a dirigency in Bergen in those days, and must have heard of it within a year or two. I was in Flanders then, getting educated in my trade." In response to a questioning glance from Toby: "You would say 'secret agent,' I think."

"Your people have many of those," said Vrispaa.

"A sufficient number." Ss'mei's smile communicated nothing. "We heard rumors about the gold in 1453, and managed to procure one of the items two years later. I left for Greenland with the first trading ship from Bremen the next year.

"I reached the Eastern Settlement that August, and spent the next year and a half trying to learn where the gold came from. If you've ever tried to get information from a Norwegian who doesn't want to talk, you know how that went." She shrugged. "All I learned was that the Tuniit sometimes had gold to trade. That's as far as I'd gotten when the ships from Lübeck arrived—and they had men-at-arms aboard."

"So you saw what happened," said Toby.

"Unfortunately, yes. The villagers where I was staying went down to welcome the ships, and they died on the beach once the men-at-arms came ashore. I was—" She shrugged again. "More suspicious, perhaps. I stayed back in the village, and kept out of sight when the men-at-arms came up to finish the job. I considered poisoning them, but my orders in those days were very strict. Two hours later they sailed for the next village."

"Over the next few weeks I found out that they'd been to every corner of the Norse settlement, and to all the Tuniit villages nearby. They killed everyone, but that wasn't all. They broke open every storeroom, overturned chests, dug in places where the ground was disturbed. They were looking for something, that was clear—but I never did find out what it was."

"The *Book of Skelos*, possibly?" Vrispaa suggested.

"Perhaps. But I did find one thing, in a Tuniit village north of the Western Settlement. Everyone there was dead, but someone came afterwards and left a message written in charcoal on a piece of caribou hide, where it was easy to find. It said, 'Torvold, if you live, flee if you can. What the wise-woman foretold has come about. We have gone with the Skraelings to the deep places to seek help, but I think we will not get it. Pray for our souls.' That was all it said."

For a while no one spoke.

"I tried to find their trail," Ss'mei went on, "but there was no scent to follow—they must have gone by boat—and I turned my attention to finding a way to leave Greenland before winter closed in and I starved. It was a long time before I came back to Greenland."

"I'm guessing that was a while ago," said Toby.

"Of course. I was with the Webb expedition in 1859 and the second Lidenbrock expedition in 1874, and again in 1948, 1989, and 2016. Then you came to visit me in Reykjavik, and I decided that another visit was in order."

Another silence came and went. Toby glanced down at the bowl of gelid grayish food in his lap, made himself start eating again. The memory of the circle of skeletons around the extinct campfire haunted him. What help had they hoped to find, there in the caverns? It made perfect sense to him just then that he would never know.

Unexpectedly, Vrispaa echoed his thoughts. "Do you know why the ones we saw, the dead ones by the treasure, came there?"

"No," said Ss'mei. "Nor why the Radiance killed everyone in the settlements." She gave Vrispaa a sidelong look. "It occurs to me that your people might have exchanged minds with one of the men-at-arms, or someone in the Radiance, and found that out."

"Our machines won't work on Radiance adepts or initiates," said Vrispaa. "Something they do shields their minds against us. As for the men-at-arms, it's been considered, but they were murdered as soon as they returned to Europe—they and the sailors both. Whatever the Radiance had in mind, they took extreme precautions to make sure no one found out about it."

They finished their meal in silence, cleaned up as best they could. The brooding darkness pressed against them from all sides. "Well," Toby said at last. "I'm thinking that those stairs aren't going to climb themselves."

"True," said Ss'mei. She got to her feet. "You're both ready? Good."

* * *

They spent all day trudging up one of the great stone stairways, stopping only when they had to. After the first hour or so, Toby's world contracted to the narrow pool of light his flashlight cast, the next few steps he had to climb, and the blackness that seemed to reach outward from there to the borders of infinity. Ninety-six steps separated each landing from the next—he counted them repeatedly to give his mind something to do—but in time the number stopped meaning anything at all. Ninety-six steps and a landing, ninety-six steps and a landing, became a leaden rhythm tapped out by weary feet on a drum of ancient stone.

Three times they stopped to eat, drink, and rest, and then hauled themselves up again and went on. Just as the thought of a fourth pause had begun to take on a hallucinatory vividness in Toby's mind, the stair came to an end, opening out into a vestibule and then a series of chambers with voormi bas-reliefs on the walls. A few words settled that they would stop there and sleep, and they started searching for a good place to camp.

"This one's dry and the ceiling's intact," Toby said, coming out of one of the chambers. "What do you think?"

Ss'mei came to the entrance, stopped, and then backed away. "I can't go into that room," she said, her voice a low hiss. "It's worth rather more than my life."

Toby gave her a startled look, but Vrispaa stepped past him, played her flashlight around, and then pointed it at the chamber's far end. "Look," she said. Toby looked, and as his eyes adjusted he saw a huge squat shape there: rather like a toad, something like a bat, a little like a sloth, gazing through half-lidded eyes, with the tip of its tongue protruding absurdly from an unnervingly wide mouth and an expression of utter indifference on its unhuman face. A frozen moment passed before Toby realized that it was not Tsathoggua himself but an image of the toad god, with a great basin of stone to either side of him.

Vrispaa bowed precisely to the idol and came back out of the temple room. "We can climb to another level if you need that," she said to Ss'mei.

"That won't be necessary." Ss'mei managed a shaken smile. "A room where I can sleep out of sight of that door will be entirely adequate." That was easy enough to find, and a few minutes later they had shed rucksack and bags and slumped to the stone floor of a room with carvings of forest scenes on the walls.

Before long one of the camp stoves was hissing and energy bars made a first course to another less than savory meal. Toby rubbed his legs and hoped the muscles wouldn't be too sore to use when morning came. After a while, he glanced up at Ss'mei. "Is it okay to ask about the business with—" A motion of his head indicated the shrine of Tsathoggua a few doors away.

"If you like," she said. A long pause, then: "You've read von Junzt, so you know my people were created by the Great Old One Yig, the Father of Serpents. A very long time ago, some of my people turned away from him to the worship of the toad god. That was not wise of them, shall we say, and they suffered accordingly. From that time onward, even entering one of the toad god's shrines or speaking his name has risks for my people." She shrugged. "So we make offerings to Yig, and then afterwards to every Great Old One but the toad god—and of course the Wind-Walker."

"So von Junzt was right?" said Toby. "About Yig and Ithaqua, I mean."

Ss'mei sent a wry look to Vrispaa, who was tending the camp stove. Vrispaa made her attempt at a nod and said, "They're a very young species, remember." To Toby: "Of course he was right. Most of your human mythologies remember the rivalry between the wind- or sky-god and the serpent- or earth-god, though they've put some odd interpretations on it."

"He was entirely correct," said Ss'mei. "There are good reasons why it's rare for any of my people to come here to the frozen lands where Ithaqua reigns."

Toby thought about that while they ate, and then again as he settled down to sleep. The fate of the people of Pine Harbor was much on his mind as he brooded on Ss'mei's words. Had they turned away from the worship of the Dreaming Lord, or in some other way offended the Great Old Ones? Was that why the Deep Ones had left them to their fate?

Time passed and he found himself again in the dark place where cold air sighed against cold stone, waiting for the faint light like distant moonlight to appear. When it came, though, it showed him shapes on the bare floor of the room he didn't remember from earlier dreams: two still forms in sleeping bags, a camp stove, traveling gear. The man in sealskin clothing and the strange circular mask picked his way around these. Instead of bending over Toby, though, he motioned for Toby to rise and follow him, and Toby fumbled his way out of the sleeping bag, got to his feet, and went with him.

Outside the room the light was stronger, and Toby was not surprised to see it streaming from the room with the image of Tsathoggua. The man in the mask led him there, bowed deeply in the doorway, went in. Toby imitated the motion and followed.

A pallid light streamed upwards from the two stone basins, set the ceiling shimmering like moonlight on water. Between the basins, the great idol of Tsathoggua seemed to hover against darkness, gazing down at Toby with unhuman patience and a hint of amusement. In front of it was a two-tiered altar on which paired censers of gold sat, sending plumes of incense up into the still air. In a dim vague way, without surprise, Toby noticed the eyes of the idol glowing red like coals, its belly rising and falling in the slow rhythm of the Great Old One's breath.

The man in the mask motioned to him, and Toby could almost hear his words: come forward. Toby nodded slowly, went up to the two-tiered altar. Tsathoggua loomed over him, the smoldering eyes gazed down at him, and all he could do was stare blankly back up at them. The one thing that passed through his mind was that wild animals prayed to the toad god—didn't the *Book of Eibon* say that? He tried to think of something to say to the Great Old One on his own behalf, but the words would not come, and the longer he stared the less he knew what he should pray for. The vast presence facing him reminded him all at once of the sea, the ice, and the bare mountains of Greenland, but it was less attentive to human concerns than any of those. Staring at Tsathoggua felt to him like gazing into the face of time.

The great hooded eyes gazed down beneath their heavy lids. Then Toby knew somehow that it was time for him to leave. The man in the mask took him by the arm and led him back out of the temple room. Once they were in the hall outside, the man turned to him. Though he made no sound, Toby could understand his words: *It is well.*

What was the ivory thing? Toby asked.

Teeth shone white behind the mask as the man smiled. *An amulet of his. I left it in my village beside the sea, thinking I could return for it, but death took me before that could happen. I needed another to bring it to me so I could do with it what I needed to do. You did that for me and I thank you for that.*

You're welcome.

I have given you a gift in return, though you will not know it until it is needed. It will not be long. Another smile caught the pallid light. *Now you should return to your camp and sleep.*

Toby managed to say something polite, made his way back to the room where Vrispaa and Ss'mei lay asleep, and climbed back into his sleeping bag. It was only when he settled down again and spent some minutes listening to the quiet breathing of the others that he realized he'd been awake the whole time.

Thereafter, until sleep took him, Toby mulled over the toad god's epiphany. Most of it left him baffled, but of one thing he was certain: if wild animals did pray to Tsathoggua, as the legends said, they didn't seek out his abandoned temples to ask for this or that favor. They simply came to gaze, as he'd gazed, on the fixed realities that defined their lives.

* * *

He woke hours later to find Ss'mei already up and the camp stove hissing. Vrispaa still slept, and Toby let her sleep as long as circumstances permitted. She looked haggard, he thought, watching her as he got his sleeping bag rolled around the six Hyperborean scroll cases and tucked it in his pack. Was it simply the challenge of the journey, or something beyond that? He knew better than to think he could tell.

Before he woke her, he left the room and found a corner a couple of rooms away to empty his bladder. On the way back from there he paused outside the temple room and shone the flashlight inside. The great squat image still rose up against the room's far wall, and the two stone basins were to either side, but it didn't surprise Toby at all that there was no trace of the two-tiered altar and no scent of incense. He shook his head, went back to the camp.

That day and the next they did nothing but climb stairs, pausing at intervals to rest and brace themselves for the next stage of the ordeal. Hour followed hour, hammered out under the slow rhythm of their footfalls. Darkness stretched unbroken above and below them, and a stream of cold air blew steady and sullen in their faces.

As the second day ended, they camped in a small room that seemed oddly familiar to Toby. He was too tired and his legs hurt too much for him to give the matter much attention, though. He shared another makeshift meal, slept like a dead thing, ate again and followed Vrispaa through half-familiar halls to yet another stair.

More hours of climbing passed, and then the stair ended in another hall. They rested there, shared out the last of the energy bars, hauled themselves wearily to their feet. No one said anything. Vrispaa led the way to the next stair, and they started up.

As with the red light before the Lowermost Gate, Toby could not have said afterwards when he first noticed the faint pallid light from above. At first he was not even sure it was real. With each flight of stairs they climbed, though, it became more evident. Time passed, and he began to glimpse a little of the stairwell as it soared upwards; more time passed, the steps themselves became clear even where the flashlight beams didn't fall, and a faint scent as of dried blood made itself known. Then the stair ended amid stiff silent shapes. The voormis had collected their dead but left the corpses of the negation team members where they lay.

A cold white glory filtered through the halls that led to the Uppermost Gate. Dim by ordinary standards, it nearly blinded Toby as he faced it. Following Vrispaa, he picked his way around the corpses. Ss'mei joined them, and the three of them went as quickly as weary legs could carry them toward the Gate itself and the outer world. The white light grew stronger, and air came cold and blustery toward them.

Then they came out of the long corridor into the pillared hall where water pooled here and here on the floor. The three openings gaped open before them, and light streamed in, white and stark. So did gusts of bitterly cold wind, and so did little dancing motes that caught the light as they spun, drifted, and sank. Toby was most of the way to the gate before he realized that they were snowflakes.

He reached the gate a little ahead of the others. Outside, beyond the sheltering arch, a snowstorm whirled and raged. Snow blew almost horizontally across the broad flat area before the gate. Off toward the edges of the flat area, though, waited half-visible shapes, facing them. Moments passed before Toby saw them clearly enough to recognize their faces: like caricatures of humanity, with staring eyes and mouths that curved in crazed grins.

"Gnophkehs," he said aloud. It looked as if there were more than a hundred of them.

Vrispaa and Ss'mei had caught up to him by then, and looked out at the whirling snow and the waiting gnophkehs. A long moment passed, with the keening of the wind the only sound. Finally Ss'mei turned to Vrispaa and asked, "The Wind-Walker's doing?"

"Toby saw him twice before we came here," Vrispaa told her.

Ss'mei nodded, as though that settled the matter.

Ithaqua, Toby thought, remembering the shape he'd seen striding through the sky, the legends he'd grown up with and the prayers he'd said morning after morning. The prayers—

A compulsion seized him then, pressing him to repeat certain words aloud, words he'd known since childhood. He tried to reason with it, then to make sense of it, but it rose in him, imperative. All at once, without intending to, he went out through the gate and stood under the archway, with the image of Tsathoggua looming high above. Words burst from his lips in a shout: "*Ia! Ia! Ithaqua c'fayak vulgtmm. Ia! Ia! Ithaqua naflfhtagn!*"

The wind stopped as if cut off with a knife. The snow cleared, and he gasped. The gnophkehs he'd seen at first, a hundred or more of them, were only the foremost rank of a concourse of the creatures surrounding the space before the Uppermost Gate. Were there a thousand of them? More? He could not tell, for his gaze was caught and held by the being that stood beyond them: humanlike in shape but titanic in size, gaunt, naked, with white hair and a white beard all aswirl about the huge haggard head, and eyes that glowed like coals.

The compulsion vanished. Toby fell to his knees. The blazing eyes considered him, and then the giant figure raised his arms. Instantly the gnophkehs turned and sprang away in great bounds, heading down the slopes to the ice. Another instant, and Ithaqua turned too, striding upwards through the air. Clouds swirled around him, and he was gone.

* * *

Ss'mei came quickly out from inside the gate and helped Toby to his feet. "I take back," she said, "some of the rude things I've said about your species. How did you know he would listen to the old prayer?"

Toby, shaken, opened his mouth to explain about the figure in the mask, the ivory image, and the rest of it—for he had no doubt at all who had put that compulsion in his mind—but the words would not come. What came instead was a wordless warning, a sense of a secret that had to be kept. "I didn't," he said. "I've prayed to him since I was little, and I figured it was worth seeing if that would matter to him."

"He was waiting for the Radiance party," Vrispaa said as she joined them. "He couldn't attack them directly himself, but

even with assault rifles I doubt they would have gotten far trying to fight every gnophkeh in Greenland in the middle of a
blizzard."

"So the Great Old Ones had a second line of defense," said
Ss'mei.

"Not surprising." She turned to Toby. "You're unhurt?"

"As far as I know," he said. Then: "I just hope the helicopter
isn't snowed under."

"You brought a helicopter?" Ss'mei asked. "Sensible of you.
I wasn't looking forward to hiking south for days along the
Eiglophians."

"It may still come to that," said Vrispaa. "Let's see."

Luck or the will of Ithaqua was with them. Snow lay knee
deep around the Uppermost Gate and for a quarter mile past
it, but further on it dwindled away to a thin layer and then
to nothing. When they reached the valley where Vrispaa had
landed the helicopter, there it sat, glinting in the pale rays of a
reappearing sun, looking not much the worse for wear for the
time it had been there. They picked their way down to it, but
before Toby could fling the hatch open Vrispaa motioned him
back. She brought something from inside her coat—an object
of metal and glass half the size of the lightning gun—and did
something with it, then waited for a moment.

"It's safe to enter," she said then. "I needed to make sure
they didn't leave someone behind up here to boobytrap it."

"If they'd left anyone," said Ss'mei, "the gnophkehs would
have eaten them. Still, no doubt it's wise to be sure."

The door slid open and they hauled themselves into the
helicopter. Duffels and rucksack clattered to rest on the metal
floor of the cabin; the door slid shut with a bang, and Toby
latched it. Vrispaa sat in the pilot's chair, turned several
switches, watched lights of the control panel blink on. "It'll be
a few minutes before the engines can start," she said. Then, as
Toby slumped into the chair next to her: "Toby."

He turned, startled by the quiet intensity in her voice.

"You've earned the highest names and privileges the Gathering of Chosen can bestow," she said. "I know you don't have any way of understanding what that means, but your name and deeds will be recorded in a place of honor in the archives at Pnakotus." She considered him. "For myself, all I can say is thank you."

He felt his face redden. "You're welcome—and thank you. It's also kind of nice to know that the Earth is still going to be around."

"True." She examined the control panel, turned two more switches. A low steady whine sounded from somewhere further back. She turned in the seat, said to Ss'mei, "Brace yourself. I'll be taking off as soon as the engine's ready."

"Thank you," said Ss'mei. "One question—your destination."

"Tornarssukalik Station," Vrispaa said at once. "If you need to go somewhere else we can leave you en route, but we don't have enough fuel to go far out of our way."

"That will be fine," Ss'mei replied. "You saw me below on the way back, I signaled, and you landed briefly so I could board." Then: "I'll ask you both to promise me not to mention my presence in the mountain, or my purpose for being there, to anyone in this time."

"Of course," Vrispaa said, and Toby: "Sure thing. We owe you that much."

Vrispaa turned back to the control panel. "It's ready." Another switch woke the engine; it growled, coughed, and then rose to a steady roar. Toby sat back in his chair, tried to convince his muscles to let go of some of the aches days of hard travel had put into them. Vrispaa reached for the stick, did something to it; the rotors engaged, slow at first, then rising to a blur of speed; she pulled back on the stick, and the helicopter rose up off the ice sheet, turned away from the soaring black cones of Mount Voormithadreth, began to retrace its route. The sun came out as the last of the clouds fled eastward, leaving the landscape etched in all its harsh clarity.

"Look!" Vrispaa said, pointing off to one side. Toby craned his neck to see. The Radiance helicopters were still where they'd landed, but a thick layer of ice glittered on every visible surface and snow lay heaped around them in drifts, marked here and there by the pawprints of gnophkehs. Huge unfamiliar shapes crouched atop a nearby ridge of black stone; as Toby watched, one of them spread immense wings and flew off, soaring through the unquiet air.

"Yes, I thought so," said Ss'mei behind them. "Shantaks."

"Those things must be the size of elephants!" Toby said, staring at them.

"Shantaks usually are," Ss'mei replied. "You really should believe von Junzt. For a human, he was surprisingly well informed."

The copter flew on, and the shantaks soon vanished behind them. Below, Greenland's melting ice cap stretched out into distance, riven with crevasses and meltwater streams. Toby closed his eyes, tried to let go of the fears he'd carried for so many days, but his mind kept circling back around to the simple fact that Vrispaa would be going back to her own time soon.

It was better that way, he told himself, better for them both: for her, so she could return to her own time and people, and for him, so that he could pull himself together and figure out what he was going to do with his life. Weeks had passed since he'd given his career so much as a single thought, and thinking of it there in the helicopter cabin felt a little like glancing back over Hyperborean times, but he had to start thinking in those terms again, he knew that. So he told himself, but none of it made the thought of Vrispaa's imminent departure easier for him.

He was still wrestling with that when Vrispaa spoke: "We may be in trouble."

* * *

Toby opened his eyes. The helicopter had reached the end of the ice sheet and the edge of the great meltwater lake—except that the lake was gone. Pools huddled in low spots, some of them more than large enough to swallow a dozen helicopters the size of the one Toby rode, but vast bare mud flats filled the spaces between them. Toby stared at the vast absence for a while, uncomprehending, and then all at once realized what he was seeing.

"That isn't just what went through the Lowermost Gate," he said aloud.

Ss'mei glanced at him. "Unfortunately not."

"There's been a—" It took a moment for the word he'd learned from Phil Dyer to surface in Toby's mind. "*Jokulhlaup.*"

"Probably," said Ss'mei. "There are three possible outlets."

"I know." Vrispaa held the controls steady. "But Tornarssu-kalik Inlet's the one the hydrologists predicted."

The helicopter flew on. The sun glinted off meltwater pools, cast long shadows from stray boulders and hillocks of mud. No one spoke. Finally, dark and jagged in the distance, the mountains of Tscho Vulpanomi came into view, and with them the thing Toby feared most: a great U-shaped gap where the Tornarssukalik Glacier had been.

Minutes passed, and finally the helicopter soared through the gap. Toby drew in a sharp breath, clenched his eyes shut for a moment. Tornarssukalik Station was gone, swept out to sea by the *jokulhlaup.* The hill beneath it and the entire northern half of the plain were gone too. Open water and a few mudflats spread out where they had been.

"Do you think there's any chance they got away in time?" he said aloud.

"I don't know." Vrispaa reached for the control panel, turned a switch. "It's possible the Radiance put explosive charges in the ice dam, and that's why Allen was disabling the alarms." Then: "But we have a more urgent problem. There's only about ten minutes of fuel left and we need to land and find adequate shelter."

"There's a quonset hut at North Station," Toby said. "Where Emmeline and I stayed."

Vrispaa glanced back over her shoulder at Ss'mei, who motioned for her to proceed. A twist of the controls sent the helicopter in a smooth arc over the cliffs south of the inlet, and then over hills and rugged ground Toby recognized dimly.

"Have you considered how to hide the copter from the Radiance?" Ss'mei asked then.

"Do you think that's necessary?" Vrispaa replied.

Ss'mei allowed a little hissing laugh. "Once they realize their negation teams aren't coming back they'll have aircraft over here in a day or two at most."

The hills gave way to low green meadows where musk oxen grazed. "Toby," Vrispaa said then, "you know how to fly this. If you were to fly it out to the sea ice and land it where the ice will tip over soon, could you swim back?"

"Sure," Toby said. Then: "How do I figure out where the ice will tip over soon?"

That got him a startled look. Of course, he thought, Yithians just know that. "I'll show you one," she said. "Once we get close to the station."

A few more minutes and the quonset hut came into view. Vrispaa turned the controls and the helicopter looped out over the sea, reached the ice a mile or so out. "There," she said, pointing to a floe a little apart from the others. "Land on the northern side ten meters in from the edge, and go well south before you jump into the water."

"Okay," Toby said. He got out of the seat, shed shirt and boots, stuffed them in his emergency pack and returned. The copter finished its arc, slowed, hovered, and touched down on the broad top of the hill overlooking the quonset hut, with the engine still going and the rotors a blur of motion. "Ready?" Vrispaa said, and Toby forced a grin and a nod.

She and Ss'mei got up, gathered the luggage, threw open the hatch, and hurried away while Toby took the pilot's seat and gave an uneasy glance at the yellow lights on the control panel and the fuel gauge, which was up against the letter E. As soon as they were safely away from the copter, he pulled back on the controls the way he'd been taught, and didn't have to force a grin as the copter rose smoothly into the air.

Another motion set it moving forward, a little more awkwardly, but before long he was out over the water again. There, he thought, seeing the floe Vrispaa had pointed out—or was it? Another one looked nearly the same, and whichever one it was had drifted with wind and current just far enough that he couldn't be sure from the patterns the rest of the ice made with it.

Yellow lights on the control panel turned red. He made his best guess, brought the copter down something like ten meters from the northern side, felt the shock of landing, and turned the switch that shut off the engines.

The engine died. Then, as the rotors began to slow, the copter suddenly lurched as the ice on one side cracked and gave way. Toby grabbed the controls to brace himself as the copter lurched again, falling half over on its side. The rotors slammed into ice and crumpled, shaking Toby hard; he clung to the controls for dear life. Another lurch, the copter jolted down a yard or so all at once, and water began to sluice in through the open hatch.

Frantic scrambling got him out before the copter sank, and that effort merely put him on a mass of unstable ice that tilted hard one way and then the other, as the copter broke free and went to the bottom. He sprawled on the ice and clung, then picked himself up and looked around as the ice began to steady. The hill where the copter had landed loomed up in the middle distance, with the quonset hut a dot of gray and rust-brown in its shadow; he went to the edge of the ice, took a running leap, and plunged into the water.

As before, his gills poured oxygen into his blood and unfamiliar senses awoke. He set off swimming hard, thinking uneasily of polar bears and orcas. Nothing larger than a young ringed seal came close enough for him to sense it, though, during the ten minutes it took him to cross the shore flaw and clamber up out of the water onto the gravel beach.

Vrispaa was standing not far away, alone, with their two packs. "Sorry about that," he called out as he pulled himself up out of the water. "I must have landed on the wrong floe."

"No," she said, turning toward him. "I miscalculated." He was still trying to process that when she went on. "And not just there. Ss'mei is gone."

He opened his mouth to speak, stopped, then said, "What happened?"

"As soon as we got down off the hill, she said, 'Thank you,' and then, 'I don't know if there's anything I can do.' Then she wasn't there. That's another power the serpent folk have. They can look like anything, and also like nothing."

Toby nodded after a moment. "Okay. And now?"

"That's the difficulty, of course. We have no way of contacting help, no one knows we're here, and winter's close."

Another pause, longer, went past. Greenland spread vast and empty around them. Wind hissed in the cotton grass on the hill, small waves rushed and splashed on the gravel beach, and the sky bent over them from horizon to horizon: edged, all of it, with the terrible indifference he'd seen on the little ivory face of Tsathoggua.

"There was food in the quonset hut when Emmeline and I were there," he said.

She glanced at him, nodded, and led the way up the slope to the door.

* * *

The battered kitchen cabinets inside the quonset hut had eleven freeze-dried meals in them, and a cardboard box over in a neglected corner turned out to have a dozen more. With the food they still had from the packs, Toby guessed, they could stay minimally fed for two months or so. They had enough fuel for their camp stoves to cook a little more than half of the meals. The nearby stream promised plenty of water, at least until the temperature dropped far enough to freeze it solid, and a few scraps of driftwood along the beach could be hauled inside, dried off, and used for fuel, along with cardboard and paper in the hut. All in all, he figured, they had enough to keep them alive until winter closed in and made the whole question moot.

Once they'd searched the quonset hut and sorted out their gear, Toby talked Vrispaa into sitting down at the table, and went to the stream with the same canvas buckets he'd used when he and Emmeline had been hiding there. It took three trips to get the reservoir full, and by then Vrispaa had fallen asleep, head down on the table and pillowed on her arms. Once he'd finished with the water and barred the door, he touched her tentatively on the shoulder, and when she blinked awake, he gently bullied her into getting into her sleeping bag and going to sleep. She nodded distractedly, got out her sleeping bag, stripped down to her underwear without a trace of self-consciousness, and settled on one of the bedsteads. Moments later, she was asleep again.

Toby watched her for what seemed like a long time. Panic jabbed at the edges of his thoughts, but couldn't penetrate far. Partly he was too tired—he could feel the ache of the long journey in his bones—and partly he found he couldn't convince himself that his life or death mattered that much. Sitting there, he remembered the lamplit darkness on the orlop deck of the *Miskatonic* when he'd told the pirates that as long as he could help kill the Radiance force, he didn't care much whether he himself survived.

You got your wish, he told himself, and it was true. The Radiance gunmen who'd attacked Tornarssukalik Station were dead: blown to pieces by mortar shells or shredded by grapeshot, torn apart by gnophkehs or shoggoths, gutted by voormi knives, drowned by the torrent that came through the Lowermost Gate, or hanged by the Terrible Old Man—it made a grim litany as he looked back over it. In Hyperborea's heroic age, so the Commoriom myth-cycle had it, the bronze-clad warriors of Leqquan and Irulat, Coriab and Aquil, met their deaths laughing if they could avenge a wrong or slay a hated foe before they fell. The comparison amused him by its absurdity; he belonged to no heroic age, and a glance at his body—barefoot and bare to the waist, since he hadn't bothered to dress again—showed only ordinary muscles and one pale scar, the track across his arm left by the bullet that had winged him.

He looked at Vrispaa then. Her face, turned toward his, reminded him of a lost child's. It occurred to him then that she'd spoken of being trained for her mission from childhood. It made sense that they would have sent a young and brave member of their species on tasks such as hers, just as humans did. Still, it stung to think that she could have lived thousands of years in her own time, instead of dying young in an age and a world that was utterly alien to her.

He blinked, and realized that his eyes had drifted shut and his thoughts had dissolved into sleep. Movement told him that his muscles had stiffened up abominably. He got up anyway, gritted his teeth to suppress a groan, got his own sleeping bag out and discovered the six Hyperborean scroll cases wrapped inside it. Those required some less casual storage, and he knew it. A little searching in the boxes and crates turned up an empty metal toolbox of the right size, some tissue paper that had once been used for packing, and some yellowing but still intact bubble wrap; he got the scrolls seen to, set the toolbox beside the bedstead he'd chosen, stripped naked, hung his clothes to finish drying on another bedstead, and settled down. After so many days trying to rest on the minimal softness of a hiker's ground pad, the cheap foam rubber mattress felt impossibly soft beneath him, and he was asleep in moments.

He wondered as he was dozing off if he would see the masked figure again one more time in his dreams. The only dream he remembered when he awoke, though, was far more prosaic. He was in his childhood home in Lefferts Corners, in the big familar farmhouse, though it kept unaccountably turning into a quonset hut at some moments and into a vast stone hall with strange mathematical designs on the walls in others. In the dream he was going from room to room, looking for something he knew he had misplaced but could no longer recall, and all the while he became more and more frightened that he would find it.

CHAPTER 11

FROG AND DRAGONFLY

He woke after many hours, and wished he hadn't. His body ached as though he'd been beaten with clubs and left to die in a ditch. Lying as still as possible struck him as the only viable option; unfortunately his bladder let him know what would happen if he did that. Stifling a curse, he dragged himself out of the sleeping bag, skinned into boxer shorts and hobbled over to the bathroom. When he was finished there, he came back out and considered Vrispaa. She was still asleep, and looked a little less haggard. That struck him as a good model to emulate, and he crawled back into his sleeping bag and tried to get back to sleep.

He managed it after a while, and woke after what he guessed was several more hours, still aching but less brutally so. After a while, sure there was no more sleep in him, he climbed out of the bag again, pulled on pants, considered his shirt and tee shirt, and decided against them. It felt good not to have cloth pressing tight against his gill slits. Besides, he reminded himself, *she knows about my gills*. The thought kindled a dizzying sense of freedom in him.

Moving quietly so he didn't wake Vrispaa, he searched the quonset hut again, and was rewarded by the discovery of two more freeze-dried dinners and a quart can of stove fuel. That cheered him, though he knew perfectly well it simply added

245

another week or so to the time before he and Vrispaa starved to death if nothing intervened. He put those with the others, then for want of anything better, got out the volume of the *Proceedings of the Miskatonic Greenland Conference* he'd read weeks beforehand and turned to the article on Hyperborean artifacts in Norse Greenland. As he turned the pages, thinking about the heap of treasure the shoggoths guarded and the harrowing story Ss'mei had told.

The shoggoths didn't know they'd doomed the Norse settlers, he thought, any more than I knew that I'd doomed my friends when I translated the *tuqqoli niunda*, or the Tornarssukalik glacier knew that it doomed me when it broke—

He wrenched his mind away from the thought, tried to convince himself that Vrispaa would figure out some way to save them, or that he would. The effort didn't accomplish much.

Flicker of movement caught his attention; he looked up. Vrispaa was awake. He said the usual things, and tried not to notice the amount of bare skin she showed as she went to the bathroom, came back, perched on her bed. "I think we should do without food today," she said.

That stung, but he knew she was right. He poured water for them both—cold, to save fuel—and tried to pretend that he didn't mind. She pulled on more clothing then, and so did he, more out of embarrassment than anything else.

A glance outside showed a storm rolling in off the ocean, dropping visibility to a matter of yards, so there was no point in searching the area for other options. Silence gathered in the quonset hut, and Toby started thinking of something to say, then stopped, remembering her words when they'd driven up to the University of Reykjavik. The memory seemed impossibly distant, an echo of a long-vanished age.

Hours passed. Vrispaa sat at the table in perfect silence, her eyes closed, as though listening to something Toby could not hear. Outside, the storm blew itself out and high thin clouds spread across the sky, turning the daylight into a vague directionless blur. Finally Vrispaa got up, went to the crates full of supplies, sorted through them, and then turned to face Toby and said, "Thank you. I know what we need to do now."

Toby blinked in surprise. "Go ahead."

"You can swim underwater without having to rise for air, and the water temperature doesn't harm you. Is that correct?" When he nodded: "Good. Then I know how you can get to Tulugaqtak. If you swim under the pack ice and stay away from open water as much as you can, you can keep away from orcas and polar bears and make it there. That will be hard—twenty-two hours of steady swimming plus stops to rest—but it will get you to safety."

Toby considered that. "And my job is to get help?"

"No. You can swim underwater. I can climb mountains—and there's enough climbing gear in the crates to make that an option. We'll leave at the same time; you'll meet me at the edge of Tornarssukalik Inlet and help me cross it on a makeshift raft. Once I've crossed, you can swim on to Tulugaqtak and I can go over the mountains and get there a few days after you. It will be a challenge, but this body has a climber's trained reflexes, and I spent the spring months climbing in the Alps to learn how to use those."

"Okay," he said after a moment. Then: "I'd be happier if you stayed here and let me go to Tulugaqtak to get help."

"I know. I would rather be the one who goes for help, but I don't think you would stay safely here and wait for me."

He met her gaze, then closed his eyes, realizing what her words implied. "No. I'd want to be the one to take the risk." The thought of the journey ahead set his nerves on edge, but he'd faced dangers enough already that he knew he could face one more. He drew in a deep breath and said, "Okay. When do you want to start?"

"Tomorrow, if the weather stays clear."

"In that case," Toby said, "we should eat. We'll need the energy."

"True." She got up and went to the kitchen, and so did he.

* * *

When they'd finished the meal—two packets each of freeze-dried spaghetti with meatballs, made more than slightly edible only by hunger—Vrispaa considered him for a while and then asked, "I would like to ask a question."

"Go ahead," said Toby.

"Will you tell me why you have gills?"

That caught him by surprise, but after a moment he thought: well, why not? "Sure," he said. "It's kind of a long story, though."

"Good," she said. "When I return to my own time the archivists will want as complete a report as I can give them."

Toby grinned. "Got it. Okay, the story starts with a man named Daniel Marsh, who moved to New Jersey with his family and a dozen others from someplace on the New England coast, I don't know where. He'd learned how to talk with the Deep Ones there, and so had the people who came with him. They were looking for a place by the sea where they could worship the Great Old Ones in peace and trade with the Deep Ones, and they settled in a little town on the Jersey shore called Pine Harbor. I don't know where it was, but there was a bigger town called Partridgeville about twenty miles away, if that helps any."

"It might," said Vrispaa. "Go on."

He wasn't sure what that implied, but went on anyway. He'd intended just to sketch out the rise and fall of Pine Harbor, to answer her question without too much detail, but one part of the tale led to another, and Vrispaa had another question ready whenever he got close to running out of things to say. Hours went by before he finished the story—how many hours, he had no idea, since the quonset hut had no clock and the storm kept the sun hidden, but it was more than two or three, he was sure of it. He ended up feeling as though his mind and memories had been wrung out like a wet washcloth.

"Thank you," Vrispaa said afterwards. "I'll see to it that all of it goes into the archives."

"Thank you," said Toby in turn. "That actually helps." In response to her questioning look: "Since I'm the last survivor and the story winds up with me—" He shrugged. "It's good to know that your people will read about Pine Harbor and the rest of it, and know that we existed."

Time passed and a long silence came and went. The sky outside cleared, letting in a trickle of light through the skylights. Vrispaa gathered climbing gear, got that and a week of freeze-dried meals stowed in her pack, and then perched on her bed and said, "There's something I want to say to you and I don't know a simple way of saying it in your language." She paused, then: "Just an indirect way."

"Go ahead," Toby said, settling in a chair facing her.

"Once when I was in France, a year after I entered this body, I went with Emmeline to a—a low wet green place. I don't remember the English word."

"Swamp?" Toby suggested. "Marsh?"

"A marsh. Yes. We sat for a while and watched the living things there. A frog climbed onto a rock from the water, and a dragonfly landed on a branch close by. I thought one of them would eat the other but—" A shift of expression hinted at emotions he could not read. "They sat there, as though speaking. I wondered what the frog could tell the dragonfly about the world under the water, and what the dragonfly could tell the frog about winds and clouds and treetops, and whether they could even find a way to speak at all."

He nodded slowly, watching her.

"I think now that maybe they did. I wondered, too, after the dragonfly flew away and the frog hopped into the water and swam off, whether they remembered the conversation and thought about each other. I think now that they did that too."

Toby's throat went dry as he realized what she was saying.

"I'll need to return to my own time as soon as I can," she said then, confirming it. "Hominid nervous systems aren't well suited to us, not for the long term, and I've been in one longer than the Gathering of Lore considers safe. I'll see you once we both reach Tulugaqtak, but the machine I need for the mind transfer is aboard the *Miskatonic* and there's a backup in Nuuk if that's needed, so—"

"The dragonfly will fly away soon," he said.

She made her awkward almost-nod.

"This frog's enjoyed the conversation," said Toby then.

"So have I." Then: "And it's a source of—discomfort? I think that's the word—for me that there will be three hundred million years between us so soon."

A lump in his throat kept him from answering immediately. After a moment: "It's also a—a source of discomfort for me."

"I guessed it would be." She paused. "You have treated me very well and I honor you for that." Then: "Have I said something hurtful? Your face is wet."

"No, not at all," said Toby. "It's a human thing. Don't worry about it."

* * *

Sleep took its time arriving, even though he knew he'd need to be well rested in the morning, and once he got to sleep he wandered through vague formless dreams that never quite went anywhere. He was just beginning to wake when the door to the quonset hut slammed open. "Toby!" Vrispaa's voice. "There's a ship. I need something to signal with."

He blinked, sat up, then scrambled out of bed as the words registered and lunged for one of the crates. A brief search found the thing he remembered: a signal mirror. He handed it to her. "Do you know how to use this?"

A quick almost-nod answered him, and she turned and sprinted back out the door. He pulled on clothes and boots, then went to another crate and after a few moments found something else he recalled seeing there: a pair of binoculars. Those in hand, he hurried after her.

Outside the sun shone low and red from the east, staining the pack ice and glinting here and there off open water. Jaegers circled overhead, making their harsh cries. He could see Vrispaa on top of the hill overlooking the sea, the mirror in her hands. He scrambled up the slope, took the lens caps off the binoculars and aimed them where she seemed to be looking. It took a little searching, but he spotted a dark shape along the horizon, adjusted the focus, looked again and saw the telltale shapes of masts and sails. His breath caught. "It's the *Miskatonic*," he said. "Or there's another barque in these waters."

"Yes," she said, acknowledging.

The mirror moved back and forth in her hands, catching the sunlight and aiming it. He didn't have to watch her to recognize the pattern that spelled SOS in Morse code over and over again. Less efficiently, he watched the *Miskatonic* and the waters closer to shore, and finally caught sight of the thing he'd hoped to see. "There's a longboat," he said aloud.

"Where?"

"Left of the ship about four lengths, there's a berg with two peaks. Just past that. It's behind another berg now—no, there it is."

"I see it." The mirror shifted, aimed at the distant craft.

Time passed. A dozen times, more, masses of ice in the pack hid the boat, but when it came back into sight again each time it was closer. The *Miskatonic* held its place: riding at anchor, Toby guessed, and wondered how the Terrible Old Man had known where to look.

Finally the longboat pulled free into the shore flaw and started across the last mile or so of bare water. Toby swung his arms, signaling, and glimpsed the same sign in answer from across the water. He drew in a ragged breath, let it out, tried to make himself believe that he was actually going to leave Greenland alive.

"I woke early," Vrispaa said then, "and climbed the hill to judge the weather. I didn't expect to see anything but ice and sea, but there it was. The crew was still taking in sails, so I think it had just arrived. Toby—I'll leave as soon as we're both aboard."

My dragonfly, he wanted to say. My shimmering one. "Yeah," he said instead.

Her glance told him that she'd read or guessed the thought. "You'll make sure the one whose body I borrowed is well."

"I'll do that," Toby promised.

"Thank you. And you'll make sure you're well."

He looked away, hard. "I'll be fine."

"Toby," she said, in a tone that made him turn back toward her. "It's important to me that you'll be well."

He opened his mouth, closed it, opened it again. "Thank you."

Another moment, and she motioned toward the shelter. "Our gear—"

"Yeah." He ran back down to the station, gathered their things hurriedly, left the sleeping bags behind so someone else could use them, and nearly forgot the toolbox in which he'd packed the scrolls but caught himself in time. Moments later he pelted back out the door and headed for the beach. Vrispaa was already there, facing the longboat.

"Toby me lad!" Long Tom shouted once they were close. "And with a wench again!"

"Of course," Toby shouted back, grinning despite himself.

The oars swept twice more, and then rose up at a barked command. Tom and Spanish Joe leapt over the side into knee-deep water to steady the boat as it grounded on the sand. "The Old Man said ye'd be here," said Tom, "and by the Black Goat's paps, here ye are. Quick, get yer scurvy bones aboard, both of ye."

They clambered aboard the bow, went aft to find thwarts to sit on. Familiar faces grinned up at Toby; further aft, Scar-Face favored him with a scowl. A shove against the bow, a sudden lurch each way as Long Tom and Spanish Joe climbed back aboard, and then Scar-Face barked an order and the oarsmen drove the longboat back away from the shore. Two more commands brought the boat around. Ahead, leads gleamed dark between masses of ice, and the masts and yards of the *Miskatonic* rose black against the distant horizon.

* * *

An hour of hard rowing brought the longboat through pack ice to the *Miskatonic*. The whole way Toby sat on the thwart in stunned silence, feeling Vrispaa's presence close beside him, trying to fit his mind around the paired thoughts that he was going to live and that she was about to leave his life forever. Once the longboat came alongside the familiar black hull, he turned to Vrispaa, motioned toward the ladder, waited for her to start climbing before shouldering his bag and following her up to the gangway.

By the time he'd climbed onto the spar deck the Terrible Old Man stood there waiting for them both. "'Tis done?" he said.

Vrispaa made her best approximation of a nod. "Yes."

"And t'other side?"

"Those who went to Mount Voormithadreth won't trouble this time again."

Coldcroft considered her for a moment, and nodded. "Aye, then, ye have my thanks, and those of a few others I might name. Ye'll go soon, I don't doubt."

"As soon as I can."

The captain turned aft, called out. "Mate Ellis!" He turned back, faced Toby. "And ye? No, ye needn't speak; go with her 'til she's gone." Then, to Ellis as he came forward: "Ye'll give Mistress Kingston-Brown whatever she needs. Gilman likewise." He turned at once and headed aft to the quarterdeck.

Ellis led them toward the aft hatch, saying, "Let me know what you'll want."

"A cabin," Vrispaa said, "with a chair, a desk, a berth. Then—" She stopped, seeing a familiar face rising from the hatch.

"And you are here!" Emmeline Grenier said, beaming. "Both of you are well? *Bien*. The others? No, they are not aboard, they wait for us on another ship. You will both want something to eat, no? I am sure Cooper can find us something."

"No," Vrispaa replied. "It's time for me to leave."

Emmeline took that in. "At once?" When Vrispaa made the same awkward nod: "Eh, well, then we will bring the machine and say our goodbye."

Toby made himself speak. "I can get that if you'll tell me where it is."

"It'll take both of us," Ellis told him. "Mistress Grenier, can you take her to the cabin aft of yours? Thank you kindly." Then, to Toby: "Give 'em your gear and come on."

Down in the hold, a watertight plastic box three feet on a side sat atop white five-gallon buckets of flour. Ellis hadn't exaggerated; Toby might have been able to carry it alone on the level but hefting it up the ladder took both their efforts. As they paused to catch their breath on the orlop deck, Toby could hear Peters' voice shouting orders and rough voices rising in a capstan shanty as the *Miskatonic* weighed anchor.

He and Ellis hauled the box down the companionway to a door Toby remembered instantly. Inside, a porthole let in daylight, showed the spartan fittings of the cabin, the berth made up with sheets and a coarse blanket, the little desk with a chair before it. Vrispaa sat in the chair, her face utterly still. She'd changed into a tee shirt and sweat pants, and left her feet bare. She looked, Toby thought, impossibly frail for someone who had saved a world.

The box went temporarily on the deck, and the foam padding inside disgorged a strange device of rods, wheels, and mirrors two feet tall and maybe half that in width and depth. A central mirror, circular and convex, didn't seem to reflect the cabin or anything in it. Toby and Ellis hefted the device onto the desk. Once it was settled, Vrispaa thanked them and began to adjust the device, twisting a rod here, adjusting the set of a wheel there. The central mirror, Toby noticed, didn't reflect her face either.

After a moment, a humming sound came from the device. Vrispaa turned to Ellis and said, "Thank you. I have what I need." He nodded and left, closing the door behind him.

"Emmeline," Vrispaa said then, glancing up at her, and then turned to face him. "Toby. Thank you. Thank you both for all you've done." He nodded, unable to speak.

"*Bon voyage*," said Emmeline, "*et merci beaucoup*."

Vrispaa turned back to the device, turned another wheel. The humming sound became a deeper drone, and something shimmered and flickered inside the central mirror. She gave the wheel a final twist, and then stiffened, eyes going wide and blank. The mirror brightened, opened up into limitless depths, then showed a momentary scene, tiny but precise, as though seen through the wrong end of a telescope. Toby stared aghast. Then the scene was gone, the mirror went dark, and the droning sound faded slowly and went silent.

A moment later the body of Wren Kingston-Brown slumped to one side. Toby lunged, got there just before Emmeline, and caught the limp nerveless shape before it could crumple to the deck. The two of them lifted the body out of the chair and carried it over to the berth, where they set it down on its back. The face that stared blindly at the ceiling belonged to a stranger.

"Did you see?" Emmeline asked him then.

Toby glanced at her, nodded, said nothing. She nodded in response, busied herself putting an extra blanket over the prostrate form on the berth. There was, Toby knew, no need to say anything further just then. She had seen, as he had, a scene three hundred million years distant, reflected briefly in the mirror of the machine: a vast dim space, a great conical body close by, and rising from it on a ridged gray stalk, an irregular yellowish globe with three huge eyes spaced around it, four slender gray stalks with flowerlike appendages rising above it, and eight greenish tentacles dangling below it. The image stayed in his mind, indelible, because he had finally glimpsed Vrispaa's own face.

* * *

He went to get Ellis, and the two of them stowed the machine back in the box and hauled it down to its place in the hold. Once it was there, Ellis said, "The Old Man says you've got your choice of berths. What's your pleasure?"

"A hammock on the main deck," said Toby. "I'd be glad for something to do, too."

Ellis nodded. "We can use a hand," he said. "Morning watch tomorrow? Good." When they got back to the orlop deck Ellis kept on climbing. Toby watched him go and then went aft to the cabin where Wren lay unconscious.

"She is well," Emmeline said. closing the door. "In twenty-four hours maybe, she will wake up. This is yours, eh?" A gesture indicated the luggage; he took his bag, shouldered it. "Now you will come with me to the galley, eat something, and not argue."

"Okay," he said. The ship had taken on a familiar rolling motion, and he knew they were under way. "You said that Phil and Leah are on a different ship."

"Yes, they are, how do you say it, out of the harm's way. We have lost so many already that I would not let those two risk themselves."

"Do you know what happened?"

He could feel her gaze on him. "I know it is over. The thing that matters, eh? What the other side wanted, they did not get, and so we still have *la Terre* to walk on. I would like to know more someday, but I think this is not the place." Then: "And I owe you the apology, *non*? I thought you might be the spy. I am ashamed to say it."

"Don't worry about it," Toby said.

She glanced at him, said nothing until they reached the galley. "But here we are. *M'sieur* Cooper? You must find something to feed us."

An amiable grunt was the only reply she got, but two big bowls of salmagundi made their appearance promptly, and two mugs of unspeakable coffee joined them a moment later. Toby wolfed down an incandescent spoonful of the salmagundi, closed his eyes for a moment and breathed a prayer of thanks to the Great Old Ones for something better than freeze-dried food. Another mouthful followed it, and then he gave Emmeline a glance with a raised eyebrow as she tucked into a bowl of her own. She said, "Waiting, it is hard work, *non?*"

That called up a bleak little laugh. "Yeah. That's why I'll be up in the rigging first thing tomorrow morning."

"*Bon.* Mate Ellis, he says you will make a good pirate. I say you will make a better scholar, but piracy, it pays better *certainement.* Maybe you can do both."

He managed a proper laugh that time. "Maybe."

They ate in companionable silence for a while, and then Toby asked, "One thing. How the hell did the Old Man know where to find us?"

"But of course the Icelanders told him." He gave her a blank look, and her eyebrows rose. "The woman, she said they were at the North Station when you and Wren arrived, and they took the little boat of theirs to go south to find help for you."

Toby forced a smile. "Okay, got it. I didn't know they were from Iceland."

"*Non?* But of course, it is your first time here. When you have been long enough in *l'Arctique*, Icelander, Dane, Norwegian, it sticks out like the lumps. But that is how."

Ss'mei, he realized. It had to be. "Do you know where they went?"

"South, I think. I did not see."

He nodded, finished his vile coffee, wondered whether he would see Ss'mei again, what form she might take then, and if he would ever know.

Afterward, while Emmeline busied herself in her cabin among her books and checked on Wren at intervals, Toby got his gear stowed in a spare sea chest, made sure the scrolls were safe, and then went up on deck and found a place to sit and stare at the gray rolling expanse of the sea. Greenland had already become a dim low presence astern, like a bank of cloud hovering low above the white line of the pack ice.

Iqqumandu, he thought: the land that the legends of a much later age called Hyperborea. Mount Voormithadreth towering over the great central valley of the Ambar River, the hills and plains of Tscho Vulpanomi descending from stark gray mountains to the eastern sea, the little village of Ulut huddled between ice and salt water in the last years of a vanishing kingdom—

He'd been there, and Hyperborea could never again be just a matter of words to him.

He watched the coast fade slowly from sight, as memories tumbled past him in the raw wind: memories of Vrispaa, those above all, but also memories of things he'd seen and people he'd met, the ones who weren't going home again and the ones who'd survived.

He ate dinner with the larboard watch, helped haul dishes and tankards back down to the galley, spent a little more time on deck and then turned in early. He expected to sleep straight through the night, but when the midnight watch was called up and the pirates around him pulled on their coats and shoes and stumbled up the ladder onto the spar deck, he woke and couldn't get back to sleep. After a while, annoyed at himself, he slipped out of the hammock, changed into clothes he'd gotten from the common store, and set off for the orlop deck in search of a cup of coffee from the galley. He'd just reached the ladder when a voice with a thick Australian accent called out of the dimness behind him: "Hello?"

Toby glanced that way, startled. One of the cabin doors was open, and he thought he knew the dim shape that leaned out of it. "Ms. Kingston-Brown?"

He could just make out her face. "That's me. Where the bloody hell am I?"

"You're aboard a tall ship off the coast of Greenland," said Toby. She took that in, nodded slowly, looking dazed.

"Give me a minute," Toby said, "and I'll wake up Dr. Grenier—"

Her face lit up. "Emmeline's here?"

"Right next door." He went to the cabin door, rapped on it, paused, rapped again. A muffled voice from within said something in French. "Emmeline?" he called. "She's awake."

A moment passed and then the door opened, revealing Emmeline in a nightgown and slippers. She blinked, looked past Toby, and burst out, "You are up so soon, Wren? But to see you yourself again, that is very much welcome. You will want water, or perhaps coffee?"

That got the first definite expression on the dazed face. "Coffee, please. Black."

"I was on my way to get some," said Toby, and went down the ladder to the orlop deck. Seeing the body that had been Vrispaa's with another person in it unnerved him. Get used to it, he told himself, but the words seemed frail.

He poured three cups, got some sugar and creamer packets for Emmeline, and carried them aft and then up the ladder. The glow of the porthole in Wren's room, spilling out through the open door, guided him. "Here you go," he said once he got to the room. To Wren: "I'm afraid it's not very good."

Wren, sitting on the berth, took her cup with a nod and a mumbled word of thanks, and held it in both hands. She sipped it, made a face, sipped more. Emmeline, on the chair, took hers and beamed at him. Before either of them could invite him to join the conversation he smiled and hurried away to drink his coffee in the galley.

He crawled back into his hammock an hour or so before the larboard watch went below, succeeded after a while in getting back to sleep. His dreams were vague and troubled, but Vrispaa did not appear in any of them.

* * *

The next morning he was up with the rest of the larboard watch in time to down a bowl of burgoo and a cup of unspeakable coffee before scrambling up on deck. The wind was raw and gusty, and shreds of cloud hurtled by overhead in a way that made him think a storm was on its way. As the morning watch went past, the wind rose, and Ellis set the larboard watch aloft to shorten sail. By the time the dog watches were over, the wind whipped spray from the crests of foaming waves, rain hammered down, and the *Miskatonic* had only half her sails raised to the wind. "'Tis well," the captain said to Ellis as the two of them watched from the quarterdeck and Toby stood at the wheel nearby. "T'other side won't dare fly in such weather."

True as that was, the storm made for long wretched hours on deck, for it blew out of the east, and east was the way the Terrible Old Man meant to go. That meant tacking, which in turn meant hauling on lines over and over again to pull the yards this way and then that, as the *Miskatonic* zigzagged across the sea into the teeth of the wind. Four hours of that left Toby winded and shivering, with a bowl of salmagundi, a shot of rum, and a few hours of sleep to help him gather his strength again before the bell called him back on deck to repeat the process.

Day followed day: six days in all, though it felt like six lifetimes before the storm finally blew itself out and a light wind out of the north gave them respite. Miserable though it was at the time, Toby was glad afterwards, for the labor on deck and in the rigging kept him too busy to think until he'd had time to get used to the fact that Vrispaa was gone.

He'd expected her absence to leave a gap like a bleeding wound in his life. The gap was there but the rawness and the pain were not. Standing at the wheel one bitter morning while the wind hissed past out of the north and clouds raced by in high thin shreds, Toby brooded over that, and finally understood part of it. There had always been three hundred million years between them, even in those moments when they had been closest, and he'd been certain once before that she was not just lost to him but dead with the others. Now she was safe, back in her own body and her own age of the world. Now, he thought, now I can finally let go—and wondered as he said it just what it was that he was letting go.

Days passed. Another, briefer storm blew by, and thereafter the *Miskatonic* headed east on light winds. One day Ellis waved him over and said, "Tomorrow, Gilman. You'll leave with the two ladies."

Toby nodded, uncertain.

"You're off once third watch is done," the mate said. "May as well catch up on your sleep." Before Toby could respond, he turned and walked away.

The last watches went by without incident, but the whole time Toby could feel another gap widening: the one that separated him from Coldcroft's crew. He was living and they were dead, and though they'd hauled on lines, sung shanties, and faced gunfire together, he would go on to the rest of his life and they would go back into the Terrible Old Man's glass bottles until Great Cthulhu rose from the deeps. That stung, but there again he knew he had to let go.

The third watch ended, and he pelted down the ladder with the rest of the larboard watch. Cooper served up one more kettle of salmagundi, and the watch sat and ate and warmed themselves. Minutes passed before Jack said, "So ye leave us on the morrow."

"Yeah," said Toby. Then, because it had to be said: "I'm glad to have known all of you. Living or dead, you're some of the best men I've ever met."

"Kind of ye, Toby me lad," said Tom. "And as for ye—why, I'll go so far as sayin' that someday ye might even make a fair sailor."

That called up a laugh and broke the tension for the moment, and a bottle of rum made its appearance and filled glasses. Toby downed his pirate-style, in a gulp, and managed not to choke on it. More laughter followed, and coarse jokes; the rum went round another time; and then the pirates finished their meals and so did Toby, and they all went to sling their hammocks.

The others, he thought then: the ones that were living and the ones that weren't. It hurt to remember the ones who'd become friends of his and then died in a hail of Radiant bullets, but it helped a little to think of Phil and Emmeline, and especially of Leah Sargent. Recalling her face turning up toward his, her arms and legs wrapped around him, sparked a pointless reaction. He managed to fall asleep anyway, and slept hard for many hours.

He was up for the dawn watch, watched the sun slide around the edge of the horizon from northeast to east. One final cup of Cooper's nameless and blasphemous coffee warmed him and ripped away the last vestiges of sleep. Finally Long Tom came to call him up from the galley, and he followed the pirate up the ladder to the spar deck.

Morning spread bleak across the sky. Miles off to starboard, the white flat-topped cone of a volcano rose up above the gray turbulence of the sea, gleaming in sunlight. Closer, a battered freighter with cranes amidships sat at anchor.

"Thar ye be," said Long Tom. "Jan Mayen Land. The Old Man wants the three of ye aboard yon ship as soon as can be."

Toby turned to face him, fumbling for words to frame what he wanted to say, but the pirate grinned and said, "Best fetch yer gear afore Mate Ellis tosses it over the side."

"Tom," said Toby, and then all at once knew what needed saying. "I don't know when it'll happen any more than you do, but if Great Cthulhu wakes up and I'm still around, come by and I'll stand you a beer."

For an instant he could see the ragged hope and longing in the pirate's eyes, and then Tom laughed and slapped Toby's shoulder. "By Dagon," he said, "I'll do that if I can." He turned, headed to the longboats. Toby watched him go, left other farewells unsaid.

The steps of the ladder felt smooth as old memories as Toby hurried belowdecks, went to his sea chest, packed the box of scrolls and the rest of his things in the crumpled orange duffel. A pause, a moment's recollection of what waited for him across half a mile of gray water, and he skinned out of the pirate gear he was wearing, left it behind for the common store, and pulled on the clothing he'd worn from Mount Voormithadreth to North Station.

A few minutes later he was up on deck again. Emmeline was there already, bundled against the cold wind, and Wren came to join them not long thereafter. By then the longboat was already in the water and crewed, and soon enough the duffels were tied to a line and lowered down to the boat.

Once they were stowed and the line hauled back, Toby went to the ladder and swung over the side. He happened to glance aft just then, and saw the Terrible Old Man standing on the quarterdeck, watching. Toby raised a hand in farewell. Coldcroft met his gaze squarely and then nodded, acknowledging, and Toby lowered the hand again and made his way down the ladder to the longboat.

* * *

The three of them settled on the aft thwarts. Scar-Face, who had charge of the longboat as usual, barked an order, and the oarsmen on the port side pushed off from the *Miskatonic*. The oars found their rhythm and the longboat danced with the waves, skimming across the water. The freighter loomed up ahead until it blotted out the white presence of Jan Mayen Land. Not until they were almost up against it did Toby think to glance toward the bow, and found himself looking at familiar words: *MV Arkham.*

Then they were alongside the freighter, and a ladder came rattling down, steel cable rather than hempen rope, with metal bars. Toby motioned to the others. Wren went up first, and Emmeline followed more slowly. Toby turned to Scar-Face. The pirate met his gaze, motioned to the ladder with a quick hard motion of his chin. Toby nodded, realizing that there really was nothing more to say, and started up the ladder.

Moments later he hauled himself up over the gunwale onto the main deck of the *Arkham.* Two of the freighter's crewmen were busy lowering a cargo net from a davit to haul up what luggage they had. Just past them, Phil Dyer stood talking with Emmeline. Wren stood nearby, watching in silence, and Leah was a little further off. She glanced toward Toby suddenly as he reached the deck, colored, looked away, and then looked toward him again.

Before either of them could do anything else, Phil detached himself from the conversation, crossed to the gunwale and took one of Toby's hands in a firm grip. "Thank God you're okay. We were sweating bullets there."

"Thanks," said Toby. "That's what we did when we saw the station."

"Oh, we got out in plenty of time. The moment we figured out what had happened and where you and Wren were going, we ran for the boats and got Captain Coldcroft to put to sea. The charges the Radiance placed in the ice dam went off about fifteen minutes later. If we'd waited any longer—" A shrug dismissed the issue.

"At least the omegasaurs are safe," Toby said.

"No argument there." With an expression that was less than half a smile: "I've decided to give them different names: *Omegasaurus elioti* and *Omegasaurus bishopi.*"

Toby nodded, catching the references to Susan and Orrin. "Thank you."

"It seemed like a good idea." Then: "But we got aboard in time—just. The *Miskatonic* was halfway to Iceland before we could do anything but ride the *jokulhlaup*."

"Do you know what happened?" Toby asked him. "With us, I mean."

"The world's still here," said Phil. "I'll want to hear the details sometime soon." He glanced to see the cargo net came back up, and said, "Okay, let's head in. We've had one storm after another, and dollars will get you doughnuts it's going to start snowing again before long." He turned to Toby. "We've got your duffel from the station, of course. If you need anything else, let me know."

Toby let himself follow the others in through the hatch and up the long familiar stair. He felt Leah's gaze on him more than once. By the time they reached the main companionway on the bridge deck, he'd also watched the others long enough to know that Wren wanted solitude, Emmeline wanted to make sure she got it, and Phil wanted Emmeline. A little disjointed conversation took care of the details, and the others headed aft, leaving Toby and Leah standing there facing each other in the harsh glare of the shipboard light. The deep rumbling note of the engines came up from below as the *Arkham* got under way.

"I'm glad you're okay," she said.

He could see past her guarded smile, past the uncertainty in her eyes, to what surged up beneath that, something too primal to be named with bland sentimental words. "So am I," he said with an uncertain smile of his own. Then: "I'm glad you got out of the station in time."

A little of the guarded quality left her expression, leaving the smile unsteady. "Thank you," she said. "Come on, I'll show you where your cabin is." Her hand brushed his as she led him aft along the companionway. He took hold of it, felt it curve around his fingers.

He knew exactly what was going to happen when they got to the cabin, and he was right. She led him to a bleak metal door and turned toward him, and her smile came unraveled to show vulnerabilities he hadn't expected. He opened the door and motioned to invite her in; she smiled again, less guardedly, and went through the door into the unlit cabin. The dim glow through the curtain over the cabin's one porthole provided just enough light for both of them to find their way. He closed the door; a moment's indecision, and then he reached out to her, offering; she took his hands in hers, and then flung her arms around him and raised her face for his kiss.

The kiss ended, and she drew back, smiled, pushed down her pants and let them fall to the floor. The rest of her clothes followed, and by then he'd struggled out of his as well. She backed up to the berth, and he lifted her up onto it and joined her there. Kisses, caresses, and low half-muffled cries followed, rising up toward the moment when he slid into her and cried out her name. Her legs wrapped around his, and she clung to him and writhed as their hips found a rhythm and took both of them to a half-familiar place on the far side of passion.

* * *

Afterwards, she lay on her back and he lay half atop her, his face resting in the curve where shoulder flowed into breast. He'd pulled the covers over them both, worrying that she'd be chilled by the cold air in the cabin. Somehow the warmth of her body didn't make him feel stifled, and all at once he could imagine himself nestling down against her and falling asleep, not just once but night after night. That startled him enough to summon up a little shaken laugh.

"What is it?" she murmured.

"You're right," he said after a moment. "We've got to stop doing this."

She laughed, too, and said, "Yeah." Silence returned, minutes passed, and then, in a quiet tentative voice, she said, "Or not."

Toby pondered that for a while, as the muffled rhythm of her pulse murmured against one ear and her body comforted and enticed him, more real for once than the whispering ghosts of his past. She wasn't Vrispaa, but Vrispaa was three hundred million years lost to him, and the strangeness in Vrispaa that had called to him so strongly meant less to him just then than the warmth and the longing he felt when he was with Leah. "Yeah," he said finally. "Or not."

Whole worlds circled around that phrase, and he knew what it would demand of him, what he would have to risk. He drew in a deep breath, sat up, forced out the words. "In that case there's—something you need to know. It—it'll be easier if I turn on the light and show you."

Leah sat up too, and for some reason pulled at the covers so they hid her still-stockinged feet. "Okay," she said, uncertain.

He reached for the light switch, clicked it on. Muted glare from the fixture in the ceiling streamed over his naked body, hers. He raised his arms, tensed the muscles that gapped open his gill slits, made himself look at Leah's face as he did so. Her eyes went round, as he'd expected, and so did her mouth. "Yeah," he said, his voice unsteady.

She tried to say something, failed.

"Yeah," he repeated. "I'm not really human."

"But—" She swallowed visibly, then: "But why did you say that you'd never heard of Innsmouth?"

If she'd suddenly sprouted feathers, Toby would have been less surprised. He burst out: "What the hell is this business about Innsmouth? I never heard of it before I came on this expedition, and every time I turn around somebody asks me about it."

Leah took that in, and a silence passed. "Toby," she said then, "where did your family come from?"

"I told you already," he replied, baffled and a little hurt. "A town up in the Catskills called Lefferts Corners."

"No." Certainty showed in the brown eyes. "Before then."

It startled him that she'd guessed that there was a place before then, but he knew there was no direction he could go but onward. It took more of an effort to say the words than it had taken him to show her his gills, but he did it anyway. "A place that doesn't exist any more. A town in New Jersey—" He choked, forced the words out. "Pine Harbor."

Her hand went to her mouth. "Oh Father Dagon."

That got a sudden shaken laugh from him. "My grand-mother used to say that all the time." Then the implications sank in. "You know about—about Pine Harbor?"

"Everyone from Innsmouth does," said Leah. "You know who Daniel Marsh was, right?" When Toby nodded, startled that she knew the name: "He came from Innsmouth. So did the people who went with him. Toby, I was born in Innsmouth. Nobody lives there any more, but that's where humans and Deep Ones first met and married in North America." His eyes went round as he realized what she was saying, and she took his hands in hers and said, "Yes. I've got family on both sides of the shore too. We all do. We—we didn't know that anybody from Pine Harbor had survived."

"Fourteen," he said. "Fourteen got into the water in time. Just—just fourteen."

"Is there anyone else—"

"No." Toby clenched his eyes shut, and his voice went thin and high-pitched. "I—I thought I was the—the only one left in the whole world. I—" His voice guttered out as the old familiar terror rose up in him.

Leah seemed to know what to do. She reached for him, drew him close and held him against her bare body. The fear rose and rose, and he had nothing left to fight it with—and then he realized that he didn't need to fight it any more, and slumped against Leah, shuddering and gasping, as the terror soared up to infinite distance and dispersed at last.

He squeezed his eyes shut, opened them again. One of Leah's breasts was pressed against the side of his face. He turned his head a little, kissed it, and realized all at once why she'd felt so comfortable to lie close to, right from the first. He'd been so worried that she might notice his salt scent that he'd managed not to notice hers.

"I can't even imagine what that must have been like," she said in a quiet voice. "Being all alone like that."

"You've got family?"

"Oh yeah. Mom and Dad, Grandma and Grandpa Sargent and Grandma Eliot, two younger brothers, one older sister, four uncles, five aunts, three first cousins, so many second and third cousins I'd have to work it out on paper, and a brand new baby niece I got to see for the first time just before we left for Greenland." She paused, then: "I'd like you to meet them."

"I want to meet them," Toby told her. She bent and kissed the top of his head. He couldn't find the energy just then to raise his face to hers, contented himself with kissing her breast again. That drew his attention to another detail of her body. "You don't have gills."

"No," she admitted. "None of my family does, unfortunately—but there's a reason I've never shown you my feet."

"Will you?" he asked, and she laughed and slid them out from under the covers. She'd kept her socks on, the only stitch of cloth she had anywhere on her body just then. It took her a moment to pull off the socks and reveal the webbed and pointed toes under them. They were, Toby thought, the most beautiful feet he'd ever seen.

CHAPTER 12

THE TWO SIDES OF THE SHORE

An hour or so later, when the sun was a pallid blur to westward and the *Arkham* drove south beneath faint flickering stars, the two of them sat on the bridge deck. Jan Mayen Land was a dim white presence astern. From somewhere down on the main deck, the shrill voice of *la cabrette noire* rose up in a slow sad melody Emmeline had written herself: *Regret du Groenland*, she'd named it, "Greenland Lament" in English. The sound of the pipes blended with the rush and crash of waves and the bass note of the *Arkham*'s engines in a music that seemed just then to give voice to the Arctic itself.

A gibbous moon stood high in the heavens to port. For some reason Toby didn't pretend to understand, that latter detail made a difference, and Leah positioned herself where the moonlight could fall on her. She had a battered spiral-bound notebook and a round silver plate like an old-fashioned mirror, and she'd handed Toby a silver bowl fashioned like a miniature cauldron, half full of water. Once a few stray clouds slid away and bared the moon, she angled the silver plate to catch the moonlight and began drawing an intricate pattern on the plate with the tip of one finger.

"Get the moon so you see it reflected in the water," she said then. "Watch it, and let me know when you see something besides the moon."

That made less than no sense to Toby, but he got the silver bowl positioned so that the moon's partial disk hovered in the water, and watched it, adjusting the angle of the bowl as the ship rolled ponderously beneath him. Minutes passed and nothing happened, but then all at once a blotch showed on one side of the moon's reflection. It slid down, tracing a line, then drew a curve and two more short lines. "There's a letter," he said, and when she gave him a questioning look: "Like a backward D with two crossbars."

She beamed. "Thank you." Her finger drew more patterns on the silver plate. Time passed, and Toby watched her, tried to keep his mind on what they were doing and not let it drift off into dazed contemplations of the lines of her body or the movements of her hand.

"Okay," she said after something like a quarter hour. "Now I'll need the bowl, and—" She opened the notebook, pulled a pen from within her coat. A few moments later, staring into the bowl of water, she copied down one strange character after another into the notebook. When that was done, she traced one more pattern on the silver disk, watched the moon in the water for a few more moments, then let out a ragged breath. "Okay," she said again. Then, turning to Toby: "Your family never talked about sending messages through the moonlight?"

He shook his head. "Not that I ever heard." Then: "That's how you got a message to the *Miskatonic*, isn't it?"

"Emmeline knows a lot about witchcraft," Leah said. "I didn't know for sure that she had a mirror and a bowl with her, but I thought it was worth trying, and the third time we had a good clear night with the moon up, I reached her."

"And—your family." When she nodded: "What did they say?"

By way of answer she stood, reached out a hand to help him to his feet. "Let's get inside," she said. "I ought to have time to fill you in before dinner."

Back in his cabin, they shed shoes and coats and sat on the berth. "I talked to them after we got aboard the *Arkham*,"

Leah said, "to let them know that I was okay, and then again to let them know the mission was a success. Mostly this time I wanted to tell them about you. They're amazed that I managed to find someone from Pine Harbor, they're sad to hear that you're the only survivor, and they really want to meet you."

"Did you tell them about us?"

"Not in so many words, but I think Mom figured it out. That's part of why they want to meet you." She met his uncertain look with a smile. "Don't worry about it."

He tried to follow her advice when they went to dinner in the officer's mess. It ached at first to sit down at the galley table and remember the people who were gone forever, but that faded into familiarity soon enough. The sheer banality of the chicken and dumplings helped, so different from Cooper's salmagundis. It helped, too, that Leah was with him, that Emmeline was her usual talkative self and Phil seemed content to sit back, eat, and listen. All those things made it easier to deal with the absences, and with Wren.

He'd seen little of her on the *Miskatonic*, and so hadn't had the chance to get used to the change. Now it was impossible for him to ignore. Every movement she made, every one of the few words she spoke, shouted at him that Vrispaa was gone and a woman he didn't know had taken her place. That was hard to deal with, but it made Leah's presence beside him all the more comforting, and by the end of the meal he'd begun to get used to the stranger in a familiar body who sat across the table from him.

As the meal wound to a close, Phil turned to Leah and said, "Can you spare Toby for a little while?" Leah blinked and then started to laugh, and Toby turned red. "Sure," Leah said, leaned over, kissed his cheek and got up.

As she turned to go, Wren said, "And that means time for me to go walkabout too, right?" She grinned. "No worries." She stood and followed Leah to the door. Toby tried not to let himself show it, but the grin left him shaken. It wasn't until then that he realized that he'd never seen Vrispaa smile.

Once they were gone, Phil motioned: shall we? Toby got up, so did Emmeline and Phil, and they left the galley and went to a cabin door further aft. Toby expected a little cramped space like the one he'd been assigned, but Phil's was larger, with two portholes, a table and folding chairs. Phil waved him to a chair, and they all sat around the table.

"Leah and Wren don't know?" Toby asked.

"Leah knew most of it all along," said Phil. "I gave her the whole story once we knew for sure that the Radiance had failed. Wren knows very little, and we figured it was safer to leave it that way."

"And it will be easier for her," Emmeline said, "if she is not the only one on the outside. You can tell Leah later, eh?"

"When you're ready," said Phil. Toby drew in a breath, started talking of Bill Allen's treachery and death, the flight to Mount Voormithadreth, the journey down into the heart of the mountain, the things they'd seen and done there, and the grace with which Vrispaa had set off the trap her people had laid for the Radiance three quarters of a million years before it was born.

It wasn't the complete story, not by any means. He kept his promise to Ss'mei, and left out any reference to the serpent folk; he kept his promise to Vrispaa, and left out the details that might give any human the least hint concerning the route to the Deep of Abhoth; he said nothing about the mound of treasure the shoggoths and voormis guarded, though he mentioned a few old scrolls he'd found, perhaps looted from a royal tomb; and even before he'd guessed what would happen between him and Leah, he'd promised himself never to breathe a word of the bond that had grown between him and Vrispaa. Even lacking those details, though, there was plenty to tell, and more than an hour slipped past before he finished and asked if they had more questions.

"I imagine you have some questions of your own," Phil said then.

"Well, yes," said Toby. He tried to marshal the uncertainties that surrounded him into neat ranks, gave up. "You said the Radiance sent people to Leng and to some other places. Do you know what happened with that?"

Phil glanced at Emmeline, who beamed and said, "But of course. The news, it is very good. The ones that went to Leng, to go to *le monastère*, they did not reach it, and not many of them came back to Laos. The ones that went to Uganda, they were not so lucky, they found what they went to find, or rather they were found."

Toby gave her a puzzled look. "What found them?"

"*Les Pêcheurs du Dehors*," she said. "The people who live by the lake, they said—oh, how do you say it? *Philippe, aide-moi*."

"Clothing and bones," Phil said. "That's what the Fishers from Outside leave: clothing in a heap, all of it turned neatly inside out—even the boots and shoes—and then bones, absolutely clean, in another heap exactly eleven hundred meters due east. It's always like that and nobody has the least idea why." Toby winced. "And the force they sent to Antarctica didn't come back either," Phil went on. "Nobody's sure why. There were shoggoths waiting for them, but the Radiance force didn't get to where the shoggoths were. We don't know why. They headed south across the ice and nobody ever saw them again."

In the silence that followed, Toby thought of the Lowermost Gate and the drowned men he'd seen there. That brought another question to mind: "What happened to the men Captain Coldcroft took prisoner at the station?"

"He left them behind to drown in the *jokulhlaup*," said Phil. "There's very good reason he's called the Terrible Old Man."

Toby nodded after a moment. Phil pulled out a hip flask, poured a shot into the silver cup that capped it, and handed it to Toby, who took it and tipped it back, feeling the golden fire of it searing its way down his throat. "Thank you," he said then, and handed back the silver cup.

* * *

Days later, as the *Arkham* drove south through heavy weather, Toby and Leah sat on opposite ends of their berth—his, technically, but she'd spent every night there since he'd come aboard and he had no interest in having her find any other place to sleep. Rain out of a dark sky drummed on the porthole and the deck wallowed and rolled beneath them. His feet were a few inches from her bare belly and the tuft of dark hair between her legs; her feet were just outside his thighs, in easy reach of his hands. Her fingers probed the scar tissue around his mutilated toes, and his hands moved more aimlessly over her delicate pointed toes and the webs between them. Feet made a convenient distraction from the thing that was on both of their minds.

"These are pretty bad," Leah said. "Does it hurt when you walk on them?"

"I'm used to it," he replied.

She winced. "That's what I was afraid of. I know witches who might be able to help, but that's a guess, nothing more." She searched the crippled toes, and he let out a ragged sigh as old tensions unraveled.

"I had webbed fingers when I was younger," she said then. "The webs had to go when I decided to head for college, of course, but the person who did the surgery was good, and it only hurt for a few weeks." Glancing up at him: "I still miss them, though."

"Why'd you decide to go to college?"

"Nobody from Innsmouth ever had that chance," she said, "not for years and years and years. Then a rich family down in Kingsport that worships the Great Old Ones made money available for scholarships. Everyone agreed that I should be one of the ones to go, and I was—" She shrugged. "Starry-eyed, I suppose. I wanted to become an archeologist and find the lost secrets of the Great Old Ones. So I let them cut the webs off my fingers, put in two years at Aylesbury Community College, finished my BA at Amherst, and then went to Miskatonic convinced that I'd be able to get a tenure track position somewhere close to home." With a little laugh: "I don't have to tell you how well that went."

"Not a bit," he said. "I've got no idea what I'm going to do when we get back to port. Well, except—"

He stopped, and the thing they were trying to avoid hovered between them.

The two of them had become a source of reliable amusement to the remaining members of the expedition, Toby knew, though that fact didn't trouble him enough to want to change the way he behaved toward Leah or to ask her to change the way she behaved toward him. Phil simply sat back and smiled, Wren watched them with a raised eyebrow that Toby was sure covered bleaker emotions—did she miss the husband she'd left when Vrispaa took over her body? That was what it looked like, certainly. Emmeline, though, took to making sly jokes at their expense, mostly said at the table in the galley just after they'd left it, when they were still close enough to hear but too far to respond without embarrassment. That evening, when Toby and Leah had finished dinner and headed for the door, Emmeline turned to Phil and said, "But it is a splendid idea, very original, and I hope, how do you say it, it catches up, or off, or whatever it catches. First the honeymoon cruise, and then afterward the marriage, n'est çe pas?"

That was the thing that hovered between them, two hours later, as Toby and Leah sat there looking at each other. "Except," said Leah, with a little uncertain smile.

"Yeah." He'd turned the idea around and around in his mind, and every time it had come up the same way. He gathered up his courage and asked, "Do you want to get married?"

She opened her mouth, shut it again, opened it and in a sudden squeaking voice said, "Yes." Then, after drawing in a breath: "More than anything else in the world."

"Okay," he said. "We can do that." Then, hoping she would remember the Hyperborean words: "*M'aqqat ish'djampa.*"

She let out a different squeak, and all at once Toby had to deal with the far from unpleasant experience of having a young, attractive, and entirely naked woman fling herself into his arms, kissing him over and over again. She drew back to ask, "You mean it?"

"Of course I do," he said, or tried to; the second half of the sentence got muffled by another kiss. By the time she drew back a second time, though, he was reddening. "That wasn't a very romantic proposal, was it?"

"I don't care," said Leah. "It was a one hundred per cent Toby Gilman proposal, and that's exactly the kind I want. I've wanted that since not very long after we met."

He blinked, processing that.

"That's why I was so brittle around you at first," she went on. "If you'd asked me to marry you back when we were both at the station, I'd have been angry with you, and angry with myself, and Mother Hydra alone knows what I would have said—" Shoulders sketched a shrug. "But I would have ended up saying yes."

"Seriously?"

Her smile confirmed it before she said, "Seriously."

"I wish I'd known," he told her. Then, teasing: "Are you angry now?"

"Oh, furious," she said, and kissed him again.

Later, he lay on his back and she lay half atop him with her head nestled on his shoulder, blankets over them but neither of them quite asleep. *Aqqat*, he thought. The love of the body, the love that's about marriage, family, home. He couldn't imagine that between him and Vrispaa, the differences between them were too vast, but it was easy to imagine sharing a home and raising a family with Leah—in fact, it was hard for him to imagine anything else just then.

Aqqat, he thought again. His mind reflexively traced the word back to its archaic roots and forward through two thousand years of Hyperborean inscriptions, but those details meant less to him at that moment than the emotions Leah's presence roused in him. He remembered the way he'd crumpled against her and the way she'd held him, and repeated the word again: *aqqat*. *Nen* also, he thought, no question there's *nen*; the soft supple curves of her body against his, the little half-sleeping movements she made, reminded him of what they'd done a half hour earlier and what they'd doubtless do again come morning; but something surrounded those bursts of frantic passion and gave them a meaning, and that was *aqqat*—or maybe it was love. He turned the English word over in his mind, pondering it.

That stirred other thoughts, and one of them made him draw in a sudden sharp breath. Leah's eyes blinked open. "What is it?"

"Something I should have thought of a while ago." Making himself go on: "Is it going to be a problem if you get pregnant before we're married?"

He could feel a smile shift her face. "Mother Hydra, no, not at all. That's one of the good things about belonging to a fertility religion." After a moment: "If we weren't going to get married it would be a problem, but as it is—" She glanced up at him. "The minute they see me again, my grandmothers are going to start pestering me about great-grandchildren, and if one's already on the way that'll make them happy." She was silent for a while, then went on in a more tentative voice. "How do you feel about that?"

"About kids?" When she nodded: "I'm still trying to get my head around the idea that I'm going to be part of a family." A silence came and went, edged by the drumbeat of rain against the porthole glass and the deep murmur of the ship's engines. "But I'm good with it. Maybe more than just good with it. And it kind of comes with the territory, doesn't it?"

That earned him a laugh. "Yes, it does." Then: "What was the thing you talked about at the station, the string that connects families or something like that?"

"*Iqqibal shalsholi*," he said. "The cord that ties the generations together."

"That's the one." Leah's arms tightened around him, and he kissed her hair. The cord was a metaphor, so he told himself, but he could feel it, spun tight by their little movements, reaching back further than Hyperborea and forward toward a future he could not see.

* * *

More days passed. The twilight blur of an arctic autumn changed to days and nights as the Arctic Circle fell behind the *Arkham*'s stern. On one of those days Toby spent an hour or so in Phil's cabin with Phil, Emmeline, and Leah, discussing the scrolls in the scroll cases.

"These are a real find," said Phil. "Have you identified the texts?"

"I've just glanced at the opening line of each scroll," Toby admitted. "*Pthagon* parchment's pretty resilient, but I didn't want to do more before I could get them properly curated. Each one starts with a line of heptameter verse, and none of them are lines I've read before, I'm sure of that. It looks like epic poetry that hasn't survived anywhere else."

Phil let out a low whistle, and Emmeline said, "But this is splendid! You will have something else to publish, *non?*"

"Can I even admit that I have these?" Toby asked.

"Sure," said Phil. "It won't be safe to let on that you were inside Mount Voormithadreth, but we can agree on a different provenance, something from the area that got washed away by the *jokulhlaup*. Let's work out a plausible way that they could be in this kind of condition and get them curated and photographed at Miskatonic, and they become one of the expedition's big discoveries." Grinning: "I want to see the expressions on some faces when they hear about this."

Toby thought about that more than once, in pensive moments when sleep was far off. Though months had passed since he'd sailed from Boston, he knew better than to think that his job prospects had changed noticeably over so short a time. One afternoon he spent a while trying to come up with topics for more papers he could write and publish—a flurry of papers, he thought, might get him a second hearing with one of the programs that had turned him down earlier—but his mind kept circling around the strange little ivory carving, the circle of skeletons beside the treasures of the Hyperborean kings, Ss'mei's troubling tale. And we still don't know why the Norse settlers and the Tuniit died, he thought. Nobody does—

Except the Radiance. The thought chilled him.

A few days later a dim gray edge of land broke the sweep of the horizon to starboard—Newfoundland, Phil announced at breakfast—but it was gone the next morning. Now and then they passed other ships tracing their own lonely routes across the ocean, but far more often than not the *Arkham* met only sea birds, porpoises, and the occasional whale.

He wondered more than once whether they'd make it to land before the Radiance caught up with them. That was on other minds, too. "The official story," Phil Dyer said one morning over breakfast, "is that the *Arkham* dropped off the expedition at Tornarssukalik Inlet, went back to Reykjavik to pick up another cargo, took it to Hamburg, carried more freight to a dozen places along the Norwegian coast, then loaded up with cargo bound for Boston and headed home. After we're ashore, we can spread the story that the *Arkham*'s radioman picked up our distress call from North Station and sent a boat to rescue us. Until then—" He shrugged. "It's a gamble. Nobody's breathed a word about the fact that we're on board, but we just don't know what the other side might be able to figure out."

"And once we get to land?" Wren asked.

"Once you're back in the media spotlight, they won't dare try anything too obvious. They can't risk publicity any more than we can. The rest of us have other ways of staying safe." He glanced at Toby, then turned to Leah. "You two'll be going to stay with your family, right?"

Leah nodded. "I've already been in touch."

That got her a puzzled look from Wren. "I thought we were keeping radio silence."

"This wasn't by radio," said Leah, smiling.

Wren glanced at her, then at Emmeline, then at Leah again. "Okay." Then, with the first unsteadiness Toby had heard in her voice since Vrispaa's departure: "Is there any way you could get a message to my husband? If someone on the other end of—of whatever you're doing could call or email him, to let him know I'm all right—"

Leah glanced at Phil, who gestured his assent. "If the sky clears up," she said, "so I can see the Moon before we get to port, I can try that. If you can write down the message you want me to send, that would help."

"I can do that," Wren said.

"Does he know?" Leah asked then. "About what happened to you, I mean."

"We talked it over before I accepted their offer. He wasn't happy about it—" A smile creased her face; it seemed alien to Toby. "But he knows I need my adventures, and he was really sweet about it all."

"If you don't mind my asking," Toby said then, "do you remember where you were?"

She glanced at him, and just for an instant an expression that echoed one of Vrispaa's crossed her face. "I'm not supposed to say anything about that," she said. "That was part of the bargain." Then, with a little smile, she nodded.

"Let me know what you want my family to say to your husband," Leah told her then, "and I'll let them know as soon as we get a clear night."

"Thank you." The smile faltered. "I hope he's been able to deal with all the time we had to spend apart."

The next two days were gray and wet, but the following night the clouds tore open and Leah was able to get the message sent. "Mom wanted to know how you were doing," she told Toby later, as they sat in their cabin. "And whether you had any plans once we get back."

"What did you tell her?"

"That you're in the same situation I am," said Leah, with a shrug and a little uncertain smile. "A doctorate that ought to qualify you for a professorship, except that nobody's hiring—and now we're both back in the job market months before we expected, and with only a few publications each from the expedition."

He winced, nodded.

"Don't worry about it," she said. "When we got the scholarships that sent me and the others to college, we all knew it was a gamble—that we might end up as schoolteachers or priestesses who had a little more education than usual. It was worth it. I just hope I can find a way to keep up with my field in my spare time, or something."

"Archeology's a pretty specialized field, isn't it?"

"Oh, it's worse than that. My field's ceramics—all those bits of pottery we were sorting were my bailiwick. My dissertation was on pottery spindle whorls from the preglacial northern Atlantic basin. I know how dull that sounds, but you can figure out an astonishing amount from their size and weight and wear patterns—what kind of fibers they spun, how they worked them—and you combine that with what you get from stone or ceramic loom weights and a few other sources of information—" She caught herself, stopped. "I'm sorry. I don't mean to drone on."

"You weren't droning," said Toby. "I don't know much of anything about ceramics, but what you're saying sounds like some of what I do." He sat back against the wall behind the berth. "Tell me more." In response to her dubious look: "No, I mean it."

It took a little more coaxing, but before long she was talking about potsherds and ceramic styles, sketching out how pottery had spread with agriculture and crude hieroglyphic writing out of the first human civilization in Nemedis, how the Hyperboreans and the other preglacial peoples of the Atlantic littoral had adapted all three to their own needs. She told him about the colorful glazed wares of the Commoriom period, the sturdy gray and golden stoneware of Uzuldaroum, the exquisite thin-walled vessels of Hyperborea's last flowering under the dynasty of Cerngoth, and the stark brown utilitarian ware of the exile communities in Atlantis, sketching out how the ebb and flow of styles and vessel types traced the whole history of Hyperborea. The whole time Toby listened and nodded, and thought about how what she was saying blended in unexpected ways with the linguistic evidence he'd studied.

She stopped abruptly, glanced at him. "Don't you dare tell me you're not bored."

"Deal with it," he told her, grinning. "I'm wondering whether the words they used for pottery track the changes you were just talking about."

"Track in what way?" she asked, eyebrows rising.

"Well, for example, they've reconstructed a good bit of Old Nemedisan, though I haven't studied it yet. If the Hyperborean words for pottery derive from Nemedisan words, then the predynastic Hyperboreans were probably trading with Nemedis directly. If the words come from proto-Nostratic instead, say, then they probably got pottery from other cultures who got it first."

Leah processed that. "Has anyone tried to correlate changes in pottery styles to changes in language?" she asked then.

"I haven't seen anything even moving in that direction yet."

"When we get home," Leah said, "whatever else happens, once we're settled I want us to try some research projects together—that one first."

Toby grinned. "When we're not doing other things."

Leah blushed, laughed, leaned forward and kissed him.

* * *

Then came the day when all five of them stood on the bridge deck, looking at the low dim line of land to the northwest. Punctuating it, a ragged mass like a low cloud rose up nearly straight from the sea and slanted back down into vague distances. The sky stretched out above, gray and cold, threatening rain. "Kingsport Head," Phil Dyer told them. "We'll be there in about an hour." Then, with a grin: "The ship's headed in to Boston, but we aren't. If the other side has something waiting for us at the quayside in Boston harbor, they're going to be disappointed."

"I hope the crew won't be in any danger," Leah said.

"We've made some arrangements," said Phil, with a look that meant he would say no more. Leah gave him a dubious look but let the matter rest.

The hour passed. Once it was gone, Toby headed down to the main deck after Leah. The others came down the stair one by one. Phil came last of all, with two sailors following him, and by the time he got there a boat was coming out from Kingsport Bay to meet the *Arkham*: a big inboard motorboat of twentieth-century make.

Fifteen minutes later the five of them and their luggage were aboard the boat. Phil and Emmeline talked enthusiastically with the skipper, a stocky black-haired man in his thirties they seemed to know. Wren went forward to stand just behind the bow and revel in the spray as the boat pulled away from the *Arkham* and plowed through the great rolling waves off the deep Atlantic. Toby and Leah sat in the open cockpit aft, his arm around her shoulders, her arm around his waist. Neither said anything for a while.

"You're thinking about the others," Leah said.

Toby gave her a startled look. "Yeah. I wish more of them had been luckier."

"So do I." A moment passed. "But they all knew the risk they were running. All of us did, except for you. Well, and that Norwegian botanist."

"Anna Slange."

"Yes. Do you know if she got away?"

He hated to lie, but the promise had to be kept. "I have no idea. I heard she was heading inland a long ways, so she had a pretty good chance."

"Good." With a shrug: "I won't say I liked her, but I hope she's okay."

Toby said nothing, thinking of Ss'mei in her many borrowed forms, and the glimpses he'd had of her own shape. "So do I," he said.

The boat threaded its way between Orchard Island and Hog Island, the guardians of the channel. Beyond them, the big tourist hotels loomed up to port. Further off huddled the roofs of old Kingsport, with a scattering of old mansions on the hills back from the shore and an empty brick shell of a building on the central hill further off, a splash of color against the gray soaring presence of Kingsport Head. Looking at the town, Toby realized he had precisely no idea where they were headed. It didn't surprise him, though, when the boat headed over toward the sea wall close to the hotels, and came finally to a quay that, from the signage, welcomed a pedestrian ferry from Salem during the tourist season.

A few moments of clambering, and Toby stood for the first time in weeks on a surface that didn't roll beneath him with the surging of the waves. He gave Leah a hand to help her ashore, offered one to Wren and wasn't surprised when she grinned and leapt onto the quay without it. A ramp brought them up to Harbor Street, all but empty now that the tourists were gone for the season, and Phil led the way across the street to the Kingsport Oceancrest Hotel, eight stories of gray concrete and blank windows staring out over the harbor.

The lobby was small and bleak, with garish abstract paintings on the walls and an unnerving marine-themed carpet that somehow reminded Toby of the seasickness he'd managed to dodge. The young woman behind the desk clearly expected them, though, and Toby found himself handed a key—an actual metal key, not a card for an electronic lock that could be hacked—and directed, along with the others, to the elevator over to one side.

"Dinner's at seven," Phil said as the elevator made grinding noises and lurched unsteadily upward. "In the Rorqual Room on the second floor. One last meal together before we go our separate ways. I hope nobody minds." Nobody did, and the door rattled open a moment later.

Sensibly enough, Phil had booked one room with a big bed for Toby and Leah, and Toby thought he'd heard at the desk that Phil and Emmeline had another. Room 412 could have passed for any other hotel room in any other tourist town north of the mouth of Chesapeake Bay. Once the door was shut, their coats hung in the closet, and their luggage sprawled across a corner of the floor, Toby and Leah sat on the end of the bed, looked at each other and said nothing.

After a little while Leah got up and went to the phone on the shabby little desk near the window. She dialed, listened, and then in a brash flat tone utterly unlike her usual voice said, "Sherry? Yeah, it's Lorraine. We just got in." She paused, listening. "Okay, good. When you get here have the desk buzz room 643 and I'll be right down. Okay? See you soon."

She hung up. Toby said, "Let me guess. Every word of that was some kind of code."

That earned him a grin. "Not quite every word, but close. Dad's going to drive down first thing tomorrow morning to pick us up. He should be here by nine or so." Seeing Toby's expression: "Don't worry about it. He's really nice."

"We're talking about my future father-in-law," Toby reminded her.

She rolled her eyes, but relented a moment later and leaned over to kiss him. "Seriously. The two of you'll get along like anything. You'll see."

* * *

Dinner in the Rorqual Room was a matter of long silences broken by pleasantries from the waitress. The food was better than Toby had expected, decent American hotel fare with just a few pro forma nods to the latest culinary fashions, and the ambience was impressively tacky, with gaudy murals of whales on the walls painted by someone who'd apparently never seen one. Phil Dyer looked haggard—he'd spent hours on the phone, calling the families of those who weren't coming back. The others simply looked tired.

They were most of the way through the meal when Toby heard someone speaking just outside the room. The voice was muffled by the door but he caught hints of a British accent, and a rising intonation that made it sound as though someone was about to land in serious trouble if the speaker didn't get something right away. Toby wasn't the only one who heard the voice, and the effect on Wren was electric. She stood up so fast her chair toppled backward with a crash, and headed for the door at a pace that reminded Toby suddenly of the way Vrispaa had lunged up out of the water under Mount Voormithadreth.

She was out the door just as quickly, but everyone in the room heard her call out, "Harold!" Minutes passed, and then she came back in with a luminous smile and red eyes, leading a lean balding man in a rumpled jacket and slacks, with the highest forehead Toby had ever seen on a human being, and dark intent eyes beneath shaggy black brows. Phil got to his feet at once, and so did Toby, a little before the others; he thought he remembered the face from a photo he'd seen online months before.

"This is my husband Harold," Wren said, confirming the guess. "I'm so very glad to be able to introduce you." Harold shook each of their hands, and said, "I understand that all of you took care of Wren's body while she wasn't in it. Thank you." Toby managed not to blush.

A few minutes later Wren and Phillips were gone. Emmeline looked at the others and said, "So that story ends. I wish them well."

"What are your plans now?" Leah asked her.

"Me? Tomorrow I will be taking a plane from, what is the place? Logan Airport, that is the name. A dreadful place. But the following morning, I will be in Paris, then home to Vyones by train. I am on sabbatical still for two years, so perhaps Miskatonic can tolerate a visiting professor come the springtime, eh? If so, you both must come visit, or I will do the same."

Leah agreed enthusiastically, and Toby said, "If I can. I have no idea what I'm going to do now that the expedition's over."

"Oh, you will find something together. I am sure of it. I make fun of you both, *non*? But you are both *trés capable*. Something will happen, you will see."

A few more bites of food, a few more desultory exchanges, and the dinner wound to a close. They all stood, hands were shaken, words said that couldn't begin to reach the immensities they'd faced, alone or together. Then Phil went to pay for the meal, Emmeline made a shooing motion, and Toby and Leah headed for their room.

As the elevator lurched and shuddered its way to the fourth floor, Toby tried to fit his mind around the difference between the familiar tackiness of his surroundings and the images that hovered in his memory: tundra and ice, Mount Voormithadreth's crown rising above the glaciers, canvas and rope straining before the wind, and the soaring shape of the Lowermost Gate in the light of flares, a moment before it opened. The gap was too great. He found himself wondering, as the elevator clattered and stopped, which of them felt more like a dream.

"She knows something," Leah said as they left the elevator. He gave her a puzzled look, and she went on: "Emmeline. Every time she's said something like that, something I thought was a joke or wishful thinking or something, it turned out she knew exactly what she was talking about. I wonder what she has in mind this time."

* * *

The next morning they were up early, showered together in straight cold water, and headed downstairs to the breakfast buffet, which was in a bare little room off the lobby with windows looking out over the harbor. It was pleasant enough, but they were the only ones in the room until just after 8:30, when Wren looked in. "Dr. Gilman! I hope I'm not interrupting. We're about to go, and there's something I'm supposed to give you."

Toby and Leah both got to their feet. Wren came in and handed Toby a package maybe a foot square and a few inches thick, neatly wrapped. Then they all shook hands and said the usual things before Wren hurried back to the lobby, where Harold Phillips was waiting for her.

"I hope they're happy," Toby said, once the main doors had opened and closed again. Leah glanced at him and smiled.

They headed back to the room to get their luggage. On the way up the elevator Toby glanced at the package. It had the words *For Dr. Toby Gilman* on it in black marker; he didn't recognize the handwriting but he was sure it wasn't Vrispaa's. He shrugged mentally, put it in his duffel when they got into the room, and all but forgot about it as he shouldered their luggage and went back down to the lobby to meet his new family.

By the time they got to the lobby a battered green Buick some decades old had pulled up in front of the hotel. Leah took one look at it, let out a wordless cry, and bolted for the door. Toby followed at a less headlong pace.

By the time he'd reached the car Leah had rounded it and flung herself into the arms of a short, sturdily built man with traces of gray in his dark hair, who'd gotten out from behind the driver's seat. Toby, reaching the car's other side, found himself facing a lean boy of fourteen whose face looked noticeably like Leah's.

"You're Toby Gilman, aren't you?" the boy said. "I'm Aaron. Did you really get to sail with the Terrible Old Man?" Toby shook his hand and admitted to both counts, and Aaron's eyes went round. "Wow," he said. "I mean, seriously—wow."

Toby was spared the need to say anything else just then by Leah, who led the older man around the car to him. "Toby," she said, beaming, "this is my dad."

"Paul Sargent." He held out a hand, which Toby duly shook. More interesting was the man's face, square and serious, marked with lines that spoke of old griefs. "It's a real pleasure to meet you—may I call you Toby?"

They got that settled. "Not a lot of luggage?" Paul said, and Toby: "I left a lot of things behind in Greenland. We had to leave in kind of a hurry."

Paul nodded. "Not the first time I've heard something like that." They got Leah's duffel stowed in the trunk, and then climbed into the car, Toby and Leah in back. Moments later the car pulled out onto Harbor Street, turned once near the gap where memory reminded Toby the *Miskatonic* should have been, turned again onto the main street out of town.

He guessed quickly enough that Leah's father was the kind of driver who didn't like to talk when he was behind the wheel, and the comfortable silence from Leah and Aaron confirmed it. That spared Toby the need to come up with something to say. Instead, he sat back, put an arm around Leah's shoulders, smiled at her as she nestled her head against him, smiled again when her breathing changed to tell him she'd fallen asleep. He glanced up a moment later to see Paul's eyes reflected in the rearview mirror, a hint of amusement in them.

Thereafter he watched the landscape roll past: the desolate hills between Kingsport and Arkham, the urban blight that was downtown Arkham, the abandoned farms and reborn forests along the Aylesbury Pike between there and Bolton, then the old highway north through Ipswich and Newburyport, where it joined Route 1 and headed north across a corner of New Hampshire into the dark fir-clad hills of Maine. Hours passed and so did an assortment of mostly small towns, until they reached the little town of Wyncliffe. There Route 1 veered north to Bangor, while the Buick turned onto a narrow two-lane road headed south. A half hour of serpentine curves among tall pointed firs ended above a harbor town maybe half the size of Kingsport: lines of clean but weathered Yankee saltbox houses huddled along a handful of streets, a little downtown district of brick and clapboard buildings three and four stories high, and off to one side, on a hill overlooking the sea, what looked like the ruins of a long-abandoned mansion.

Leah woke up as the Buick picked its way into town, blinked, and then let out a little cry. Toby glanced at her and said, "Home?" She nodded her delight. Another few minutes and the Buick rolled to a halt in the driveway beside one of the saltbox houses. Toby gave Leah a squeeze and opened the door on his side, meaning to go around and open hers, but long before he got there she'd flung the door open and gone pelting up the walk to the house. He watched her, closed the door, went with her father to the trunk and helped gather up their luggage.

"Welcome to Collinsport," said Paul as they headed for the front door and Aaron trotted alongside them. "You haven't been up this way before, have you?"

"No, never. It seems really pleasant."

"Collinsport's been good to us. I imagine Leah told you—"

"Toby," said Leah, smiling and wet-eyed, as she came out the door with someone else behind her. "This is Mom."

Before Toby had quite finished processing this he found himself on the receiving end of an ample hug. Mrs. Sargent was in her forties and her curves were more substantial than Leah's, but the resemblance was otherwise impossible to miss. As she drew back to arm's length, beaming, Toby considered the likelihood that Leah would look much the same in twenty years, and decided he was good with it.

"Toby," Mrs. Sargent said. "Welcome home." Then, releasing him: "Please call me Ruth. I bet you haven't had a bite to eat since breakfast, have you? Come in, get that coat off, and let me see about some lunch."

They headed inside. Coats went into a closet off the entry, the duffel got handed to Aaron who made off with it, and Toby and Leah had a moment of privacy in the parlor, a comfortable room with plaster walls, well-worn furniture, and a cast iron Franklin stove filling the fireplace on one end, radiating a pleasant warmth and a familiar hot-metal smell.

"Are you okay?" Leah asked him.

"Yeah. It's just—" A gesture reached for the inexpressible. "'Welcome home.' I'm going to have to get used to that."

CHAPTER 13

THE GIFT OF THE WITCH-KINGS

Tea made a prompt appearance, and so did Leah's youngest brother Simon, who plopped down on the floor next to his brother and watched Toby with wide eyes. Ruth bustled back and forth from parlor to kitchen, bringing with her gusts of scent that made Toby's mouth water. Leah nestled up to him, and her parents seemed untroubled by that, which soothed some of Toby's worries. Over the tea, they worked their way past the usual pleasantries.

"I think we're all still a little bit in shock," Paul said. "We'd almost given up hope when we heard from Leah, and then it wasn't long afterward that we found out she'd be bringing someone home with her."

"I hope that isn't any kind of problem," Toby said.

A shake of Paul's head denied it. "Not at all. It was just a little sudden. I'm going to guess it wasn't quite so sudden for you two."

"Not really," said Toby. "We met at a clambake in May when I came to Massachusetts, got to know each other at the station in Greenland, fell in love aboard the *Miskatonic* after she and the others came aboard, and once we were both safe on board the *Arkham*—" He shrugged, hoped all the things he'd left out weren't too obvious by their absence.

Paul nodded as though it was the most ordinary thing in the world. "Well, there you are. Ruth and I, our families knew each other and we went to school together, but since everyone had to leave Innsmouth that sort of thing's not so common as it was."

"I'd like to hear about Innsmouth sometime," said Toby. "My family didn't know anything about it." Despite everything that had happened, it still took him an effort to go on. "And I imagine you'll want to know a thing or two about Pine Harbor."

Paul's gaze met his. "Quite a few people are going to want to hear about that," he said. "Once the two of you get properly engaged, we'll have some of the elders and priestesses over."

Just then Ruth ducked out of the kitchen and said, "Paul, if you could—" Leah's father extracted himself from an armchair and headed for the kitchen. Before Toby could turn to Leah and ask her what it took to get properly engaged in Collinsport, Simon said, "Dr. Gilman—"

Toby turned to the boy, said, "Please. Toby'll do."

He got a grin in response. "Okay. Were you really a sailor on Captain Coldcroft's ship?" When Toby admitted this: "Up in the rigging and everything?"

"Yeah," said Toby. The two boys clearly expected to hear more, so he went on: "When the *Miskatonic* rescued me and Dr. Grenier," said Toby, "I thought your sister and everyone else who'd been at the station was dead. I was pretty torn up about that, and I couldn't stand the thought of sitting around doing nothing." Remembered bitterness caught at his voice. "I wanted to do something to hurt—" He paused.

"The other side," Leah interjected.

"Yeah. I'll be honest, I wanted them all dead, and I didn't care much whether I was still alive after that happened. So I asked the captain if there was anything I could do, and about five minutes later I was helping to haul up one of the sails."

That got even wider eyes than before, and a flurry of further questions, at the end of which he'd promised to teach the boys the cutlass drill if they promised not to hit anyone. Paul came back from the kitchen then and sent the boys to set the table. Leah turned to Toby and said, "I hope you realize you've just become the best brother-in-law in the history of Collinsport. They're going to be telling all their friends that their sister married a genuine pirate."

Lunch followed shortly thereafter, an astonishment of lobster chowder, fresh-baked bread, and slices of raw fish dipped in an assortment of sauces. On the way into the kitchen Toby caught the scent of the chowder and stopped cold in the doorway, assailed by memories. Paul glanced at him and said, "Long time?" Toby clenched his eyes shut, nodded, went on to the table once he was sure he could do it without bursting into tears. The food tasted just as good as it smelled, and the glasses at each place and the big pitcher on the table were full of salt water. He sipped some, gave it a startled look. "Sea salt?"

"Friends of ours make it down east where the water's cleaner," said Leah. "I used to take a big sack of it with me every time I went away. It never lasted long enough." She shrugged, but Toby could sense the emotions beneath the casual mask. "Put it down to homesickness."

"How'd you get by in New York and Ohio?" Paul asked.

Toby laughed, shrugged also. "Not very well. I bought sea salt at the grocery when I could find it, and plain table salt when I couldn't."

Ruth made a face, then: "No need for that any more. We've got this for everyday and Breton salt for special occasions, and if you're starved for sea water, why, there's a fine beach south of town, with cliffs all around it for privacy. We can all go there Saturday if you like."

Toby managed to indicate how much he'd like that without choking on his chowder. "Leah mentioned that you've got gills," Paul said then.

For Simon, that was apparently the last straw. "That's not *fair!*" he said, outraged. Both his parents looked at him, and he put a hand over his mouth and turned red.

"I'd give you a set if I had spares," Toby told him, getting a general laugh. Then, more seriously: "I know it's not fair. The thing is, I had to hide my gills from everybody."

"One of my great-grandmothers had gills," said Ruth. "She was a Deep One's daughter. None of her children had them, though, and Paul's family hasn't had them for I don't know how many generations. It's one of the things that comes and goes." She smiled. "We can borrow artificial gills from the Deep Ones, and swim down just as far as you please."

* * *

After lunch, Ruth and Leah took Toby's measurements and sent Aaron with a note to someone in town; Toby gathered from their talk that people coming to Collinsport with not much more than the clothes on their backs was nothing out of the ordinary. A little later, Leah's grandparents came over to meet Toby. Ruth's mother was plump and smiling, Paul's mother thin and frail, and Paul's father, a muscular balding man who leaned on a cane, moved like one of Coldcroft's pirates. Once everyone settled down in the parlor, Toby's first guess turned out to be correct. "Yes, I worked in the merchant marine for a good while," Joel Sargent said. "Diesel freighters for most of it, but I started on one of the last schooners to work up here." He leaned forward. "So tell me about the *Miskatonic*. Do I remember right that she's a barque?"

So Toby talked about the *Miskatonic*, and since the boys begged for a story of a battle, he told them about the fight at Tornarssukalik Inlet: the tense hour in the mist drawing near, the roar of the mortars, the great rolling fireball from the fuel tank that ended the battle.

"I wish I'd seen more of that," Leah said when he finished. "I was belowdecks the whole time, and all that happened was that every time the guns fired the whole ship shook."

"You were down below?" Simon asked, in a disgusted tone.

"Captain Coldcroft put her to work," said Toby. To Leah: "You and Cooper were taking care of the gunpowder, right?"

She nodded, turned to the boys. "Cooper's the ship's cook, and he's got a wooden leg. No, I'm not making that up. A wooden leg and a kerchief over his head, and he looks at you like this." Her face twisted momentarily into a piratical glare. "The two of us were down in the hold. He was scooping up gunpowder from a barrel with a wooden scoop and I was holding the cartridges for him, then closing them up and handing them to somebody to run up to the deck."

"Her job was to make sure the gunners had something to shoot with," Toby said. "That's how they could keep pounding the other side until they gave in."

"What Toby hasn't gotten around to mentioning," said Leah then, "is that he was at the ship's wheel the whole time."

That got amazed looks from the boys. "*Steering* it?" Aaron said.

"Well, more or less," said Toby. "I stood there holding steady, and every so often the Terrible Old Man would say, 'Point to port, Gilman,' or something like that, and I'd turn the wheel to put her on her new heading and wait for him to say something else."

"While bullets went whizzing past," Leah added.

"We didn't take a lot of rounds, but there were some," Toby admitted. "I've got a scar."

"The two of you had quite a series of adventures, I gather," said Ruth, returning from the kitchen with plates of apple pie. "I hope you don't develop a taste for it."

Leah considered that. "Well, not dodging bullets or negation teams—but I wouldn't mind going back to Greenland someday. It's really beautiful in its own way."

Plates found their way to everyone. "Don't mind me," said Ruth. "I just can't help but think that any gathering goes better with pie."

Toby turned to Paul. "You're a very lucky man."

"Leah," said Paul, "has been helping her mother in the kitchen since she was five. I don't think you'll have any cause to complain."

Later, they talked about Collinsport and the strange old family who had founded it; later still, with a solid dinner and a glass of local whiskey to brace him, Toby told them as much as he knew about Pine Harbor, the flight of the survivors to the Catskills, and what had happened afterward. Finally the boys walked their grandparents home, and Ruth and Leah led Toby upstairs to a hall lined with doors. "This'll be your room," Ruth said, gesturing toward one of the doors with a smile. "Pleasant dreams." She turned to go, and Leah went to him. "See you soon," she whispered, kissed him, and went through the next door. Toby watched her go, then went into the bedroom he'd been given.

The room was comfortable, with faded green wallpaper, a twin bed with the headboard against one wall, a dresser on the facing wall. A window on the third wall looked out toward the dim restless ocean. He closed the door, got undressed, turned out the light and slipped under the covers, and was just beginning to feel warm and sleepy when the door opened again.

It was Leah. She was wearing pajamas, but the faint light from the window was enough for him to see her pull off the top and drop it on the floor near the doorway, and shed the bottom and let it fall beside the bed. Naked, she slipped into bed next to him, and before he could think of a question to ask, said, "You have no idea what any of this is about, do you?"

"Not a clue," he admitted cheerfully.

"It's an old-fashioned Innsmouth engagement. The young man gets an invite to stay the night at the young lady's house. If the parents can't stand him they can just not invite him, and then the couple can give up or elope and settle somewhere else. But if they're willing to see the match, they invite him to stay the night, and how much distance there is between her room and the room where they put him tells him how hard he's going to have to work to get their favor. As soon as everyone else goes to bed, the young lady tiptoes over to his room and spends the night with him, and then her mom walks in on them the next morning." Sensing his reaction: "Don't worry, she'll listen to make sure the bed's not creaking. But once she walks in on them, of course they have to get married, right?"

"Okay," Toby said. "And she has to come to his bedroom?"

"Of course! That way everyone knows that it was her idea and he didn't force things. That's why the pajamas go on the floor, too."

"Okay," he repeated. "I'm good with it."

"Thank you. I know it's old-fashioned, but both my grandmothers have been hoping I'd do things the old way since I was little. You know how grandmothers are." A frozen moment, then: "Toby, I'm sorry. You don't, do you?"

"Not really," he admitted. "But I want to find out."

"What do you think of them so far?"

"They're very nice people. Your whole family's been really welcoming."

"My family," said Leah, "is impressed as hell. Did you notice that Mom and Dad put you in the room right next to mine? That works out to 'marry our daughter with our blessing.' There'll be a big party tomorrow with lots of relatives."

Toby considered that, then thought of the one potential problem. "Are you sure this bed creaks loud enough for your mom to hear?"

"We'd probably better find out," she told him.

Laughing, he reached for her.

* * *

The bed creaked quite adequately, but it was properly silent by the time footfalls, a little louder than they had to be, ascended the stair. Leah caught the sound first, winked at Toby, and moved a little to her side of the bed, and they both made sure the covers were pulled up. The footfalls paused at the top of the stair, came closer.

The door opened and Ruth looked in. Her glance took in the two of them, the bed, and the pajamas on the bedroom floor. "Good morning," she said. "Breakfast in an hour?"

"Please," Leah said, and Ruth smiled at them both and closed the door. More footfalls moved back down the stairway, quick and light, almost dancing.

"There," Leah said. "Now we're officially engaged."

"That's all it takes?"

"That's all it takes. Well, there's breakfast with both—" She caught herself. "With my family, lunch with relatives, and then dinner with everybody—there'll be people falling out the windows this evening. Then everything's settled, and it's back to normal until the wedding."

That seemed promising enough. Toby's questions about what he would wear that day were settled promptly, too. Leah slipped out of bed, pulled on her pajamas, left and came back a moment later with a capacious bathrobe for him. "There's all kinds of clothes for you in my room—well, ours, starting tonight. I bet Dad finds a spare dresser before lunch."

It took most of the hour to get washed and dressed and ready for the day, but just before breakfast they went downstairs. From the clothing they'd found for him, he'd picked slacks, a long-sleeved shirt and a knitted vest; the shirt and vest fitted a little more loosely over his ribs than he was used to, and he drew in a deep breath and then realized that for the first time in years his gill slits didn't feel crowded against his ribs. He was still pondering that when they got to the foot of the stairs and Leah's parents and brothers, standing in the parlor, started to applaud.

Breakfast was lavish, with pancakes, sausage, and applesauce in volumes Toby was sure no six people anywhere could eat, though the two boys did their level best. Lunch outdid it, but by then Leah's grandparents had returned, and so had her aunts, uncles, and first cousins, along with her older sister Carol, brother-in-law Matt, and little Anna, the infant niece she'd mentioned aboard the *Arkham*. By mid-afternoon close to thirty people had come for dinner, all of them Leah's relatives in one way or another, and tables for the children had to be set up in the parlor. Toby wondered at first how to explain the absence of relatives on his side, but gathered that news had spread. A few times, someone said to him, "I'm sorry none of your family can be here." He thanked them, and that was as much as the situation required.

The day turned to evening, and a third gargantuan meal made its appearance, this time with the help of various relatives who'd brought pots and pans and boxes and then labored alongside Ruth in the kitchen. Afterwards, Aaron and Simon begged him to repeat the story of the battle of Tornarssukalik Inlet—Toby gathered that some doubts had been raised at the parlor tables about his bona fides as a genuine pirate—and he obliged. Things wound down gracefully thereafter, the guests departed, and Toby and Leah stumbled up the stairs to bed.

The next morning over breakfast they talked over dates for the wedding, and settled on one in two months—Leah's period was already several days late, and Toby thought he could guess why. Once breakfast was over Paul left for the boat repair firm where he worked, Aaron and Simon headed off to school, Ruth busied herself with household tasks, and Leah and Toby sat in the parlor and talked about things that didn't matter.

Leah had blossomed since they'd reached Collinsport. That was easy to see, and the reason was as easy to divine: she needed her family and her home town as much as she needed salt water. The elders who'd sent her to college, Toby guessed, had weighed her mind carefully but her personality not at all, and it didn't take much effort to imagine what would have happened if she'd gotten a position at a distant university— the drinking, the self-destructive relationships, early successes paid for with a long slow spiral toward misery and failure.

"You look sad," Leah said to him then.

"Just thinking." Then, when her expression didn't shift: "About what we're going to do after the wedding." She nodded and said nothing.

Days and nights passed. Twice Toby woke in darkness shaking with inexplicable dread, and both times Leah reached for him and held him until the terror passed. Twice, too, Toby woke early while Leah was still asleep, sat up, and watched her for a while. She was pleasing to look at but not beautiful by most definitions, and the feelings she roused in him had nothing of the intensity Vrispaa kindled in him, but the soft curves of her body and face waked reactions of their own. Hyperborean words came to mind—*aqqat*, the longing for home and family; *nen*, the longing for sexual release—but something less easily categorized made him want to nestle down against her, to comfort and be comforted. Love, he thought. The word would have to do.

Saturday they went to the beach Ruth mentioned, a crescent of dark sand and shingle walled in by ragged cliffs. Leah had explained that nobody from Innsmouth wore swimsuits, but watching the whole family strip off their clothes and head for the surf still took getting used to. Before long, though, he had salt water rushing over his gills again, and the artificial gills the others used, Deep One devices that fit over nose and mouth, let Leah match him dive for dive.

Sunday the Grand Priestess and a few of the elders of the local Esoteric Order of Dagon lodge came over for coffee. They all wanted to know as much as Toby was willing to tell them about Pine Harbor. When he'd recounted everything he'd learned from his family, and a silence with harsh edges settled in the parlor, Toby broke it by saying, "I don't know if the Deep Ones told you what the people at Pine Harbor did to make them turn their backs, but if they did—" He made himself go on. "I'd like to know what it was."

That earned him startled looks. "We got some news in Innsmouth," said the Grand Priestess, a plump grandmotherly woman with white hair in a long braid. "What the Deep Ones told us is that they never got the call for help from Pine Harbor. They didn't know anything had happened until no one showed at any of the usual meeting places undersea, and they sent some Guardians ashore and found the town burnt to the ground."

"But—" Toby began, and then stopped, seeing the answer in their faces.

"Somebody made a mistake," one of the elders said, confirming his guess. "Or some bit of bad luck got in the way. Things like that don't have to have a good reason, you know."

"Yeah," said Toby, nodding slowly. "Yeah, I know."

Then there was the day not long after his arrival when he called the Case Western professor who'd chaired his dissertation committee, reassured her that he'd gotten back from Greenland in one piece, told a few carefully evasive stories about what had happened, and got in return a few pieces of astonishing news. "Dr. Broward's announced that he'll be retiring at the end of this school year," he told Leah. "That's what Dr. Prasad told me. She said word of the Ulut inscription's already all over the discipline, and a lot of the old guard's looking at taking retirement." Knowing how inadequate the words were: "I'm sorry."

"Don't be," Leah told him. "Ham was wrong. It was an honest mistake, but he was still wrong." She shrugged. "And I know he was kind of a jerk about it." Toby knew her moods well enough by then to reach for her, and she closed her eyes, nodded, and huddled against him.

Less difficult was the afternoon when a small parcel with Toby's name on it came in the mail from Miskatonic University's Department of Geology. It contained a letter from Phil and a USB drive, and when that latter went into Leah's spare laptop, up came a complete set of photographs of the scrolls Toby had brought back. "This is amazing," he breathed, as Leah looked over his shoulder. "Commoriom period, fairly late from the grammar, and heptameter verse like the epic literature, but it's a comic work, a mock-epic about the master-thief Satampra Zeiros, who's just a name and a few passing references in the other literature."

"That's got to be worth a few publications," said Leah.

Toby grinned. "At least two books, and plenty of articles." The grin faltered. "Once we get our future straightened out, I can get to work on those."

Other days were less memorable but no less busy. All in all, two weeks passed before Toby remembered the package that Wren Kingston-Brown had given him just before she'd left the hotel in Kingsport and his life.

* * *

That morning he went back upstairs after breakfast to choose clothes for an event that evening: the ceremony welcoming him to the first and lowest degree of the Esoteric Order of Dagon, which everyone else among the Innsmouth families received when they were seven. The family pictures Ruth had shown him a week before included snapshots of Carol, Leah, Aaron, and Simon, looking solemn and well-scrubbed, on their way to the ceremony in the Collinsport equivalent of their Sunday best, and he meant to match them.

A few moments in the closet turned up most of what he wanted; he was hunting for a tie in his dresser when he found the package with his name on it. Had Leah put it there? That seemed likely enough, and after a moment he remembered a comment she'd made in passing days back, when they were about to head downstairs for a meal.

He set the package on the bed next to the jacket he meant to wear, continued his hunt for a suitable tie. Once that quest was successful, he picked up the package again. It had plenty of padding in it, and hard uncertain shapes inside that. After a moment spent staring blankly at it, he found a pocketknife, cut the tape and the paper open along one edge, and pulled out a mass of bubble wrap. A few moments of effort disgorged the first of several circular shapes neatly wrapped in tissue paper. He got the wrappings off, considered the object in his hand.

It was a ring five or six inches across made of a metal he didn't recognize, of a color that was related to black the way copper was to red and silver to white. Harsh abstract patterns decorated most of it, but at one point the ring thickened and a snarling face, half animal and half human, bared crudely fashioned teeth to the world. Baffled, he turned it this way and that, and then headed downstairs to ask Leah about it.

She was in the parlor, paging through a leatherbound volume from the Esoteric Order of Dagon library, when he came down the stair. Sounds from the kitchen told him where Ruth was. Leah glanced up at him with a smile as he came over to the sofa, then saw what was in his hand and jerked as though someone had slapped her. An instant later she was on her feet, pressing a finger against his lips in a demand for silence, and all but marched him back up the stair.

Once they were in their bedroom and the door clicked shut, she turned to him and in a whisper said, "Where the *hell* did you get that?"

"The package Wren gave me," he whispered back. He gestured at the bed, where the package still sat. "What's the big deal?"

"You don't recognize it?" He shook his head. "That's an Atlantean liege-ring." He gave her a baffled look, and she went on: "If it's authentic, it's probably worth more than this town and everything in it."

A silence passed. "I think there's more in the package," Toby managed to say.

She stared at him and forced out, "Show me."

There were five more: four of them identical to the one he'd taken out first, the fifth ornamented with five of the snarling half-animal faces. "Father Dagon," Leah said in a shaken whisper. "A complete set. If they're authentic, those are really old even by Atlantean standards. That's got to be native orichalcum, hammered from nuggets, not smelted."

Toby glanced at her. "You're not just a ceramics expert."

"That's my specialty, but—" She shrugged. "Material culture generally fascinates me." She drew in a breath. "Okay. Let me get some tape, and then we've got to get these into a safe deposit box right away. Are you up for selling them?"

"Yeah. They're pretty ugly."

"Everybody says that," said Leah. Then, with a little laugh: "All right, yes, they're ugly. But there are collectors who'll pay unbelievable amounts of money for things like this."

Once the liege-rings were wrapped again and the package taped up, she tucked it into a shoulderbag and the two of them went back downstairs. "We're going to take a walk," Leah called into the kitchen. "Just around town a little. Toby hasn't seen much of it." Ruth called back something approving and reminded them to be home by lunchtime.

Outside a salt-scented wind danced down Collinsport's streets and chased clouds toward the hills to the north. A few blocks brought them to the town's commercial district along Water Street. At first Toby was sure he knew where they were headed—a three-story brick building with stone cornices that practically shouted "old bank" loomed up ahead—but by the time he got close enough to read the words COLLINSPORT BANK on the front cornice, he could see that the lights were out and the building hadn't been tenanted in years. The bank, a little storefront branch of a national chain, huddled in a commercial building a block further down.

It took them half an hour to get a safe deposit box rented, although that was because the clerk was one of Leah's cousins and wanted to congratulate them on their engagement and ask about Greenland. He accepted without question the half-truth they'd settled on—"some things that belonged to one of the people who didn't come back with us," Leah said with a look at the floor, and the clerk nodded and handed her some paper-work. Once the package was stowed inside a locked box, Toby held out the key to Leah, who nodded and tucked it in her purse. Moments later they were outside again, walking down an empty sidewalk.

"What next?" Toby asked.

"After lunch, once Mom's gone over to Grandma Eliot's, I can call a dealer down in Arkham who handles things like this. I've done work for him a couple of times, authenticating Hyper-borean pottery, and he's one of the best in the business. He can come up, do an appraisal, and then contact the collectors he knows and see who's willing to offer how much." With a glance at Toby: "If that's okay with you. They're not mine, after all."

"They will be in six weeks," Toby reminded her, and she beamed, leaned over and kissed his cheek. "But that's better than anything I've come up with."

"It's all I could think of," she admitted.

They walked on in silence for a short distance. Ahead, Water Street ended where Frenchman's Bay curved inward, and a city park with a little arc of beach faced the troubled waters of the Atlantic. As they approached it, Toby motioned toward the beach and gave Leah a questioning look, and she nodded. They crossed the grassy strip between sidewalk and shore, clambered down a slope onto dark sand and shingle, and stood there watching the waves.

"So what's a liege-ring?" Toby asked then.

That got him a smile. "You know Atlantis was a patchwork of tribal societies in Hyperborean times, right? Back when the Witch-Kings weren't much more than chieftains, each of them had five warriors to defend them in battle and cut their throats if they broke tribal law. Each of the warriors had a liege-ring on his right arm, and their master had one on his left. By the time of the Hyperborean settlements that was ancient history, though. I wonder how on Earth a complete set turned up in her luggage."

"Vrispaa got them the same place I got the scrolls," said Toby. Leah gave him a puzzled look, and only then did he realize that he'd spoken the name aloud. It doesn't matter now, he reminded himself. "That was the name of the Yithian who borrowed Wren's body—well, one of her names." She asked him to repeat it, and he spelled it for her for good measure. "The tombs of the Commoriom dynasty weren't far from Mount Voormithadreth, and some things ended up in the tunnels. I'm pretty sure she found them there."

Leah nodded after a moment, and then slipped an arm around his waist. He gave her a startled look, but put an arm around her shoulder anyway.

* * *

He didn't hear much of the phone call that afternoon, just Leah's voice saying carefully guarded words into the mouthpiece, but two days later they went for another walk after lunch, stopped at the bank, and then headed for the Collinsport Inn, the one hotel in town, a big rambling place on Water Street just past a small stone church of eighteenth-century date. A thin balding man in a tailored jacket and slacks got up from a chair in the lobby to greet them. He had, Toby thought, the air of an old-fashioned schoolmaster: the wire-rimmed glasses, the broad smile, the creases and lines of a face used to concentration all suggested that.

"Toby, this is Dr. Amos Wentworth," said Leah. "Amos, Dr. Toby Gilman." Hands got shaken, and a few moments later they were on their way up the elevator to a second floor room, where Wentworth put out the DO NOT DISTURB sign, locked and bolted the door, shed his jacket, got a jeweler's loupe and a little box of paper strips, and then sat at the desk and turned to Leah with a smile. The package came out of Leah's shoulder-bag then, and she extracted one of the rings, handed it to him, and gave the tissue paper that surrounded it to Toby.

For the next hour none of them spoke more than a few words. Leah handed over the rings one at a time. Wentworth gave each one a meticulous examination, pressed moistened paper strips against the metal, watched them turn colors, and took photos with a digital camera. Each ring then went to Toby to be wrapped and put away. The first two went in smoothly, but the third caught on something; glancing in, Toby found a slip of paper he hadn't noticed before. A glance showed the angular characters of Hyperborean script. Leah was watching Wentworth just then, so Toby extracted the paper, tucked it into a pocket, and slid the ring into the package.

When Wentworth finished with the last one and gave it to Toby, he turned in his chair and said, "A very impressive set."

"Are they authentic?" Leah asked.

"Oh, very much so. The metal's orichalcum with traces of copper and antimony, which means they were made using nuggets from riverine deposits in the eastern plains—the mines in the Poseidonian uplands had a different set of trace elements. The designs are typical early geometric period work—I'm sure you recognized them from pottery. All in all, quite the treasure." His smile stayed fixed in place, but something less genial stirred beneath it. "I trust you're interested in selling them. The other options may not be entirely safe."

"I'd like to see them go to someone who values them," Toby said. "And I'll be honest, I could use the money."

"Of course." Wentworth beamed at them both. "Certain arrangements will have to be made, you understand—a cash transaction would be difficult to explain to the authorities, and might draw the attention of certain others who should certainly not find out about this." A little shake of his head dismissed them. "It's purely a matter of finding an organization or a company that can receive the money and then disburse it in some plausible manner."

"Amos," Leah said then, "how much money are we talking about?"

"Eight figures," he said at once. "And not necessarily small ones." He met Toby's startled look with a smile. "As I said, this is a very fine set, one of the only complete sets in the world and certainly the only one of anything like so very early a date. I expect spirited bidding." He put away the loupe and the paper strips, extracted papers from a stack on the desk, and handed them to Toby. "If you're ready to proceed, we can fill out the necessary forms."

It took another few minutes for Toby to sign papers agreeing to sell the liege-rings to the highest bidder who exceeded a minimum bid, and he managed to keep his face and his voice from betraying his feelings when Wentworth wrote *Ten million and "‰* on the minimum bid line. Once that was done, though, hands got shaken again and Toby and Leah left the hotel as quickly as they could without attracting attention. Once the package was back in the safe deposit box they both breathed easier, and headed back home.

That evening, while Leah and her mother sat together in the parlor with needles in hand, embroidering Leah's wedding dress, Toby went up to their bedroom, sat on the bed, and got out the paper he'd found in the package. It was in perfect Middle Hyperborean, as he'd expected, and the writing was Vrispaa's. It read:

> *Perhaps you remember my words on Mount Voormithadreth, when I said that you and your lineage had earned the highest names and privileges the Gathering of Chosen can confer. Your people have their own ways, but I think these gifts will bestow something of the same kind. I said then that your name and deeds will be recalled in the halls of Pnakotus as long as those last, but I wish to say this now, that I will remember you also. May your gods favor you, my frog.*

Toby sat there for a long moment, half aware of the wetness on his face, thinking of how they'd first met at the clambake, thinking about all of what followed from that, up to the moment when he'd helped lift the body she'd borrowed and seen the first traces of a stranger's presence there. *Ilul*, he thought, the Hyperborean word coming easily to his mind: the love of the mind and spirit, the love that demands adoration. And what does that mean when the one you adore is three hundred million years away?

He could think of no possible answer. After a while, he got up, put the slip of paper in a private place in his dresser, and went to wash his face so Leah wouldn't know.

* * *

The phone call came two weeks later. Ruth picked up the phone, came out of the kitchen and asked, "Leah, do you know an Amos Wentworth?" Leah got up and hurried into the kitchen. Toby sat on the couch with a printout of one of the photos from the scrolls and a spiral notebook where he was writing a first tentative translation. A certain test had come back positive the day before, and Toby was trying to keep his thoughts distracted while he dealt with the fact that he'd be a father in another eight months or so. Still, he set the book aside and listened, as much to the tone of her voice as to those few words he could hear.

He wasn't surprised to see the luminous smile on her face as she came back to the parlor after the call was finished. "Good news?" he asked.

"Really good news. He'll be here tomorrow afternoon to make the final arrangements." She sat down next to him and whispered a number in his ear. He turned to stare at her in atonishment, and she nodded, beaming.

The next afternoon they met in the lobby of the Collinsport Inn again. Wentworth had someone else with him, a muscular, broad-shouldered man with an anonymous face who shook everyone's hands but didn't introduce himself. All four of them proceeded at once to the bank, where one of the town's notaries watched paper after paper being signed and put her seal on each of them. The bank clerk goggled as a gargantuan security deposit went into a temporary account, and then let Toby into the safe deposit room. The package came out; the nameless man opened it, examined each of the rings with utter concentration, put them one at a time into white archival boxes and those into a briefcase, signed a few final papers, and then got out a cell phone and made a call. Two minutes later two big late-model cars drove up to the sidewalk and stopped, and he thanked them, left the bank, got into one of the cars, and drove away.

"Excellent," said Wentworth then. "I wonder if you've considered how your side of the transaction might best be handled."

"I've been thinking a lot about it," said Toby. "Do you think it would work to have the buyer use the money to found and endow an institute for research on the prehistoric Arctic?"

Wentworth smiled like a schoolmaster whose pupil had just mastered a difficult lesson on the first try. "Why, yes," he said. "That would be quite suitable, of course, and it would have tax benefits for the buyer, which will be very welcome to him. I assume the institute would hire you and pay for your research."

"Both of us," Toby said. "But I'm not sure how to set that up."

"Why, that will be easy enough," said Wentworth. "I can have a lawyer come here to make the arrangements in the next few days. You'll need a board of trustees, and your salary as executive director shouldn't be too far out of line with what's standard in the field, but with those in mind it should be straightforward to set up." He paused. "You understand that confidentiality is important in this business, of course, but the buyer requested that if there was a donation, it should be made in the name of his late grandmother, Mrs. Vivian Ritman. Perhaps you can keep that in mind as you proceed."

They assured him on that point, the ordinary formalities followed, and they left the bank. Wentworth headed back to the hotel, head up, looking as though nothing could be better than that day. Leah and Toby stood on the sidewalk and watched him go, then turned and went the other way down Water Street. "This institute," Leah said. "Where do you think it should be?"

"Here in Collinsport," Toby said at once; he'd settled that point in his mind days earlier. "The money'll go a lot further here, and it's an easy drive to Arkham and Boston."

She stopped and turned to face him, then all at once buried her face in his shoulder. He could just make out her muffled voice: "Thank you."

"Do you know if the Collinsport Bank building's for sale?" he asked.

She drew back, looked up at him. "Yes, I think so. That would be a really good building to use, too. If the vault's still there, and I'm prety sure it is, you've got a good safe place for collections that might be at risk from theft."

"That's what I was thinking," Toby said.

They started walking again. "Well, Mr. Executive Director," Leah said then, smiling.

"You could take that job," Toby pointed out.

"Not a chance. Administration isn't something I'm good at."

"What job do you want?"

She paused for a little while. "Director of collections," she said. "That's the part of archeology that's always interested me most."

"You've got it." When she kissed him: "I'll take that as your letter of acceptance."

She laughed, and they walked on.

"I want Phil and Emmeline on the board of trustees," Toby said.

"I was about to say the same thing."

"And Dr. Ragnhild Ormsdóttir from Reykjavik," he added, thinking of Ss'mei.

That got him a luminous smile. "Good. She has a great reputation. I know a few other people who might be good trustees, too." Then: "The institute'll have a library, right?"

Toby grinned. "Start making a wish list. There'll be a serious book budget."

"Oh, I will. But it's not that. One of the other people from Innsmouth who went to college when I did, Sally Marsh, got a masters in library science. She's really good, but she's spent the last two years in one of those miserable library systems where they're always culling fine old books from the collection and pushing the latest cheap media schlock on the patrons, and she's sick of it. If we can use a full-time librarian she'd be a fine candidate."

"We can use a full-time librarian," Toby said. "If we're going to do serious research, and I want to do that, we'll need a really good collection of books on the prehistoric Arctic, and that means someone has to run the library." A thought occurred to him. "You've got a high school here in Collinsport, right? We could see if they're interested in doing student internships in the library. Maybe some other fields, too."

"You're going to make yourself really popular here," Leah told him.

They walked on in silence a little further, and Toby thought of another possibility he'd been considering. "Do you think the Esoteric Order of Dagon could use a lot of money?"

"What are you thinking?" Leah asked.

"The scrolls and the liege-rings aren't the only things down under the mountain." The image of the heap of treasure he'd seen hovered before his mind's eye. "There's a lot more. It belongs to shoggoths, but they're willing to trade. I got those scrolls for six pounds of cheese."

She stopped, staring at him, and then laughed. "You're serious, aren't you?" Then, taking his hand again: "Yes, the Order could use money. If it had the funds, there are a lot of people who used to live in Innsmouth who could settle down someplace, and there are other groups that worship the Great Old Ones who could use some help, too."

Toby nodded. "Once the institute's up and running, we can figure out how to get in touch with the shoggoths. They know worshippers of the Great Old Ones in Newfoundland."

"Those are ours," said Leah. "There's a lodge of the Order at a place called Dunkeld." She shook her head in amazement. "You're going to make yourself really *really* popular here."

Ahead of them, Water Street ended at the little park beside Frenchman's Bay. Across the water, hills dark with firs rose up from narrow beaches. The wind carried scents of salt and seaweed, and great masses of cloud loomed above them, glowing in the afternoon light.

"I know what to call the institute," Leah said. "The Vivian Ritman Institute for the Study of Prehistoric Arctic Antiquities."

It took him a moment to parse the initials. "VRISPAA," he said. "Yes, please." Then he realized what it implied. "Oh my God. That's why she knew she could trust me. Somebody they sent to our future must have brought back the name of the institute, and she knew before she got here that she would tell me her name. And—" The rest of it tumbled through his mind, from the first wary confidences to their conversation the night before the *Miskatonic* arrived.

He realized then that Leah was watching him with a smile he couldn't read. "She meant a lot to you, didn't she?" she asked.

He reddened. "Not the way you do."

"Toby," she said, gently chiding. "I saw the way you watched her. What was the Hyperborean word? *Ilul*?"

"Yeah," he admitted. "You don't choose it, it chooses you."

"I know." When he gave her a questioning look: "When we first met at the clambake, I knew right then that I wanted to marry you, and you know how long it took me to deal with that. I'm just glad you're here now, and not hundreds of millions of years in the past."

The only answer he could think of started with a kiss. When they drew back a little, she said, "So there was that. And there's—what's the one that's about home and family?"

"*Aqqat*," he reminded her.

She nodded. "That's something I've always known I needed, and once I realized the two of us could make something that would last, that shouldered its way to the head of the line."

"I think there's some *nen* in there somewhere, too."

She blushed. "Well, yes. But what I meant to say is that if what you can bring to this—to our marriage—is *nen* and *aqqat*, I'm not going to fuss."

"We could just call it love," said Toby.

She looked up at him, her brown eyes solemn but a faint smile bending the ends of her mouth. "You know," she said, "I think we could."

AUTHOR'S NOTE

This novel was originally drafted as the sixth volume in *The Weird of Hali*, my epic fantasy with tentacles, with Justin Martense playing part of the role that ended up going to Toby Gilman, and other characters from that series—Jenny Chaudronnier, Belinda Marsh, Asenath Merrill, and others— having their own parts. Two complete drafts later, it was clear that there was too much story to fit within the limits of the series, and Justin and the others went to New York's Red Hook neighborhood instead, leaving Greenland to a different cast of characters.

Readers of *The Weird of Hali* may find it helpful (or at least entertaining) to know that this novel is set seven and a half years after the events in *The Weird of Hali: Innsmouth*, and thus falls between *The Weird of Hali: Dreamlands* and *The Weird of Hali: Providence*, the fourth and fifth books in that series. The Esoteric Order of Dagon's real estate purchases, which are mentioned in *Providence* and *The Nyogtha Variations*, may be less obscure in the light of this volume.

Like the other works I have set in my own quirky version of the Cthulhu mythos, this novel depends even more than most fiction on the labors of previous writers. Most important among them, of course, was the inimitable Clark Ashton Smith, who created the preglacial realm of Hyperborea that forms the background to my tale, and stocked it with enough marvels to fill a far larger book than this. Smith's friend and correspondent H.P. Lovecraft also contributed a great deal, including a passage in his notebooks that he never developed into a story but that provided the climactic events of this one. Other authors who helped me stock postglacial Greenland with eldritch possibilities were Robert E. Howard and Jules Verne, whose *Journey to the Center of the Earth* was a boyhood favorite of mine.

As I have little experience of tall ships and none at all of the North Atlantic and the east coast of Greenland, I am indebted to a number of nonfiction authors for relevant details. Books on sailing vessels by the incomparable Alan Villiers, especially his *The Way of a Ship*, were invaluable, as was Richard Henry Dana's classic sea story *Two Years Before the Mast*. My portrayal of Greenland and the voyage there drew extensively on Barry Lopez' vivid *Arctic Dreams*; Lopez' book was also my introduction to the Tuniit, the vanished people of the New World's arctic regions. The details of a Greenland deglaciating under global warming depended a great deal on E.C. Pielou's account of postglacial North America in *After the Ice Age*.

The sea shanties Long Tom and the pirate crew sang aboard the *Miskatonic* have a complex origin. According to Stan Hugill, the last of the old-time shantymen, the shanties that survive today mostly date from the mid-nineteenth century, long after the great age of Caribbean piracy. I therefore used Hugill's notes on the history of the sea shanty, as compiled in his books *Shanties from the Seven Seas* and *Shanties and Sailor Songs*, to fill in the gap. I am indebted to Robert Mathiesen for pointing me toward Hugill's invaluable works. (I am also grateful to Dr. Mathiesen for help with the details of Hyperborean linguistics, and to him and Dr. Dana Driscoll for guidance in the equally abstruse subject of American university staff hiring procedures.)

The song sung by the pirates in Chapter Six, however, is from *The Pirates* by Douglas Botting, which also provided many details relevant to the Terrible Old Man's crew. Those sung by Long Tom and the crew in the following chapter are classic shanties fitted with new verses. I had already inserted "What D'ye Do With A Drunken Deep One" into the tale before I ran into the H.P. Lovecraft Historical Society's album and songbook *Peculiar Sea Shanties of Innsmouth, Mass.*, which has a different set of words to the same tune. Folk song collectors like to talk about "the folk process," which creates so many variants of every folk song; clearly that same process is at work even when tentacles are involved. The poem recited by Phil Dyer in Chapter Two is the epigraph from Robert E. Howard's tale "The Pool of the Black One."

A more personal debt is owed to Sara Greer, who read and critiqued the manuscript. I hope it is unnecessary to remind the reader that none of the above are responsible in any way for the use I have made of their work.

Printed in the USA
CPSIA information can be obtained
at www.ICGtesting.com
JSHW031913240424
61831JS00006B/21

9 781915 952028